Loft Island

Set on the Salcombe (Devon) Estuary in the 1950s. Rescued from a flood, Mary (11) comes to live with the father and 13 year old son who saved her, though her parents and brother were drowned. The land they farmed is now an island. Practical and emotional help with their losses comes sometimes from unlikely sources. They are faced with a variety of attitudes from authorities and friends.

The long established friendship between the children develops slowly, innocently, with neither of them realising. Gradually life becomes stable, only to be ripped apart again.

"Loft Island" is the first book in the Island series.
This, "The Island and the Town", is the second.

Change at Tide Mills

Near Seaford, 1963: a chance, fleeting glimpse of a girl from a train brings Owen running back from Seaford to Bishopstone Tide Mills. His interest is matched by his father's interest in the failing Mill. For the Tide Mills in the story is still fully built.

The youngsters explore, finding evidence of the past which leads to a search for the past inhabitants. It unearths a story of lost love, a tyrannical husband and his mistreatment of a wife and the child.

Gradually the site is restored and ready for its next chapter. The characters of the old story are brought together and find surprise after surprise. This is a tale of families, of the ups and downs of life, of some little adventure. But it's also a tale of the real Sussex of the time, with its old customs, its history, and some of its Characters.

The Suspects

A light-hearted story, but with spikes. A group of mid-teen friends camp illicitly in a wild, private estate. Despite being discovered and evicted, they later need to hide from an adult criminal gang and return to lie low.

Encounters with their evictor whose life they save, the gang, Police, hospitals, a hotelier, a dog, truffles and copious thorns and brambles bring a maturity they never realised. It also brings friendships and relationships.

Available online at rw2.co.uk, or at Amazon

The Island and the Town

Richard Harbroe Wright

Cover painting by Alla Atkins
Alla.Atkins18@gmail.com

Published by Richard Wright
Seaford, Sussex, UK
richard@rw2.co.uk

First edition 2020

ISBN: 979 8 57236 344 9

Dedicated to Judy Wright for… everything.

Dedicated also to Stella Bateman, long-time friend of both my wife and myself and fellow book-lover, with copious thanks for the coffee, reviews and proof-reading. And the friendship.

In addition the book is dedicated to the RNLI, Salcombe, whose now-retired Lifeboat *Samuel and Marie Parkhouse* I remember well from Salcombe holidays in the 1960s and which I have 'used' in this book but peopled with fictional characters. The RNLI is an organisation which deserves our thanks and support for its unstinting, round-the-clock voluntary engagement with the entire maritime community: commercial and leisure. It needs and deserves our continuing financial support.

This is the second part of a story started in *Loft Island*. Every effort has been made for it to be complete in itself, but you will know more about the families if you have read the first book.

All characters are fictional. Common local surnames have been used but any resemblance to a real person is coincidental.

Kingsbridge

Squares
Quay

Crabtree
Quay

Balcombe Creek

N
W   E
S

The Estuary

Sketch map showing the major
towns, villages and creeks. Lofts
Island and the extent of the
Beales' land is shown, with the
adjoining old roadways shown as
dashed lines

Frogmore Creek

Collapit Creek

Extent of
Beales' land

Farmhouse

Blanksmill
Village & P.O.

Blanksmill Creek

Loft
Island

Lincombe

Milk staithe

Halwell point

Tosnos point

The Bag

Batson Creek

Snapes point

Ox Point

Scoble point

Shadycombe
creek

Island Quay
& Edgar's Yard

Salcombe

The Hard

Southpool Creek

Marine Hotel

East Portlemouth

Small's
Cove

North
Sands

Mill
Bay

South
Sands

The Bar

Open
sea

Contents

1 – Chepstow

"You're from Devon, then?"

It wasn't the response Martin was hoping for, having just asked for directions to an address in the town.

"Yes. Kingsbridge. But can you..."

"Ah, that's where they had all the trouble with the water, isn't it?"

"It was. But..."

"Duw, that was bad. We have troubles enough with the water people by here, see, but nothing like that. Affect you, did it?"

"Not me, but some friends of mine. They lost a lot of land and their neighbours were drowned." By being blunt he hoped that the porter would be stunned into silence, and then might answer his original question.

"Drowned, is it? That's bad. Why d'you want the Williamses then? Is it Williams the Town you want, or..." he man's eyes seemed to narrow ..."or his wife or daughter?"

"Who is Williams the Town, please?"

"He is the Town Clerk, see. Very important."

"I know Mrs Williams – Dolly, and Bronwen."

"Dolly, is it? Well, now..."

"Well yes. I know her brother, you see. Solicitor, in Salcombe. Very important." He smiled to himself, feeling he'd at least tried to trump the porter.

The man nodded. "So you want to know where they live?"

"Yes please."

And finally, almost grudgingly, Martin received the directions.

He trudged into the old town of Chepstow and down the hill towards the River Wye. He had come to Wales to try and find Bronwen without meeting her father, having had two letters returned marked "Return to Sender" despite being sent correctly to the address she had given him. Subsequent letters to her seemed to have vanished into thin air.

Ever since Mary's sixteenth birthday, when the Lofts had thrown open their home to Mary's and Stephen's friends, [told in *Loft Island*] Martin had been trying to write to Bronwen. They had met on the island originally the previous Christmas and had found common ground. Just a month later they met again at Mary's party, and despite the short acquaintance had discovered that they were somehow attracted, despite Bronwen being raised in a comfortable home and Martin as a farm worker's son. The two had spent most of the time talking, or walking on the island – sometimes hand in hand.

When the mother and daughter had left after the party Bronwen had quietly warned him that her father was 'old fashioned' about his daughter's friends, particularly male friends, but that she wanted to write to him and if possible visit again. But letter had there been none. He was now all but certain that it had been the father who had intercepted those he had written to her, and if that were the case, he thought, perhaps he had also intercepted hers to him. So Martin had begged a day off work and had spent some of his hard-earned money on a train journey to Chepstow, that being the only way left to him to contact Bronwen.

The area by the old chain bridge that carried the main road into the town had

1

some smart houses, though behind them were many smaller, poorer cottages. Martin had timed his arrival to try and coincide with what he hoped might be a suitable time to make a call, early afternoon. Bron would have been unlikely to have started a job, he thought. From what he understood, a father such as hers would have seen a job for his daughter as unthinkable. He was also hoping the father was at work.

Mr Williams had not been impressed with Bronwen's admission that she was becoming close to a young man who was a builder. Bronwen had protested, and that had made matters worse. Arguments from a child were not tolerated by him and as such had hardly ever been heard in that household. He recollected having heard some other strong opinions being expressed by his now nineteen-year-old daughter, and he was concerned. Opinions were in his view the province of the male of the species and not to be countenanced from the weaker gender, especially those opinions that concerned his household. That was the rule that had held sway throughout his own upbringing. His long-held beliefs had become entrenched during the years he had spent regulating the conduct of a town.

He was very patriarchal; Victorian in outlook. He had never met Martin, of course, and to his mind such a meeting would be unnecessary. All that he needed to know was that a common builder had made a pass at his daughter. That was enough.

As Martin neared the street he found he was becoming even more nervous. His worrying had really started as he joined the old train at Kingsbridge and endured its plodding journey to the main line. Now in Chepstow and nearing his goal he felt as though there were butterflies flapping wildly inside his stomach. Once again he tidied his tie – almost unworn since he'd left school two years previously – and pulled his jacket straight, checked his shoes and rubbed a smudge from one of them onto the back of his trouser leg. If he didn't impress by looking smart it wouldn't be for the want of trying.

He found the house.

A small iron gate gave onto a paved pathway. The gate groaned as he opened it and again as he closed it behind him. The path was long. He felt exposed to anyone looking out of the windows. The front door was guarded by an old fashioned mechanical bell pull. He persuaded his hand to pull it.

After a while scurrying steps could be heard. The door opened and a young, black-haired, attractive girl in a plain black dress with a white apron appeared.

"Yes?"

It wasn't a very good welcome. Martin swallowed.

"May I speak to Mrs Williams, please? Or… or Miss Williams?"

"Who shall I say it is?"

He was unused to dealing with domestic staff. There were now few to be found anywhere in Britain, besides which he was a farmer's son. Indeed, most girls who might have been candidates for such positions had found during the war that there were more interesting jobs open to them.

"Please can you tell her it's M… it's Mr Rawle, from Loft Island, Salcombe." This last was a sudden inspiration. He was sure the family wouldn't know his surname, yet the address would tell Dolly and Bronwen who he was.

"Mr Rawle from Salcombe," she repeated, looking appraisingly at him before

2

turning away. He waited at the door.

Steps approached. Male steps. Martin's heart sank. A tall, thin, ascetic man appeared.

"Yes?"

"Er... good afternoon sir. I was hoping to speak to Mrs Williams, please. We met last Christmas near Salcombe and again at Mary Beale's birthday party."

The man looked at him.

"My wife, is it? And how do you know her?"

"As I said, sir, we met at two parties recently and as I was in the town I thought to... to look her up."

"Are you the builder fellow?"

"I beg your pardon?"

"My daughter spoke of a builder from Devon she had met. Are you he?"

Arghh... Martin's brain raced. "I'm... doing some work with a building firm whilst my application for a course in architecture is being considered."

"And you wrote several letters to my daughter, I believe?"

"I have. But how did you know? I have had no replies."

The man ignored the question. "So why did you ask for my wife?"

"Because..." he was faltering now, wilting under the man's steely gaze. "Because it seemed the more polite thing to do."

"Did you now... well, I am telling you that until you have fully qualified as an architect – if you ever do – you are not welcome to correspond with my daughter. You are at the moment a builder from Devon and as such unsuitable for her. Is that understood?"

"But... but once my course starts it will take *years* for me to qualify. And I need Bronwen to know what my plans are and... and what my prospects are. Now."

"And I say that your attentions are not welcome until you have a suitable career and genuine prospects. Being a builder shows no prospects."

"Who is it, dear?" The voice came from inside the house.

"No one to concern you, Dolly."

Martin saw a movement past the man and moved to one side so he could be seen. There was a pause.

"Oh, Martin! I didn't know it was you. You should come in. Eli, he is a friend. Come..."

"He is an unwelcome suitor for our Bronwen. I have told him so and that his attentions will not be received until he has demonstrated that he can keep her in a suitable manner."

Martin saw her jaw drop. The father continued looking at him.

"Yes, dear," she said to her husband's back. Then, mouthing silently: "*Wait around the corner.*"

Martin blinked. What now?

"I see you have understood what I am saying. Do not try writing to Bronwen again as the letters will not reach her. And do not return unless you have something better to offer my daughter than a life with a Devon builder. Good day."

The door started to close.

3

"Sir… may I at least just say hallo to Bronwen?"

"You may *not*. Just go."

And the door slammed. The only thing that kept Martin from kicking at it in rage was Dolly's instruction to wait round the corner. He was fairly sure that was what she had mouthed to him. Slowly he retreated down to the gate and had to make himself open and close it without slamming it. Various words he could apply to the father swam across his mind and he mouthed them silently to himself.

He looked both ways. Which corner? Further along the road a path appeared to run beside the house and he wondered if it led to a back door. He walked past it and looked back. Windows were still visible. There was a movement at one of them. It looked like waving. He wondered whether to wave back. But it could have been the father.

Having walked further along until the house was out of sight, he waited. The occasional car crossed the old chain bridge. Birds sang. Someone coughed, making Martin jump. He looked back towards the house. Was that a shadow, moving, on the pavement near the little footpath? It was. He frowned. Man sized? Smaller? Would it be that father of hers?

But it wasn't. It was her. Bronwen. She looked cautiously away from him, then towards him and saw him at last. A smile lit up her face and she ran towards him.

"Quick! Come away from the house. He's told me not to go out but I have. Oh Martin, you're so brave, coming all this way!"

He was hurried away from the house, up the hill and towards the castle. Bronwen found a bench to sit on, hidden from the road.

"I often come here, when I've had enough," she said. "Was he very rude to you? I didn't hear anything, but Mum told me he'd sent you away and that she'd told you to wait round the corner."

"He thought I wasn't good enough for you," Martin said bitterly, his supressed anger threatening to pour itself over the girl. He was so pleased to be with her, almost euphoric, but her father's attitude still hurt and mystified him.

"He has this thing…" she started. "He wants me to marry someone who's rich and works hard. It doesn't matter about anything else. I keep getting told to get to know people, quite old men, some of them, and see how I get on. When…"

She stopped and looked at him.

"When I met you, you were just a breath of fresh air. Happy. Natural. Different from anyone I'd met in boring Chepstow."

He sighed. "It's been hardly boring for me so far. But now – now I am talking to you and it's certainly not boring. It's *so* good to be with you. You said I was happy? Well yes I am. Now."

"Now?"

With a rueful grin he reminded her of his sudden departure from his own family home in Kingsbridge after many rows with his own father about his never being *enough* for him; about his being required to earn money for the family; about his future and his education. The father hadn't even wanted him to sit his GCE 'O' Levels which had been a mere month away. Hesitantly he even told her about Alice, who had been his fiancée for a year until she had found someone else.

When he'd had his say he just sat silently looking at the old castle walls with their circling seabirds and wondering what the reaction would be, hoping for understanding.

A warmth came to his left cheek and he felt lips touch it.

Cautiously he looked at her, almost wondering if this was true, if this was their first real kiss. He let their foreheads touch.

"I was so worried what you would say. Especially when you heard about Alice."

"She was a fool to let you go. But I'm glad she did."

They kissed properly.

A roar of anger came from the roadway.

"How DARE you? How dare you touch my daughter when I told you to leave immediately? And you, Daughter; I gave you instructions not to go out, not to try and follow, and you have disobeyed me. And here you both are, canoodling in public like two animals..."

Martin had jumped up at the first sound of the voice, startled and now protective. Shock stung him into expressing the anger he had felt at the first meeting with this man, and the treatment he had received. He spoke with heat, in a tone he'd last heard himself use when arguing bitterly with his own father.

"Yes, we are in public. Not in your house. In public. And we are attracted to each other. And I want to get to know Bronwen better. And I will, one way or another."

He was amazed at his own courage. Or was it foolhardiness? The man was about to shout him down when Bronwen spoke, also with some force.

"Father, we have met, and we like each other. I like him better than any of the older men or the rich younger men you have tried to pair me with. And I *will* do what I can to meet him, to write to him, to know him..."

She was interrupted by another shout. "You will *not*! You will go home now and I will deal with you later. And you, Devon builder, will leave my town immediately and never, ever return. Do you understand?" It was said in a crescendo and finished at full volume, but was followed by a silence.

Martin allowed it to continue as long as he dared. The desire to continue in a heated tone evaporated with the man's obvious loss of temper. He was used to that from his father; it had almost always meant that the son's argument was won.

"No," said Martin quietly, in the way he used to at home. "I do not understand. And I will not leave. My father fought for freedom in this country. He said so frequently. You probably did, too. So it would be wrong for anyone to try to forbid another person to visit anywhere that is public. And I don't understand..."

A further roar. Martin hadn't been prepared for that.

"How DARE you question what I did in the war, boy? How dare you accuse me of deliberately avoiding the fight?"

Now *that* was news, thought Martin. Especially as he had made no accusation.

Still managing to maintain his quiet tone, he answered. "I don't know of your war career ... er... *sir*. But you see, my father was a pilot and was shot down.

Twice. The aftermath of his wounds are what led to his bad temper which, eventually, led to my having to leave home. I've just explained that to Bronwen. But that aside, your daughter and I have an understanding. No more than that, yet. But we *will* be in contact with each other. In two years she will become an adult officially, as will I a year later. So at the very latest, if she agrees to see me, I hope we shall be friends still. Perhaps more.

"Will you please now pass the letters that I addressed to her, on to her? Or shall we have to contact each other without your knowledge?"

"You little…" he took a step towards Martin, his hand raised, and tried to slap his head. With the agility of youth Martin sidestepped. The blow almost spun the old man around. Bronwen screamed.

"Father!"

He stopped, recovered and looked at her. "You will come with me. You will not stir from your room until the Police have ensured this urchin has left the town."

"I will not. You will not keep me prisoner in my own home."

"If you do not return there with me instantaneously I will ensure that it will no longer *be* your home. You will have disgraced yourself and will be unwelcome there."

"Then I shall go and live with Uncle Algy in Salcombe. Mother might want to come too."

The man looked at her, his face blanching.

"How DARE you…?" He looked almost incoherent with rage.

"You know she would. Like a shot. And Uncle would have both of us. Or I will ask Martin if I can share his house in Kingsbridge."

This time there was a long silence. Father and daughter looked at each other; the father with an expression of speechless rage, the daughter with both disdain and determination.

"You will come with me." It was a quiet and threatening tone.

"When I have said goodbye to Martin, yes."

Uncomfortably now, with the man watching her, she crossed to Martin, who looked into her eyes with admiration.

"There will be a row," she said softly. "I'll try and write, but you must please send letters to me at 16 High Street. It's a friend's shop. I'll tell her later. But please – do write. Tomorrow. And I'll tell you what happens. And I'm sorry. About him. And thank you for coming. It means so much to me, more than you'll realise. But perhaps you will, one day."

She lifted herself onto her toes, cupped his face in her hands to pull it down to her level, and kissed him. Just the once, on the lips.

He was about to say something but she turned and walked back towards her father. Giving him a wide berth she walked purposefully down the hill towards her home. Her father, still red-faced with rage, gave him a last glare and followed her at a distance.

He endured the long journey back to Kingsbridge and was late to bed that night. His first letter to her at the High Street address had to be completed and he hoped he would wake in time for the first post the next day.

6

Next morning, as he was walking from the Post Office, a voice called to him. "Come on, son, you'll be late!"

The foreman at the job they were still doing for Peter and Dot Loft was a friend, really, but liked to encourage the young man to toe the line.

Martin grinned. "If I run, Ian, I'll still arrive before you can cycle there!"

"Cheek!" the man threw back over his shoulder. "We'll see about that."

Martin did get there first, but it was a close thing.

They were working, when time from other jobs permitted, on modernising a pair of cottages for Peter and Dot Loft, elder son and daughter-in-law of Henry Loft of Loft Island. The arrangement was that once the improvements were complete Martin would rent one. It was to have been a home for him and his fiancée, but having been dumped by Alice before Christmas it was now just possibly somewhere to live if he could afford the rent.

Having been thrown out of his family home two years previously Martin had been given a home on Loft Island by Henry and Susan Loft – their son Stephen had been a school friend. Susan was expecting an addition to the family later in the year so he knew that space there would be at a premium. That made him even more determined to have a place of his own, even given the loneliness that sometimes overcame him on the occasions he camped out in the still-unfinished cottage.

If only he could have persuaded the Williams patriarch that he really was good enough for Bronwen. If only she would agree to be with him, even after just two – three now – meetings. If only her family would allow her to move to Devon. But then it almost sounded as if Bronwen would consider coming anyway.

He shook his head. Too many 'ifs', he thought, following the older man up to the part of the roof they were working on. How could he improve his chances? He enjoyed what he was doing – it was his first job. He wasn't scared of hard work – years of helping his father at the family farm had seen to that. It hadn't stopped his father from throwing him out when the arguments about stopping education and earning money became too much to stomach, though. A grin came to his lips; a wry one. One boy and one girl, each with father problems. One in Devon and one in Wales. Each attracted to the other. She *was* attracted to him, wasn't she?

He was due to visit Loft Island again after work, after taking the last ferry down the estuary. He would return the following morning on the school bus. It was an arrangement that suited everyone and kept him in touch with old school friends. Stephen Loft was one of these, of course, though he would be leaving school in July after the exams. Mary would stay on, as would others, and not for the first time he smiled at the events of that cold, moonlit, romantic January night where his two friends had announced their engagement.

At school and engaged! And with Mary just sixteen! They had all been asked not to spread the information as it would have been unfair on the two. He put it all out of his mind and concentrated on the work in hand.

Tea break had him thinking again, though, and his responses to the others were short and sporadic. At last Ian, the Foreman, took him on one side.

"Now, last time you was like this you got careless and bust your shoulder.

7

Wassup, son?"

"Oh, it's nothing. Well, not really."

"So it's nothing that's keeping you thinking about it rather than about the work you're doing, is it?"

"I've not made any mistakes, have I?" he asked anxiously.

"I'd have bawled you out if you had, son. No. There's summat going on."

So Martin explained to the man, who nodded sagely.

"Well, whatcher expect? That's how that sort of person thinks. He doesn't want to see his daughter living with someone who's a rough old workman when she could have someone else who's...what? An architect? Someone with smooth hands and a big salary comin' in? Thass prolly it, son."

"But he doesn't know *me!* He doesn't know what I'm going to do, what I'm going to be."

"Nope. And d'you know what? Neither do I. But do *you?* Are you going to be a builder at this firm all your life? 'Cos you'll never get this gal if you do. That's the honest truth."

Martin let that sink in.

"What am I going to do, Ian?"

"I should start with talking it over with that Peter Loft. Or his father. They seem like decent people. But at the end of the day it's got to be *your* decision. And what that is might depend on what you really want to do. Or it might depend on how much you really want this girl. Would it be enough to persuade her father, maybe?"

"After what happened yesterday I don't think he'd welcome me if I was royalty. But I do want to... to make what I can of myself. Do what I can to... well, to make sure she wants to be with me,"

"Ah, but don't think you've got to be a moneybags to get her. If she thinks that way you'll need to think hard before taking her on."

"She really isn't that sort of girl, Ian."

"Hope you're right, son. That sort's no good to a man at all."

So that night Martin sat with the Lofts and talked. And as usual Susan suggested talking to her father. Not only for guidance but because he was Bronwen's uncle.

"Uncle Algy," he said. Susan smiled.

"I think this is something better discussed face to face," said 'Uncle Algy' when Susan phoned him. "It combines family with what other people might regard as careers advice. May I come over next weekend? And will Martin be there?"

Susan assured him he was welcome any time, and that they'd make sure the subject of the conversation was there too. The latter grinned; he knew he was being talked about.

2 – The family grows

"It's a long, hard slog to becoming a qualified architect," Mr Merryweather told him. "Firstly, you may find you need an Advanced level GCE, but much will depend how you set about it. Had you thought about applying to an architect for a job? You have some 'O' level GCEs behind you, have you not?"

Martin admitted that he had six. Fortunately his teachers had always commented on the neatness of his artistic drawing and his skill in geometry, and one of them had suggested he tried technical drawing. It had caused some head scratching at the time but with the addition of a correspondence course to his normal school studies he had achieved his 'O' Level. However, the extra time studying when his father had thought he should have been out earning money for the family had been one of the many differences between them that had led to the full-scale rows.

"See if you can ask your employers for a reference," was the next piece of advice. "If they can say some nice things about you. We can copy their letter and send it with your application to someone and see what the result is. You'd need to take the original with you if they ask you to go for an interview, of course."

"Do you think anyone would even think about me, sir?" asked Martin.

Mr Merryweather looked at him. "Well, you told me you wore a suit and tie when you went to Chepstow. That means that you know when and how to make a good impression. You have been working ever since taking the GCEs. Your employers approached you with your current job – you never applied for it. They obviously think well of you; after all, the owner let you live in their office when you broke your collarbone. I'm told by Peter that you've made some suggestions that would improve the cottages, and seem to have used the one you'll be in for a few trials…"

Martin grinned.

"…And you come over as a decent, honest chap to whom, in my opinion, anyone should want to offer a chance.

"Now, you may find that the money you get to start with isn't much. Maybe not enough to live on. But it is your decision whether or not to accept a low salary on the basis that eventually, if or when you prove yourself to them they will increase it."

Martin thought. "But if I'm not paid enough to live on, how can I continue with renting Peter and Dot's other house? And what do I use for food?"

"There are ways of making it work, if you want it badly enough," the old man said with a smile. "People like you. For example, in exchange for some part-time work making the two cottages habitable once the builders are finished, Peter might offer you a low starting rent. Henry and Susan regard you as one of the residents on Lofts' anyway, so that's another bolt hole. And if you and Bronwen think that you might have a future together, that will make you part of Susan's family, and therefore mine. In my book, families help each other out."

Martin thought again, warming to the old solicitor. "But sir, Mr Williams is part of your family too."

Mr Merryweather pursed his lips and gave a wry smile. "There is a saying, you know: 'God gave us our relatives. Thank God we can choose our friends.'

Last Christmas I tried to bury an old hatchet and asked him down to visit us, along with Dolly and Bronwen. He declined as he viewed his duty to his Chapel as more important than his family ties. I was relieved, but now wished he had come so that he could have met you informally and gained an idea of your character. He wasn't asked to Mary's birthday party since it was for her friends only. And I cannot foresee a day when he would be welcome here, to be frank with you. But that is between us only."

He let that sink in.

"Thank you, sir," said Martin. "I appreciate what you are saying, and your confidence. But it seems that to go for a job with an architect..."

"Not a job, young man, a career. A calling, if you like."

"A career... a career start... with an architect, I will have to be a burden on a lot of other people and come to them for charity."

It was Mr Merryweather's turn to stop and think.

"Would it be charity? Would it not be, more, an investment?"

"An investment? Me? Do you really think someone might invest in me?"

"I really don't see why not. If someone knew you and knew the history of how you applied yourself, they might well do. In fact..."

He looked out of the window, down to the estuary's mud and up to the encircling rooftops, thinking. Could he? Should he?

His had been a successful Practice for many years. He was wealthy, he was almost ashamed to say. There were few outlets for the money. It took almost a full minute, but a decision was made.

"In fact I might well invest in you myself."

Martin sat bolt upright, like a dog who had heard the key in the door.

"But... but that wouldn't be right, sir. Neither you nor I would know if I would be able to pay you back. It would be unfair. I suppose if Bronwen and I were married maybe you might consider it... but no..."

He paused whilst trying to think of how that would work.

"It would mean that I would be paying some kind of dividend to you and the Lofts and Peter and Dot. I don't even know if I could afford that..."

His mentor held up a hand.

"As you get older, and I speak with experience in this, you learn that money isn't everything. Oh yes, when you're young and starting out, and have all that energy, you go hammer and tongs after it. And rightly so, as you need shelter, you need to live, to love and to thrive.

"But there are other rewards. Rewards that are even more worthwhile than accumulating wealth." He smiled softly. "Yes, I speak with the experience of ageing, but also with recent experience of such worthwhile rewards.

"Firstly I have seen my only daughter fall in love and marry. Can you start to imagine how that feels? Men aren't meant to shed tears, yet I did when it happened." He smiled. "I managed to disguise the fact as a sneeze, however.

"Secondly I was able to help somewhat to obtain justice for a young lady who had been very badly treated. And I was given, freely, the honour of being asked to become an honorary grandfather to her and to the remarkable young man who is now her fiancé.

"Do these things put bread on the table? No. Do they give me a lightness of mind, after all those years of just doing my job as a solicitor? To quote our American friends, you bet they do!"

He paused, embarrassed at the unexpected exuberance with which that expression had come out.

"What I am aiming at telling you is this. I believe in your abilities and character. If I can make it possible for you to live in reasonable comfort and feed yourself, over a period during which you work for very little and study hard and gain respect with a different employer, I am happy to do so. I believe – no, I know – that at the end of it we shall all see a successful young man, well able to look after himself. And who knows? He might by then have a fiancée to look after too."

Martin looked straight ahead, his face expressionless.

To have someone invest money in him and to have the strings of repayment and interest attached would, he felt, have meant a permanent debt. But to have nothing attached to the offer except the expectation of his success… well, that was different. But it did mean that should he fail to do well it would let himself down in the eyes of someone else. Someone he could respect.

Did he have the ability to deliver? He thought so. And if not, it wouldn't be for the want of trying.

He thought back to what the now gently smiling solicitor had said. Suddenly he blurted out, not having thought about saying it: "I can see why Mary and Stephen value you so highly; why they asked you to be their grandad."

He stopped, embarrassed, wondering what he'd just said, and why.

But his mentor just smiled deeper. "I regard that as a down payment. Good. That's agreed, then. You need to go into the bank and start a bank account. If you need a reference, I'm nearest, but Henry or even your employer will provide one. And there will be payments into that account once you've taken the plunge."

"But sir – I haven't taken you up on your offer yet."

"You made a down payment by giving me an insight into what my adopted grandchildren say about me. And you said that you understood why they said it. That means you agree with their view, I believe. That means that, unless you say 'no', we are in business. May we shake on it?"

Martin looked at him, dazed, and saw how he had been out-manoeuvred, how he didn't have to say 'yes' or agree or anything else. Wordlessly he held out his hand, which was taken and shaken, and he put his other hand on the old man's. It seemed to him a token of sincerity.

The old man smiled again.

"Good. That's settled. All you need to do are three things. Firstly, tell me when you have been engaged and what as, secondly tell me how the finances are going and whether you need more or less, and thirdly, tell me when your income will support you on your own.

"Now that's settled, we'll go and beg a cup of tea, shall we?"

"Thank you," Martin almost whispered, unsure whether it was relief or emotion in his voice that caused the quietness. He received another smile.

They joined the others in the kitchen. Susan and Henry Loft, Henry's son Stephen and his fiancée Mary Beale were at ease, chatting. At this stage of the year they had the time. The island's café business didn't open until the end of

11

April.

"All sorted?" asked Henry.

"Thanks to this gentleman," said Martin, still looking rather dazed. "I'm going to be an architect. Actually I should say that I'm going to work for an architect, if one will have me. And work my way up, get qualifications, and – well, see what I can do."

"I know you were good at tech drawing," Stephen commented, "so that's a good start. And if you're going back to being a student that means you'll be coming here to eat more often. So that's good, too."

Susan looked at them both, then at her father who had the grace to look embarrassed. But she said nothing.

Henry looked at her and raised his eyebrows, and she nodded. They seemed to be able to communicate about some things in this way.

"A long time ago we said you had a home here as long as you wanted one, Martin," he said. "That still applies. If it means that the cottage in Kingsbridge has to take a back seat for a while, so be it: Peter will cope. He might have to get a tenant in for a few years but you'd get first refusal after that, I'm sure."

"I... I don't know if that would be necessary," Martin started. "I... really I just have to clear my head after this afternoon, and after the last few weeks. And sorry – that sounds as if I don't want to be here: that's not the case at all. It's very kind of you indeed, and thanks. It depends on where I end up working, really. First thing tomorrow I need to draft a letter to apply. I know there are two architects in Kingsbridge but I don't know who to apply to first."

"Draft the letter," said Mr Merryweather, "and first thing on Monday I'll make a phone call to a colleague of mine, a solicitor in Kingsbridge. He's dealt with the local people and can recommend the better of them. If you're here tomorrow night there will be a message waiting for you."

"Thank you, sir."

"And while I'm at it, please will you stop calling me 'sir'? We're business partners now, don't forget." He smiled again.

"But I can't call you by your Christian name. I suppose it could be Uncle Algy..."

"Where *did* you learn that from?" the old man asked, surprised.

"From Bronwen."

"I should have known... that imp! Well, until perhaps one day you can rightfully call me great-uncle in law or something, it'll have to do."

Everyone laughed, except Martin, who just looked thoughtful.

They had that cup of tea. Mary, Stephen and Martin washed up, then Martin quietly asked the two of them to come for a walk.

Once outside, he heaved a large sigh. "He's going to support me," he said. "Just until I'm earning enough to support myself. It was all done before I had a chance to say yes or no. I don't really know how he managed to do it, but before I had a chance to comment he just told me it was finalised and he wanted his tea."

"He's a lovely man," said Mary. "That's why we adopted him as our grandad."

"I know," Martin replied. "I told him you rated him very highly and that I could see why."

Stephen grinned. "I bet that pleased him."

"It did. He said that was a down payment."

The other two looked at him quizzically. He grinned.

"He said he was going to invest in me. Not to get something out of it – well, not money, but just the pleasure of seeing me succeed..." A grimace. "...if I do."

"You took on tech drawing and got a good grade at 'O' level," Stephen reminded him.

"Yes, but there are too many if's. I've got to get a job – start a career – with one of the local architects. I've got to go for a correspondence course again, and this one will make the tech drawing one look like child's play. And to be fair, I've got to do it in a reasonable time so he can see some results."

"He's not going to expect quick miracles, Martin," said Mary. "He's a wise old owl and just...kind."

Martin nodded, and paused.

"I wanted to ask you... you know he doesn't want to be called 'sir'? Well, I don't like 'Uncle Algy' either. It just sounds like something I'd have to call him if I was an eight year old. The thing is... what would you think if I adopted him as a grandad too?"

The other two looked at each other. Two pairs of eyebrows lifted. Two heads nodded: an echo of their elders' communication earlier.

"What did you say earlier about a down payment?" asked Stephen. "I imagine he'd view that as a year's interest, or more. Do we want you as a brother? Ah... you hadn't thought of that, had you?" He grinned again. "I think we rather like the idea, don't we Mary?"

She smiled up at them both. "I'd not sure I'd want him tickling me like you and Greg did when we were kids, but yes, I like the idea."

"Quite right," said Stephen. "No one is allowed to tickle you except me... *ouch!*"

And she put out her tongue at him too. All three laughed.

Back inside Martin told them that he had come to terms with Mr Merryweather's offer and was about to launch into profuse thanks but the old man just held up his hand with a grin.

"And I thought it was going to be 'Uncle Algy'?" he said sorrowfully.

"I've been thinking about that," said Martin slowly. "If I was still eight, rather than eighteen, maybe. But I've been talking to my newly adopted brother and sister, you see. And if I've adopted them, then if I may I'd like to adopt you as my honorary grandad too."

The look Susan gave him was unfathomable. It hadn't occurred to any of them that it meant she and Henry could now have another adopted, near-adult child.

Martin looked at his mentor. The old man's eyes were suspiciously bright. There was a silence.

"I know I surprised you with what I said earlier," he started in a slightly husky voice, "but you certainly have surprised me, just like these two did when they asked me the same question. And if you turn out to be half the man I think you are, then I shall be honoured, just as I am honoured to call these two my grandchildren.

"In the course of less than a year my family has grown exponentially, and is due to grow again, soon - " he bowed to Susan " - thank you, Martin. I am indeed honoured."

To Mary's disgust, Henry found the Scotch bottle again.

"When you told me you were expecting," Henry suddenly said to Susan, "you said that we would need to expand the house again. Have you actually thought any more about that?"

Susan shook her head. "We'll need another bedroom somewhere. And it would be nice to be able to offer people a real bedroom when they stay, and not have to ask them to sleep on the floor in the café!"

Stephen bit back the nearly shouted words 'Mary and I can share a room…'

"I could live full time in Kingsbridge," Martin offered.

"Martin, there is no need for that at all. You have your freedom, but space here is not one of the things you have to consider. No, we need to think. We probably need an architect…"

Martin found every eye in the room focussed on him. He held up his hands in defence.

"Give me a chance!" he laughed, "One step at a time!"

"But you've had a lot of building experience and you can draw plans if we tell you what is wanted."

"But not the detailed plans architects have to draw."

"No, but you can take ideas and map them out…"

There was the clearing of a throat.

"May I interject?" said Mr Merryweather. "I think that if Martin and you got together and he found out what was wanted, it would be useful for all of you. For you, because he might come up with a plan that worked with the existing building, and for him because it would show prospective employers what he can do."

Two generations of Loft family and Mary considered this.

"You know, that's a very good idea," said Henry. "We'd pay you, of course…"

"No." said Martin forcefully.

Henry looked at him, surprised.

Martin clarified. "I don't mean that I won't try and do it. I mean that I'm not going to be paid for it."

"But…" Henry tried again.

"No, Henry. Or is it Dad? No. I'm not qualified or anywhere near. I'm still just a mere Devon builder, as Mr flipping Williams would say, but one with some ideas of his own. But more than that, after all you've done for me I absolutely refuse to be paid. And another thing: if my new Grandad says that money is not the only reward, just think. If it works, in a few years' time I'll be able to turn to people and say 'that was my first ever design, and I did it before I even started training'. If it works. And there's absolutely no guarantee."

"Let's just see, shall we?" asked Henry.

"No, sir; I do not want to be paid for this. This is for you and Susan. And Steve and Mary."

Henry looked at him, surprised at such vehemence from him, but nodded, crossed to him and shook his hand.

"Thank you. If it works, fine. If it can't be made to work, also fine; no blame attached. Deal?"

"Deal... Dad."

Henry clapped him on the back and went to sit down.

"But what do you actually want to add on?"

That simple question started a discussion which involved them all and lasted until Mary started yawning.

After church the next morning, which Martin felt that he now had to attend with them despite the heavy rain, they continued that same discussion. At last Martin stopped making notes and started sketching.

The floor plan they agreed on realised that the café was now part of their lives and their income. It was Martin's idea to extend the front of the house to bring the café inside so that it formed a part of the house. It would also be made to cover a larger floor area than the existing cafe. That included making a separate kitchen and servery area to cater for it whilst retaining the family kitchen and living room behind.

A new entrance for the house, with a porch and small hallway, would be added to the left side of the building. It would lead into the present living room and the stairway. That would give room on the floor above for a larger landing, another bathroom, no fewer than three new bedrooms and a storage area.

"And all that work I put into extending along the front will be wasted," Henry said in mock disgust.

Martin, tied up with the sketches, said seriously: "The drainage from the new roof wouldn't work if we kept it. Sorry."

"I was joking, Martin."

He looked up, realised what had just happened and grinned.

"If you made the storage area bigger, we wouldn't have to use my old room for storage and I could have a bit more space," said Stephen.

"*We* could have a bit more space. Eventually." Mary said quietly in his ear.

Martin, just the other side of him, overheard.

"I'm a fool," he muttered, and pulled a blank piece of paper towards him. "May I go up and have another look at the load bearing walls, please?"

"You're family, Martin; you don't have to ask."

The lad looked at Henry, surprised, pleased. The look that Henry received was enough to make him smile too. Martin walked towards the stairs, then hesitated.

"Mary? Steve? Can you come with me, please?"

Upstairs they crowded at the end of the landing.

"Look," Martin started, "the central load-bearing wall – well, it's not quite central but you know what I mean – is this one. It's the kitchen wall downstairs and the bathroom wall up here. So your room could actually start as it is, but once over the outside wall where we're extending, it could widen out and be as long as you like."

"You mean I'd have more space?" asked Mary.

"I mean... it'd be big enough for... well, for both of you. But it'd still be your room. As it is now. But bigger."

"I grew up in here," said Stephen thoughtfully. "I even had to share it with Peter for years."

"And I shared it with you for ages, until…" Mary had spoken without thinking. Martin looked at her, surprised. Her hand came up to cover her mouth.

Stephen looked uncomfortable. "That was different. We were kids."

Martin's face was a picture.

"Please – don't tell anyone else. Not even Susan. You see, when I was rescued from the flood…" and after all the years that had passed, she still shuddered at the sudden, unguarded recollection "…there was nowhere else for me to sleep. Steve and Henry were as exhausted and shocked as I was, so Steve and I shared. And with all the horror and the inquest and the funeral it was just so comforting to have him there that we never really…well…"

Stephen continued. "Until Dad insisted, and built the extension so he could sleep downstairs and Mary had his room. Then Mary was taken, and he came back upstairs again."

Martin nodded. "I thought the room might be a bit special to each of you. But it's also special to both of you, isn't it?"

They worked this out, then smiled and nodded at him.

"Okay. And no, I won't tell anyone. What I'll do is to put the door in the end of the landing here, on the present outside wall, then the original room won't be disturbed. Let's go down to the sketches again and I'll recalculate."

It meant a dogleg in the extended landing passageway, but gave more scope for the three decent size rooms and another, smaller room over the new front of the house.

"Damn!" said Martin suddenly. "I've forgotten lavatories for the café!"

It had become a real nuisance having to allow customers to access the only bathroom they had, on the upper storey of their private quarters. Martin set to with an eraser and fitted in two basic facilities against the end of the new kitchen. It reduced the kitchen's size a little but still left a very useable space.

"We *could* make that upstairs storage room into another lavatory with a bit of jiggery-pokery," muttered the budding architect, reverting to the upstairs plan. "That would be more convenient."

"That's what it is," said Mary.

Stephen looked up. "Pardon?"

"A convenience."

3 – Bronwen

The Royal Mail was very busy that weekend. Through the letterboxes of all those who had been affected by the bursting of the two dams four years previously came letters from the local Water Board detailing the compensation payable. They had been forced into action by national government following years of procrastination. Through the letter box of Susan's Salcombe café also came letters from two insurance companies, one addressed to Henry Loft Esq and the other to the Guardian of Miss M Beale.

Martin was still awaiting advice about which was the better of the two architects in Kingsbridge before he could post his drafted application letter.

Susan went to collect the mail once she had delivered the junior members of her family to the school bus. She smiled to himself again at the idea of having achieved another eighteen year old son, but the expression turned to a frown as she looked at the envelopes. Bills? The appearance and size was different. Should she be patient and wait until late afternoon to be able to discover the contents, or just worry about what they might contain. She decided to phone Henry and was pleased when he told her that of course she should open them.

Discovering what they contained she scanned them avidly. The amounts on the insurance offers, particularly Mary's, made her gasp. But then, she thought, with what she had lost it was only right. Henry's was less, of course, as there had been neither loss of life nor buildings.

The file of papers from the water board... now, that would be interesting. She read through it swiftly to discover the acreage they deemed the farm had lost. It also quoted a compensation amount per acre. Being a solicitor's daughter she frowned at this last figure.

"That can't be right," she said to herself, and reached for the phone again.

Forty minutes later Henry was with her and she was explaining what she knew about land prices.

"So they think they can still base their rates on pre-war prices, do they?" he asked bitterly. "Do they have no idea how we have suffered? And how long we have had to wait for this... this mockery of an offer?"

She held up her hands. "Don't shoot the messenger! I think we need to talk to Dad about this, don't you?"

"I should be able to fight my own battles," he muttered.

"*Our* own battles, Henry. And we're not the only ones. I imagine everyone who lost land has had the same acreage price offered to them. And speaking of that, where is Mary's?"

Henry looked at her. "Isn't there one there for her? It should have been sent to us, as her guardians."

"No. That's all we had. Do they know she's been adopted? Or don't they know she's a minor and has had to move..." she laughed bitterly "...because of the flood *they* caused? I doubt if they do."

"You don't mean they've actually addressed it to Beales' Farm?"

"That may be it," she said.

"Should we try at the post office?"

"Would they release it to us?"

"Hmm... Perhaps we do need Dad after all."

Was that the first time he had called her father Dad, she wondered.

Another phone call. The old man was silent when they had explained the terms of the Water Board's offer. There was a muffled exclamation when Henry explained that Mary's was missing and why they thought that should be. Henry was about to ask him if he was still there when his voice came over the line again.

"In my opinion as a solicitor they are attempting to minimise their losses at the expense of those to whom this would appear to be a large amount. As a local resident I would say that it is an attempt to swindle a lot of ordinary people whose loss they have caused, but you may not quote me on that."

He paused again.

"We need to convene a meeting of everyone affected and I will ask if they want me to take action on everyone's behalf. With the usual legal fees split between about eight families I imagine this would be an inexpensive way of attaining justice.

"I wonder, would you be able to assist by attending my office and helping to persuade the others? It is in the interests of everyone to ensure we have all parties present as a part of the counter-claim. It will come as something of a surprise to them to realise that they are not dealing with farmers whose inclination is not to fight with authority, even when that authority is trying to... er... minimise costs."

"To swindle."

"I did not say that, of course."

Henry laughed. "Of course not. And of course I will come up. Is now convenient? And what do we do about Mary's letter?"

"Good heavens, yes. I had better call the local sorting office to find if it has been returned there as being undeliverable, as seems likely if it was addressed to a drowned and probably demolished building. The answer may well be here when you arrive. I shall see you soon."

The answer was indeed there when Henry arrived. The solicitor's secretary was in the middle of typing a letter of authority for Henry to take to the sorting office. "He's on the phone," Mrs Damerell explained to him. "And is likely to be for a while. He says that this introduces you as the legal Guardian for Mary Beale, late of Beales' Farm, and the rightful recipient of any post directed to the family."

When it was complete, Henry left for the sorting office and presented it. He was surprised to receive a box of mail as well as the letter from the Water Board.

"This is stuff we couldn't return," said the clerk. "Thought someone might be in for it eventually."

"You don't know about the Beales, then?" asked Henry, dangerously quietly.

The man looked uncomfortable. "*I'm* Salcombe, so yes, I know. But the Royal Mail has regulations and we have to stick to them."

"Not an unofficial word to someone? Like the solicitor who took the inquest?"

"Sorry, sir; not allowed to."

"Is there a record of what has been returned to sender?"

"Oh no, we don't keep that."

"So if there were unsettled bills that have been returned, the Beale parents and maybe the children too have black marks against their name, and all because of Post Office regulations."

"Looks that way, sir."

The man withered under the look that Henry gave him.

For once the solicitor shrugged his shoulders when Henry described his disgust. "It may be wrong. But it has been wrong a long time, I should imagine. During the last war, for example, addresses just vanished. But with respect we have more local and more immediate windmills to tilt at.

"I have spent an interesting hour telephoning some of the landowners I know and have suggested a week tomorrow for a meeting. Perhaps we could take over the Shipwrights' bar in the morning? I suggested that to my contacts. Would you be prepared to try the others? If you find it easier, refer any technical questions or awkwardness to me. And would you be happy working from my Secretary's office as I have to talk to a client about a *very* different matter in here." He smiled wryly as he said it, so taking any sting out of the relocation.

He found it quite easy talking to the others who had suffered in the same way the Lofts had. They were all pleased to compare notes but some regarded the idea of complaining to be pointless. "It's something. Better than nothing," seemed to be their attitude.

Henry had equipped himself with some local land prices – and had discovered in doing so that there was a parcel of land near the Island that would shortly become available for sale. The difference between its acreage price and the Water Board's offer was marked.

He told the other affected landowners that if none of them would accept the figure in the Water Board's letter, then the Board would have no option but to increase their offer. They were left in no doubt, too, that if any one of the other farmers accepted the first offer it would create a precedent. Everyone else's offer would suffer.

There were a few more grumbles from those who didn't like the idea of arguing with any authority, and some misgivings about how much it would cost. Henry explained patiently that the cost would be miniscule compared to the additional compensation they would be paid by the Water Board. Eventually he won them over enough at least to come to the Shipwrights the following week.

Henry reported his success and the reactions.

"Good," said Mr Merryweather, "that means we should have them all on side. I'll do a few sums on the acreages we know about and present some contrasts if we can be sure of the current price of land per acre. Estate agents can help with that."

"Do you want me to visit the Salcombe ones?" asked Henry.

"That would save a lot of time; thank you. And we do need their most accurate, not their best, estimates, based on experience. It has to be factual, it has to be on their headed paper with as much details of source as possible, and it must be signed and dated by a Partner or similar."

Henry blinked. "I think I'd better go home and put on a suit," he said jokingly.

"Good idea. But don't show any interest in a piece of land first; that would likely skew the prices. I see there's land on sale near Lofts' you might want to look at later; it's a bit hilly, but gets better towards the summit. Might do for a dairy herd…"

Henry gaped at him. "Is there anything you don't know? I'd already noticed it was for sale."

The old man smiled. "I like to keep my wits about me. But that enquiry needs to be dissociated from your enquiry on behalf of this firm of solicitors; I'd suggest waiting at least a day, please."

Henry nodded. "I'll go and get ready, then."

Wearing his hated suit, he spent a careful afternoon visiting the few estate agents in the town. Careful because the first, slightly suspicious reaction was to look for any hidden reasons behind the requests.

He found the easiest way of disarming them was to be honest without going into details of the Water Board's offer; just saying that it was derisory and those affected would be taking legal action as necessary. They were inclined to become interested when he casually mentioned that landowners should be more able to afford current prices once the offer was increased.

"But, of course, we have to back up all the evidence we provide with actual figures and dates," he told them. "It would be pointless either you or Merryweathers inflating the rates artificially, with no evidence."

The senior partner in one of the agents nodded. "And of course you would be interested in regaining some farming land once this compensation is received, Mr Loft. Apart from the Beales, you lost most."

Henry squirmed a little. "I want to keep that totally separate from gathering evidence for Merryweathers, please."

"Indeed. I mention it because we have a parcel of land shortly coming up for sale that is close to you."

Henry sighed. "I know. But until this is over and we actually accept an offer I'm in no position even to look at it."

"But you have thought of it, of course. Don't forget that with many landowners seeking to replace their lost acres we shall find that demand for land in the immediate area will outstrip supply, and prices will be forced up as a result. There's precious little land available in the area anyway – as you doubtless know."

Henry gritted his teeth. "I *do* know. And if I had the money..." He shrugged.

"Well, sir, you know where we are. You also know that none of the others are in the same position as you. And we must just hope that there are no outside buyers attracted to the area."

This was a point that Henry had missed. Thinking, he asked: "Would the seller be agreeable to sell only to a local farmer, in view of the situation?"

"I think we could ask them. As locals they'll know what the others have gone through."

When the besuited Henry reappeared in the solicitor's office, the old man did a double-take. "I didn't think you were serious about changing, Henry!" He smiled. "I'm sure it showed them you were serious on my behalf though, especially if they'd known how you hate wearing one. Did you manage to persuade them?"

Henry told him the story, including the mention of the parcel of land.

"Hmm... well, they understand the situation. And they are correct in believing that local land is likely to increase in value because of the inundation.

A simple matter of supply and demand. Very well, that's all we can do with the case today. Thank you so much for being my researcher. It has helped me considerably."

He stopped and changed tack.

"Tell me – do you think I'm being a fool with the Rawle boy?"

It was a sudden question that took Henry off guard.

"Er... no. I don't think so..."

"Only think not?"

"No... not *only* think... Look: he's a friend of Stephen's, and he wouldn't remain one if he was two-faced. He's had plenty of bad luck, but we both know he's really put the work in, both at school and since becoming a builder. What he did last night showed that he's engaged and enthusiastic. I think he's a really good bet. And he's just a nice lad. Isn't he?"

There was a smile on the questioner's face. "Please forgive the question coming out of the blue. A professional technique, I'm afraid. The question asked which gives no time for prior consideration is the one that usually achieves the truth. I'm glad that you agree with me, especially as he's paid me the compliment of becoming another grandson!"

"Yes indeed," Henry smiled in return. "You do seem to be gathering grandchildren rather. Don't forget you'll have a real one soon."

"How could I forget a little matter like that?" the solicitor almost crowed. "Now, go and have a tea or something with that wife of yours in her café or my smile might just meet at the back, and you'd hate to have to render me medical assistance."

Henry laughed and left.

Before she closed the very quiet café, Henry had his cup of tea with Susan.

"Are you visiting the Kingsbridge estate agents tomorrow?" she asked.

"I suppose it would give a complete result. Bother. That means a suit again."

"You could take the three youngsters into town by boat. That'd be a change for them."

"Good idea. I'll warn Stan not to expect them on the bus."

"Yes, we could."

He looked at her, then suddenly understood.

"Sorry... it's just that I spent so many years as the sole adult in the house. I do know we're in it together, you know. And I do love you."

She just smiled. "And I shall keep reminding you of it."

As they walked down to the bus stop they each had to pull their coats around them. March had been kind up to that point, but not only was it raining unpleasantly hard but the forecast was 'changeable' according to the BBC. In the notoriously stormy month of March that threatened bad weather of any sort. The message was delivered to Stan and the five of them returned to the island.

"Had we better moor the boats in the lee of the island?" asked Henry, having difficulty controlling the launch to allow everyone to land.

"Might be as well. Good that we've got running moorings there too." Stephen was making ready to bring Mary's smaller dinghy to the stern of the launch and secure her for towing to sheltered water.

"Change first, you lot!" Susan called. "No need to get decent school clothes even wetter, and you most certainly will."

They looked sheepishly at each other and followed her to the house. Martin, about to shut the door against the wind, heard a voice say his name. Eyes widening he looked out and saw a bedraggled, windblown figure appear around the corner from the pigsties. He had to look twice before realising with a shock who it was.

"Bronwen!" he shouted. "Oh Bronwen."

When the embrace finally broke and he looked at her face, he was aware that other eyes were also watching, surprised.

"Come on," said Susan, "let's all get inside and get warm."

"I'm sorry…" she started.

"No. No more words until we're all sitting down and having something hot. Come on in now. Be fair to yourself."

The girl nodded, aware that it was not just Martin with his arm around her waist, who was looking after her. She was sent upstairs to change, and given some clothes of Mary's to wear until hers were dried.

Twice more, as they were preparing the meal, she had to be stopped from talking about her experiences. But when they had sat at the old farmhouse table with food in front of them, nothing would hold her back.

"Martin told you about his visit?" she asked. "I went home afterwards, and my father just walked behind me. I saw some people looking at us both, people from his Chapel as well, but I just didn't care any more. I went straight upstairs to my room. A short time later he was upstairs and came into my room without knocking.

"That's when we had the row. He repeated all the things he'd said by the castle in front of Martin, and a great deal else, and we finished off with his slamming my door and locking me in.

"And there I stayed. He brought in a sort of meal that evening after I heard raised voices from downstairs. Eventually I slept. The door was still locked in the morning. More meals were delivered – by Angharad our maid. Not by him, though he was there unlocking and locking the door. She was really embarrassed to have to be doing it, I could tell. She couldn't say anything but the look on her face told me what she was thinking.

"Each time they came I asked him how long he was going to keep me there." She blushed. "It's just as well I have a bathroom leading from the room. After the third time he said 'Until you apologise properly and promise never to see that boy again.'

"There was no chance to reply – he'd gone immediately. So I stewed it over and thought to myself that this was it. I wasn't going to be his 'thing' any more. I wasn't going to be controlled like a stupid little girl. So I thought of what I was going to say when he next appeared. And said it.

"His reply was as I thought it would be: 'In that case you will just stay in here. I will not have a child of mine being so disrespectful and rude to me as you were. You *will* apologise.'

"I shouted after him that I would be an adult in two years and was he going to keep me imprisoned until then, but he'd gone. He remained in the house until the Sunday, and I suppose had told Mum she wasn't to come near me. I heard footsteps approach the staircase to my room occasionally, but so did he; he would always come out of his study. But I knew nothing would keep him from his Chapel and that Mum would have to go with him as usual."

She smiled. "You know those spy books, where the prisoner escapes by sliding a sheet of paper under the door, twiddling the key with a bit of wire until it falls, then bringing in the key on the paper? Well, it works. He'd left the key in the lock, stupid man. So I got out. And I locked the door after me.

"He keeps the church collection in his study, so I'm sorry to say I took money from there. But I left a note telling him to top it back up by using my next two months' allowance."

She nodded, as if to confirm that she had done what she could to remain honest.

"I hurried to the station and caught the first train to anywhere," she admitted. "I just wanted to get away from the town where I was known. It was only to Gloucester, but I felt free for the first time in ages – since Mary's party, in fact. And even then I wasn't really free because Mum had been with me. Except when Martin and I… went for walks.

"Then I realised where I was, and that I was going in the wrong direction if I was coming down here." She blushed again. "I thought my geography was better than that. Anyway, I found a train to Bristol, having discovered that I should have gone the other way and under the Severn. It took me two hours, going the long way round.

"Anyway, I walked around Bristol until it was dark, then wandered into a Church which was still warm after evening service, then I hid and went to sleep."

She shuddered. "It wasn't very comfortable. And it got colder and colder. At dawn I just had to get up and walk around to get the blood moving. And then had a cat nap, then got up and walked… At last I heard a key in the door, hid again, and escaped when they weren't looking.

She smiled. "Thinking of Mary's journey, I got back to the station and tried to trace her steps. There was no ferry due at Kingsbridge but I was lucky enough to find someone bringing a pleasure boat back from being stuck fast in one of the creeks, so I asked if they could drop me off here. They did."

She took a deep breath and a forkful of food.

"Whew," said Stephen.

Martin just hugged her again as best he could from his chair by her side.

"I'm pretty sure that what you underwent was false imprisonment," said Henry, slowly. "Your uncle needs to know, of course, and he's the best person to advise on the legal aspect."

"But if he does, he's bound to tell Mum and *him*. And I am *not* going back there to be treated like that."

"But your Mum is going to be worried about you," said Susan. "You wouldn't want that, would you?"

"I *think*… I think that Mum might well guess and follow me down here. I think she's had enough of *him* and is only staying because they're married. She could stay with Uncle Algy."

"Yes, but at the moment she'll be worrying, scared." Stephen remembered how he'd felt when Mary had been taken.

"I suppose we should tell Uncle, then," she said reluctantly.

"His chickens have come home to roost," was her Uncle's response when she had explained everything to him on the phone. "I will telephone to Chepstow. It will probably mean speaking to the man. I know he insists on making the telephone his own, so that your mother has to view it as a special favour to be able to use it. But this time I hope he will have the humanity to let me speak to her. I would not want to tell him where his daughter is because he will probably insist I put you straight back on a return train."

"Which I would leave at the next stop, of course," she told him.

"Indeed. Which is the other reason why I would not attempt it, the first being that it would be completely unfair on you. And I would lose a grandson..."

She looked puzzled, so he explained about Martin.

"I feel it would be best if you stayed with me, though. There is very little room at Lofts' without using the café. I at least have spare rooms. And it will not stop you seeing Martin when you want, of course."

"But if my father comes to get me..."

"He will have to enter the house against my wishes if he does. And that would be a legal matter. No: either tonight, or tomorrow late afternoon, I suggest. You may have the room you liked when you last stayed with me."

It was evident to everyone that Martin didn't want her to live in Salcombe, but he had to accept that there was no room for them all at Lofts' as it was – not without using the café as a bedroom. He remained very attentive to her and finally managed to persuade her to come for a walk with him.

It was colder now. The wind was gusting but at least the rain had eased off to a thin drizzle. There was silence for a while.

"You know I want to get to know you properly, don't you?" Martin asked suddenly, as if scared of the lack of speech. "So that we can really find out about each other?"

"I know.. I know... I knew that when you turned up at home... at Chepstow."

"I just had to find out what was happening. Why my letters had been returned. You never said that you didn't want me to write, so I thought it must have been your father."

"You know it was."

He nodded. They walked on in silence.

"Are you all right? Really? You're very quiet."

"Martin, I've just had a row with my father, at last; I've left my home, spent a frozen night in a church, and travelled to Devon, the only other place I know where there are friendly people and family. And the only place I feel safe. Everything's topsy-turvy, and I'm really tired."

She drew breath. "I do like you. A lot. And the fact you made that journey showed me just how much you think of me. And I want to get to know you properly too. But all I really want now is to sleep. And at this stage I almost don't care where."

He looked at her, smiled uncertainly, and led her back to the house.

Susan was on the phone again. "No," they heard her say, "it's not safe to make the journey tonight. The wind is too strong – must be almost gale force by now. We can cope. If it's safe in the morning she can come then... Ok... ok. I'll see you tomorrow afternoon, I hope."

She turned to Bronwen. "That was Dad... Uncle Algy. He had a long, acrimonious conversation with your father who seemed to think you could be put on a train back to Chepstow tonight. Even telling him that it would be impossible to do so, and you would not agree to it anyway, did not persuade him. He didn't allow Dad to talk to your mother, so I don't know what is happening there. He was making noises about coming down and taking you back, but Dad told him that you would not go and that anyway he would not be permitted inside the house."

She stopped for breath.

"Are you going to try and make me go back?"

"No, Bronwen. Both Dad and I agree that holding you prisoner was the last straw and that you are better off here, in Salcombe. You are safe now."

The girl heaved a sigh. "Thank you. Thank you both – all – more than I can say. I just feel so relieved. I'm so tired after yesterday and today that I don't think I could have argued."

"You need to get into a warm bed, Bronwen. And soon, I suggest. Mary, would you mind if she used your room? It's more out of the way and she wouldn't be disturbed. You can sleep in the new room here, and Steve and Martin can use the café. Is that all right for everyone?"

Two lots of bedclothes were changed and an exhausted girl thankfully heaved herself into the small upstairs room. She had just settled down when there was a knock at the door.

"Come in," she said sleepily.

"I just wanted to say goodnight." Martin was unsure about crossing the threshold into what he viewed as a very female room.

Despite her tiredness, Bronwen smiled.

"I'm sorry I was irritable outside, but I really had had enough for one day. You are allowed in, you know."

Cautiously he crossed to the bed and knelt at her side, watching her face.

"Thank you for coming up. And for everything else you've done. *R'wyt ti fy machgen hyfryd.*"

Martin smiled a little uncertainly. "What does that mean, please?"

"You'll find out, some time."

He raised his eyebrows. "Say it again?"

She did. He repeated it as "ruity fer markyen huvrid".

She smiled and closed her eyes. "That's good enough. But now... good night."

"Good night," he whispered, and was about to stand. Instead, he leant forward and lightly kissed her forehead. The eyes flickered open; a smile appeared.

"I shall sleep better now," she murmured, and her eyes closed again.

It was all he could do to stop himself climbing in beside her to hold her and chase some of the hurt away. He knew he couldn't, but...

Swiftly he stood, stole another look at her and quietly left the room. He never saw the smile reappear on her face.

4 – Trees

The BBC had been right: the weather remained 'changeable'. Next morning had changed for the worse and even the voyage up to Kingsbridge was at times very wet. Indeed, it was the sort of weather that had prompted Henry to insist they all wore the hated lifejackets which had proved so unpopular when he had first obtained them.

There was no mutiny, though a rather strained silence held for the first few minutes.

Susan and Bronwen would have had to use the smaller outboard dinghy to reach Salcombe, but Susan decided it was too rough. She had to call and ask a friend in the town to run the café there.

She made up for the enforced idleness by a large baking effort, and was pleased and surprised that Bronwen was not just a help but had ideas of her own.

"It's *bara brith,*" she explained as one of her concoctions came from the oven. "Literally 'speckled bread'. It's very Welsh. Mum and I love it, Da… my father just turns up his nose at it."

"Doesn't he like Welsh things at all?" asked Susan.

"If it's to do with Chapel or the town, yes. But he insists as far as he can, even now, that people don't speak Welsh at school. Or in Chapel. But the main church has a Welsh male voice choir, and they love singing in Welsh." She laughed. "It seems they do it especially when he's there."

Susan laughed. "I didn't know Welsh was still spoken."

"It isn't. Not much. But there were a few of us who felt that here we were, with centuries of tradition, and we couldn't enjoy it properly because it was in a foreign language. Imagine – the language of your own land and it's called 'foreign'. We learnt French at school, of course; but France is miles away. Wales is all around us."

"So did you learn Welsh?"

"A little. We got so far, then one of the girls thought she'd surprise her parents by a Welsh poem, which she translated. They were furious she'd learnt it and seemed to think that anyone who could speak Welsh was destined for the gutters. They told the other parents, and I was forbidden ever to speak it or mention it. But our maid Angharad spoke it, and when I was in the kitchen with her we would practise. It was only Mum who came in there, so I knew it was safe."

This was all a new concept to Susan, but she could understand there was a conflict – not just in that family but throughout Wales, or so she thought. It had not been long since the Welsh-Not was finally abolished.

"So what does Welsh sound like?" she asked.

Bronwen smiled. "I'm not fluent. You need to come from a country area, as Angharad does, or from North Wales for that. But I told Martin he was my beautiful boy last night – *r'wyt ti fy machgen hyfryd* – and he didn't know what I meant. He just repeated it – sort of! And I'd had to ask Angharad how to say that."

Susan smiled. "You're fond of him, aren't you?"

She paused. "It seems crazy, but yes, and I've only met him four times. Twice here, once in Chepstow – you've got to admire someone who comes to check

26

that you're all right, haven't you? – and here, now. But he's good looking and intelligent and nice to be with, and I want to know him properly. He seems to like me."

"Understandably. Yes, he's a nice lad. I really hope he does get a job with an architect so he can use some of that intelligence."

"I'd give him a job if I was them. Perhaps if he does, I could ask if they want a typist."

"Do you type?"

"No. But I could learn."

"I think you may be able to do better than that. Don't forget we're not in the 1930s any more! Women can do all sorts of things nowadays... perhaps you could train as an architect too? Or... or how about a solicitor?"

Bronwen's eyes widened. "*Me?* An architect? Or a Solicitor like Uncle Algy?"

"Why not? If learning together doesn't get you to know each other, nothing will!"

"I could ask him what he thinks..."

"Do. But remember..."

What she was about to be told to remember, Bronwen never did discover. Outside there was a noise of snapping, then creaking, then a distinct tearing noise; but all were ten times louder than mere words can describe.

Then the house shook as a loud crashing, rustling impact rocked the very ground, far too near to the house for comfort. A cup jumped from the centre of one of the dresser's shelves and smashed on the floor.

The two looked at each other, scared.

"Was that a tree?" asked Susan, shakily.

"I... I don't know. Is it safe to go out, do you think?"

They listened. Apart from the wind which still seemed as strong, and the rain which was still falling, there seemed to be silence.

"Come on," said Susan, and crossed to the door. She opened it and, to her credit, stifled a scream; it emerged as a gasp. Bronwen hurried to her side.

The outside door was half off its hinges. A branch protruded through the gap, nearly the length of the short lobby. Beyond it was a maze of other branches blocking their view but with a massive tree trunk just visible, running at an angle almost towards the house.

"Can we see more from upstairs?" Bronwen suggested. Susan tore her eyes away from the sight and shut the inner door on it.

"Yes," she admitted, still very shaken. "Yes, perhaps we can."

From her and Henry's bedroom they gazed out onto the corner of the house. One of the island's massive, historic oak trees had given up its hold on the ground, narrowly missed the corner of the house in its death throes, A few yards to the east and it would have crushed part of the building.

Susan shuddered. Bronwen looked at her sharply.

"It's done no harm, except that we'll have to get out by using the back windows."

"But it could so easily have done. It could have demolished the place. We could have been killed..."

This was not like the Susan she knew. Carefully, in case it might have been unwelcome, Bronwen offered her arms to Susan and just held her, hoping the nightmare vision might recede. The breathing subsided, grew normal and Susan detached herself.

"Sorry. I'm usually better than that – I can stand up when things go wrong. But I just couldn't help thinking: what if the whole family had been here and it had hit the house? You, Henry, Stephen, Mary, Martin… and the baby…"

She took a deep breath.

"But you're right. It didn't. But we are going to get some specialists to look at the other trees after this, and I don't care what it costs."

Bronwen nodded. "I think that might be a good idea. If there are any others as old as that one it would be good to know."

"Come on. We'll go out of the window and make sure there are no others loose and threatening. It's the least we can do."

"Should we tell any of the others?"

"Nothing anyone can do – except perhaps Dad – Uncle Algy. He might know a company to cut it up and remove it."

"But – well, what about Martin's company? Would they want the wood for building?"

Susan looked at her, surprised. "I would never have thought of that. Yes. If we can sell it to them it'd save the cost of carting it away. We'd best wait until Martin gets home, then."

They climbed out of the window, Susan with caution in view of her pregnancy. The tree, when they arrived at it, had left a considerable mess. The roots had brought a lot of earth from the ground, and without touching it they could see how wet it was, how the ground was sodden with the recent rain.

"We were lucky it brought no others down with it," Bronwen remarked.

"I never thought of that. I suppose it didn't weaken any, did it?"

"Difficult to say. Is anything hanging down?"

They scanned the branches but nothing was obvious.

"I'm still not happy about it," Susan said. "We need to get someone out here today. I'm going to phone Dad. He'll know who deals with trees."

They climbed back through the window. Susan made the call and explained what had happened. Her father was alarmed, but thankful they were both safe. He thought, but didn't know anyone who was anything but an ordinary gardener.

"Best to wait until Martin returns," was his suggestion. "or maybe even phone the office."

"But would a building firm know about trees?" asked Susan.

"They might know someone who does," he replied.

So she made another call. To her surprise Martin was there, having had to return to Salcombe to call into his employer's office. He too was worried to hear of the fall, and his first question was about Bronwen. Susan smiled.

"She's fine – we both are, but we're worried that the tree might have hit others on the way down, and that there may be others that are dangerous. We really need a tree expert."

"I'll see who knows anything about them," Martin told her. "Hold on."

There was a long pause. Susan wondered if she should have asked him to call her back.

"Hallo Mrs Loft," said a voice. "I hear you have a tree problem. I've got a company looking for decent wood, and they fell trees to get it, usually. They'd be pleased to get rid of yours, I'm sure."

"But that's only half of it," Susan started.

"Ah yes, but they also have to look at the trees they want to see what health they're in, and make sure they're not just going to fall over as soon as someone climbs up into them. They're as good as you'll get."

Susan paused. "So if there's anything else that's dangerous, they'll be able to tell us?"

"That's right."

"Very well. Can you tell me who they are, please?"

He dictated the details over. Bronwen was about to ask if she could talk to Martin when Susan put the receiver down.

"Should we?" asked Susan.

"It's the only way if you want peace of mind,"

"You don't think Henry will mind?"

This was unlike the usually decisive Susan. Bronwen shook her head.

"By the time he gets back it'll be too late for them to reach us today, so we'd have to hope for the best overnight. No, I think we should get them out as soon as possible."

Susan dialled the number. Explaining the situation took some time but the result was an offer to come out as soon as one of their people returned from another job. "Probably this afternoon," said the man. "But if you're on that island, how are we going to get to you?"

"We'll come and fetch you," Susan told him. "Where's your nearest point? Ours is Lincombe but that's very out of the way."

"We're up Alvington, so it's no skin off our nose whether we come to Salcombe, Kingsbridge or Lincombe. Kingsbridge is nearest to us, though."

"We can get you from Kingsbridge. It's only a small boat, so I hope it's big enough. How many people will there be?"

"Just me. Thinking about it, if Lincombe's nearest to you that'd be best, so if we need to do any cutting it's quickest to ferry the tools over from there."

"Thank you. When might you be able to come?"

He hoped they should be there in three hours, but couldn't promise.

While they were waiting Henry phoned from Mr Merryweather's office, almost beside himself with worry about their safety. Susan calmed him down, then told him what they'd done.

"Good for you," he said. "Well done. Let's hope they find nothing else. Or rather, let's hope that if there *is* something else, they find it."

Susan paused, slightly confused. "Ahh, yes, I see what you mean. Yes, that's the general idea. I hoped you didn't mind our phoning."

"We work as a team, you, Steve and me. What goes for one goes for all three – and for Mary and Martin."

"We *are* growing our family, aren't we?"

He laughed. "There is one particular addition I'm particularly looking forward to."

"I'll be glad, too! Speaking of family, why are you in Salcombe? You've not forgotten about the others later, have you?"

"They'll be on the school bus."

"Did you arrange that with them?"

"No – why?"

"Because you promised you'd collect them from Kingsbridge in the launch."

Silence.

"Henry?"

"I'm absolutely daft. I forgot all about that. I'll have to go back up there."

"You will, or they'll not let you forget it! How did you forget?"

"Everyone in Kingsbridge was so quick to give the figures we need that I left there an hour ago to come back down here to report in. Sorry – I'll head back to the island now and back to Kingsbridge later."

"Good," said Susan, "that means you can have a look yourself and make sure I'm not over-reacting."

"Since I don't know enough about trees, I would have done the same as you. If your chap is coming soon we can both talk to him. I'll see you as soon as I can get there."

"Hallo Martin." The old solicitor smiled as the lad poked his head cautiously round the office door, having been instructed to go in by the firm's receptionist.

"Hallo Grandad," he replied cautiously, and was rewarded by a broadening of the smile.

"What can I do for you? You have not run out of money already, surely?"

Martin looked at him worriedly, but was relieved to see the smile still there.

"No... It's... were you able to find out who was the best architect for me to try first, please?"

"Do you know, I've been so busy so far today that it had slipped from my memory. Wait there. Let me make some phone calls. If you sit there, nobody else can interrupt.

He made the calls. One of the Kingsbridge solicitors was surprised that he should want to involve himself with finding someone a job, and gave him the names of the two architect companies in the town – information he knew already. When pressed for an opinion on the better of the two he said there was nothing between them.

Henry shrugged and politely ended the call.

"I never did like them," he said, and reached to dial the other number.

The tone of this conversation was altogether different, Martin thought after listening for some moments.

"Another one!" he heard the surprised comment. Then "Salcombe!" followed by another pause. A few moments later he pointed to a pad of paper and a pencil. Martin readied himself and wrote as an address was dictated. At last the phone was replaced.

The old man sat for a moment or two whilst Martin waited, wondering.

"Hmmm... I don't know what to think, in all honesty. It might work, or it might be a complete waste of time."

He paused again. Martin raised his eyebrows and looked at him.

Slowly, he started again. "I am told that a young man, quite brilliant, has started working as an architect from his parents' home. And it's here, in Salcombe. You have the address. He has recently qualified, but instead of the time-honoured way into the profession that I outlined to you, he has decided to set up on his own and offer his services around the South Hams. My colleague in Kingsbridge has a client for whom he has just done some work. His description was that the client sees him as a maverick, but that he was very, very efficient whilst being innovative in bringing the client's wishes to a design.

"Apparently it was quite a major job, well done, and the lad's had a good deal of work on the back of that. So much so that he's now looking for someone to help in the office. But he can't afford another qualified architect."

He let the conversation hang.

"When can I go and see him?" Martin asked.

"You have yet to hear the disadvantages of working for him. There are a few, and they are potentially serious, though in view of the situation you might feel that... Well.

"You see, he is young, inexperienced, and still finding his way. It may be that he makes mistakes in a client's work which prove disastrous; there is after all no one to check his work. If that happens and he goes out of business, you would be out of a job, and, which is definitely worse, you would be 'the man who worked with that solicitor who made the mistake and the house fell down'. That sort of stigma is difficult to shake off. You would find it difficult or impossible to join another firm, particularly locally.

"So, you see, there are risks. If you joined an established firm it is just that, established and reliable. So you have a choice to make. And it has to be a decision *you* make."

"But... without making the decision for me, what would you do if you were in my position, Grandad?"

The old man smiled again.

"I think... I think it would do no harm to go and talk to him, if you can make an appointment. You're not bound to accept any offer he makes – if he does. But also talk about it to that adopted family of yours. They have horse sense."

"But..." Martin was nothing if not persistent. "... but if you were eighteen, a builder with about two years' experience, and wanted to qualify as an architect, what would you do?"

"It is not my decision to make. When I was eighteen I was being told what to do. I vowed I would never direct my children in that way."

Martin noticed a sudden unexpected note of bitterness. It sounded as if the man's life course had been decided for him early on, and that he didn't have the strength to resist the decision.

"Were you... did you have an argument with your father too, just like me? And Bronwen?"

Silence. The eyes that now looked into his over the desk were serious, unsmiling. Martin felt as if he were being tested, or that he had crossed a line of some sort. He felt, though, it was important not to break that eye contact.

A heavy sigh. "I was not in an argument. Arguments were not the done thing. Not in my youth, not in my family. It was essentially the same atmosphere that

Bronwen suffered. Like her, I just did what I was told. And I regretted it for years, until I managed to leave my father's practice and set up my own. You see, at University I was a cricket player, captained my side, and was picked for the County, and then... well, I may as well tell you... for England. But when I told my father he was furious and told me I had to give up any ideas of that and get back to my studies. As time went on all hope of cricket as a career ebbed away and I was forced to use my law degree in my father's firm of solicitors.

"Yes. I did what I was told. And it was done through gritted teeth until I qualified on my own account and had ten years' experience under my belt. I had met Susan's mother during all this, and increasingly we felt indomitable, untouchable. One amazing day I knew I had developed the strength to tell my father that I was going to get married, that I was moving away, and that I was setting up a practice in a small town in Devonshire.

"By that time my fiancée and I had made all the arrangements. Not just for the practice but for the wedding too, and the first my father knew about it was when the banns were read."

He paused again and gave another grim smile.

"I never went back to the practice. He forbade me. It left him with cases to complete about which he knew nothing, but he refused to back down. My mother came to the wedding; he did not. I tried to build bridges between us once I was down here, but he declined all contact."

He gave another grim smile. "Sounds a little familiar, I imagine."

Martin, appalled, nodded.

"So you see," he said, suddenly warming to his original point again, "I don't want to give advice based on what I feel about a situation. I will give facts, and suggest outcomes. That is all, and you will understand why, now."

It was Martin's turn to sigh, and to think.

"Forgive me, Grandad, if I say this. I know it's maybe tactless, if that's the right word. But you came down here, leaving a successful firm of solicitors, with a new wife... to a situation which you believed – *believed* – would be successful, knowing that if it wasn't you would be unable to return."

He paused, waiting to see how this would be received. The steady, smile-less gaze was back, and once again he held it.

"You have intelligence, my adopted Grandson. And you are unafraid to present an argument. Yes, of course; with the self-assurance of youth – well, thirty years of life, anyway – I took a massive chance. And I believe you are saying to me, without actually doing so, that if *I* took such a chance, so should you be able to.

"And depending on how you and this young architect get on, it may well be a very, very attractive and exciting prospect, just like mine was. And not to have the dead weight of an old fashioned firm which might stifle you – well, that's an exciting prospect too. It was more exciting for me, for I had come from a situation where I had experienced that dead weight. You have not, and I hope you never have to.

"You asked me the question 'what would I have done?' I think you probably know the answer by now. But there are still risks."

Another silence.

"Yes, Grandad, just as there were for you in coming here. But mine are fewer than yours."

"How do you work that out, pray?"

"Because, if it all fails and crashes, I would still have you. You're not the sort of person who gives up on his family. Oh yes..." He could see the look on the old man's face "...you've said some really nice things about me and that means... well, a lot. More than you could possibly know... or maybe, on reflection, you do. I hope I can live up to them. But just as you've... you've complimented me like that, I can understand more about you – especially now. And I have opinions too. So..." he gulped "...I feel I might be able to pay compliments in return."

He looked into those grave eyes still.

"Even if it's only by talking to myself. And I have Susan and Henry, and Mary and Stephen. And, I hope, Bronwen. So I admire your courage in building up what you have. Tremendously. But you see now that you've helped me to come to... No. To weigh my choices."

Once again there was silence. The gaze was still straight into Martin's eyes and not for the first time he wondered what his adopted Grandfather was going to say, and whether he'd be bawled out. But then he saw a smile appear, very gradually.

"I have no idea where you learned to decide on a course of discussion like that so quickly, based on new information you have just heard in the course of a conversation. I also have no idea where you developed the courage to present it so gently to a man with whom many others fear to argue – in Court, anyway. But you have done so and have once again proved me right to have invested in you. Please, though, never do anything that would bring you against me in a Court, because I fear that I could possibly lose an argument against you."

"I hope I would never come up against anyone in any Court," Martin protested. "And certainly not you! But they'd never allow that, would they?"

"These things are sometimes overlooked. But yes, I am sure we shall never have cause to face each other like that. Particularly as you will be an architect, not a Solicitor."

He smiled. "I still think you should talk to the others. But if your mind is made up, you need to write a letter to your potential employer to explain the position. And tell him what you have to offer him. And include your ability to discuss matters without becoming confused – and you may want to quote me in that."

5 – Mike Alexander

The tree specialists had still not appeared by the time Henry moored at the island. He examined the damage and went white when he realised how close the immense old trunk had come to demolishing the house. His inexpert eye looked at the remaining trees and their branches, one or two he thought might have been damaged in the fall.

Susan looked at her watch. "They should be there by now," she told him. "Shall I go?"

"No, I will. I spoke to him, after all. He might think it odd if a man turned up."

He nodded and she set off for Lincombe in the boat.

"I hope they're not too long," he said to Bronwen. "I have to get to Kingsbridge for the others fairly soon."

"It's only two of them. You could take Susan's dinghy."

"In this weather? I'm not so sure. Apart from the safety angle they'd get their school clothes wet for sure."

She smiled. "That wouldn't worry them!"

"No, but they'd need washing and drying before tomorrow."

Twenty minutes later Susan was back. Ed Luscombe admitted to being the brother of the lady in the Blanksmill Post Office and seemed just as pleasant and easy going as she. Presented with the situation he did a lot of head scratching and looking up into the branches. Then the notebook came out.

"Henry! Kingsbridge!" Susan called suddenly.

He looked at his watch. "Oh damn. It really isn't my day, is it? I'll be late."

"'Ere, you're not marooning me, are you?" said Ed Luscombe.

They explained the situation and said there was a smaller boat on the island too. Henry ran to the launch again.

Three branches, said Ed Luscombe, needed to come down so they could be sure of being safe. Another nearby tree seemed to be showing signs of being loose in the ground.

"There was all that rain and wind four years ago," he said, "and this lot's just carried on where that let off. If you like I'll have a walk round and have a look at the others while I'm here, just to make sure. If we've got to get any others down it'd make sense to do all of them when we have the men and tools on site. And then we can start them all off seasoning together so we've got a load when we need them."

"So will you be buying them from us?" Susan asked.

"Well, that's for you and the guv'nor to talk about," he said cautiously. "Chances are if the wood's in good condition – and the main one's an oak – then it might at least reduce the cost to you. And if we find more – well…"

"So you can't give us an idea yet?"

He shook his head. "Not till I've had a look round, leastways."

"And what about the damaged branches?"

"There's one worries me, but the rest can wait a day or two. I'll get some ropes and a saw and sort that one out, if that's okay?"

Susan assured him it was, and thanked him. She fetched her little dinghy and took him on the spray-soaking and bumpy voyage to Lincombe and back.

Henry's late arrival at Kingsbridge was greeted with a round of applause from his son and daughter, though the laughter was stilled when he told them the cause of his lateness. They asked the usual concerned questions and were assured all was well, but then asked about Martin who was meant to be making the journey with them.

"He had to go to Salcombe," said Henry. "We'll get him later. I don't even know where he'll be."

"Town Hard, most certainly," said Stephen. "That's where you'd pick him up if he'd come back by bus with us."

Henry agreed, and cast off again. The wind, though in their faces, seemed to be dropping, though there was still quite a chop to the water. Their arrival found Ted Luscombe just completing his circuit of the island, much to the young couple's surprise. Henry had to explain again.

He had discovered two more quite ancient trees which he felt needed attention, but wasn't sure if felling them was necessary.

"We need to get up there and have a closer look," he said. "We'll do that when we've got some help here, see? I've taken that branch down that looked damaged. Wasn't *that* bad, but better down than uncertain. Next, I'll talk to the guv'nor and see what we can do. He'll write in a day or two."

Henry thanked him.

"I'll take him back to Lincombe, Dad, then go down to Salcombe and get Martin. I'll take the dinghy – it's fun in this weather."

"Make sure you wear a life jacket, Steve. Mary going with you?"

"No. She said she wanted to change and get warm. We had a bit of a wait at Kingsbridge, you know…" He held up is hand "…And yes, I know it couldn't be helped!"

Martin's journey to the solicitor had taken place when he had left the builder's premises. He could have returned to Kingsbridge by bus but his arrival would have coincided with knocking off time. His boss agreed he should stay in Salcombe and have the time off. He had spent the best part of half an hour at the solicitor's office. Realisation dawned as he left the building that he was stranded in the town and he wondered who would come and get him – if anyone. Surely Bronwen would remember eventually?

Rather uncertainly he started walking down towards – and then past - the Hard, deep in a daydream, and unusually for him looking into shop windows. Later at the foot of Market Street's hill, still thinking hard, he was shaken to the core to hear a loud report which echoed round the buildings. A moment's confusion and he realised it was the Lifeboat maroon sounding. A man behind him was already running.

With time to kill, Martin followed him, also at the run, then slowed as he thought others might think he was another crew member. Down Fore Street, Union Place and round the corner at the Fortescue he hurried, down to the Customs Quay where the crew was clambering into their gear and awaiting transfer out to the Lifeboat, which was moored as always in deep water.

He watched them, wondering if he'd ever have the nerve to join in what looked like real-life adventure. A small boat appeared past Snapes Point, the only one of its size moving in the choppy water of the harbour. His attention was drawn to it. Was that Stephen? Dividing his attention between it and the scene in front of him he came to the conclusion that the person was the right shape for his friend, and the dinghy looked like theirs too. And it was headed towards the Hard. He muttered something and set off there himself.

"Lifeboat's just going out," were his first words when the two met.

"Thought there was something going on. Will we be in the way if we go now?"

"Don't think so. It didn't look as if they were casting off straight away."

Stephen pushed the boat off and steered back towards the north. Martin looked back at the Lifeboat crew and saw their launch also setting off. He told Stephen, who throttled back. They bobbed up and down like a cork whilst the Lifeboat tender sped past.

"I'd like to join that," said Martin.

"You'd need to live in Salcombe, then," he was told. "It'd take too long to answer a maroon if you were on the Island – and we'd not hear the maroon."

Martin nodded. "Suppose not. One day, perhaps."

He looked again back towards the Customs Quay. There seemed to be another crew member there, kitted up and waving furiously.

"Steve – look; there's another of the crew who's missed their boat. How about us taking him over?"

Stephen looked. Certainly the man was agitated. Was he waving at the tender – or was it to them?

"Hang on to your hat!" he called, and put the throttle on full, turning the little dinghy as he did. They made a beeline for the quay.

Those four years of boat handling had taught Stephen a thing or two. The manoeuvre to get to the steps was as well done as anyone could wish for. The man scrambled in, and Stephen set off without a pause.

A very cultured voice shouted to them, making itself heard over the noisy outboard. "Look, I'm most frightfully grateful to you. I only realised there was a call when Dad shouted at me. I was working, you see, and I concentrate so hard that I haven't a clue what's going on, usually. I'm Mike Alexander, by the way."

Martin made a sort of gasping noise. The man looked at him.

"Are you okay?"

"Yes… er… Martin Rawle and Stephen Loft. I… I'm about to write to you."

"What, to send me a bill for the petrol? Surely…"

"No, no, no! Hardly! I… Now isn't the time. But when you get a letter from Martin Rawle, that's me. And it's good to meet you." He grinned. "Even if we're going hammer and tongs across the Salcombe Estuary, it's good to meet you."

"You want some work done?"

"No… well, maybe Steve's Dad does, but I want to train to be an architect."

The man laughed out loud. "As you say, here we are hammering over the water trying to catch up with a Lifeboat and I get a job prospect and the offer of help. Salcombe's amazing. Do you think I'd be able to choose one without the other?"

"Er... well, I'm not in a position to say no, er... sir."

"If you're a hard bargainer you might. But look, don't bother with a letter. Got the address? Come up. Saturday if you can – I try and get a day off then. Oh damn... the tender's coming away already. Will this boat go any faster?"

"Sorry," said Stephen. "I'm at full throttle now."

"Well, we'll just have to hope they wait... there's someone pointing at us now. Good. Look, when we get there, there won't be time for fond goodbyes. I'll just do an undignified scramble up the ladder and turn into a good little crew member. But I really do thank you for coming to rescue me like that. In fact, when you come for a chat about a job, you come too. We might nip out to a pub instead of tame tea and biscuits at home. So come at lunch time on Saturday and I'll treat you."

"I'd like to," Stephen started, "but I hardly get to see my fiancée during the week. Not properly. So..."

"Bring her too. I'm sure we can chat while you two play darts or something."

"Are you sure?"

"'Course. Now look, here we are..."

There were shouts from above. Stephen executed another turn to bring his port beam alongside, bumped gently into the ladder and before they knew it Mike was gone. The dinghy lurched to starboard and nearly let a wave top in, but Martin shifted amidships and disaster was averted.

"Thanks!" was bellowed down to them as Stephen cautiously moved away to the Lifeboat stern. Water boiled from under it as their anchor was weighed and he hastily increased speed to avoid being swamped.

It was a lumpy sea in the centre of the Estuary after the Lifeboat had sped away from them. In weather like this the flow in the narrows between Snapes Point and Scoble Point runs fast on an ebbing tide. With the wind battling against it the water was quite troubled. Coming south, Stephen had hardly noticed it, being borne along by the current, but heading against it was noticeably uncomfortable. They were glad to reach the comparative peace of The Bag, after which it all calmed down and their voyage was almost quiet. Darkness had all but fallen by the time they arrived at their mooring at the north of the island. Each of them now carried a torch so as to be prepared for the stygian darkness of moonless nights.

"I was getting so worried about you." Bronwen's comment to Martin made him smile happily. He held his arms out and was even happier when she allowed them around her.

Over the meal there was a lot of news to share round. There were congratulations to the two boys about their escapade with the Lifeboat and particularly to Martin on making a good impression with their passenger.

He smiled happily. "It was one heck of a coincidence. I hardly believed it when he said who he was."

"I thought you were choking," Stephen told him.

He shook his head, grinning. "I'm looking forward to Saturday... do you think he'd mind if Bronwen came too?"

"He invited Mary, as well as me. I don't see why not, if they want to come?"

"We can always go shopping. Window shopping, at least. How about you,

Bronwen?"

"That'd be nice."

"Bronwen…" Henry started slowly "… do you think Saturday would be a good day for you to move to your Uncle's place in Salcombe? I mean, we love you being here, but… well, you know what he said."

There were two straight faces in the room at that, and Bronwen looked as if she was about to start a discussion. Susan was quick to forestall her by offering another cup of tea round.

"You'll still be able to visit each other, obviously," she told them. "Either here or at Dad's. But you know we just don't have room here on a day-to-day basis. What we do for special event or in an emergency is one thing, but sleeping in the café day by day is another."

Bronwen nodded, still rather glumly.

Martin reached for her hand. "I shan't be far away. And if I do get to work with this chap Alexander I'll be in Salcombe every day."

"And we'll be expecting you back here on Sunday, with Dad," said Susan, remembering something.

Martin looked at her, a smile appearing on his face.

"No, the others may have forgotten your birthday," Susan continued, "but I hadn't."

By Saturday the weather had settled down to its normal March self. Susan had phoned her father yet again and had confirmed that Bronwen could move down to his house, but that he and she were expected at Lofts' to celebrate Martin's eighteenth birthday the following day.

"We'll bring you back after Church," she said.

Martin settled down with a lot of paper and made a neater job of his plans for extending Lofts' farmhouse.

The younger contingent made the journey to Salcombe late that morning. In Martin's case he was partly nervous and partly buoyed up by Mike Alexander's casual attitude. Alone of them, he was in a suit and tie, though the others were far from scruffily dressed. It was impossible for any of them except Bronwen to walk through the town without being greeted by acquaintances and friends. Bronwen received many inquiring glances, as did Martin's suit.

The four of them appeared at the Alexanders' house just after 12.30. There was a long delay before footsteps approached, and by the sound of them, running.

"Sorry," Mike said, "I was working again and only just conscious of the bell. Come in a second… We can make introductions on the way down."

He showed them into a living room and told them to make themselves comfortable.

"Well, *he's* not wearing a suit!" Stephen observed.

Martin felt over-dressed.

They waited in silence apart from one or two remarks. Footsteps approached, the door opened and a figure said: "Oh! Oh, sorry"

He was a man of about fifty, and looked so like Mike Alexander that they did a double take. The brown, slightly wavy hair, the nose and the pleasant expression and voice were so alike.

They stood "Er... we're just waiting for Mi... for Mr Alexander," said Martin.

The man laughed. "Ah well, that used to be me. But so many people come to this house now that I suppose it's Mike you really want. He knows you're here, of course? He's not gone back to that drawing board of his, I hope. I'll go and find him."

Before he had a chance to move their host returned, grinning.

"You've found Dad, I see. Or he found you. Sorry, Dad, I never had the chance to warn you. This is Martin Rawle, who wants to see if he can stand working with me, and this is Stephen Loft – is that the family on Loft Island who were in the news some years ago?"

Stephen admitted that they were, then introduced Mary and Bronwen.

"I know of Mary. You are the young lady who spent an unhappy three years in Scotland, forced there by a relative, I believe? You see, Dad, I don't spend *all* my time at the drawing board."

"Only because you don't want to miss any design work that might come out of a case," his father retorted.

"Discovered. My guilty secret. Anyway, Miss Loft, I'm glad to meet you. And Bronwen... I imagine you might be something to do with Martin?"

"I am," she said shyly. "We like each other."

He nodded. "So now we all know each other. I suggest we go to the town and have a drink and something to eat. Perhaps Martin and I can have a quiet chat whist the rest of you play darts or something. Is the Shipwrights okay for everyone?"

Mary had only once been in a pub, and technically that was a hotel in South Brent. She had bought a snack there as she neared the end of her escape from the school in Scotland. Bronwen had never been allowed anywhere near a pub. So when they were ushered in in front of the men they were both rather reticent until Stephen, with the authority of just three visits to that same pub with Henry, led the way.

"My treat," said Mike. "I have a petrol bill to pay."

Stephen and Henry laughed. The girls looked at him with enquiring looks on their faces but smiled anyway.

They found a table. "First thing," said Mike, "I'm Mike. I'm not that much older than any of you so let's just treat each other as friends, may we? And that includes you, Martin. If we do end up working together the last thing I want is a sycophant. But we need to get to know each other first, I suggest."

He asked them about Loft Island, and who lived there. Martin told his story and Mike was sympathetic, and intrigued that Martin had wanted to return to school to take the exams. Soon he understood more about them than they probably realised. It was when Stephen started talking about the need for more accommodation and to have the café as part of the house that he really started talking, rather than just listening.

They heard about his interest in buildings as a child and how he had ensured that his school provided technical drawing and that it could form part of his curriculum. Martin smiled to himself but said nothing. Mike had naturally had the opportunity to continue to Advanced Level GCE's and had followed his dream into a University course.

"Not Oxford or Cambridge," he admitted. "I couldn't find the right course there. But Exeter did, and they were very good."

He described the luck he'd had since graduating and ended by telling them that he seemed to be attracting work of all sorts that he could hardly keep up with.

"And that's me, up to date," he finished. "Except that I kept on saying that I really needed help, but that I couldn't afford to take on someone qualified. And then along come two useful blokes who help me out in an emergency, and one of them wants to become an architect. So I'd be silly to ignore that.

"May I talk to Martin now? I don't think it'd be fair on him to have to lay out his stall in front of everyone. Shall we move to another table, or do you people want a game of darts, or Devil-Amongst-the Tailors?"

They looked at the nearby table.

"The people behind the bar will tell you how it works," he told them.

"Now then Martin," he started when they had gone off, "tell me about yourself. More about yourself."

Martin thought. "Well, you know about how I got to be living at Loft..."

"Yes, some of it. But if it's not prying too much, what were the real problems that led to it?"

"My father is a farmer. He was shot down twice in the war and injured the second time. He's never really recovered and when he's in pain it comes out as a bad temper. I was at school, working hard on exams, and more and more he was telling me to make a real contribution to the farm or go and get a job so we had more money coming in. At last I couldn't stand it any more and we had a blazing row.

"He said if that's how I felt I'd better go and look after myself, and not come back when I got hungry. I called Stephen, and they told me I could live with them."

Mike nodded. "And then?"

Martin shrugged. "I went back to school and got my six 'O' Levels."

"What are they?"

"Maths, English, French, Technical Drawing, Geography, and History."

"A good school if they offered technical drawing."

"They didn't, actually. Someone saw I was good at art in a clinical way..." He laughed at the memory. "...and suggested I should try tech drawing. It sounded like a good idea, so they asked if I wanted to do a correspondence course. I tried it, loved it and it seemed I was quite good. The extra work was one of the things my Dad hated me doing."

Mike grimaced. "But you got the GCE. You didn't go on to Advanced?"

He shook his head. "Didn't seem right, really. It would have been more expensive for the Lofts, and they needed the help with building the café. Steve and I had done some of the construction work at weekends when we weren't at school."

"Did you? Had you done any before?"

"No, none. It was the firm I work for now that built it really. We were just labouring for them. But it was interesting. And tiring!" He remembered back to those muscle-aching Monday mornings after weekends of heavy work.

"But didn't you think of going back after that? After the café season? Either of you?"

"Oh, Stephen did. That was always his and his Dad's plan. But me... it never really occurred to me. I was at a loose end, but then the boss – my current employer – came and offered me some part time work and I jumped at it. I've been doing that ever since."

"So you work for a building firm at the moment?"

"Yes. Just a labourer really, but I've seen a lot of the things they have to think about. And one of our jobs has been on a pair of cottages that Stephen's brother is buying. I'm going to rent one of them – I think I am – and I've been thinking about things and making suggestions as the work's gone on."

"So you've been adding your own touches to it?"

"Yes, though it's more a case of making careful suggestions to the foreman. It caused some comments to start with, but he now thinks of me as a sort of assistant, though he laughs at the idea if anyone mentions it."

"Hmm. I'd like to see them, and see what you've done."

"We can go up at any time. Peter's let me have a key."

"Peter?"

"Peter Loft."

"Ah. That would be good. How about tomorrow?"

"Yes," Martin said, surprised at someone acting with such speed. "Why not?"

"Okay. Car from my place at eleven o'clock. That suit you?"

"Yes," said Martin, surprised again. "That's fine. It's only just in east Kingsbridge, so it's not far. I can come with the rest of them when they go to church."

"How about getting back?"

"Oh, I can work something out."

"You can phone from the house when we're done."

"Thank you."

"Now, earlier Stephen mentioned wanting to extend their farmhouse. I imagine you've been involved in that?"

This was Martin's moment. "Well, yes..." he started, thinking of the paper bag sitting against the table leg. "I have. You see, Henry and Susan are expecting a baby. Stephen and Mary can't really get married until Mary leaves school. So they need more rooms. And the café is really a quickly built glorified shed and needs to be more a part of the house. So I thought immediately that we could combine the two.

"We talked a lot about it, and what they wanted. I had a look and roughed something out. Then Stephen said something and I thought again, went to have a look at the load bearing walls and made some adjustments. Well, actually I started again.

"At last we came up with something that would do what they wanted, all in rough sketch form, and yesterday I made a rather better drawing so I could show you."

"You did, did you?! Better let me see, then."

Almost reluctantly, almost fearing his drawings being rubbished by an expert,

Martin drew the drawings from his paper bag.

"I wondered what was in that," Mike chuckled. "I didn't realise it was a brief case!"

Martin was about to say something but realised that Mike was already scanning his drawings. He stole a look over to the others. Bronwen caught his eye and her eyebrows lifted. Martin smiled and nodded slightly, a nod she returned.

"Where are you going to tie the extension into the existing building?" The question was more barked than asked.

"That's something I don't know... well, I know where I *want* to but I haven't got the knowledge of how to do it."

"What materials would you use?"

"The farmhouse is stone, like all the others around. But it could be done as a timber framed building as that might be cheaper – I think."

"What makes you believe that?"

"I don't *know* if it is, but I thought it might be. You see, there are trees that need felling on the island – one's down already – and I thought we might be able to trade the wood in for seasoned stuff to build with."

Mike nodded. "Roofing?"

"I hadn't got that far. The main roof is slate."

"Is it a pitched roof?"

"The existing one is. I'd want the new one to be the same because I don't trust flat roofs."

"With a valley in the middle?"

"I beg your pardon?"

"Which way is the present ridge pointing? Parallel with the new one or at right angles?"

"The way I've visualised it, it would be parallel."

"That means you'd have a valley over the join of the two buildings. Instant trouble. If either part moves even a tenth of an inch you'd have leaks all along it. No, better to have the extension's roof tied into the existing one and at a right angle. Adds variety and is easier maintained."

Martin thought furiously. "Wouldn't that be more expensive?"

"In the short term, yes. But rather that than a jerry-built leaky affair."

"But surely if the new walls were really tied in well, and the new centre beam the same, wouldn't that hold the roof in place? So that a centre valley could drain outwards if it was peaked in the middle?"

Mike looked at him, grinning. "Good. You're thinking, and not afraid to argue. In fact we can think about that. I know it's been done elsewhere. But I meant what I said about not really liking a centre valley, especially if we do use wood for the extension, because it moves. And I'm relieved you never even suggested a flat roof or I'd have poured the remains of that pint over you."

Martin smiled. "But what about the layout of the actual extension?"

"Oh, that's fine. It'll probably need some tweaking once we're certain what materials we're using, but we can't do that without talking to the client."

That was enough for Martin. He smiled happily. "So you think the design's all right?"

"As I said, it's fine. Was that your first go?"

"I'd roughed it out quite a few times before."

"Don't we all? I meant, how many extensions or buildings have you designed?"

"Just this one."

"Then I'd say that it's good. Probably a bit more than good. And it's a tidy bit of drawing, but I'd expect that given your GCE in the subject. What do you actually want to do?"

"Get this designed properly for the Lofts."

"No... I mean what do you want to do about becoming an architect?"

"Oh. Well, Henry – Stephen's Dad – mentioned an 'A' level, and then perhaps... well, I don't know about University. I couldn't afford it."

"There are ways, I think, without that. We'll ask some questions. If it's a correspondence course, or maybe evening classes somewhere, would you be prepared to do it? It'd mean a lot of hard work."

"I'm prepared for that. I've worked on a farm as well as going to school and doing the tech drawing course at home. So yes, I can do that."

Mike was silent for a while.

"Can you make it an earlier start tomorrow? Because after we've been to Kingsbridge we could come back to my study and I'll set you some exercises in real life problems. See what your drawing is really like and how you take to it."

"Yes, I can get here when you want."

"Then make it ten o'clock. I'll be outside waiting. The Parents don't like me working on Sundays really, but this is exceptional. And do you think you could take me to look at Loft Island some time? I'd like to have a look at the building."

Martin thought. "If Stephen agrees we could go this afternoon."

Mike laughed. "Strike while the iron's hot, eh? Okay, you arrange it, I'll come. Now I think we could do with lunch, don't you?"

6 – Ted and Ian

That seemed to be the formal side of it out of the way, at least for the moment, Martin thought. They watched the others, playing a slightly raucous game of Devil-Among-the-Tailors. Mary saw them watching and shushed them.

"Sorry!" mouthed Stephen.

Mike grinned. "I'm usually louder than that."

"Want to play?"

"Wouldn't you rather have lunch?" Mike asked. "I would – I'm hungry!"

"Okay… we'll finish this game."

"I'll see what they've got, shall we? Then you can decide while you're at it."

Stephen nodded his thanks and carefully swung the chained ball in an arc. Mike crossed to the bar and made enquiries. Martin asked Stephen about Mike coming to the island that afternoon.

"Dad would say it's your home too, so you can bring who you like. Mike seems like a nice chap."

"He is. I think I could work with him. He doesn't mind being questioned and he's fair, I think. All I need to do now is see what he thinks of my work."

"Have you shown him the drawings?"

"Oh yes." He described their discussion.

Stephen smiled. "Sounds like you gave as good as you received!"

"Well, at least I can ask questions and make suggestions without having someone jump down my throat, like Dad used to."

"Your turn, Stephen," Mary interrupted. Then when Stephen was once again calculating angles Bronwen joined her and Martin, and asked how it had gone. He was in the middle of explaining when a voice interrupted.

"He probably thinks I'm an ogre with too strong opinions and can't wait to get away."

Martin wheeled round, mouth open in surprise. He was about to protest that he was thinking no such thing when he saw the challenging grin on Mike's face. He took a chance.

"How did you guess? You read my thoughts exactly." It was his turn to grin.

Mike laughed. "Well, one thing; I'm as sure as I can be that we could have a good working relationship. I think we both realise when it's work and probably time for being serious, and when we can relax as two friends. That's a major advantage as far as I'm concerned."

"Thank you," said Martin, and meant it.

"So all I've got to do now is to get you to do some real draughtsmanship that I can use on a real project, and we could be home and dry. They've got pies and bits of salad, they say, and we can add some crisps to that. Is that okay for everyone?"

They all nodded.

"But you mustn't pay for lunch," said Stephen.

"Why not? I can stand lunch for a prospective employee, why not his friends?"

"But…"

"And I'm still paying for petrol, remember."

Stephen laughed.

"That's the second time you've mentioned petrol," said Bronwen. "Is it a private joke?"

Stephen explained and she and Mary laughed.

Mike was taken to the Island that afternoon and looked carefully at the building. He grinned at the temporary extension that had been added to provide an extra bedroom.

"Is this your work too?" he asked Martin.

"No. I think it was done by Henry – Mr Loft."

"Ah. Good. Instant problems there with the join onto the main building once the wood starts moving. But with your design that would go anyway. The original building is good and solid; proper South Hams work, and well built too. We can work with that. Now..."

He and Martin continued to talk about roof designs and pitches and materials, and gradually the others drifted off. Mike was pleased that Martin continued to question and even criticise his comments and proposals, the more so because what he was saying was based on common sense. Both learnt: Martin about Mike and house design; Mike about Martin and how his lively brain worked.

Eventually they were called to a Devon cream tea, even if it was out of season and the cafe was closed.

"Tomorrow, ten o'clock," Mike reminded Martin as he left the boat, much later and in near darkness, at Salcombe.

"I'll be there," Martin grinned, raising a hand in farewell. He made the journey back to the Island, rigged the launch to their running rigging and rejoined the others.

"Well?" he asked, once surrounded by what he increasingly regarded as his second family.

"Nice chap," came from Henry and Stephen.

"Good looking," from Bronwen. Mary made no answer, just smiled.

Martin looked at Bronwen sharply, and she blushed.

"Not my type. Not in that way."

"Glad to hear it!" said Martin.

The following morning Martin left the others by the Church. They continued, very early, to the Victorian building whose vicar had rallied the community to help four years previously, when floods had left Mary Beale and Henry and Stephen Loft shocked and in need of a boat.

Martin made his way to the Alexanders' and found Mike outside, waiting by a small red sports car.

"My pride and joy, this MG," he told Martin who was looking at it as if he was still a thirteen year old schoolboy. "Do you drive?"

"No," said Martin regretfully, "I don't. But I want to learn."

"Need a car on a job like mine – ours, if things work out. Chances are you'll be desk bound to start with, but when you get to go to clients' houses you'll need something to drive in. Many of them are nowhere near bus routes."

Martin followed Mike's lead and climbed into the car. Soon they were haring out of Salcombe on its main road. There was little opportunity for talk on the journey as with the hood down it was too noisy. Martin had to shout directions as they reached Kingsbridge.

To his surprise Peter and Dot were at the cottages when they arrived and Martin had to introduce Mike as his prospective employer.

"We can't afford an architect, I'm afraid," Peter laughed. "though we've had a lot of ideas from Martin – and from the rest of the builders of course."

"And that's what I've come to look at, if I may," said Mike. "You see, I'm looking for someone to work for me and Martin is looking for a path into architecture. I want to gauge the scope of his imagination."

Peter grinned at them both. "Well, he's done a good job in this place. He's taken some of Dot's and my ideas and made them better, and put a lot of his own to us, most of which we've agreed to. Come and look."

They embarked on a tour of the two cottages with Dot and Peter pointing out features and Martin trying to explain his thinking behind them. Mike said little, just nodding now and again but asking the occasional pertinent question. Martin was quite pleased with what reaction he noticed, though still unsure what Mike was thinking. They bade their farewells to Dot and Peter, and set off again at some speed towards the town centre and therefore once again unable to chat. Speed had been reduced so as to navigate the narrower streets when Mike swore. Two youngsters jay-walked across the road, causing him to brake hard to avoid them.

Martin gasped as he recognised the two.

"Stop!" he shouted to Mike above the noise of the car. "Stop, please – they're my brothers."

Mike complied and Martin opened the door and climbed out. At the sound of the door the two boys looked round furtively, as if ready to run. The elder did a double take and said something to the smaller. They turned and faced Martin.

"Hallo, Ted, hallo Ian. You nearly got run over... here, what's the trouble?"

Ian, the younger of the two had sunk to his knees and was looking white. Ted stood there, defiant, facing his brother, but also looking white and ready to give up.

"What 'you doing, riding in a car?"

"What are *you* doing nearly getting run over by it? And you both look ill. What's being going on?"

Ted shrugged and almost staggered. Martin rushed to support him.

"What's Dad been doing, Ted? You look all in."

"He's been on at me so much this last week. And he's not made any food since Wednesday, Martin. We're both so hungry. And yesterday we went out and left the key indoors so we can't get back in."

"Where did you sleep last night?"

"Shop doorway. Look, we've not seen him since Tuesday night. He said he was ill and in bed, but didn't want anything to eat. He told us to go away and leave him in peace."

"Is there a problem?" said a voice behind him.

Martin swung round. "My brothers haven't eaten since last Tuesday. And now they can't get back into the house. Dad seems to be ill, or something."

"Hmm... okay, what can we do? Do you want to get to the house to see what's going on? I can take these two home with me, if they're happy with that. Or how about the Lofts where you're known?"

"I can't burden them with more people! They've taken me in already."

"From what I hear around Salcombe they're the sort of people who would be almost offended if you didn't ask them for help. Look, if you sit in the dickey seat these two could cram in the front. If I go slowly we can reach Salcombe and with any luck they'll have waited for you. If not we can call from my house and they can come back."

"What about Dad?"

"Is there no one else with a key?"

"My aunt has one. You two could have asked her to let you in."

"Didn't know she had one," Ted said indignantly.

"Okay, okay... sorry. Can you cope if we go back quickly and get her to let us in? That all right, Mike?"

"Yes of course. Climb in the back, Martin. You two – can you fit in the front? It's not very comfortable. Perhaps if you have your brother on your lap, Ted..."

It was surprising to find a Police car and a white van by the farmhouse when they arrived. Mike stopped and had leapt out before the others had a chance. He ran over and was asking for news, having explained that he had the sons of the household in the car.

"We had reports of animals in distress, sir. The vet's checking them out now but from what I heard they just need milking."

By this time the brothers had caught up with the conversation.

"Milking!" Ted exclaimed. "We milked them from Wednesday until Saturday, but this morning... Oh, God, how could I have forgotten?"

Martin put his arm round him, and hugged Ian too. "You can't do everything, boys. Look, if it's all right with Mike, go back to Salcombe now with him..." Mike nodded "... and he'll make sure the Lofts, who have been looking after me, take you in. I'll stay here and sort things out with the Police."

"But Dad won't want you to be anywhere near! You know what he was like when you broke your collarbone."

Martin's expression was grim. "I do. But we're still family."

Mike ushered the two back into the car and they were gone. Martin had to go over his experiences with the policeman, telling him the story of his leaving home and what happened afterwards. He mentioned that his aunt had a key to the farmhouse. The policeman took him in the car to see a very confused and concerned aunt, who produced a key and returned with them.

After discussion they allowed her to open the door and to call inside the house. No reply. The policeman asked to go inside. She made room for him. He crossed the threshold, paused to gather breath to shout, sniffed twice and stopped.

"Oh."

A small word, but both of them were suddenly aware of what it meant.

"Everyone out, please. We need to call for an ambulance. I'm afraid there is no doubt, though, that there has been a death, Martin. I'm really sorry to have to tell you both this. I need to get a colleague here and we will go and do what we have to."

Martin and his aunt didn't know what to do. Martin had experienced what felt like a kick in the stomach at the policeman's words. Estranged they may have been, but a father is still a father; he had already lost his mother. At eighteen the realisation that you have lost both parents leaves you rudderless.

His aunt just sat on the grass outside. She was aware that her brother had been changed by his experiences in the war, only too well aware. His burns had seen to that, together with the near-constant pain that went with the shrapnel still inside him. She had become increasingly unwilling to visit him and risk enduring his impatience and shortness of temper with nearly everything. Yet he was still her younger brother, and losing him hurt more than she realised it would.

She found a presence by her side and an arm around her; a surprisingly strong arm, she realised, thinking back to the times when Martin needed just that sort of comfort having been the victim of his father's angry tongue. She had known then the reason for the outbursts, but it hadn't helped with the unhappiness of a young nephew.

The authorities soon arrived. Death of Mr Rawle was certified, cause to be identified by post mortem. The original policeman stood in front of them.

"I'm really sorry to say that we need the... deceased formally identified. Would one of you be prepared to do so now? I have to warn you that the body has lain there for some days so the sight is not pleasant."

They both shuddered. "I... I don't think I can," Miss Rawle said. "And I don't think it would be fair on Martin to ask him. He's under twenty-one anyway."

"Then I don't think his identification would be acceptable. It will have to be done using dental records."

She was relieved.

"Are you both all right now? I know this has been a horrible shock."

"Well no, of course not. Not really. I think it'll take time to sink in. And we've got to tell Ted and Ian! They don't know anything about it yet."

Martin's heart sank even further. He was not ready for that responsibility. Thinking about responsibilities, he gasped.

"What about the farm? What about the cows?"

"I can sort that out," said Miss Rawle. "Unfortunately I know the landlord. He's not a nice man but at least he can make arrangements for the moment – God knows your Dad paid him enough rent over the years. And your family – the Lofts. They're farmers, aren't they? You could take the cows and add them to the herd there."

Martin knew the state of the Lofts' and the Beales' cattle. They were being looked after by neighbours until permanent arrangements could be made – if indeed they ever could be made in view of the continuing lack of suitable land since the valley had flooded. He nodded, thinking that at least he could help his new family by providing new stock. *If* his estranged father had left them to him.

"Auntie, why don't you come to Lofts now, with me? We can get you back home later, you know."

"Me? But I'm not dressed for visiting. I would be the laughing stock!"

"Neither am I, and I was on a job interview of sorts. The Lofts don't worry about things like that – you'll see."

The policeman took pity on them, took them back to Miss Rawle's house to use the phone to tell Henry the state of affairs. He was shocked, insisted they both return there and told them he would make arrangements about the milking and looking after the cows.

Then they were taken to Crabtree Quay, from which they knew the ferry was due soon. They also knew that the two people in charge of it would happily divert to Loft Island.

Their arrival at the Island's landing stage brought quite a crowd. His brothers were not amongst them, Martin noted, and was thankful that his unwelcome duty would be at least postponed.

"Where are they, please?" he asked Susan.

"In bed, having had a snack," she said. "It wouldn't have been good to give them a big meal after four days on nearly nothing, and they wouldn't have slept well either. So they're together in Stephen's room. Mary offered it. It seemed the best thing to do."

"May I see them, please?"

"Martin, it's your home, and they're your brothers. Of course!"

He gave her one of his sudden, happy smiles and felt better. She really was a nice person.

The two boys were sound asleep. Even Ted, at fourteen, looked angelic. His arm was protectively over his brother's back. Ian, eleven, also looked angelic, and Martin was pleased to see that the whiteness of his face had gone. He was also out for the count. Satisfied, he tiptoed away.

Mike was still on the island, and when Martin rejoined the group he was chatting to Bronwen. She excused herself as he appeared and went to put her arm round him.

"How are you feeling? I really felt awful for you when I heard. And poor Mary has been beside herself – she knows better than any of us what it's like."

"Hmm. I still don't know, really. It's just a bolt out of the blue. I can't think about it except to be sad about so many things."

She nodded, waiting for him to continue if he wanted.

"He just was so awful to me. And it sounds as if he might have been getting onto Ted too – maybe even Ian. And now... well, it just seems to be so wrong. He was in pain, obviously, and it made him take it out on us. But before it got really bad he was a good Dad."

She just hugged him.

Mike was chatting to Stephen and Mary about Martin, trying to get more background. Stephen, who knew him best, was positive about him but cautious. He had his friend's privacy to consider, and told Mike so.

"Oh, I understand, really I do. But you see I need to know as much about him as possible if we're to work together."

This set Mary thinking. "But then, I didn't know Martin except as someone much older than me at school. But when I came back, Martin was there, living in my home, and I had to get to know him. Stephen told me he was a good person to know, so that helped because I trust Steve's judgement. So I had to find out a lot about him too, stuff that Stephen wouldn't think to tell me."

It was Mike's turn to think. At last he smiled. "So what you're saying is that I should trust Stephen and you, and talk to Martin myself."

"Yes," she said. "And finding out about someone isn't something you can do in one conversation."

"I stand corrected."

"Oh... I hope you don't think I was being rude."

"No. Not at all. Honest, but not rude. I value honesty very highly, and prefer argument to sycophantic agreement every time. That's one of the things I discovered about Martin very quickly. He says what he thinks, even when you disagree with him."

"Well, I try to," said Martin's voice. "It's easier that way and you find a lot out about the person you're talking to."

They hadn't heard the two come to join the conversation.

"Sorry," said Mike. "I was talking about you. That's not fair and I apologise. Look, you'll need some time to sort things out before you come and join me for a work trial. And coming back today for a look and a bit of practical stuff is out of the question now. Would you like to give me a call when you're ready?"

"I... I need to talk to my brothers, and we need to find out what we can do with them. But I really, really want to get started, and working will take my mind off – well, everything. I know I was meant to be coming tomorrow morning, but would the afternoon be all right instead? I could at least do some drawings as you suggested and then you can tell me if I'm good enough or not."

"Yes, that would be great, if you're sure. If you do start with me I know it'll likely be difficult for the first few weeks while matters have to be attended to and you must take off what time you need."

Martin nodded. "Thank you so much, Mike."

Mr Merryweather had taken Miss Rawle under his wing.

"I'm so pleased to be able to talk to you," he told her. "When we were trying to sort out Martin's property all that time ago it was more of a formal talk than a chat. I wish now that I had had the time to get to know his father as I feel I could have pointed him in the direction of someone who could have helped him recover better."

"He was a very independent man, my brother. And so attached to the farm that it came before everything else. It was not particularly good land, you see, and so very difficult to make pay. A shame. A swindle, really, as there was so much good pasture in the area which could have been attached to the farm; but the landlord wanted that for himself. Natural, I suppose, but a kick in the teeth for someone who had fought in the war and been injured."

"And, unfortunately, entirely legal," Mr Merryweather rejoined. "If there is anything I can do to help ease the tenancy to its end you must tell me. I suppose the details will come out in the will. But it's early days yet."

"It's the boys I'm most worried about," she said. "It's very good of the Lofts to have them here and so on, but what will happen to them in the long term? I have a small cottage – I never needed more space – and three of us would be jam-packed if we all lived there."

The old solicitor was silent. So was she.

At last he continued. "You know, I have lived alone since my wife died and Susan left to live above her cafe. Bronwen joined me yesterday and after just a few hours it's made me realise that the house is just far too big for one person. Even for two. God knows I have bedrooms enough. Why don't I give them a home, if you and Bronwen will look after them?"

"Me?"

"Er... I mean... well..." He appeared untypically confused, embarrassed. "Now it seems that, unlike my usual self, I have overstepped the mark. But I think we might agree that the boys need a family presence there; you, as their aunt, would seem to be the best person to fill that void. I am talking about possibilities here only, you understand. Your ties in Kingsbridge may make it impossible and you may not even want to take on the responsibility. But before they went to bed just now it was obvious to me that there was a feeling between you and them, so perhaps... Well, I may have said too much."

He was starting to feel as if his voice had run on before his thoughts could catch up. He was not sure where the idea of throwing open his home had come from. Bronwen was family, and there was a reason for her being there. The boys – well, they had to live somewhere and the idea of officialdom taking them over filled him with horror. It had a lot to do with Martin who, he felt, would not forgive him if he agreed to their being taken to some sort of orphanage.

And if the boys, why not their Aunt? He had found her helpful and intelligent when they were dealing with Martin's possessions all those years ago. Talking to her for even a short time that afternoon had shown that here was a woman who was surprisingly similar in outlook to himself, and the idea of having her come as part of the package, as it were, was a pleasant one.

But she would doubtless baulk at the idea of living in the house of a complete stranger, he told himself. Even if it was to look after her nephews.

For her part, Miss Rawle had no idea what to say. She could see that the two boys needed someone to look after them. Even if the elder was already fourteen he could hardly be expected to care for an eleven year old. And to have them live with her seemed a fitting tribute to her brother, whom she remembered being a cheeky, happy fourteen year old just as Ted usually was now. How he had teased her in those long gone days, but how he had stood up for her when she was in trouble...

She felt tears approaching, and swallowed hard.

The boys... yes. Having the opportunity to be a mother to them for once would be wonderful. She remembered how they would come to her occasionally since Martin left home, when the atmosphere at home became too harsh, and how they allowed her to comfort them and to make up for some of the shortage of food at home. And how her brother would accept no help for himself – or them – insisting they could manage.

The old man found that his ability to offer support to someone in distress was as effective then as it had been when he was married.

"Sorry," she whispered eventually, accepting the handkerchief that was offered.

"Tears are only natural, at any time, for a proper cause," she was told. "The loss of someone close to you is a proper cause, I would say. So you have nothing to apologise for."

"But you... you are a solicitor. I shouldn't be..."

He interrupted. "Before a solicitor, and more importantly than being a solicitor, I am a man; human, and open to human emotions. The human comes first, the man later, and the solicitor later still and only then as a means to earning an income. So it is only another human being who can comfort another. Unless there is a dog in the household. I'm told that they are wonderful at being comforting and also that they repeat no secrets. Just like solicitors."

It took a few seconds, but she had to laugh; shakily, but still a laugh.

"I have had few dealings with solicitors, but none has ever made me laugh before. Thank you."

He nodded gravely, by instinct back in solicitor mode, then caught himself and said "It is nothing, really."

"But it is. To me it is."

She had never met anyone like him before. Perhaps if she had, all those years ago... She shook her head, a movement taken by him to mean that she had cleared her mind.

But she was still thinking. If she took up an offer like that, to up sticks and move to Salcombe to be with the boys, what would happen? She would have to look for a new job to make up the difference between her investment income and her needs... and what would she have to pay as rent? For the boys and for herself? And if Bronwen was also living with her uncle it seemed likely that Martin would want to move there as well – if Mr Merryweather would allow that. She counted up. Five bedrooms! Did he have enough room?

"Do you... is the house *really* big enough for that number of people?" she asked. "Even if the boys share, there's Bronwen, maybe Martin, me, and you."

"It is, alas, a large house. You see, my wife and I intended to have a large family, but after Susan was born we knew that there could be no others. So – yes. There are enough bedrooms to start a small hotel, but I never wanted to do that, nor did I see the need. So yes, there is plenty of room. And when young Ted needs the privacy of his own room we can still cope."

She paused. "I think I need a day or two for all this to settle down in my mind before I come to a decision."

"Naturally. And the boys need some stability and a few days more rest before they return to school. And the rooms need to be looked at too. Bronwen and I can do that – in fact it will be Bronwen alone since I have to run a Solicitor's practice. She will enjoy it, I'm sure."

"You make it sound as if I'm going to agree."

He smiled at her. "I admit to hoping you will. Bronwen isn't the right person to look after them and I don't think I am either at my age."

"You do yourself an injustice. You are not that old."

It was his turn to smile. "Still of grandfather age, it seems; for Mary, for Stephen, and of course now for Martin. But the boys have not had the chance to anoint me as their grandfather yet. And it is not something into which they should be led. I must emphasise that to Martin."

"Indeed. It is and must be their choice."

"Which is exactly how it was with the other three. They adopted me, I am glad to say, of their own free choice."

"If I do come, I will need to adopt them properly."

"That would be simple. You would have accommodation for them and you are the nearest blood relative. I assume that is the case, anyway."

"Yes," she said, "I am."

"Then there would appear to be no difficulty."

"You are very persuasive, without seeming to be so."

He laughed. "It is part of the job, I'm afraid. You should guard against it. But I really hope you won't in this case."

She raised her eyebrows and smiled. "I will consider the suggestion when you are not there to influence me."

"Very wise, very wise. But there…"

7 – Plans 1

He was interrupted by Susan calling for everyone's attention. When the conversations had paused she said in a quiet voice: "We have all forgotten that today is also Martin's birthday. I have been wondering how to reintroduce the subject – it seems so inappropriate under the circumstances. But I really feel we should eat some of the tea that has been prepared, and wish him well for the future; to wish him many more, happier, birthdays; and to respect and commemorate his father and his life in happier times.

"I will start taking things through to the café, but will someone please help?"

It was a muted celebration. He was helped by Susan's words but Martin realised the possibility that he could never have a carefree birthday again with the shadow of the anniversary of a tragedy on the same day. He did his best, but he was secretly glad when Henry left to take his father-in-law, Mike and Bronwen to Salcombe in the boat, even if it meant being without Bronwen.

The others returned to the house. Martin was sitting with Mary and Stephen when the door opened again. All three looked round.

Bronwen.

He jumped to his feet. "Is everything all right?"

"Yes. Yes, they've gone. But I begged to stay and help look after your brothers. Your Aunt has to get back to Kingsbridge later tonight so she won't be here when they wake. And I thought… I thought…"

She just looked at him, lost for words. He went to her and put his arms round her.

"You thought that I might need some help too?"

She just nodded, worried that she had overstepped the mark. A kiss landed on her forehead. She looked up.

"You are amazing."

"*R'wyt ti fy machgen hyfryd.* I told you."

He pulled a wry face. "I still don't know what that means. But to me you are just my beautiful girl and I want you in my life *so* much."

"You mean *r'wyf i ei merch hyfryd*?"

"Er… that's nearly what you said to me, isn't it? Did I say the same to you?"

"I told you that you are my beautiful boy. You said that I was your beautiful girl so I translated it. I asked if you meant I am your beautiful girl - *r'wyf i ei merch hyfryd*? You should say 'yes' if you mean it."

He kissed her again.

"Yes."

The other two looked at them, understanding, and pleased.

"But…" she started again. He put his finger to her lips.

"No 'buts', please. Not today. Please let me just live in this glow for today. These two have had hell for months now – probably years – and when they wake I shall be involved in their unhappiness. Let me enjoy *some* good in the day. I think I need it."

"I think you do, too," she said. "So let's all four of us just sit and enjoy what we have, shall we?"

They were about to sit again when there was the sound of footsteps on the

54

stairs. Ted. Mary smiled to herself to see him dressed as she had found herself dressed having been rescued, in one of Henry's old shirts. For her to have worn it, then aged twelve, it had been enough. On Ted, at fourteen and quite tall, it served for technical decency only. He was taken aback to see his brother with his arm round a girl, and two strange young people in a room he couldn't remember.

"Where are my clothes, please? And where am I?"

Not 'where's Dad', Martin was part glad and part sorrowful to notice.

He released Bronwen and crossed to his brother, who looked alarmed.

"Don't worry, Ted. Everyone here is a friend. You and Ian were so tired and hungry that Susan gave you some food and then Henry took your dirty clothes and put you to bed."

"Who's Henry? Who's Susan?"

"Henry Loft. He and Susan are the people who have given me a home all these years. This is Stephen, my friend from school, and Mary his fiancée who also is at the same school."

He looked more closely at Stephen, then nodded. "I sort of recognise you, but you were younger then. Ian is scared of you."

"Scared of me? Why?"

"Ian jumped in a puddle and soaked you once. You looked so angry that he was scared."

Stephen laughed. "I remember now. It was the day of the flooding. Everything was wet and this little kid jumped into a puddle and splashed me all up my legs. Well, that was about four years ago and I think I've forgiven him by now. In fact I'd forgotten all about it until you said."

"Sure?"

"Sure."

"Good. I'll tell him."

"So will I. And I'll shake his hand on it."

He nodded again. "Who.. can I ask... are you?" This was to Bronwen.

"I met Martin at Christmas last year, and again on Mary's birthday. We got to like each other. I'll tell you the full story some day but now Martin is my beautiful boy."

Martin's eyes opened wide and he was about to protest.

Ted spoke first, his face full of amazement. "Martin? Beautiful? Are you pulling my leg?"

"Thanks, Ted," his brother managed. "What's the saying? 'Love is in the eye of the beholder'?"

"Attraction, I think," Stephen put in.

"Well, it's love in this case," Martin said firmly, then blushed. "I'm sorry... I never meant it to come out now, like that. But – well, it's true for me, and I just hope it is for you." This last was, naturally, to Bronwen, not to his brother.

She just smiled. Ted shrugged theatrically in mock dismay, an incautious move in view of his state of dress.

"Anyway, where are my clothes?" he demanded, "and how is Dad?"

This was the question Martin had dreaded.

"Can we wait until Ian is here too?"

Silence.

Then: "He's dead, isn't he?"

Martin sagged.

"Yes," he whispered. "He is. I'm most dreadfully sorry."

"Why?" The suddenly treble voice was almost trembling. "You hated him."

"Ted, we argued. Years ago. You know that. He didn't want me back, so I didn't go back. I met you and Ian at Aunt Annabelle's from time to time because I couldn't go home. But any hate that I'd felt faded over the years. Believe me."

"But we kept on getting told 'If Martin was here, he'd have been able to do that'. We just felt so useless. All the time."

This was news. Martin was astounded, and caught his breath.

"But these last few days, you kept the farm running," he said. Martin was desperately trying to keep his emotion on an even keel.

"Huh! Not last night, I didn't. Forgot the cows... How could I *do* that?"

"Ted: I said this morning, you can't do everything. And you're not useless, neither of you. And I'm sorry he used me – my name – to try and make you feel awful."

Another silence.

"What are we going to do now?"

"You haven't eaten properly for days," said a quiet voice behind him. Ted spun round and found Susan looking at him. He read care and comfort in her face. "We're going to give you food when you want it and let you rest – you've had a dreadful few days. Then we can all think what's going to happen."

"Will we go to an orphanage?" The tremble was back in his voice.

"No," said Susan and Martin together. They looked at each other, each waiting for the other to continue.

"Not while I'm around, you won't." Martin sounded as positive as he had about anything.

"And not while there's breath in my body," Susan confirmed. "Let's just wait those few days, shall we? Then we shall all know what can happen."

"Poor old Dad..." Ted sounded shaky again. He looked at his elder brother.

"Poor old Dad indeed... He must have been suffering."

"I know. But he never said anything."

"I wish he had."

Both sets of eyes were downcast. Martin moved carefully towards his brother and enveloped him in a hug. The others turned way to give them privacy.

"Does Ian know yet?" asked a shaky voice.

Martin shook his head. "He's not been down yet. Maybe he'll sleep through."

A few more moments, then Martin asked: "Feel better now?"

"No. Not really."

"Well, best get dressed in something and come and join us properly."

Ted looked down.

"Oh."

He pulled the shirt down.

"There's some of my old stuff you can use until yours are clean and dry," said Stephen. "Come upstairs and we'll have a look."

"I don't want to be a nuisance..."

"You're not. Martin's family is our family too. Come on."

Carefully, holding down the tails of the old shirt as he climbed, Ted followed Stephen upstairs.

"Nice young chap," Susan commented. "I think he's probably caught a little of his father's impatience but that should disappear with time."

"It's something most of the Rawles have, apparently" said Martin. "That and an independent nature."

"Independence isn't necessarily a bad thing," said Susan, "so long as the streak of independence doesn't mean turning down help or a bit of support when it's genuinely offered."

"Like me at first, when I broke my collar bone, you mean?"

She smiled. "Something like that."

He smiled wryly.

The noises made upstairs by drawers opening woke Ian.

"What 'you doing?"

"Finding some clothes for us, if Stephen's got any our sizes."

"Stephen? Who's Stephen? Where are we?"

"We're on Loft Island, where Martin lives."

"But he... Stephen Loft... Oh."

"What's wrong with Stephen Loft?" asked the name's owner, but gently.

"Nothing... but..."

"If you're still worried about having jumped into that puddle four years go, or whatever it was, don't. I'd forgotten all about it by the end of that day. That was when the flood happened and killed my friends – remember? I had more important things to worry about."

Silence. Then: "But you've remembered it now."

"Only because Ted warned me you were still scared of me, and why. I didn't even know who it was."

Another pause. "Have you forgiven me?"

Stephen laughed, again gently. "If I'd forgotten all about it, how could there be anything to forgive? But if it helps: yes, I've forgiven you. Friends?"

Ian nodded. Stephen held out his hand. The boy looked puzzled for a moment and then cautiously held out his hand to be shaken.

Some more rummaging around in cupboards and Stephen managed to find old pairs of shorts which nearly fitted each boy, and a variety of T-shirts in a variety of states of repair.

"I don't know why these have been kept," he muttered, half to himself. "The state of them..." He apologised to the two and then left them to dress properly.

"They're getting dressed," he announced to the others downstairs.

Martin sighed heavily. "I'd better go and give the news to Ian before Ted blurts it out. Wish me well."

"May I come too?" Mary asked suddenly. "I've been through the loss of two parents and a brother, so I might be able to help."

She found everyone's eyes on her, and blushed.

"Well, I have," she said defensively, "and if I can, I'd like to."

"Yes please," said Martin thankfully. "I'd really like that."

Upstairs they found the brothers sitting on the bed. Ted's arm was round his brother's shoulders. Ian was looking down at the floor.

Martin bounded up the last few steps and went to sit beside Ian, cautiously extending an arm round him from that side. Ian checked who it was before looking back down at the floor. Mary let them be.

"I had more time with him when he was a good Dad," Ted said. "He wasn't always like you remember him."

"And I had even more time," Martin confirmed. "He was a good father then, and loved you to bits when you were born. Then Mum died and he got busier, and the pain started... He changed."

Silence came again. Mary noticed that tears were dropping from Ian's cheeks and longed to be there to offer support. She knelt in front of the two younger boys and looked up at them.

"Now is the time to cry," she told them in her quiet voice. "Now and whenever the loss strikes you. It's better that way."

Ted looked straight into her eyes. "You lost your parents and a brother too, didn't you? I remember being told about it."

Mary nodded. "I did. And I felt lost, and hopeless. But thanks to Henry and Stephen it slowly got better. But we all did a lot of crying over the weeks. Something would set us off. We understood what was happening though; Stephen's mother had died a few years before so he could share with me. It helped."

It was Ian's turn to look her in the eyes. "What's going to happen to us?" he asked simply.

Again two voices answered, interrupting each other. Mary let Martin explain. "Well, the thing that *isn't* going to happen is that *none* of us is going into an orphanage. Not me, not either of you. And no one's going to send you overseas to start a new life either. Too many people are on our side for that."

"But what about the farm?" asked Ted.

"The farm is leased. That means that anyone running it has to pay rent each month. You know that a lot of the land we had wasn't very good. So at the moment the farmer Henry knows is looking after it all, along with Henry's cattle still. Eventually I suppose the livestock will come to us – it depends on Dad's will. And then we can decide what to do. In the meantime we think that Aunt Annabelle will come to Salcombe where Stephen and Mary's grandad has offered to give her and you a home. We hope so."

"But the farm..." Ted asked again. "I want to be a farmer."

"You sound like Stephen, and me." Mary smiled at him in a way that woke something inside him. "He wants to farm, and so do I. When we have the money we're going to build a house and farm the land there."

"I have no chance of doing that."

"You never know. Martin says that your farm would be difficult to make pay. But there are other ways into farming. And you could find one to lease, like your father did. Or work for someone on theirs."

"How about yours?"

"Well, it's a possibility. We've got to build it and get the land first! How about you, Ian?"

"Don't know. Farming's hard work."

"Yes, it is. But it's a way of life. Anyway, neither of you have to make any choices yet, and when you do you can always change your mind."

They were both looking a little less sad now, though neither had a happy expression, naturally.

"There's still food downstairs," said Mary cautiously. "It was for Martin's birthday and it seemed a shame to waste it. We've had some, but you were catching up on sleep. How about coming down?"

Ted jumped to his feet, and after a moment's hesitation so did Ian. Downstairs, they were welcomed.

"Good. Hallo, Ted and Ian. Please come to the café where the food is, and help yourselves. We don't want it all for breakfast." This was from Susan who was pleased to see them looking better. As was their aunt.

"Are we all really going to live in Salcombe? With you?" asked Ian.

She smiled fondly at them both. "It's something I want to think very carefully about. Would you like it if I did?"

His eyes opened wide. "Yes. Yes, of course!"

Ted was smiling – shakily – too, so she took that as approval from him. "Well, it's Mr Merryweather's house. He's a solicitor. And it's a big house, almost like a small hotel. Perhaps we can go and see it next weekend."

"Why not tomorrow?" asked Ted.

"Tomorrow's Monday. He'll be at work and you'll be at school… won't you?" She looked round at the other adults.

"I *think*," Susan started carefully, "they might be allowed a day or two to recover, don't you? What do you think, boys?"

The answer was, unexpectedly, unanimous.

When Henry returned to take Annabelle back to Kingsbridge he found most of the birthday food gone and the three Rawles much happier than he expected. Martin asked if he'd mind if he took his Aunt back to Kingsbridge himself.

"You've done enough for one day," he told Henry, "and anyway I'd like a chance to talk to her."

Henry readily agreed, knowing that Martin was by then as good at navigating the Estuary in the dark as he was. After many farewells the two left.

"Are you sure about leaving Kingsbridge and living in Salcombe?" was Martin's first question.

"It's all happened so quickly that I've not had a chance to let it settle in my mind," she said. "But the boys seemed to like the idea, and Mr Merryweather seems a real gentleman."

"Oh, he is. He's been extraordinarily good to me. You've heard the story?"

She admitted that she hadn't, and was soon astonished when she had learnt it. "But we can't let him do that!" she exclaimed.

"That's what I was thinking when we were talking, him and me. But somehow he just failed to let me say no. It was only after I'd shaken his hand that I realised just what he'd done. It was that, and all the things that he said, that made me think that I should follow Stephen and Mary and adopt him as a grandad."

Another shock. "You didn't!"

"I did. It seemed the right thing to do. And he regarded it as a compliment."

"You never knew your real grandfathers, did you?

"No. But I know they were both killed in the first World War."

"My father was a lovely man and I loved him to bits. Then he went and got himself killed four months before the war ended." She heaved a huge sigh. "I think he would have liked Mr Merryweather. They share the same quiet positivity."

"He wasn't a cricketer, by any chance, was he?"

"How did you know?"

"Because grandad – Mr Merryweather – was. He played for the College and was so good he was selected for the county, possibly for England. But *his* father wouldn't allow him to continue."

"Silly man. But Dad was just a good club player. He was never even selected for the county. But it means that I still like cricket to this day."

"You'd be good company for him."

"For whom?"

"Mr Merryweather."

"I should think he's going to have all the company he needs if he takes in two young boys, Bronwen, possibly you, maybe me."

Martin laughed. "You're thinking about it, then?"

"I'm going to give it careful consideration. Let me sleep on it."

He nodded. "I don't know what Ted and Ian would do otherwise."

"Just let me sleep on it, Martin."

"I'm not going to let them go to an orphanage."

"No, and nor am I. But there are more ways than one to skin a cat, you know."

"What?!"

"It's a saying," she said, surprised he'd never heard of it.

"Surely people don't… Imagine eating a cat."

She shuddered. "It *is* rather bloodthirsty. Just as well I have no cats."

He laughed.

He dropped her at the Town Quay, and started back, having made sure she didn't want him to escort her to her front door. Inevitably his thoughts turned to the past, and to his father. He found that the only way he could remember him with affection was when he was himself much younger. To think of him during the last year or so that he had lived at home left him unhappy and resentful; his father's already irritable nature had become so destructive. He knew that since then it had remained so and affected his brothers too.

He shook his head and concentrated on navigating, dashing away the blurriness from his eyes with impatience.

Annabelle Rawle sat alone and silent into the late evening, thinking.

At last she took herself off to bed, a decision made. The little cottage she had rented for years was surely just a convenience for her. She had few local friends. It was near her work and had been near her brother. Its main attraction was that it had become a bolt-hole for three unhappy nephews on occasion. If that was so, then obviously the most sensible thing to do was to continue to be available for the two younger ones. There was no room for them to live with her in Kingsbridge, so Salcombe was the place she would need to be. None of the other potential occupants of Mr Merryweather's house put her off: quite the reverse. And the host himself; well… An attractive gentleman, albeit older, who could make her laugh. After so many years of being alone she was suddenly aware that there was an emptiness in her life – not that she was seeking marriage or anything like that. But his company on occasion would be rewarding.

Despite herself, she wriggled in the bed and was immediately embarrassed.

8 – Aunt Amble

Early the next morning Mr Merryweather answered the phone. What he heard pleased him.

"Yes, please do come down at lunchtime," he told Annabelle. "It will need to be a fairly brief visit as tomorrow is particularly busy, but possibly we could ask one of the Lofts to take you back to see the boys on the island. No: better still, why not ask one of them to collect you from Kingsbridge – or take the ferry – and you can bring the boys with you? It's only fair they should see where they might be living, after all."

"I can telephone them, and catch a ferry which they can join at Loft Island," she told him. "That would be a bit of an adventure for them, I should think. Should we see you at your office?"

"A far better idea. Then we can walk up the hill together."

For a reason she couldn't fathom she was pleased by the last word.

"That would be pleasant," she said.

"The pleasure is mine," he said, and meant it.

She made the promised phone call.

The ferry wasn't due to call at Loft Island until the café there opened at around Easter, so it was only by explaining the reasons and her plans that she engaged the crew's full support.

"We know young Martin," said old Charlie. "He's a good lad and a credit to his Dad if only he hadn't been so pigheaded about it. I'm sorry to speak ill of the dead and apologise to you, but it is a fact."

She had some more explaining to do about the likely reasons for his bad temper, and silenced the old man by doing so.

"That bloody war…" was all he could mumble, half to himself and half to her, and then apologised for his language.

They approached the sloping landing stage which was really the old road that had once led to Lincombe. A small boy was jumping up and down and a taller one hopping from foot to foot, trying not to appear too excited. Annabelle smiled. They had been so cloistered when living in Kingsbridge with their father. Outings were rare, almost non-existent. Small wonder the idea of sleeping on an island and travelling by boat to town was a real event for them.

"Hallo, you two," she called when within hailing distance, and they shouted their greetings back.

Charlie helped them aboard and asked them to sit reasonably still or else they would rock the boat. "You might be able to swim, but I can't," he told them.

Ted frowned. "But everyone can."

"Not me. When I first went to sea fifty years ago they told us that if we ended up in the drink it'd take longer to drown if we could swim. I never learnt."

"But that's cruel."

"Things were different then. It's too late now, I'd never learn."

"I could teach you."

Charlie grinned. "That'd be a turn up for the books, wouldn't it! Here am I at seventy, and a little lad of – what – fourteen? – teaches me to swim. You be careful, lad, or I'll take you up on it."

"I'm sure I could."

"Well now... look, that's Halwell Point we've just passed, next on the west side is Tosnos, then east is Ox, Then Snapes and Scoble on either side. Got that? 'Cos if you're going to sail or motor around on this estuary, as it now is, you'll need to know."

"What are they again?"

"Halwell, Tosnos, Ox; Snapes and Scoble. Starting on the left, the east, and then alternately."

He repeated the names to Charlie's satisfaction and was echoed by Ian.

"Which is east?" asked the younger boy.

"Face the direction we've come. That's North. Spread your arms either side. How do you spell 'WE'?"

"W... E..." came a puzzled voice.

"Which way do you write it?"

"What?"

"Which side of the paper do you start to write it?"

"On the left," he said indignantly.

"And that's how West and East start. Face North, then West is on your left and East is on the right. W – E across your page. Turn round and where are west and east now?"

He thought, then the penny dropped. "They're reversed."

"And which way are you facing?"

Another penny dropped. "South."

"So all you need is to know where North is and you know where the others are. And what tells you where north it?"

"A compass."

"Good lad. Next time you get on board we'll do the intermediate points. Then the points between them, and finally you'll have boxed the compass."

"Boxed a compass?" asked Ian, feinting left and right with his fists.

"Wrong boxing," said Charlie. "No room for that on a boat. Or in a ship for that matter. Boxing a compass is quoting the points of it, in order, from North."

"But why?"

"So you can prove you know."

"No, I meant why's it called 'boxing'?"

Charlie shrugged. "You find out, then tell me. I don't know."

"If we find out, can I teach you to swim?" Ted this time.

Charlie looked at him for a long time until he felt uncomfortable. "You find that out, boy, and I'll let you teach me."

"Why are you so anxious to teach Charlie to swim, Ted?" Annabelle asked.

"So he can save himself if he's ever in the water." It was said in such a matter-of-fact, it-should-be-obvious voice that she was both taken aback and reminded of her brother. Settling herself to recover from the memory-stab, she looked over the water towards where Salcombe should be.

"Where's Salcombe gone?" she asked, half to herself.

"You can't see it until we're through the Bag," Charlie told her. "That's the big pool of water before the two last points, Scoble and Snapes. It was always called 'The Bag' even when there was just a stream through it and farmland everywhere else. Now you can see why."

It was almost an inland sea when the tide was high as at that moment. A large, grey expanse of ruffled March water. A Bag of water.

Thanking Charlie and Bert, they found they were early for lunch. Annabelle showed Ted and Ian around the small town, walking them past Susan's café and Mr Merryweather's office, down Fore Street and to the Customs Quay. One of the new tourist shops that sold nautical and mock-nautical items to tourists had opened early, before the season, and they went in to look at the clothing and gadgets on display. Ted and Ian were drawn to a rather splendid compass, over which they spent ages trying to learn how to box it.

"It's very expensive," called Annabelle from the other end of the shop. "Better look at some decent waterproofs before you buy that."

"On holiday?" asked the shopkeeper.

"No – they live in Kingsbridge and have just been through hard times, which is why they're here with me. I need to buy them some better clothes. Their waterproofs might have been all right on a farm but not here, or on the water."

"You're not anything to do with poor Mr Rawle, are you?" he asked.

Annabelle was shocked. "What do you know about that?"

"It's in the paper," he told her.

She sighed. "I had no idea it would get around so quickly. Yes, I am Simon Rawle's brother, and these are his younger sons."

Looking around, he said quietly: "Clothes are better bought from one of the ordinary shops in town. Ours are for tourists and are more expensive. Unless they want a good seaman's jersey, that is. We do them for locals at a lower price. But they're still expensive."

"Thank you. That's very kind. I think once they've stopped growing might be a good time to think of that sort of thing – or I might take up knitting again and do them myself."

"If you do, and if you enjoy it, you could make some for us."

"Really?"

"We always need more hand-knitters. Ganseys are very popular. If you decide to, let me know and I'll show you some of the local designs. Everyone uses them nowadays but it's good to have the originals here if you can."

"I will think about it. Knitting was something I did as a girl, so perhaps I should take it up again"

A clock chimed.

"But now we must go. Thank you again. Come on, Ted, Ian; time we went. You'll be able to come back.

As they walked up the street Annabelle was looking for the clothes shop she had been told about and the boys were talking about compasses. Comments like "no, that's South East," and "No – he said west is on the *left!*" made some fishermen heading to the Victoria Inn for a liquid lunch laugh. "Tell us when you've got it right, boys. We'll sign you on!"

The carried on comparing notes – in other words squabbling – all the way to Mr Merryweather's office where his waiting presence made them stop.

"Ah, good," he said. "I confess to being a little early since I know the ferry arrived some time ago."

"I hope we haven't kept you waiting too long. We knew we were early so spent some time in Sea Chest – I think it was called that."

"A little expensive, but quite pleasant. I think they cater mainly for visitors."

"So I was told. I must buy some more clothes for these two but I'm told that the ordinary clothes shop is less expensive."

"Indeed, but if I might suggest, I should allow Ted to make his own decisions on clothing – within reason, of course." He smiled at the elder boy, who liked him the more for his comment. "He might also relish choosing for Ian – or *with* Ian – too. I found that leaving her to her own devices with clothes was the best way with Susan when she was a similar age. I was never an expert on young ladies' clothing, just as I expect you have limited knowledge about what the young gentleman wears nowadays."

She smiled at him, encouraged by Ted's attitude.

Chatting happily, with the boys still arguing about compass points, they climbed the short distance to the substantial house, itself on a hill, that Mr Merryweather called home.

"Now then, boys; I very carefully opened every door this morning that you could pass through. That means most of them. Those that are closed are Bronwen's and mine. You may go and explore, and go anywhere with an open door. And if you like a room, make a note of where it is and its compass bearing from the Church which is just up there – " he pointed " – and we'll think about it as a possibility for you. All your own stuff will be brought down eventually, and we'll have a think about furniture then."

Politely they waited for more, but all he said was "Go!" and they were leaping up the stairs within a split second.

"If you would assist me, I think it would be a good idea for us to prepare some lunch for all of us. Then we can go and find them to see how their choice of rooms compares with one I will suggest for you. It has a superb view. And if it works out, there is a rather pleasant room that you might want to consider as a family room for times when you feel that a little solitude is needed."

"But surely you wouldn't want me to share your living rooms? I rather expected we would inhabit two rooms – a bedroom for them and a bed-sitting room for me, and for them to socialise in."

"But, no... I would not dream of enforcing boarding house customs on you. I envisage, even if we don't know each other too well, that the downstairs living rooms are there for use by you, Bronwen and me, and the boys too. My niece has a large room, and I have a study. We each have a space where we can be alone if we wish. And the boys need a large play area. There is a loft which extends over the house. That can be partitioned off so that boyish footsteps avoid bedroom ceilings, but the remainder could be theirs.

"And so far as bedrooms are concerned, Ted is, I believe, fourteen. That is an age where privacy might start to become desirable for him. He could have a small room of his own now. Indeed, I have left some clues in two of the rooms which might make them more attractive to what I believe a fourteen and an eleven year old might want."

"I hardly know what to say. You are being very kind."

"Not at all. It seemed to me there is little point in your coming from a small home in Kingsbridge unless you have come to a home with more room for you all in Salcombe."

"Does Martin figure in all this?"

He sighed. "He will want to, of that I am sure. And I believe Bronwen will want him to. It does make complete sense that if he is working in Salcombe he needs to live here too, especially in view of the likely random finish times of his daily work."

"I really hadn't thought of it in those terms. It would be fair, but if there is an ill-advised development in their relationship, let us say, then it would be undesirable."

"That is a consideration, but they are both strong characters who know what they want and have common sense. Eventually, if the relationship develops then we should be little better than Bronwen's father if we attempt to stifle it. But I hope the financial pressures would weigh heavily on their minds before there were to be a *reckless* liaison.

"Turning to the Lofts, we have also to consider that until their compensation is actually credited to an account, work on their extension cannot start. And my grandson or grand-daughter is due in October. That gives seven months – hardly a long time for the design and build process alongside an operating café. In my opinion any pressure on space that can be relieved, should be relieved."

Annabelle nodded. "These are all very pertinent points. I am concerned, though, that you are opening up your home to a lot of people. As I understand it you have been living alone here for many years. It will be a strain on your routines and your peace."

"And that is what I relish most of all."

"You do?"

"Yes. It took a few hours of Bronwen's presence to achieve a feeling that all those years of a near hermit's existence have made me even more of a dusty old solicitor than I naturally am." He smiled. "Have you any idea how much hearing a young voice in your home again brings the things of youth – well, the things of a younger person – back again?"

"Alas, I have never had children."

"But you have enjoyed the company of these three young gentlemen; Martin, Ted and Ian. And they like you and enjoy your company. And your decision to come here means you enjoy theirs – even when it's noisy!"

This was in response to even more arguing about compass bearings that were audible in the landing above. They both smiled.

"You are being very frank with me, Mr Merryweather, something I appreciate. I wondered, yesterday, whether you were encouraging me to bring the boys here just in order to be a housekeeper."

He looked shocked. "That is something I would never do. If that was in my mind I would say that I was looking for a housekeeper. In my practice I deal with truth and lies on a daily basis and have come to the conclusion that I prefer truth. It has a more wholesome feel to it."

She bowed to him, unconsciously echoing one of his own professional foibles. He laughed.

"We are both being extremely formal. To bow in thanks is one of my ploys.

I hope we may be honest with each other and less formal. Please – the name I am cursed with is Algernon. Bronwen calls me Uncle Algy, particularly when she is annoyed with me. I regret that my second name is Bertram, which I also detest, but I have not told her that yet. Perhaps Bert is a nickname which, to my regret, I'll have to bow to and use. Please take your pick."

This made her laugh. "And I am Annabelle, a name which is at the best a long one, if perhaps not unattractive…"

"It is very attractive."

"… but to many people who heard Ted and Ian try to pronounce it when they had just started talking, I am 'Amble'.

It was Mr Merryweather's turn to laugh. "That is a lovely story. Amble and Bert. Bert and Amble. For goodness sake keep that from my clients!"

"Keep what from your clients?" came a voice from the door. "May I prepare lunch, or have you?"

"Hallo Bronwen. Yes please, that would be really nice. We were about to do so but were sidetracked. There are two potential navigators upstairs examining bedrooms for suitability and trying to work out the bearings from each to the church."

"Why, may I ask?"

"To give them something to think about so that we can have a chat in peace."

"Ahh… and what should be kept from your clients?"

"Oh dear… My dreaded Christian name and its possibilities."

"What's wrong with 'Uncle Algy'?"

"I have always detested it, that's what is wrong. I think your father coined that from my full name."

"Oh. In that case I won't use it."

"Thank you. My middle name is just as bad, but at least can be contracted to 'Bert'. That's what my wife used to use when we were alone."

"Uncle Bert? Well, that sounds better to me, and has nothing to do with my father."

"Indeed."

"And I have decided to trade under the name of Aunt Amble," said Annabelle, "at least so far as those two are concerned. It's what they used to call me when very young indeed. Some local people in Kingsbridge still call me Amble to my face."

Bronwen was still taking all this in and wondering whether it was appropriate for the laugh that threatened to overtake her smile when there was shout from above.

"Can you come up, Aunt Amble?"

Though there was no alarm in the voice, the three exchanged anxious glances before hurrying up to find that the call had come from the top floor. They found the two in one of the rooms, looking out over the Estuary.

"Can we have this one, please?" asked Ted. "It's just a lovely room."

"I rather expected you'd want a room on the first floor, not way up here." The owner of the house was amused that his decoys in the rooms he had chosen for them had apparently both failed.

"Oh no. We like being out of the way, don't we, Ian?"

"Yes. It means people can't just pop their heads in all the time and tell us off."

"Ian!"

"Well, it's true. This is a great room, anyway."

"So who is having this one?

"We are – please."

"But we have enough rooms for one bedroom each." Mr Merryweather was determined to give them the chance.

Ian's jaw dropped. His brother looked uncertain.

"We've always shared a room," Ted said thoughtfully, looking at his brother. Ian plainly didn't know what to say.

"Why don't you share for now, and settle in," said their Aunt tactfully. "But decide on another room to use for playing in and making things and so on. Then if you decide to, one of you can use it for sleeping in as well."

Two broad smiles were all she needed as an answer and the two scurried off again, only to the bigger room next to it, where they nodded to each other.

"This one, please," said Ian.

And so it was decided. They had lunch. Mr Merryweather was late back to his office and received a look of reproach from Mrs Damerell. Bronwen asked if she could return to the Island with them. "I'm getting bored here," she admitted.

The Rawles noticed, at the Hard, that the small motor boat that Susan had bought years ago was tied to one of the pontoons.

"We could wait and see who's here," said Ted, hoping he might be allowed to be at the controls on the voyage.

"It might be Martin," said their Aunt, "and if it is he will be at work. His first day at being a trainee architect. We'd better go round to the Ferry steps – there's one due at about two-thirty, I think."

But there was none on the timetable. She hesitated.

"Can we phone one of them on the Island?" Ted asked hopefully.

"Unless... bother, I have almost no money with me. We could have let you choose some new clothes. I suppose phoning is all we can do."

"I saw the post office earlier," said Ian. "We could phone from there."

They did. They heard Henry ask Susan if she could come down to the main Hard. "I'm dealing with tree people," he explained.

Annabelle knew nothing of their recent near miss. "Three people? Have you opened the cafe early?"

The crossed wires were eventually sorted out, to much mirth from the boys when she explained. Half an hour later Susan swung the launch alongside the Hard. They boarded and she made her way through the moored boats.

"Susan..." said a wheedling voice. She looked across at Ted who had carefully placed himself opposite.

"Please may I steer?"

She realised that one of the many opportunities the pair had missed was to take to the water. Why should these two be denied, when Mary and Stephen had become such natural watermen?

The journey was made in fits and starts as each of them received tuition at both tiller and engine. Susan only took over as they arrived at the Island. Ian heaved a sigh of happiness as he climbed ashore.

"Thank you. Can I have another go some time?"

She smiled. "Even if you're living in Salcombe we hope you'll come up here regularly, like my Dad does. Even if we can't, I'm sure Mary and Stephen can take you out until you're safe enough on your own. Can you both swim?"

They assured her that they could.

"That's all right, then."

They were on their way back to the house when there was a shout of "Timber!" from the other side of the Island and a moment later the ground shook.

"It's all right," said Susan, "they decided they would take the weak trees down today. We don't want another accident." She explained what had happened. Annabelle was horrified.

"That's why they've all been looked at," Susan reassured her, "and the three weak ones are being taken out."

"That's what Henry meant earlier on the phone. He mentioned tree people. I thought he said 'three'."

"There are five… oh, I see what you mean! But we've been hoping the tree people – this is getting confusing – would come before the next high wind," Susan explained. "It's quite a miracle nothing came down when the flood happened."

At the house they found that Henry had just put the kettle on.

"Shipping order," he said. "Five tree fellers and me. And now you four."

9 – Trees and Fellers

They were chatting still when the phone rang. Susan answered it, then handed the receiver to Annabelle. "Police," she said in a stage whisper.

It seemed that the Police had finished in the Rawles' cottage. They had been about to leave when the landlord had arrived, wanting to know what was happening.

"So far as we're concerned you have access to it again," the Policeman told her, "but I should warn you that the landlord is very keen to clear it and let it again. We told him that we had just released it back to you and that you would need time to remove your property. He didn't seem very interested in that, so we told him that any removal of property without your consent would be theft. That rather shut him up. We felt you should be made aware."

Annabelle thanked him. After finishing the call she explained the situation to Susan and the boys. Susan told her to waste no time and phone Mr Merryweather.

He was pleased to talk to her. "No second thoughts, I hope?"

She reassured him and described the phone call from the Police.

"Do you know the landlord's identity?"

"No, but Martin does."

"Could you find out... no, I can. I know Mr Alexander's phone number."

Forty minutes later he phoned back. "I have set Mr Wilson straight. He is in no doubt that any property remaining belongs to Martin, Ted and Ian, and that it will be collected without undue delay. In practice that means as soon as arrangements can be made to do so. It is a pity that the rent was already due, otherwise there would have been less of a rush."

"It is also a shame," Annabelle told him, "that Mr Wilson is not at all a reasonable man or one given to Christian behaviour."

There was a laugh at the other end of the phone line. "But he knows now that the boys have a legal eagle working for them. That is inclined to exercise the mind somewhat, even if it is only me."

"*Only* you! I have heard stories that make the juxtaposition of those two words wholly inappropriate."

A chuckle. "Oddly, I find myself bowing, and I am holding a telephone. Please consider yourself bowed to in thanks. Bother – my next client has been announced. I must go. Please could you remind Henry about tomorrow? He will know what I mean."

She assured him that she would and walked from the hallway smiling.

"I wonder..." Henry stared when he had heard the news. "If our tree people are free tomorrow, could they help out with their rather large truck? Would they be prepared to? I can't help, I'm at the meeting and I need Mary with me. She's one of those who have been caused losses by the water board."

Mary frowned, suddenly deflated. "And Stephen needs to make the decision of whether to come with me or help you move."

Stephen was torn. Mary was needed at the meeting of landowners and what affected her affected him too. On the other hand the Rawles' move needed able-bodied helpers.

Cautiously, not knowing if another tree was about to come down, Henry, Martin, Ian and Ted took the tray of tea and went to find the team of tree experts. Their quarry had stopped for a breather, so he shared the tea round and explained the situation. The boss was with them, fortunately, and smiled ruefully.

"Seeing as we can't get a boat here until next week now, not one that's big enough to take these big old trunks to start their seasoning, we're at a bit of a loose end for two or three days. So yes, if you pay for the fuel, we'll come and help your lads. Especially Martin. He's a good'un. Knows what he's about. Where's the stuff all going to?"

"Mr Merryweather's house in Salcombe. It's at..."

"I know where he lives," said the Boss. "He's my solicitor too but he plays cricket, just like I do. So I've been to his house, discussing tactics. He's good, too. Didn't help us, mind; we still lost against Paignton."

Henry hurried back, leaving the boys watching events, and remembered that another client had just entered the inner sanctum of the solicitor's office. He phoned Mike Alexander instead, apologised profusely and asked to speak to Martin again.

"We're just about to come to you," Mike explained. "We need to have another look at the house and Martin's plans."

"Won't they work?"

"Oh yes, and he's done really well today, on your build and on other schemes. But we had one or two ideas... May we come and beg a tea from you? And was it urgent, your message for Martin?"

"No, when you get here will be fine. We'll put the kettle on."

Martin was at first indignant about the landlord's attitude, but pleased to hear the view of the police and the actions of his own solicitor. He was even more pleased to find Bronwen on the Island.

"Good old Grandad," he said, having kissed her. "It's wonderful having him so much on side. But what do we do now? Hire a removals firm?"

Henry cleared his throat. "Er... well – it seems the tree people – there are five of them..."

It was Martin's turn for confusion. Everyone else laughed.

He was delighted and grateful for Henry's intervention and the woodsmen's agreement to help. He and Mike requested *carte blanche* to investigate Lofts' farmhouse and its structure. Mike requested a ladder and torches so as to access the roof space and an elderly wooden affair was brought in from the pigsty. Susan eyed it doubtfully and set to with a cloth.

"Best test the rungs as you use it," Henry told them. "If you get stranded up there we'll be begging favours from our five three people again."

"Us injuring ourselves is a minor matter, I suppose?"

"Well, naturally. Now we have the NHS."

They grinned at him. Martin wondered about putting out his tongue as he would have done in private had it been Ted, but decided not to.

They found the ceiling trap to have been painted in situ so that it was securely stuck down. "Draft-proofed" as Henry described it. An illicitly procured kitchen knife, carefully applied, cut through several layers of paint. Finally, amid a cloud of dust and paint flakes, the trap yielded.

"I know I'm teaching my grandmother to suck eggs," Mike told Martin, "but make sure you don't try treading between the joists. If we need to work up here we can get some boards to span them. But I don't want a bill from Mr Loft for ceiling repairs."

It proved to be a quite simple roof structure which would easily allow for what Mike was aiming for: a roof for the extension running at right angles to the original to avoid the problem of a trough between them. They made notes and sketches, and a few cautious measurements and prepared to descend. Martin's attention was drawn to a dusty lump in one corner of the void.

"What's that?" he asked.

Mike looked. "None of our business. Been up here years. It's not structural."

"But they don't know it's here."

"No. We can leave the ladder there, though, and let Henry know."

"I'll come up with him."

Back downstairs they were firmly directed outside by Susan and Bronwen to brush each other off, after which they told Henry about the item in the corner.

"What is it?"

"We didn't look."

"I know who would love to be there – Mary, Stephen and the boys. Shall we wait until they're back?"

"It's nearly time to fetch them from Salcombe anyway. Shall we take Ted and Ian again?" Susan knew that Henry would want to stay and supervise the five tree fellers, as she described them to her husband, who laughed.

"We need to do a few more measurements," said Mike, "then if you can run me back I'd be grateful. In fact as I know Martin will need to be busy tomorrow and probably the rest of the week, could he run me back so we can talk about employment on the way? There's no doubt that I want him!"

"Thank you... thank you. Is that all right, Susan?"

"Of course," she smiled at him. "And you won't want Ted and Ian with you, will you?"

"Let them come, if that's acceptable to Martin. They need the practice with the boat and it'd leave us free to talk."

"Don't forget they're only just starting to learn!"

"I know," said Martin. "And why that should be when I learnt to sail all those years ago, I don't know."

"Probably your father's health getting in the way of that side of things," Susan reminded him gently.

He shrugged. "Any opportunity to set that right, we should take."

They all instinctively ducked as another shock went through the ground.

"Another tree? I hope those two were safely out of the way."

"I'm sure our fellers, no matter how many, would have made sure of that!" said Susan.

Mike and Martin elected to go to the felling area and find the brothers. Mike took his opportunity.

"Now look, Martin: based on today and how we work together, I want to offer you a job. You need to be busy this week, but can you call me on Thursday and tell me if you want to accept, and then start work the following Monday? If I haven't put you off too much, that is."

Martin had all but forgotten that he wasn't actually already working for Mike so he had a moment of confusion. The offer was there, though.

"Yes... yes please. And thank you!"

"I think I'm going to be in the situation where I'll be thanking you. You have just the attitude I need – and the neatness of drawing too. The rest of it we can sort out over time. Deal?"

"Deal... except that I don't know what wa... salary to expect."

"No – we've not discussed that, have we? I have in mind a monthly figure plus a share of the fees we are paid. How does that sound?"

"Well, yes, I think so..."

"Naturally as you get more useful the percentage share of the fees would increase, as would the basic sum. Now, I need to work out exactly what can be afforded as we stand, so I won't be able to tell you the amounts until Thursday. It won't be a large salary to start with – but I'm pretty sure you're expecting that. If that proves to be acceptable I'll draft something out formally and we can both sign copies. Is that okay?"

Martin nodded, suddenly almost deliriously happy. He felt that at last he was on his way. Would there ever be a time when he could shout at the Williams father that he was a qualified architect, earning hundreds a year, but that as Bronwen would then be over twenty-one he had no need of her father's permission to marry? And that he didn't want to see his new father-in-law, ever?

"That is wonderful. Yes, it's very okay. Thank you." On an impulse he stopped and offered his hand. It was firmly shaken.

They found Ted and Ian happily sorting out cut branches into piles.

"May we borrow your workforce today as well, please?" asked Martin. "The youngest ones will do!"

"We're enjoying ourselves," Ted protested.

"Well, we need some trainees to take the boat into Salcombe to fetch Mary and Stephen, so we thought you might like to be those trainees."

Ted and Ian shared a look.

"Can I come?" asked Ian.

"Of course. Ted?"

He looked undecided.

"You can stay here if you want."

"Is that all right, Ian?"

"Yes. I want to learn how to steer the boat properly."

"So do I, but I can do that any time. This doesn't happen often."

Ian was given the helm as soon as they had slipped their moorings. Without his older brother watching he was less self-conscious and with one-to-one instruction he quickly improved. They let him reduce speed and find a way through the moored boats and the few moving ones as they headed toward the Hard.

"When Stephen and Martin rushed me from the Customs Quay to catch the Lifeboat that time, they did a very skilful manoeuvre – a sort of half circuit that leaves the bow facing the way you want to go. If Martin stands by to guide you, will you have a go?"

"I'll try," said Ian.

Between the two of them they made a passable attempt at it, with a surprised Mary and Stephen watching. Stephen had to grab the gunwale to stop the boat overshooting, but the accuracy of the turn was good.

Mike jumped out and held the boat whilst the others climbed in.

"Soon have you in the Lifeboat crew, Ian," he said.

"After me!" Martin answered.

"If you're serious, you need to talk to the Coxswain. I'll talk to you on Thursday. And thanks."

Ian steered all the way back to the Island. He managed to adjust speed and course so that picking up the buoy attached to their running moorings was done without incident. There were complimentary comments from the others and he smiled happily.

The tree fellers – they went through the gamut of jokes again for Mary and Stephen – were waiting, wanting to return to Lincombe and their lorry. A happy, tired, dirty Ted was with them. He and Stephen ferried them over, with Ted under instruction this time.

During the meal that Bronwen and Susan had hastily concocted Martin explained why the ladder was still at the roof space. "If we go up there we need a board so that we spread the weight. Otherwise we'll forget about the ceiling and someone will go through." He avoided looking at anyone in particular.

"How about a few planks?" Henry suggested. "We could get whatever it is to the hatch so it's easier to see, and maybe get it downstairs so we don't need to worry about the joists."

Carefully the investigation was made. Stephen thought himself inside a treasure story as he saw that the dusty, wooden lump with iron bands was a chest. It caused so much excitement that it was Martin whose foot strayed off the joist and nearly caused damage.

"Oops..." he said.

It proved to be a reasonably light chest, despite the metal hoops. It was slid carefully to the trap on the planks.

"Can we get it through there?" Stephen asked.

"It went up, so it should come down," Martin observed.

"What have you got? And is it dusty?" called Susan from below.

"A chest of some sort, and yes; very."

"I'll put a dust sheet down."

"We need two people down there and we can lower it down to them," Henry suggested.

Henry and Martin climbed down with Ian. Susan brought an old sheet and carefully they manoeuvred the chest down the ladder.

"Do we open it here?" asked Stephen.

"It'd be easier to take the contents downstairs separately – if there is anything."

It wasn't locked, to the boys' disappointment. To them it meant that there was no treasure inside. The clasp was undone, the lid was lifted.

The first thing they saw was a piece of paper. In large writing, all copperplate capitals, was written:

TO MY SONS, OR THE MEMBER OF THE LOFT FAMILY WHO OPENS
THIS FIRST IF MY SONS ARE NO LONGER LIVING.

Stephen looked at his father. "You're the head of the family, Dad, it should
be you.
"But Martin and Mike saw it first."
"But that's not what it says, it says 'who opens it first.'" Henry was glad he
hadn't mentioned the family difference, but nevertheless opened it.
Trying not to damage the old paper he opened it up and read:

*I had been a seafarer since first I left my home in London, from which I ran
away when I was just twelve years of age having been used badly by my father.
Now I have seen enough of life and death in His Majesty's Navy to want no more
to do with it. I have been cautious with what fortune I earned, not wanting the
release from the treatment we received that my early shipmates found, in dubious
women and strong liquor, but instead purging my soul in study, music and
tranquillity.*

*My sea clothes are in this chest. I have hidden them away knowing that now
I shall never be tempted to return to that life.*

*With my savings I have founded a farm which I ran first with my wife and
you, my sons. It is run from here; Loft Island. I made bold to name it so and am
proud to have done thus.*

*They planned to drain the old estuary. I invested in the scheme so that the
land uncovered will provide ample good grazing and fertile soil once it has been
purged of the salt. It will allow our higher lands which are more distant and less
convenient to farm to be released to others.*

*Ten years have now passed since the works were complete. The sweetness of
the exposed land is now confirmed and we have driven our animals from the
higher lands to the valley floor where they flourish.*

*Our Bailiff and our solicitor in Exeter, Maxwell and Sons, have arranged all
this and now our high land pastures have been sold.*

*I have written this for my sons, Albert and Henry, to await their return from
fighting with the King's Navy. I am told that I am now sick unto death. If they do
not return, then this affidavit remains for their children to find when they achieve
their majority or for a future generation of Lofts to discover and use as they will.
My Bailiff will put this in my seaman's trunk, which has seen as many violent
seas and violent men as I, and carry it to the loft of the house on Loft Island. A
fitting hiding place.*

*The remainder of my goods and chattels will have been distributed in
accordance with my will.*

*Joseph Beale Loft
In the year 1785 anno domini: the thirty-first of May.*

"Joseph Beale Loft..." The name rang in Mary's and Stephen's mind. Beale? Did that mean they were related? Would that affect their plans to marry?

"Can we look at the clothes?" asked Ian.

The others put their thoughts to one side and the things were carefully removed. Trousers – dark blue. Jacket – gold braid...

"Good heavens!" Henry exclaimed, "he was a captain! Look at this."

The braid was examined, but only Henry knew its meaning. The boys were still looking into the chest.

"There are two wooden boxes at the bottom," Ted said with excitement in his voice.

"Go on, then," said Henry.

Ted brought out the larger one. It had been well protected from the dust and was very smart, with an inlaid design to the lid. He opened it.

"But what is it?" he asked.

"It's a sextant," Martin told him. "It's used for finding your position at sea." He had seen photographs of one during his later school years.

"How does it work?"

"I have no idea. You'd need to ask Charlie, or Edgar at the boatyard."

Ian was already delving into the chest again. The other box came up and was opened. He gasped.

To call it just a compass would be a complete injustice. It was of brass, pivoted at four points onto a bracket which looked as though it could be mounted on something solid.. The main case could therefore swing to allow the housing to remain upright. The card on which both degrees and the 32 points of the compass were inscribed was mounted in a fluid and stayed true despite any movement of its case.

It was an instrument, not just a compass.

"Wow," said Ted. "That's a real compass."

"They're both antiques," said Martin, "and worth a lot of money." Ian and Ted were still just looking at it.

They took the items downstairs and the trunk was manhandled down too.

"For the moment the uniform needs to go safely out of the way," Susan told them. "There's nothing we can do with it, and a decision needs to be made about what happens to it."

"It'd be nice to display the sextant and compass," said Henry.

"In the living room where cafe customers can't see them," said Susan. "We don't want them walking off."

Henry, Mary and Stephen left with a full boat the following morning. The three of them were to attend the meeting of landowners and the remainder were to travel to Kingsbridge, meet up with their volunteer removers, and clear the Rawles' house.

It was exhausting, sad and exhilarating for them. The sadness came with the knowledge that the boys' home of 11, 14 and 18 years respectively was to be theirs no longer. The sadness was crowned by the need to clear their father's bedroom, the room in which he had died, along with everywhere else. It was while they were doing so, as quietly and reverently as they could – it seemed only right – that there came a loud knock at the door. Susan was downstairs and answered it.

"How long are you going to be?" demanded the visitor with neither introduction nor preamble.

Susan blinked and entered Solicitor's daughter mode.

"How pleasant to see you? It seems we have yet to be introduced, Mr...er..."

"Mr Wilson."

"Sorry, I didn't quite catch that. Mr...?

"Wilson!" He almost shouted it.

"Ah, *Wilson*. Wilson, of course. I believe you spoke to my father, Mr Merryweather, yesterday. He will have told you, and will repeat the message in writing in a Solicitor's Letter if you require, that the house will be cleared without undue delay. That means, in legal terms, as soon as practically possible. In fact you are very lucky that we have been able to arrange for assistance so quickly, since I have known cases – for example where someone has died intestate – that have resulted in many months where the landlord has been unable to regain possession of the deceased's home. Indeed there have been cases where the landlord has had to clear the deceased's property in his own time and at his own expense."

"I want to get in as soon as possible."

"Which is precisely what is meant by 'without undue delay' of course."

"What does that mean?"

Susan raised her eyebrows. "I was under the impression that we had just covered that. Legally, it means 'as soon as it is practically possible to do so.'"

"I mean, how long are you going to take?"

"At this stage I really cannot say. It is a shame you never knew Mr Rawle well. Had you done so you would have known something more of the extent of his possessions when you visited him socially. Since he was a war veteran I'm sure you would have found him most interesting. It is a very great tragedy that he has died, since now all that first-hand knowledge has died with him, of course."

"I want to get into this house as soon as possible. Today, preferably."

"That will not be possible. There are delays we have to face, and not undue delays, either."

"What do you mean?"

"Just that. However, if you can reassure me that you will not attempt entry whilst Mr Rawle's family are away from the property, I will reassure you that no attempt will be made to change the locks to avoid such an illegal act."

He blustered: wordlessly, Susan was pleased to notice. She felt she had gained the advantage.

"*Good* day to you." She closed the door, very nearly in his face.

Martin emerged from the room nearby. "Thank you, you were marvellous," he said. "I was wondering when he was going to push you aside and barge in, but he didn't."

"I think he realises that would be illegal. He is an unpleasant man."

There was another knock at the door, more circumspect this time. Martin and Susan exchanged glances. He went to the door.

"Who are you?" came the barked question from the same man.

"Oh, just one of the clearance people, he said in as much of a cultured London accent as he could. That seemed to confuse the man.

"Look: tell that woman I was just talking to that I want to bring some people round this afternoon to look over the farm."

"Is that an instruction for her, the daughter of a solicitor? If so, I think she would make charges for working for you."

"Just who are you?"

"I imagine you are the man Wilson, who we've heard so much about. If that's so, and if we are here when you arrive, I imagine we'll assist in showing your prospective clients around."

"I don't need your assistance. I want you out."

"The lady you spoke to mentioned the principle of 'without undue delay', I think. Currently we are trying to work as fast as we can but your interruptions will probably add another two days to the clearance of the property."

"What?"

"Well, of course. We're here to assist in clearing the house and you're interrupting us."

"Just get out of it. Quickly."

"Once again you are giving orders. We can't respond to orders except from our boss. If you cease interrupting us we will complete the task without undue delay."

Mr Wilson glared at him, receiving a smile in return. He turned and fumed off.

"You're not too bad at arguing yourself," Susan called to him from her place in the front room where it seemed a heavy candlestick was in her grasp. She called for a break and a conference. There was some muttering from above and a clatter of approaching people.

"Do you want us too?" asked the boss of the tree-felling gang.

Susan nodded. "That was the delightful landlord. He seems reluctant to take no for an answer. Ted, do you know if your father changed the locks at all recently?"

"No. He's never done that."

"So Wilson has keys to this place?"

"He came in without knocking once," Ted said. "He swears he knocked but he can't have done or we'd have heard him."

"Do you remember when?"

"Ages ago. I don't know when."

"I see. That's still good. Anyone know anything about changing locks?"

"I do," said Martin. "It was one of the first things we had to do on Peter and Dot's place. They got me to do it."

"Can you buy some cheap locks that will replace these?"

"Just the front one, that's all you need. The back door can be bolted as well as locked."

"Very good."

A swift transaction and ten minutes with a screwdriver, and the front door was made private again.

10 – The move

In Salcombe later with the first load of furniture it became obvious that that would be the only load of the day. The sheer hard work of lifting large items from the farmhouse and into a three-story house was enough to tire anyone. As every room was already furnished to an adequate level it was also awkward deciding where the items should go, and wondering what their host would say. Uncle Bert, Mary, Henry and Stephen rejoined them just after lunch. Bronwen had taken time from the removal effort to make sandwiches.

The large contingent, including those drafted in from the tree company sat around the kitchen table, discussing progress so far.

"It went well, apart from one particular landowner, of whose holding we were unaware," the solicitor announced. "He was most concerned that he hadn't been told and seemed not to want to listen to the reason that if we were unaware of him, we couldn't inform him. It seems that there is a small sliver of land which he had let out, on which the tenant had recently defaulted so leaving him out of pocket. It had only been used for the summer grazing of horses so they were absent when the flood occurred.

"For the sake of this one man we had to go through all the pros and cons again. Everyone else knew them. He found it difficult to see why he should contribute to a case when the advantage to him was minimal. It took a lot of argument to try and stir him, to appeal to his community spirit but the more everyone tried, the more entrenched he became. I could see Mary getting more and more frustrated and angry and was really pleased when she stood up."

He looked at his honorary granddaughter and smiled. She took up the tale.

"I was furious," she admitted. "He was being so *selfish* and pig-headed. Oh yes, I stood up. Gradually people stopped talking and looked at me. I told him that the difference to me, to my case, having lost my entire family and possessions, was more to me than he could possibly realise. I asked him if he really wanted to be known as the man who rubbished the legal case for a lot of good people, people who really deserved to be treated to a fair amount of compensation, not the derisory amount that we had been offered.

"I asked him what the difference in money would be to him if we didn't act together and argue the case, and after a bit of to-ing and fro-ing he told us it would be about a hundred pounds. So I asked him what he would do if one of his tenants owed him a hundred pounds for four years."

"And that," the solicitor resumed, "made him more annoyed still so I told him to play along with Mary." He turned to her. "I apologise for making that sound condescending, but I know the type and I knew he would have difficulty in responding to an argument presented by anyone apart from a man, and a man over thirty at that.

"Anyway: the man said, from between gritted teeth, that the tenant wouldn't last in the property for four years."

"'So you would take legal action to evict him?', I asked. He replied vehemently that he would so I asked him if that would be the same one hundred pounds he was prepared to wave goodbye to in our present case.

"That stopped him in his tracks. One of the others, one of the reasonable, large landowners, knew him and said something quietly. Then, with bad grace, he agreed."

There was a murmur of approval and Mary got some admiring glances.

"Well, why not?" she asked indignantly. "He was being a selfish pig."

"Anyway," Mr Merrweather continued, "we have agreement that my firm will act for the consortium of landowners – the Salcombe Landowners' Action Consortium. It took ages even to reach agreement on that."

Ted was thinking, and interrupted. "Er... excuse me, but if anyone shortens it, it will be S-L-A-C. Slack. Is that the right thing to call it?"

Mr Merryweather looked at him, eyebrows raised. Ted squirmed in his seat as the others laughed.

"I hope you're not laughing at Ted," he observed. "He is right, that is not what we should be referred to. Bother. I shall have to ask them again." He sighed. "I foresee another round of arguments."

Reassured, Ted raised his hand again and the solicitor looked at him, this time with a twinkle in his eye.

"What about Justice?" he asked cautiously. "Salcombe Landowners' Justice Consortium."

Pause. No laughter this time.

"You know, I think they might go for that, Ted. Good. Common sense comes from those with the clearest sight. And including the word 'justice' will persuade some people in the Water Board of how our minds are working. I will write to the clients tomorrow, inform them of the – er – complication and give them the obvious solution. If you'll forgive me, I may not credit you with it or we might encourage dissent. But I would like to." He bowed to Ted who smiled at him.

He made a quick tour of the house with the Rawles and made some suggestions about moving some of their furniture round, offering to give away some of his own items to make room. "Though we shall have to make sure all the new items are labelled with the owners' name," he said, "just in case. And if you have a good, honest kitchen table that's larger than this, it would be really useful as we're now a larger family here." He smiled happily. "We could put this one upstairs for you two – perhaps for a model railway?"

Both sets of eyes opened wide. Stephen's did too, as Mary noticed. She smiled. Perhaps he wasn't quite so adult as he seemed at times.

"We've still got another load to come tomorrow," said Martin wearily. "And our kitchen table *is* larger. We need to take it to bits to get it out, I should think."

"Leave that to us," said one of the woodmen. "We'll take an axe to it. We're used to that." He grinned at Martin.

"And there are my few sticks," said the latter's aunt. "Some pieces were our parents', Simon's and mine. I believe they might be quite good, but don't really know."

"We will label them and decide between us, shall we?" her host asked.

"It appears that we have missed your delightful landlord with his prospective clients," said Susan suddenly. "That will annoy him."

"He gave you some problems, I hear."

"Nothing I can't handle, following in your mould," she told her father. "I confused him, then Martin did some more, and the *coup de grace* will have been the changing of the locks."

"That could be an unwise thing to do," said her father. "If locks are changed the tenant is in duty bound to provide a key to the landlord."

"Oh, Martin has a spare key for him," she said innocently. "To save time we agreed to wait until he appeared again this afternoon, didn't we, Martin? Or of course, as he failed to appear this afternoon whilst we were there it could always be posted. Tomorrow."

Her father looked at her and quietly muttered the word 'incorrigible'. She smiled sweetly at him.

With Henry's and the woodmen's help the remainder of the furniture was cleared from the farmhouse the next day in two loads. Although Mr Rawle's will hadn't been found Henry had arranged for the cattle and as much as possible of the farm machinery to be moved to join the farm where his and the Beales' cattle were still being cared for.

In the afternoon the landlord arrived with two bemused people in tow.

"We need to look round," he started. Since the comment was aimed at one of the woodmen it produced just a grin. Mr Wilson's way in was blocked by one end of the kitchen table and since the woodman, Alf, was walking backwards, was at least a head taller than the landlord and had no intention of putting the table down the man was nearly trampled. He started blustering.

"Careful, will you? This is my property and I need to gain access."

He was ignored. Alf just continued backwards, toward pavement level. At the other end Martin and Ted were trying their best to cope with the weight. They too ignored him.

Henry came out next, carrying another, much smaller table on his own. He looked at the three and cautiously lowered the table to rest on the path.

"You tried to bully my wife yesterday, I understand. That is something I will not put up with and I warn you that if you do so again, or try to bully me or anyone else here there will be a breach of the peace." He allowed no gap for the man to interrupt. "And if you are trying to let this farm as a going concern to these people they need to hear the Rawles' experience in trying to get it to pay. The land's no good. Wilson has all the really good acreage which I assume he now farms himself."

He picked up the table again and held it across himself, almost as a battering ram against the angry man who was drawing breath, and marched off down the path.

Susan, listening inside, heard the husband of the visiting couple ask: "is that so, Mr Wilson?" She smiled to herself and walked out, arms full of table legs.

"That's what led to the previous tenant having to send one of his sons to live elsewhere," she told them. "There wasn't enough income to feed them."

"We heard there had been a death. Are you...er...?"

"No, just a friend of the sons'."

"You have no right to talk like that to my clients!" shouted Mr Wilson.

"Mr Rawle fought the Nazis for freedom of speech," she told him coldly, "and the truth is a part of that. Now, excuse me..."

She marched past the trio, noticing the look that the couple exchanged as she did.

When Alf, Martin, Ted, Henry and Susan returned from the truck being used to take the furniture to Salcombe the couple were walking away from Mr Wilson, who was speechless. He recovered enough to swear at Alf, a move which caused a wince from Susan. Alf walked up to him and towered over him.

"Only a coward uses language like that in front of a lady."

Henry also moved up.

"I warned you that if you bullied my wife again there would be a breach of the peace. Now you have used foul language. Apologise now, then go, or face the police and a Public Order charge."

The man looked at him and up at Alf, seemed about to say something but instead retreated to the pavement.

"There's some agricultural stuff still to move," Henry called. The man continued walking away "And we know what's there. The key will be under the mat when we've finished." The last was shouted after him. He hadn't turned round.

The solicitor returned late from his office, tired, and found Mary and Stephen back from school and with the others. A new, larger kitchen table had been installed and the original was now upstairs in one of the larger bedrooms.

"That's just to get it out of the way," Susan explained, trying not to look at Ian's pleading eyes. "There's so much else to find a home for."

"Uncle Bert..."

Even the addressee of the unanswered question knew wheedling when he heard it. Martin was used to it, though in his experience the answer was almost always a snapped "No!"

Uncle Bert looked at the wheedler, otherwise known as Ian, and smiled tiredly.

"Hmmm?"

"You know you talked about a model railway? And this table?"

He waited. So did his subject. He had to finish the request.

"*Please* could we use the big room upstairs for it? It won't really fit into the bedroom we chose, or even into the other one that you said Ted could have."

"Hmm... I suppose we could cut it in half so it *did* fit into the other rooms."

The boy's mouth dropped open. "Oh." He looked down at the carpet.

"But that would mean that all the trains would have to be driven into a wall, doesn't it? And that seems a very bad idea."

The eyes looked up again, hopefully, and saw the twinkle in the eye and the start of the smile.

"Dad, you're teasing him." Susan laughed.

"I know. But it got us both thinking, didn't it Ian? Because if it was in that big room – I take it you mean the attic room – and if we really wanted to, we could have another table in here and build a model bridge across the gap, a bit like the Tamar Bridge, perhaps. Then it'd be bigger; lots bigger. And that means I could come and play as well. How would that be?"

A large, astonished grin. "Yes! Yes please!"

"It'd take some building, though. Are you ready for that? Maybe next autumn? That means we could save up for some track and some engines and carriages to run on it."

The grin spread further round the face. "Yeah..."

"Now, are you two happy about moving here? Or is it too early to say? Your Aunt Amble has agreed to come."

"Aunt Amble's bed is still in Kingsbridge," she responded. "I need to move everything here first and create even more havoc. But I have no compulsion to start a model railway layout, you'll be glad to hear."

"So far as railways are concerned I think one per household is adequate. We shall have to share Ian and Ted's if they'll allow us. Bedrooms are a different matter, and I do have two fully fledged spare rooms downstairs, you know, apart from Bronwen's that is."

"I don't want to put you to any trouble..."

"You would not. The Rawles and I would value your company and presence."

She held up her hands in surrender, then thought. "I have no possessions with me."

"And now it is dark. I will run you to Kingsbridge to retrieve what you need, or of course we could make do with what I can find."

"I...well..."

"Go on, Aunt! Let Uncle Bert take you to Kingsbridge."

"Ian, you are a bully. Mr Merryweather is tired."

"But she needs some pyjamas and..."

"Ian! That will do!" She blushed, and turned resignedly to their host. "Unfortunately he is right. I either need to go back to Kingsbridge to sleep tonight, or to bring some possessions here. By road would be quicker, but we could go by boat, I suppose."

"I'm not sure about navigating through the mud flats to Kingsbridge at low tide and at night," Henry said, "nor does anyone else, I imagine."

"Then I will take you. And perhaps Bronwen could work her magic once again and cook – with Ted's and Ian's help, perhaps – then we can all eat when we return. Would you be prepared to, Bron?"

"I'm sure I can, but I'm really not an expert cook, even if I did help out with Angharad when I could."

"You've done very well so far. I'm sorry to have to ask you to cook so much, but then – well, we can take it in turns."

She bowed to him, then laughed at herself.

Over the meal he admitted that he had written to the water board with a demand, a counter-claim for the losses suffered by the members of the Consortium – the SLJC, as he named it with a bow to Ted. "I have written to the members additionally, telling them of the adjustment to the name and the reason for it, and the fact that we had all missed something that Ted Rawle, at fourteen, spotted."

Ted gave a sudden, Cheshire-cat grin.

"I have yet to tell the others but I have calculated an allowance for the bank interest lost for the years from 1954 to now, and an allowance for hardship and interest on unpaid insurance claims for the same period. We'll keep that to ourselves for the moment, even from the Lofts. It may be contested; certainly the

Water Board will not like it, nor will they like the pressure from our MP who has also received a copy." He laughed. "I may be a very unpopular solicitor in a building in Exeter in the morning."

Ted, in a strange room, wasn't sleeping well. When the first maroon went off he jumped, and lay back, disorientated. Had he been asleep? Or had it been that he was awake but with his eyes closed? Befuddled, he remembered what Martin had told them earlier about the Lifeboat maroon so hoisted himself to his feet and to the window. There was another trail of sparks as the second charge was sent skywards, to explode moments later. Despite himself, he jumped. Some minutes later three bicycles sped down the hill, but although he watched for any more activity none was visible. Shivering, he returned to bed and this time slept soundly until morning.

Annabelle, Martin, Ted and Ian arrived at Aunt Amble's Kingsbridge cottage next morning there to find an official looking envelope on the mat. The Coroner desired Annabelle's and Martin's presence at a meeting to discuss the death of Simon Edward Rawle the following Monday. She carefully put the letter away and continued packing her personal belongings.

After the run to Salcombe, Martin decided to visit Mike to tell him about Monday, to apologise and to talk about starting the day after. His ring at the bell was answered almost immediately by a strained looking, white faced Mr Alexander who looked at him as if he was the last person he wanted to see.

Martin was put off his stroke. "Er... I've come to talk to Mike, please. I'm the... one he has offered a job to..."

The man's face cleared, partly. "Yes, yes Martin. I remember you of course. But Mike went out with the Lifeboat last night and they're not back yet. To be honest..." He gulped "... I thought you might be the bearer of bad news.."

Martin's jaw dropped. "No. Sorry – I had no idea. Have the Lifeboat station told you anything?"

He shook his head. "I haven't phoned, and I didn't want to go down."

Martin thought.

"I'll go down," he said. "You stay by the phone and I'll bring you any news there is."

He was sorry for the strong and capable looking older man, a man who seemed to have had the stuffing knocked out of him. Is this what possibly losing a son did to you? Is this what happened to his own Dad when he lost his temper and told his son to leave?

"Thank you," the man almost whispered.

Martin rushed down the hill to the Lifeboat station, almost tripping over his feet at speed on the gradients. He bumped into a group of people standing by silently.

"Excuse me, but what's happening?" he asked one of those on the outskirts of the group.

She looked at him searchingly. "You're a reporter."

"No," said Martin, "I'm an employee of one of the crew. Mike Alexander."

"Young Mike... Well, we don't really know yet. She went out about one o'clock this morning to a coaster in trouble. They say they're towing her into port, but we don't know where, see? There's something wrong with their radio."

"So we don't know if they're all right, or anything?"

"No. And one of the harbours should know. They've phoned everywhere between Exeter and Plymouth, but no one's seen them."

Martin nodded, and thanked her. He was running back up Union Street when he heard shouts behind him. Looking back he saw the woman he'd spoken to waving furiously and ran back, half hopeful, half in dread.

"She's been sighted off South Sands," she said with relief in her voice. "They got a message to us in Morse so we know they're all safe. They even asked for breakfasts for ten." She laughed. "I'm that relieved I could hug anyone."

She proceeded to hug him, although Martin would rather have been running to the nearest phone. When he was back at the Merryweather house he called the Alexanders. A scared voice answered almost immediately.

"It's Martin," he said. "It's all right. They're safe. They've just passed South Sands, someone's contacted the Station in Morse code and they're all safe. And hungry. All is well."

There was silence on the phone. Listening, Martin thought he could hear sobs. At last a voice came back, though it sounded strangled.

"Thank you, Martin. I'm an old fool, I know. But he's... he's very special to us. We'll go down to Customs Quay now. And thank you again."

Glad to have been the bearer of good news Martin wondered whether he should also return to the quay, but knew that there was another load to collect from Kingsbridge and a weekend of sorting out to do. He looked forward to being able to bring his own belongings to the house so as to be near work. And Bronwen.

He went to see Mike the next day, hoping he hadn't woken him. Mr Alexander was effusive in his thanks for his help the previous day. "I'm sorry I was such an emotional wreck," he said. "I almost wish he hadn't joined the Lifeboat. It can be so dangerous."

"But such a worthwhile thing to do," Martin observed.

"Yes, I know. That almost makes it worse because I can't really argue with Mike. He at least is saving lives. His brother joined up in the last year of the war and was killed two days before Berlin fell and it was all over. There was no one to save *his* life."

Martin was horrified, but guessed at the depth of feeling the man had showed the previous day. If you've lost one son... He didn't quite understand the connection between Mike saving lives and his brother going to war, though. Surely if you were called up, you went.

Mike was tired, but at work, and was pleased to see Martin. He was even more pleased to hear his offer to start work the following Tuesday, after the visit to the Coroner.

Mike shook his hand, and the two discussed terms. To start with he would be on quite low salary, as Mike had said, and neither of them knew what the first month's share of fees would be. But Martin was just pleased to start.

"We can find out about correspondence courses later," Mike told him.

11 – Martin and Dolly

Saturday was a time for furniture shifting in Salcombe. Annabelle telephoned the local removal company to bring her belongings south, and after some intakes of breath through his teeth their manager agreed to meet her on Monday to judge the scope of the job.

They all met at church the following day and the vicar was surprised to see how the Loft family had grown. Explanations were given afterwards.

"Typical of you two," he told Susan and Henry. "And a good thing for Mr Merryweather. I just hope all those extra people don't tire you out."

"I relish their presence," said the subject of the comment. "It's about time I had some young voices around the place. And some adult company as well."

Mary and Stephen had slipped away, as they did every time after the service, to a part of the church's grounds overlooking the Estuary. Here they stood in front of a wide slab of untrimmed Dartmoor Tor granite with a boundary of smaller stones well heeled into the turf. Although each of them knew it by heart the inscription was silently read again.

"To remember:
John Hunter Beale, born 4th September 1916
Cicely Marriott Beale (nee Fortescue), born 22nd February 1919
Greg (Gregory Michael) Beale, born 3rd July 1940.
The beloved parents and brother of Mary Elizabeth Beale who were tragically killed in the inundation on 11 March 1954 which flooded the Estuary again, demolishing their home.
Rest now in Peace with the love and respect of your family and friends."

After all this time and having visited the grave so many times before, still Mary's eyes misted over. Now though, her emotions carried pride with loss; a remembrance of happiness in youth; a pride that so many people in the town should want to contribute to provide this, for it was the town's and her own memorial. It made her parents and brother even more special to her.

As always, Stephen's memory was of the lost, close friend of his childhood and early youth, his constant companion, and of the sun-blessed times of all those years. He knew that he had come from that tragedy with honour and, better still, with the girl who had been his friend, then his companion, then his fiancée. He felt sad too, but very lucky in what he now had.

As always his arm circled her shoulders. She looked up at him and smiled mistily.

"Thank God you are still here," she said.

"I always think the same about you. Twice I nearly lost you."

"Twice?"

"Once then, and once when you were taken."

"Oh."

Silence fell, but a happier silence this time.

"You still love me, don't you?"

He answered her by pulling her to him and telling her without words.

As usual they all gravitated to Loft Island for lunch. Ted and Ian made a beeline for the compass, to see how much they could remember. The younger couples found they were redundant from the kitchen, so sat and talked. Uncle Bert and Aunt Amble were pleased to be referred to in those terms by the two boys "Though actually Ted is as old as Stephen was when he encountered the flood," said their honorary Uncle thoughtfully.

Ted and Ian were invited to stay the night on the island. That Monday was to see the excitement of a dumb barge being towed to their landing point to take the four heavy tree trunks that had now been stripped of boughs and branches. It gave the boys something else to think about and be involved in – Ted particularly had been genuinely helpful during the felling and clearing, the woodmen had declared, and had become an effective wielder of machete, axe and saw in a very short time.

Martin and his aunt found that the Coroner was the same man who had been kind and accommodating to Mary and Stephen years before. His attitude to the present two was equally considerate.

"I just need to get an informal idea of the family background and the difficulties you had all experienced," he explained. They discussed their situation with him and noted his smile when the name of Loft was mentioned.

"Is the actual cause of death known yet?" asked Martin suddenly.

"A post-mortem is necessary, I'm afraid, and it will be carried out soon. That will tell us, though there are no suspicious circumstances. He died naturally."

Martin thought back to those occasional views of his father's scarred, red-blotched torso, the vivid red patches showing the extent of the burns he had suffered.

"I don't think war injuries come under natural causes," he said bluntly.

"I take your point. They were treated, I suppose, as best they could be at the time. Maybe now, thirteen years after the war, we could have done something better for him. But what I really meant was that there was no foul play within the house that caused the death."

"There can't have been. Only my young brothers were there. Surely you don't think…" His aunt laid a hand on his.

"I wouldn't dream of making such accusations, quite apart from which it is not my position to do so. I meant that there had been no intruder in the house who may have been responsible."

Martin looked down. "Sorry," he said.

"You are right to be angry. You are right to want to know the cause and that is exactly what a post mortem will do: find the time and the cause of death. If there is anything untoward then an inquest will be held to establish what happened."

Eventually they were released. Passing a café, Martin almost dragged his aunt inside and asked her to choose lunch.

"On me," he said. "I have some savings and I want to thank you for everything you've done for me and my brothers over the years. And for agreeing to move to Salcombe and look after them."

She started arguing about saving for his own house, using the money to have fun, for saving for a rainy day, but he would not listen. He just smiled and said it's what he wanted to do. The appointment with her removal company was not until half past two so they enjoyed a leisurely chat, spending longer in each other's company than they had been able to for years. He knew at last what he had guessed as a boy. She had been and still was deeply concerned about her brother's young family. The comfort that each of the boys had found with her when their father's temper had grown too much, was based on love.

"I wish now that I'd been able to visit regularly, and have you do the same," she told him. "But he was never very welcoming, and there is a limit to the number of times you can be a prod-nose. It's just a relief I was able to be there as a sort of long-stop."

At her small rented house there were a few more intakes of breath from the removals company manager as he saw the limited amount of possessions to be shifted. He took the details and thought, came up with a price which Annabelle accepted, and told her that the earliest he could make the move was in seven days' time.

Once again Annabelle agreed, signed a contract and a cheque, and matters were settled.

Her news was warmly received that evening as they all, including Martin, Ted and Ian, tired but happy from a day's woodsmanship, sat down to another meal concocted by Annabelle and Bronwen.

"I really am most grateful for this," said their host as he entered the room. "Once again it seems most unfair that you should have to do the cooking. It has occurred to me that none of us is a really experienced cook – and I'm not talking about an ability to feed one person here, you understand, but a family which now numbers six. I am considering whether we need to engage a cook, or a housekeeper."

"But I'm sure with a little practice I could do the cooking..." Annabelle started.

"But why should you? You have a good brain, as do Bronwen and Martin. I cannot help but wonder whether you would wish to spend your time on more rewarding pursuits, salaried or otherwise. The gentlemen of the house are inexperienced in anything except sandwiches – in my case, that is, and probably in Ted's and Ian's cases as well."

To punctuate his comment he performed one of his trademark bows in their direction. The two looked at each other, jumped to their feet and bowed back. His face was a picture, his mouth widened, he gave a most un-Merryweather bellow of laughter and collapsed into his chair, chuckling gently.

"Boys!" said their aunt in a critical tone that was nevertheless tinged with laughter.

"Don't criticise them, Annabelle. They are exactly what I need. Thank you, gentlemen, for pricking this overinflated balloon with such pointed humour."

They smiled, but looked cautiously at their aunt, but who was now laughing openly.

"And how did it all go today, Martin?" she asked when they had all subsided.

"Very well, thanks. It's such a change to know that someone expects you to disagree if you think they're wrong about something. Usually, he was right, and I didn't know enough about what was needed, or what the customer had specified, or the limitations of materials. He gave me a lot of information, but I got him to think about some of the designing, too."

"Do you think you'll enjoy it?"

"If he goes on like he's started, yes. Very much."

Mr Merryweather nodded. "Good. That is pleasing to hear. But to resume about the cooking, your working hours will be very approximate at best if Mike Alexander thinks you're good, so even given that you can create cream teas it wouldn't be fair to expect you to cook as well. No, I think a cook-housekeeper would be the answer."

Bronwen broke in. "I wonder if Angharad would come? You know – our girl in Chepstow."

"But she'd be needed by your parents still, wouldn't she?"

"I doubt it. And she might be prepared to come. She was quite glad to escape from her family home when Mum offered her the job with us. I don't think her particular school suited her and at home there were so many brothers and sisters. And she can certainly cook – the eldest daughter is always best trained.

"Anyway, at my old home there are only the two of them, and I imagine Mum will escape soon when she realises I'm not coming back. It might take her some time to make plans. I'm convinced that the only reason she stays is because she's old fashioned – you know, the promises made in the wedding service. There can't still be any love left for him. Not after what he's done."

"Well, she too is welcome here," said her uncle. "In fact I was rather wondering why she's not made an appearance so far. It's rather worrying."

"Could someone phone?" asked Martin.

"Each of us is *persona non grata* with that... well let us call him a gentleman, shall we?"

Bronwen snorted, then apologised.

"Mike could," Martin said. "Or... Bron, do you know anyone who could ask to talk to Angharad in Welsh? Make it appear that they couldn't talk English? That way a message could be passed to Mrs Williams without the man knowing."

"My friend in Chepstow could," she exclaimed. "But don't you think he might just put the phone down on her? He hates Welsh, as you know."

"It's worth a try, I think," said her uncle, "and of course we'll pay her for the call."

The call was made. Her friend laughed and said she'd enjoy trying and would phone back when she'd been able to speak to Angharad. "I think what I should do is wait until the Chapel is on," she said. "Then it might be that he has gone to it, see? It's more of a chance there'll be that he's not at home."

"I like that idea," Bronwen said. "And I don't know why we never thought of it before."

"Ah well, it's the Welsh way to think before we speak, see. Of course, he might not go to the Chapel meeting. But Sunday is the next service and I'll try then."

They agreed that she would call them whatever the result.

"I must go," said Martin suddenly. "It's dark and I'll be late back to Lofts."

His adopted grandad looked at him approvingly. Bronwen pulled a face.

"I wish you could live here," she said. "It would make more sense, surely, as you're working just up the hill."

He sighed. "Yes, it does. But you have a house full now, and besides..."

"Besides what?"

"Just besides, that's all."

"We'll never get to know each other properly if we hardly ever see each other. And besides, they don't have a lot of room at Lofts."

He looked hopelessly at the old man, who just smiled back at him.

"What do I do?" he asked.

"I think you need to think. And then I think you, Bronwen and I could talk. But for tonight, they're expecting you at Loft Island. They may even try and give you a meal."

"I hadn't thought of that!"

"Off you go, then, and be careful."

"Yes, Grandad. Good night everyone."

"I'll see you off," Bronwen told him.

Leaving the house took him a long time.

He received a warm welcome by the Lofts, as always.

"We've eaten," Henry told him, "but if you want anything please help yourself."

It made him wonder if he should stay there and help with everything, especially with a baby due in the autumn. But Bronwen was always at the front of his mind, as was the convenience of living in Salcombe. He was contributing little to the sporadic conversations around the room, and eventually Stephen asked him outright.

"Something's the matter, isn't it? It can't be Mike – you've told us that's going well. Something else has happened."

Martin gave a sigh. "It's Bronwen," he said. "That and travelling. It seems so silly to come all the way back here when I could stay in Salcombe. I can walk to and from work from Grandad's. And according to Mike I'll never really be sure when work will finish for the day."

"And Bronwen lives there."

He looked sharply at his friend. "Yes. And if we're going to get to know each other better… well, at the moment I see very little of her."

"And your brothers and aunt live there."

He nodded. "I don't want to move from here again, but…" he shrugged his shoulders. "I don't know what to do."

Henry, listening to the exchange, answered him. "You'll always have a home here if you need one, whether for a day or two or for years. I think I'm right in saying that, aren't I, Susan?"

"Of course you are. We've said this all along."

"But if you think that staying in Salcombe is better in the long run, talk to Mr Merryweather – grandad – and put it to him. I *suspect* that one of the reasons he's not suggested it is that no one knows how your and Bronwen's friendship will develop."

"It never will if we don't meet more often," he protested.

"I know. But see what she thinks, too."

"I know what she thinks. And yes, I mentioned the possibility of moving there tonight. He told me I should think, and then come and talk to him."

"There you are, then. You have done what he's asked. I know you were thinking, or worrying, all evening. If you've come to a conclusion, talk to Dad. Grandad. Oh, this is confusing."

Martin smiled. Happier now, he took a greater part in the family chat until it was time for the news and, along with millions of others, was astonished to hear that Elvis Presley had been drafted into the American army.

Early next afternoon there was a tentative knock at the door of the Solicitor's house. Annabelle, taking the opportunity for a wash and mending session for some of the elderly clothes belonging to her nephews, was the only person at home so put down her work and hurried to open the door. An agitated-appearing, middle aged woman, smart of clothing, was standing there, a woman who was taken aback to see her. Annabelle smiled at her and wished her a good afternoon.

"Er… er…" She sounded like one of her nephews when at a loss to explain a domestic breakage. "Er… is Mr Merryweather in, please?"

"Not here, but his office is at…"

Her visitor held up her hand. "I'm sorry, I know the office. I hoped he might be at home."

"Then I'm sorry to disappoint you. He will return at about five thirty."

She looked at her watch. "Oh…oh dear. It has stopped. And the glass is broken. He must have… It is saying that it is later than that. Oh, I'm so sorry. You have no idea who I am, have you? I'm his sister, Dolly Williams."

Annabelle started at the name, composed herself and smiled.

"I am Annabelle Rawle. I think you know Martin? My nephew. You must come in. I shall make a pot of tea."

Dolly looked relieved. "I… I should be most grateful. It has been a long journey."

"Then please sit in the living room and relax."

Dolly was looking in puzzlement at the fresh pieces of furniture in the room. Good furniture, antique. Furniture that, had Dolly only known, bore the initials A.R. in chalk underneath to prove ownership.

"They are mine," she said simply. "It is a long story, best told over a cup of tea and a piece of cake."

"I really don't want to intrude," Dolly said faintly.

Annabelle laughed. "It is not an intrusion, believe me. They are here as a matter of necessity and your brother's generosity."

Her guest was intrigued, but couldn't ask more as Annabelle had returned to the kitchen.

Over the promised tea she explained what had happened and was pleased at the reactions.

"Poor boys," her companion kept saying. "Poor boys."

"With Martin now effectively one of the family, and Bronwen here too, it seemed this was the best place for them to live. The Lofts, bless them, can't take in every one that comes to them for help."

"Especially with Susan expecting."

"You knew that? Of course, from last Christmas. I was really only in Kingsbridge because it was convenient for the boys and for my little job, and so when Mr Merryweather suggested I should help look after them here it seemed most logical."

"I understand completely. And Bronwen – is she recovered?"

"Yes, she seems to be. It must seem rather boring for her here at the moment, but it is early days."

"And now, it seems that her mother is throwing herself on the mercy of her daughter's saviour as well," admitted Dolly. "I imagine the story is known to you from Martin and from Bron. I have done my absolute best to do my duty to my husband and to the vows we made to each other all those years ago. But now he has proved that he is not interested in living by those vows and... what on earth is that?"

The door had crashed open and one treble and one slightly less treble voice were arguing in the hall.

"It wasn't my fault! I was going to knock."

"You just leant against it."

"You pushed me, trying to get there first."

"If you've broken anything you can take the blame."

Footsteps. A pause. The door opened and two faces looked in.

"Sorry," said Ted, "we didn't know the door would be unlocked. Oh..."

He had noticed the visitor.

"Ted, Ian; this is Mrs Williams, Bronwen's mother. She is coming to live with us,

"Hallo, said Ted, undaunted. "It's good to... How do you do?"

"We were talking about you last night," said Ian. "Uncle Bert said..."

"I think that'll do for the moment, Ian," his aunt interrupted. "Wash hands, please, and then there's tea here. With cake."

The brothers looked at each other, smiled at the two sitting and rushed upstairs.

"So those are Martin's brothers," said Dolly. "Lively youngsters, aren't they?"

"They're still getting over losing their father. As I said earlier, the last few years have not been happy ones for them. My brother was badly injured in the war and the pain and difficulties he must have been enduring affected his patience levels with all three of them. Suddenly, they've been freed from a lot of unkind restrictions and from farm work, and are enjoying being boys again. Like they were, indeed, before Simon's health started suffering."

As if to underline what she was saying there were sounds of arguments from upstairs. Her eyebrows rose and she left the room.

Bronwen had never been allowed to be so wild, so noisy in the house, thought Dolly. She had been forcibly trained by her father to be so compliant and well behaved. Perhaps that explained some of the reports from school when she was described as very active and a little mischievous, but happy. She could be herself there. Dolly sighed, not for the first time.

Footsteps, quiet now, came downstairs.

"We want to apologise," said Ian. "We've been very noisy."

Dolly smiled at him. "I think we're all been through some really horrible times just recently, so a little behaviour that's out of the ordinary is to be expected. People react in different ways. Your aunt and I have had a lot more years behind us than you, years that have taught us to be patient and to count to ten before arguing with people. But if you're Martin's brothers you'll settle down quickly." She smiled again. "Just don't become too tame! It's good to have some life around the place."

"That's what their Uncle Bert said," explained Annabelle.

"I thought you said you were their only relative."

Annabelle laughed. "It's the name your brother suggested. He hates his Christian names – as you obviously know better than I. It was Mr Williams who told Bronwen to call him Uncle Algy, it seems. He… he wanted not to be reminded of that so has shortened his middle name for easy use."

Dolly gave the first full laugh she had felt like using for days. "Well, it's certainly nice and short!"

"And this is Aunt Amble," declared Ian. "I couldn't say Annabelle when I was little, and it came out as Amble."

"Uncle Bert and Aunt Amble," Dolly chuckled just as Bronwen had the previous night. "It sounds very pleasantly domestic."

Both Uncle Bert and Martin were pleased to see her. The solicitor and she spoke privately and he emerged from the discussion with an uncharacteristically dour face. Ian noticed, nudged his brother and they went and sat either side of him. He looked to left and right, and gradually the unhappy expression left him.

"And what, pray, are you two after now?"

Ian looked up at him and just smiled as angelically as he could manage. Ted looked seriously at him.

"You looked so unhappy we thought we had better try and cheer you up. Has anything happened?"

He sighed. "Yes and no." He paused. "I see no reason to keep it a secret; nor does Dolly. It is a tragedy when a man and woman fall out of love, especially when one of them is willing to work at the relationship. But that is what has happened between my sister and her husband. So yes, I am sad. But I am pleased that Dolly has chosen to come here to her daughter and me – I suppose I should say to all of us – to live."

Ted nodded. "You can count on us to help, if we can."

He gave one of the Rawle family's trademark, honest smiles, a move which softened the old man's expression. He smiled back and looked to be back to his usual cheerful self.

"Thank you Ted, Ian. You are a tonic."

12 – Angharad

Angharad thought that her master must have finished his meal by now. The previous day her mistress had left, telling her quietly that she was going for good and giving her the address and telephone number of her brother's house in Salcombe where she was going to live. At the mention of Salcombe she remembered that good looking boy, the one who had come to see her mistress but had been thrown out by the master. That was when the troubles had really started.

The master had been silent and moody – even moodier than usual – when he had entered the dining room earlier, and had watched her every move as she brought the plate, the serving dishes and his carafe of water to the table.

Cautiously she entered the room again but was shocked to see him still sitting there, staring out of the window. He looked around as she appeared.

"You may clear," he said in his usual haughty tone. Then, to her surprise, added "And I will help you."

This was not typical of him, of any of them. They would expect her to get on with her work. It was in a state of some anxiety that she knew she was being followed to the kitchen. She put the plates on the draining board, he put the serving dish next to them, standing too close to her.

"Thank you, sir," she said.

"I think we can dispense with the 'sir'" he said, in a tone she didn't understand. "And in our… our changed situation I think it only right that I ensure that your accommodation is still up to standard. We might be able to make it more comfortable for you."

"My room is fine, thank you sir," she said.

"Nevertheless, I wish to look at it for my own information. We will go now. You may lead the way."

Why did he want to do this now, she wondered. Any time would have done. She had work to do – the washing up, the bed-making… But there was no refusal possible. He wasn't that kind of man. Meekly she climbed the stairs and entered her little room, and stood by the bed. He stood facing her, just inside the door, breathing noticeably heavier; she thought it was because of climbing the stairs.

He took a step forward, looking, not at the room, but at her. All of her. His expression had changed and there was something in his expression she didn't like. Nervousness grew in her. He partly turned away, but it was only to close and lock the door. Her eyes grew wide.

The Williams residence was one of a row of detached houses, with plenty of space between them. The smart garden at the front meant that the house lay comfortably back from the road. The back garden, less well cultured, was even further from any building.

No one heard her screams. No one heard his shouts as she bit the hand that covered her mouth. No one came. No one interrupted.

When he had gone she continued to lie on the bed that she had once regarded as her own, her sanctuary. There was a feeling of sickness to her. She felt violated and mentally numb. The front door clicked shut and at last she knew she was on her own. He could do no more. And then the tears came.

When, later, she tried to stand she still felt dizzy and sick, and there was discomfort in her too. That was when the shame hit her. How could she face her family after what had happened? How could she face anyone?

With difficulty she walked to the door.

It was locked.

A shock went through her. A mental shock. But at least she knew what to do if he had left the key in. Bronwen had told her. She found a piece of newspaper and a hairgrip, and set to work.

He can't have realised how Bronwen had escaped. The key was still there. She followed what she had been told and soon was outside the door. She locked it again.

Now what?

She thought. Her mistress... no. That meant something to do with *him*. She couldn't face that. And her brother was there too and he might be as bad... no, that didn't follow. She leant on the bannisters to support herself. Her friend in the town... that was it. Cerys would know. Cerys would understand and help.

Blindly she ran downstairs, almost stumbling as she went. Out of the house she flew, leaving the door open, up away from the river towards the town. Initially she looked neither left nor right but realised suddenly that she didn't know where *he* had gone. She started looking out for him, her feeling of sickness increasing with the terror that would hit her if she saw him. She was peeping round corners before entering each road. At one, the nausea overcame her and she relieved herself of her breakfast down a drain in the gutter.

With a relief that was almost overcoming, she reached High Street without seeing him and ran up to the shop where Cerys worked.

It was half past nine. Cerys looked up as the door rang its bell. Her smile of recognition, of welcome vanished as she saw her friend's face.

"What on earth has happened?" she asked. "I was going to phone you next Sunday!"

"Can we go somewhere? Please?"

Shocked, Cerys just said "Come into the store room." She raised her eyebrows at the shop's owner who nodded.

It was in that untidy room, there on their own, that all the emotion, all the hurt, all the hatred burst out of her. Cerys held her, hugged her, listened to her, was shocked with her. Time passed. Angharad cried herself to a standstill and had to sit down on the floor. Cerys sat beside her.

"Have you told the Police?" she asked.

Angharad shook her head. "I came straight here. I had to get away... my family won't want me back now."

"But the Police. They must arrest him."

"They won't believe me over him."

"You must try."

She shook her head again. "He's Williams the Town, Williams the Chapel. How would they believe me?"

"Angharad, you must try. He must not get away with it."

"No... I just need somewhere to go."

"Where is all your stuff?"

"Back there. I just left the room and ran."

Cerys thought.

"You must come back with me. Now. And we will look after you. But I still think you must go to the Police."

Angharad shook her head again. "I can't. They will want to look."

"A doctor would do that."

"No." She shuddered. "I can't."

A pause.

"Well, come with me, then. I'll ask for time off and take you home."

"What if he sees me?"

She thought. "My elder brother is at home. He can come down and walk with us."

"Is he… will he stand up to Williams if he sees us?"

"I'll make sure he does. You stay here – or in the little kitchen. That would be better. I'll tell the owner what's happened. Stay there a moment."

Angharad was taken to the kitchen, right at the back of the store near the only lavatory. Once she was there, Cerys slipped out. Angharad became more agitated the longer she was gone, yet it was only two minutes before she returned, to be greeted by a scared, hunted gaze which dropped as soon as she recognised her friend.

"Mrs Rees will make you a tea and look after you. I've warned her about Williams and she knows not to let him in – not that he comes into this shop, ever. I'll go and fetch Dylan and then we'll get you home."

The doorway darkened and Angharad looked round in alarm. Mrs Rees. She said nothing but put her hand on the girl's shoulder as she crossed to the kettle.

Dylan proved to be a large, capable looking lad of about seventeen. He was at home, he said in a surprisingly gentle voice, because he was looking for a job. Angharad thanked Mrs Rees and they set off, with Angharad taking frequent looks behind her. The journey passed without incident.

Cerys' Mum was as agitated as her daughter had been. "You must stay here as long as you need to," she said.

"But I can't. I've got to leave here. He'll find me."

She had no answer.

"What about Mrs Williams?" said Cerys suddenly. "Her brother is a solicitor and she's with him now in Devon. They wrote and asked me to call you at the Williams's so we could talk."

"I don't know… I'm scared she'll believe him, not me."

"She's just left him," said Cerys bluntly. "There's hardly any love lost, surely?"

No answer.

"I've got to phone them, anyway. Before Mrs Williams went they wanted to know if you were all right. So I owe them a telephone call. Let me?" she pleaded. "I'll be able to understand how they feel about it. And your parents – they need to know, even if they think badly of you. Though why they should, I don't know. Maybe you don't want to visit them, but you must write and tell them."

Reaction to the events of the morning had now set in. Angharad was exhausted. The knowledge that she was now safe for the moment contributed.

She sat, and just nodded her assent. But there was one last thing.

"Please – may I have a bath?"

Mrs Rees looked at her and her eyes filled. She crossed to the chair and hugged the girl as best she could.

"Of course, my dear. I should have thought of that. Dylan, could you heat the water, please?"

He nodded and went into the kitchen.

"If you need anything, Cerys will look after you. I'll go and make the phone calls."

She was away at the phone box for about twenty minutes.

"Well," she said as she came in the door. "That's stirred up a hornet's nest. I need to sit down. I've spoken to Mrs Williams. She said some very unladylike words but the first thing she asked was 'are you all right?' I told her you were as all right as you could be. She started apologising for her husband and then stopped and said no, she wasn't going to apologise for him. He should do that himself, in court."

Angharad looked horrified and was about to speak, but there was more to come.

"She said that of course you must come down to Devon so as to be safe from him, and asked me to speak to her brother. When he came to the phone he was very businesslike once he'd asked how you were. He told me that you need to see a doctor, firstly to make sure you are not injured, and secondly so that it's recorded for evidence. He said you must do that before you have a bath, if possible."

Angharad started to say something else but Mrs Rees carried on as if she'd not noticed.

"And Mrs Williams is coming up with Martin, who you met, and Stephen, a friend of his, and Stephen's father. They will stand up to Williams if he's there whilst you get your things. They'll take you back to Devon with them. It sounds like there's quite a few of them there already."

Finally Angharad could see her escape route clearly. To go to Devon… she'd hardly ever been out of Chepstow, except now and again to Newport and a very few times to Bristol.

"Thank you," she whispered.

"That's all right, *geneth*," said Mrs Rees. "Least we can do, isn't it. But we need to get you to our doctor to make sure that… that *man* hasn't injured you. That's important, according to Mr… Merryweather. Can that really be his name? So when you've finished that tea, get your coat on – and you, Dylan – and we'll nip up the road to the doctor. I…" She cleared her throat. "I took the opportunity of phoning them too. Hope you don't mind."

"But a doctor… I don't need to see a doctor!" She was shying away from the horror of having to strip in front of him, of having him look at… everything.

"If you're all right, then no harm done. But if you're not, he'll know what to do. And don't forget, he's seen most people around here. Doctors are one of the few people who are used to seeing… things."

"But… But if I do, will it help get that man into prison?"

She had recovered to the extent that she could just accept the idea of seeing a doctor, if Cerys or her mother were with her. And Dylan's solid presence would be a comfort on the journey.

"It certainly will. In fact it's the only way, probably."

A pause. Then in almost a whisper: "All right, then."

"Good. We'll go now."

"Can Cerys come too, please?"

"Of course," her friend said. "I was expecting to."

"Thank you. Are you sure they won't mind you being away so long?"

"Bad luck if they do. But she's all right, is Mrs Rees. She understands."

The time in the waiting room seemed interminable. Finally they were announced and entered the surgery to find a grave man in a white coat waiting for them. She told him what had happened. Was about to tell him who was responsible, but he stopped her in time.

"Don't tell me. It's better that I don't know. It might be another patient of mine. Tell me what happened, and what he did, then I'll need to examine you. Your friend needs to go, please."

"I want her to stay."

"I need to do the examination and I can't have her here."

"But she could be behind a screen, or something… I need her here. Please?"

"I can't have another girl in the surgery while I'm carrying out an examination. See sense, girl."

"Then I won't have an examination. That means that *he* will go free and do the same to someone else."

"An examination is a private thing. Nobody else can be in the room."

"Nonsense!" A third voice piped up: Mrs Rees. "You've been my doctor for the last forty years and you've helped me bring two children into the world. There was you and the midwife at Cerys' birth – yes, and a nurse as well. So you let my daughter, or me if she'd agree, to come and comfort Angharad from the other side of the screen. And I want notes made too, for her solicitor."

"Solicitor, is it?" said the doctor thoughtfully. "So this is serious, is it?"

"Ever been raped?" asked Mrs Rees in a voice that would have cut through bone. "It's serious, she's in a state, and we're going to get that ba… *man* behind bars. With or without your help. And if you refuse to treat her…"

"I'm not refusing to treat her…"

"She won't let you without a friend there to give her the courage she needs."

If looks could kill, the doctor would have fallen on the spot.

He took a deep breath.

"Very well. She shall be in there. But it's most irregular. And I don't want any comments. From either of you."

Despite the rocky start he was very gentle. Samples were taken, notes were made. Angharad felt worse than she had since it had happened. When the doctor stepped away and asked her to dress herself again she found she was sobbing. She rushed into Cerys' welcome hug and once again cried herself out.

"I'm sorry," said the doctor, more gently than she had expected. "I know it's upsetting, and horrible, and all the other things. But it's better that you know you are all right. Bruised, but no lasting damage. You need no treatment. There are traces of… of what happened, and I've removed what I could see and we'll keep that for the police. But now, I imagine you want a bath. You should, and a good hot bath at that."

They all returned to the Upjohns' to allow her to do just that.

When the call had come, the Merryweather household went into meltdown. The old man, usually so old fashioned and artificially doddery in his ways almost to the point of maddening some of his younger clients, became concise and authoritative.

"It's no good my going," he said. "The best I can do is to be on the end of my office phone to act as a referee in case of problems. You need to go, Dolly, and so should Martin and Stephen. And Henry too. They will act as a defence, both force and brains. We need to warn Stephen's headmistress, and get hold of Martin at the Alexanders'. I'll contact them – they know me better. Get yourselves ready, please."

Henry Loft said they'd do anything, immediately he understood what had happened, and gave his blessing to Stephen's being picked up at school *en route* to the station.

"Best wait at the Hard. They can pull in there and find you," he was told.

Mike, a little confused when he first answered the phone, said a rude word when he understood.

"Yes, he is," was all Mr Merryweather answered.

"Martin and I will both come, of course. Just a moment – hold the line."

Footsteps receded, there was some indignant conversation, and footsteps returned.

"I'm borrowing Dad's car," said Mike firmly. "It'll be quicker, and as it's quite large we can fit the six of us in it. It is six, isn't it? With Angharad?"

"Are you sure?"

"Yes. One in the front, three in the back. Martin and Stephen can squash up on the front on the way back. Ah, here's Martin now. Are Henry and Stephen with you?"

"No, Henry's on his way from the Island and Stephen should be in school."

"Good. We'll pick him up on the way. We'll be there in a moment."

Martin was bemused when told to put his coat on again. For a moment he thought he'd made some terrible mistake and was being given the sack. Mike explained as he struggled into his own coat, accepted the keys and a warning from his father to drive carefully, and went to unlock the garage.

It was a large Wolseley, and as roomy as Martin had suggested. Its appearance in narrow Fore Street caused something of a stir. They pulled into the Hard's car park as instructed, and waited.

Normally, any period spent there, looking over the Estuary and watching the comings and goings of craft of all sizes, is time well spent. Today, though, the three of them were at the water's edge, waiting impatiently for Henry to appear.

Finally he did appear, moored and joined them, straight-faced. Mike set off up the one-way street like a rocket until he realised it was hardly safe and slowed – at least until the houses had thinned out and he was on a proper main road.

Outside his school Stephen was pacing up and down impatiently, and joined the others in the car with very little spoken welcome.

Mike cursed the winding roads as they progressed to Exeter, then joined the only slightly straighter one towards Bridgewater.

"It's more direct from here," he said. "The A38 takes us a lot of the way, then we can get to Bristol, over the Clifton Suspension Bridge then head to Aust and the ferry, and that's more or less Chepstow. Saves going all the way through Gloucester. I just hope the ferry's not too busy. It's only small."

The others – and indeed at times the driver – were sliding from side to side on the shiny leather bench seats as the car cornered. Sometimes the corners were accompanied by tortured sounds from the tyres.

"Here's hoping," said Mike as they at last saw a turning signposted "Aust. Severn Ferry."

They joined a queue. Mike stopped the engine and they all climbed stiffly out. A foray to the water's edge gave the information that there would be a 45 minute wait.

They spent the time looking over the wide estuary, so much more daunting and wild than their own even when in its bad moods. A short, terse discussion had concluded that the road via Gloucester would take longer than that 45 minutes. Besides, they were there now and in the queue. It was frustrating to realise that Chepstow was almost visible.

At last they realised that their turn had come, drove down the slipway and, with a sharp left turn which landed them facing broadside across the small vessel. But two men appeared, pulled and pushed at the car and they realised it was on a turntable which enabled Mike to drive into a slim parking space.

The crossing was choppy. The estuary, daunting as it appeared from above, took a different view when they were cruising their way over it. A vast expanse of muddy water, swirling past the boat diagonally, so strong was the tide. The centre of the channel brought back memories of sea voyages to France for Henry, and he shuddered.

"Are you all right, Dad?" asked Stephen.

Ruefully Henry thought back to the times when it had been his duty to ask his young son that same question. How had the tide turned!

"Yes, old son. Just thinking back to certain channel crossings. I think there was less chop in the Channel than there is here."

Gradually the other side could be seen drawing nearer. At last, just as Stephen was beginning to hope they made land before he was actually seasick, the crew leapt ashore.

"Right," said Mike. "Now we're all but there."

'All but there' they may have been, but there was still the length of the Beachley peninsular to drive before running up the side of the Wye to cross it at the old iron bridge.

It was mid-afternoon before they arrived. Dolly rushed to Angharad who, despite herself, pulled away. In her mind, Dolly was too close to her husband to be immediately acceptable as a comfort.

"Angharad, I am not *him*, and I hate what he has done, and I hate *him*, even more than I did when I left home. There is no love between us, no regard, no respect; nothing. He is beyond the pale so far as I am concerned."

She looked at her, saw the honesty in her eyes, and the care, and with a sigh allowed the hug, aware that she also knew one of the men who were entering the room. When it was possible she looked at Martin.

"You came to the house, and he told you to go away. Mr... Mr Rawle?"

"Martin," said Martin quietly. "Yes, he did, but Mrs Williams told Bron and she came to see me."

"I know. He was furious. Good."

"That is what made Bron come to Salcombe. And Mrs Williams after her."

"Is Bronwen all right?"

"She's fine. Horrified, like the rest of us, but fine."

She sighed again. "I'm sorry to be such a nuisance."

"You are *not* being a nuisance," Martin said fiercely. "The only nuisance is Williams, and we're going to settle him."

"One moment." A new voice entered the conversation: Henry's. "One thing we are *not* going to do is engage in some sort of retribution. We need to keep on the right side of the law. We will go to the house and we will get your belongings. If we need to protect ourselves we will, but that is all. We will take Dolly – she is needed to give us the authority to enter – and we will take Mike and Martin and my son Stephen. Not Angharad. She will stay in safety here.

13 – Angharad (continued)

Dolly and the others drove down to the house. There they found the door open just as Angharad had left it in her flight. Dolly opened it wide and looked in every downstairs room whilst the others waited in the hall. One was locked.

"Are you in there?" she called, so differently now from the tones she would have used whilst still living there. "Unlock the door. Now."

There was no answer.

"He must still be out," she said. "Good. That will save unpleasantness. This way."

She led them to the top of the house and to Angharad's room.

It was unlocked. She hesitated. "Didn't Angharad say that she had locked the door again after her?"

"I heard that," Martin replied.

"That means he's been back," said Henry. "I'll go first, just in case." He didn't specify what he was worried about.

Cautiously he opened the door. The room was unoccupied, giving them all cause for relief.

"Touch as little as possible." Mike had obviously been listening to detective stories on the radio. "If the Police investigate they will need it just as it was."

"He's right," said Henry. "What are we looking for?"

"A case, clothes in the wardrobe and cupboards," said Dolly. "Let me. I know what's hers and what's ours. Bron's and mine, that is."

She found Angharad's case on top of the wardrobe and was about to put it on the bed so as to fill it.

"Not there!" said Mike sharply. "It could damage evidence. Put it outside the room and we'll fill it if you pass things out."

The case was packed as carefully as they could. Martin had to sit on it before it could be properly closed.

"Is that it?" asked Henry.

"I think so… no…" Dolly had seen something else. On the floor by the bed was an object; furry, with semi-circular ears that stood up.

A teddy-bear.

She looked at it unbelievingly. "She's so young," she said, almost to herself. "So young that she brought her childhood toy with her. And we just thought of her as our domestic and cook. She hadn't been a person, a child, so far as we were concerned, all through the months she was with us. And he… he…" Her eyes filled. Henry's arm went around her and she buried her face in his shoulder.

Stephen and Martin, just two years Angharad's elder, had emotions of their own. Stephen thought back to becoming sixteen. He had enjoyed a loving home and a father who succeeded in persuading him to decide for himself to continue his studies. There had been no need for the comfort of a toy, yet oddly he remembered that from time to time he had rediscovered the things of his childhood and would look at them, smiling. They were a reminder of having his mother as part of the family too, and had been a comfort.

Martin, by sixteen, had left the family home. It had been a home where there had been little warmth, either spiritually or physically, except occasionally from

102

his brothers. That teddy-bear reminded him that there had been good times, that somewhere there might even be a teddy-bear of his own which he could resurrect. But he felt even more protective towards Angharad. For him she had suddenly become a child let down by adults. By *an* adult. If anyone did anything like that to either of his brothers, he thought, there might be murder done. Thank goodness they were boys.

There was a distant footstep on the stairs.

All five of them straightened as if electrified.

"Quietly – outside the room," whispered Henry.

They complied as the steps reached the first floor and paused.

"Who is up there?

Dolly stiffened, as did Martin.

Henry held his finger to his lips.

A figure reached the lower landing and looked round and up. Light from the window behind him illuminated the group. They looked down on him, saying nothing.

"What are you doing in my house?"

At last Dolly stirred.

"I do not wish to speak to you ever again. You are no husband of mine. Once the Police have finished with you, my solicitor will start. And whilst you are in prison you will have little opportunity to fight a divorce suit. Not that any court in the land, not even in the town you call yours, will find in your favour. You will leave this house now, for we are going. You have lost your daughter and your wife, for we never want to see you again. And if you have left that young girl with child, be assured you will never see the baby or watch him or her grow into adulthood."

She paused.

"And as for your Chapel, you proved today without doubt that you are no Christian. They will disown you. They will remove your name from their records. They will remove the plaques that contain your name. As will the Town Hall. I will ensure it.

"Now, go!"

He stared at her, unable to believe this was really the same person he had lived with all those years. The hatred, the scorn in her voice made something inside him wilt. What she had said hit home despite the iron will that he had wielded for so long. His hope, his intention, had been to brazen it out, to rely on his authority within the house, within the Chapel and within the Town in beating down his wife's will as he had done for so many years. Her sudden assurance, authority and the sincerity and anger in her tone amazed him.

He knew, by instinct, that there was to be no arguing with her, that imposing his will on her as he had done increasingly since their marriage, would no longer work. And there were was that man, with those young toughs too… he recognised one, one who would have no respect, no love for him at all.

He turned and blundered down the stairs, followed by Martin, Stephen, Mike and Henry with Dolly, slower, behind them. At the door they found a policeman, but he was pushed out of the way. The others stopped.

"That man, my husband, raped our maid this morning. Arrest him, please."

If it was meant to galvanise the man into action, it failed spectacularly.

"Williams the Town, that is. I can't arrest him. Ma'am."

"Didn't you hear what I said? Williams the Town is now Williams the Rapist. He raped Angharad Pugh in her room this morning. She has been seen by a doctor who will provide the evidence. Because this *will* be dealt with. If not by you then by your Chief Constable. You forget, perhaps, that I am still Mrs Williams the Town, and I too have influence. Especially when there is evidence to prove what I am saying."

"And who are all these people?"

"It doesn't matter who they are – friends, if you must know. We have come to retrieve Angharad's possessions. But the important thing now is that you arrest Williams – Williams the Rapist – and hold him so that other young girls are safe."

"Well now, serious, that is… and you have been in a room where a crime has been committed…"

"Ah, at least you now admit that a crime has been committed."

"But he's also Chapel…"

"*Was* Chapel. And never a Christian."

He looked at her, doubt passing over his face.

"Well, you need to come to the Police Station and give a statement then, I suppose."

"Will you not arrest that man? Now, while he's somewhere near?"

"Well, see: I don't know where he is."

"Then you need to wait here and make sure he doesn't disturb the crime scene," said Mike quietly. "If it was disturbed by anyone, any court would blame you for not securing it. We will go and tell them where you are and why, and give a statement."

He ushered the others past the astonished policeman and into the car and as soon as he could, before there was a chance of further questions or objections, he moved off.

Their route took them first down towards the Wye. Mike looked left, across the bridge to check for traffic and saw a group of people at its centre, watching, pointing. A police Wolseley passed in front of them, bell jangling, and sped over the bridge toward the group.

Mike screeched to a halt.

"Surely not…"

He was out of the car and running before the others realised what he was doing, let alone thinking. He sped after the police car and looked in the direction the people were pointing. A figure was in the water, thrashing about, but being carried downstream by the current, the fast ebb of the tide. It had been too far away to recognise and was now so far away as to be almost out of sight.

An officer was in the car, using the radio, describing the whereabouts of the victim. Mike pushed past him, now followed by Martin and Stephen, and approached the staring spectators. One of the women was weeping.

"Excuse me, but did you see what happened? Who it was?"

One of the men looked at him in distaste.

"Our business, that is. You go back to where you came from."

"Maybe it's mine too," said Martin before Mike could say anything. "This

104

morning, Williams the Town raped his maid in her room. His daughter is my girlfriend. His wife is in the car over there." He pointed behind them. "Was it Williams?"

The man looked at him, not knowing what to say.

"Come on, please," Mike asked. "Don't you think we need to tell Mrs Williams one way or the other?"

Finally the man sighed heavily. "Yes. It is Williams the Chapel. He jumped. But he wouldn't rape anyone. He's Chapel. And Town."

"We know better. We have evidence. The Police will too, soon."

The other police officer had overheard this.

"And you are?"

In turn they identified themselves and reminded the man that Mrs Williams was in the car, waiting. The two officers conferred.

"Back to your car, and wait, please. We need to get details from these people then we'll come and talk to you and Mrs Williams."

They walked back to the car and Henry, carefully, broke the news to Dolly whose eyes and mouth opened in an unspoken "Oh" of horror.

She took time to compose herself.

"It's a coward's way out," She said finally.

Some time later the police car backed its way over the bridge, releasing a queue of cars from the north which had been unable to turn so as to divert via the distant Brookweir Bridge. They took names and addresses, including Angharad's, and agreed that they could all give statements in Salcombe. Henry remembered the lone police officer outside the Williams' house and mentioned it.

At last, much later than anticipated, they returned to the Upjohns' house and Angharad. All were worried by the delay and horrified when they heard the reason.

For Angharad, the first emotion she felt was relief. Relief that *he* was no longer a threat to her. She felt sad for Dolly, and said that she was sorry.

"You have no need to be sorry, Angharad. I sorrow at the death of anyone, but he was no longer my husband when he took the coward's way out. Not in my mind, anyway. And from what Bron said this morning he's no longer her father either. Be sorrowful for the loss of a life, but not for the loss of a probable threat to other young girls."

She nodded her thanks, and thought for a moment. Then: "What am I to do, please?"

Henry took over. "Now there is no danger, I think it would be good if we take you to see your family. You need to spend some time with them. They deserve it, too. Then, it's your decision. The invitation to come down to Salcombe and see Bron and recover is still there, and maybe it would be possible to stay there if you want."

Again she thought. "May I see my family, please? And would Mrs Williams come with me?"

It was by now late afternoon. Henry knew he should give a progress report to Susan and his father in law – he smiled as he thought of that – and really they should start the homeward journey soon.

Mike stirred again. "Come on then. Let me take Angharad and Dolly – if I may call you that? – to her family."

"I had rather hear my Christian name used than my married name, to be perfectly honest."

He smiled grimly and stood, ushering the two to the front door.

Whilst they were away Henry and Martin went to the nearest phone box. Henry's call to Susan produced sympathy and concern, and resignation that their return would be late. He had a brainwave.

"Would it be helpful if Ted and Ian came over to join you and Mary? Don't forget they're used to farms, and Ted wants to go into farming."

He could hear the smile in her voice as she answered. "And it'd get them out of the way when you return from Chepstow, late. And help take their minds off tomorrow."

"Tomorrow?"

"Their father's funeral.

"What! Is it tomorrow?"

"You know it is."

"I'd forgotten," he confessed. "So has Martin I should think. We've had a lot to contend with here. But I was thinking of the farming jobs too."

"I know, and yes, if they could it'd be rather nice. Oh, there are the pips. You must go. I'll see you tomorrow."

"Good night. I love you. Sleep well."

Susan's reply was cut off.

Martin almost swore when he was told. He *had* forgotten the funeral in the course of all the extraordinary events and trauma of the day. His call to his honorary grandad was businesslike until he had explained what had happened. Inevitably there was a silence as the news sank in and the emotions were weighed up.

"I never liked him. But it does sound as if he had gone completely off the rails to do something like that. Of course you must do what is best for Angharad. But please don't forget that it's your father's funeral tomorrow afternoon and you would want to be back in time for that."

"I had forgotten, until Susan reminded Henry. Here, will you talk to him?"

Henry, too, was businesslike, aware that he had few coins with him. Swiftly he arranged that the boys should go and help on Loft Island and stay overnight, and that they would drive through the night if necessary, grab some sleep and ensure they were present at the funeral in good time and not exhausted.

"Please can you tell Mike's parents? They will worry otherwise."

They broke the connection and looked at each other.

"Where do we eat?" asked Martin. "We've got to have something." It was a thought that had crossed Stephen's mind too.

"A hotel, I should think, if any of them serve food for non-residents. We need to wait until Angharad gets back, then set off immediately."

They returned to the Upjohns' house. The smell of frying onions came to their nostrils as they approached the front door. Each privately wondered how he was going to endure the wait for the others with empty stomachs and a smell like that in the house.

It was Cerys who opened the door. Her mother called from the kitchen. "I'm doing enough for ten," she told them. "You must have something to eat before you start back. Or are you staying in Chepstow the night?"

"That is very kind of you, Mrs Rees. We were just thinking that we needed to eat somewhere. We need to return tonight, though, as it's the funeral of Martin's father tomorrow afternoon, and we have to be there."

"Martin's dad, is it? Oh Duw, there's sad. Such a lot of death he's seen recently. Is he the only?"

"I've got two brothers. Younger."

"Oh, sorry Martin; I didn't see you there. I *am* sorry..."

Whilst she cooked he told her the story and she clucked sympathetically.

"There was a lot went on in that war that we never knew. People came back, yes, but changed. And never for the better. Except that Leonard Cheshire, look."

"From bomber pilot to near saint," said Henry unexpectedly. "He's quite a man."

"And your Dad must have been quite a man to have faced all he did, even if you eventually saw the side of him that was suffering," she told Martin. "Not easy, I know, but don't be too hard on him. Apart from the pain, farming bad land is soul-destroying. We know. That's why we left and came to town."

"You're not really from Chepstow, then?" asked Martin.

"No. We speak Welsh. No one else does by here except the Pughs – Angharad's family. They're from farming too, see. That's why we were so glad Cerys met her and they could speak their own language together."

They talked easily for some time. Her husband returned from work and was told of the day's events.

"I'd heard something about it," he said, "but it was all so confused I thought it to be just talk – you know, *clecs.*"

Martin looked puzzled.

"Ach, sorry," said Mr Rees. "Gossip. But shocking, it is. We all thought better of the man, even if he hated Welsh for whatever reason."

He was interrupted by the return of Angharad, Cerys and Mike. Angharad's expression was blank.

"Her Mum didn't want to believe that a man of God would do such a thing," said Mike grimly. "To start with it took us long enough to prise her away from her housework so we could talk alone, then she came up with that. Then she said that Angharad must have made eyes at him. Angharad ran out, in tears..." he put his arm around her and she didn't resist. "Cerys followed her and they bumped into her Dad in the garden, Angharad told him and he went mad, said he would go and kill Williams with his own hands. It took us a time to calm him down enough to explain that it wouldn't be necessary, and why. That took the wind out of his sails.

"Cerys explained as tactfully as possible what Mrs Pugh had said about making eyes and he went silent. We told him we were taking Angharad back to Devon with us, if that's what she still wanted, and he just nodded.

"We thought it was a bit odd. He just stood there silently. We all said goodbye as there seemed nothing he wanted to say or do, and were nearly leaving the garden gate when he rushed up and, thank goodness, kissed Angharad."

"He said... he said there would always be a home there for me," she said almost in a whisper. "I didn't want to see Mum then, not after what she had said, so I told him so. He just said 'leave her to me. She's had a shock.' Then we came away."

None of the others could trust themselves to say anything. The silence was interrupted by Mrs Rees' cheerful voice. "Come on in here, you, and eat before it gets cold."

With Henry sharing the driving, and after a few wrong turns, they arrived at Salcombe well after midnight. Henry and Stephen spent the night at the Merryweathers'; now, with Angharad needing a room too, they had to share. The supply of rooms in the house had finally been exhausted. Henry phoned Susan, waking her from a worried, light sleep and told her where he was and that he would return in the morning. She returned to bed and fell at last into a deeper sleep.

Angharad too was beyond exhaustion. Dolly tended to her as if she was a child and told her not to worry, that she should call her if she was scared or needed anything in the night as she was only in the next bedroom, and that she would be there for her at any time. And once in the comfortable bed, even with the worry of a door with no key to lock it and so many men in the house, she fell asleep almost immediately.

14 – Funeral

Martin had low expectations of the turn-out for the funeral. Those he knew and had spoken to had hinted that they had been avoiding his father if possible. His demeanour had changed so much since the year before Martin left home, and had worsened as the years progressed. In consequence Annabelle and he had arranged a very simple service, a plain coffin and just a wooden cross for the grave.

They arrived at the church with thirty minutes to spare before the service. Mr Merryweather had insisted on driving, so the augmented family had made the journey from Salcombe in good time. Henry, Susan, Stephen and Mary had used the launch from the Island and were expecting the others for tea there afterwards.

They all waited outside the church and were pleased to see a couple arrive whom Annabelle recognised as near neighbours. She was chatting quietly with them when subdued voices were heard approaching. Stephen looked round and his eyes widened. Seven young men were walking up from the road, young men many of whom he had last seen as boys, before they had left school. They were the seven who had been chosen after his entire class had volunteered to carry the coffin of Mary's brother Greg almost four years previously. Despite the solemnity of the day Mary, Stephen, Bronwen and Martin welcomed them eagerly. Hugs were exchanged. They didn't notice a small group of younger boys of two age groups dodge round them and surround Ted and Ian, whose mood lifted immediately. With them was Miss Armitage, still the Headmistress of the Kingsbridge school they all attended or had attended.

Eventually the vicar asked them all to take their places. It was left to Annabelle, Martin, Ted and Ian to follow the coffin down the aisle and slip into their places.

The comfort and unspoken support from their friends made the simple service more than just a sorrowful affair. It added to the dignity, somehow, and although tears were spilt it was a farewell with love and goodwill rather than being just the necessity that Martin had feared. When the vicar spoke of the wrench it must have been for Annabelle to lose a brother, Ted and Ian were seen to look at each other in sudden realisation. They never saw their new uncle's hand reach out to take hold of their aunt's. Ted did look round at Martin, though, and saw a look on his face he'd never seen before, and which comforted him.

When the sad business of the burial had taken place there was a drifting back to the path. One of his contemporaries asked Martin if he and his family would like a drink. Henry overheard.

"We were just going back to the Island," he said, "but there's nothing to stop us from going to the hotel – they might rustle us up some sandwiches too. Is that all right with you, Annabelle? It seems a shame just to disperse when these people have been good enough to support you and the boys."

She agreed. They made their way to an hotel. Mary smiled when she saw it; it was the same place she had visited on her way back home after her flight from Scotland almost a year previously.

Over half an hour the solemnity of the occasion slipped away from the younger people for a time. The boys, allowed into the back room that a startled

109

hotel manager had found for them, were particularly cheerful, although told to be quieter on a few occasions by Miss Armitage. She was herself startled, having been given little escape from the invitation to the hotel even with a group of youngsters between ten and fourteen. More alive to the feelings of others, Ted noticed that their Uncle Bert and Auntie Amble were sitting quietly together looking more serious, but even they were seen to smile at each other frequently. He wondered, amused but pleased, if they were getting soft on each other.

During a lull in his conversation Martin raised his eyebrows to his younger brothers and jerked his head towards the door.

"Give me a few minutes alone with them?" he asked Bronwen, who understood. He followed them, took the lead and led the way outside into the hotel's small garden. They followed him, wondering.

"How are you feeling?"

It was a blunt question, and in its suddenness was difficult to answer. Both of them considered what response to make. Ted, unsurprisingly, was the first to find words.

"Better now, I think. It seems like something's happened to make it complete. But in a good way."

"Ian?"

"All right, I think. P'raps Ted's right."

Martin nodded. "It's been a very odd time. You've been busy moving, I've been doing the same and starting work. And all the time there's been this... this knowledge at the back of everything. That's been horrible.

"But after the service there, that feeling's gone, sort of. We know more about him, what he was going through and why it affected us like it did."

He paused to think.

"I forgive him." Ian's unexpected comment surprised him. Ted nodded.

Martin hadn't thought that way; it had been two years since he had escaped to Loft Island so much of the distress he had borne had leaked away in that time. But he too understood now, and prompted by Ian's remark he felt a layer of hurt and resentment evaporate.

He nodded. "The person I'm really worried about is Aunt Amble," he told them. "When we were in the church and the vicar talked about her losing her brother it just struck me how I'd feel if it had been one of you two in there. In that coffin."

Unwonted, tears came to his eyes. Ted saw, and remembered the expression on his elder brother's face when those words had been spoken in church, giving each of the brothers that same epiphany moment.

Despite knowing he was near tears himself, he heard himself say "but it wasn't us. None of us. We're here." Clumsily he gathered Ian and went to Martin, enveloping them both in a hug, a hug that lasted a long time. Breaking away, each of them rubbed their eyes, Martin and Ted with handkerchiefs and Ian with his sleeve. Martin handed him his handkerchief; Ian wiped his yes, blew his nose and offered it back. With a shaky smile Martin told him to keep it.

Wordlessly they returned to the room and were in time to crowd around the table where snacks, quietly ordered by their new Uncle in consultation with Henry and rustled up hurriedly by the hotel, had appeared.

Martin saw his aunt was now sitting alone and removed himself from the crowd to join her. Once again he asked the question.

"Easier now, I think," she said with a smile. "Thank God you have no idea what it's like to lose a brother."

"But... well, in the service, when the vicar said what he did about losing a brother, I nearly did. I could imagine it suddenly. It was horrible. We've just talked, the three of us, and we all felt the same: what would we have felt like if one of us had died?"

He stopped, overtaken by the stab of that emotion again.

"So although we're all here, we were made to think. So I wanted to know that, now, we're here for you, just as you've been there for us all those years."

She looked sharply at him. To his surprise and slight embarrassment her eyes filled: he knew that what he had said was the cause of it. He did the right thing and let her rest her face against his chest until she had partly recovered.

"I am an old fool," she said.

"No you're not. You've just bur.. you've just said goodbye to your brother. And as we said, we three can only try to imagine that and... and don't want to think about it. Losing one of us three. If we had..." He grimaced. ".... I think I would be a wreck by now."

"Is everything all right?" asked Mr Merryweather's voice. They looked up. He looked gravely down at them.

Martin wasn't sure what to say but his aunt spoke up.

"We were just talking about losing a brother. It rather hit home with both of us. And with the other two."

He pulled a face. "It must be desperately hard. I have no idea what I should feel if Susan died, so I can only try and imagine your feelings. And no one should tell anyone else not to shed tears, by the way. In my occupation I have dealt with many emotions. I've discovered from experience that those who hold them in are inevitably the worst off in the long run. Are you both feeling better now? And are Ted and Ian all right?"

The two people of concern were alternately in animated conversation with friends from school and filling their mouths with the food from the table. Their lack of concern was so marked that their brother, aunt and honorary uncle laughed. And, doing so, themselves felt better.

Some time later Miss Armitage came over. "I really must take them back to school. If we don't leave very soon we shall be late for the buses home and parents will be annoyed. On their behalf, thank you so much for laying this on. It's probably done Ted and Ian a lot of good to have their friends around to support them; and beside that, the best way to any boy's heart is through his stomach. I really do hope things settle down for you all now. Once Ted and Ian are back at school we'll keep an eye on them, of course, and if you need me to do anything you only have to ask."

"I think you were marvellous to think of bringing them all," Annabelle answered before anyone else was able to. "Their being here has made the day more bearable for those two – and for the rest of us, in fact. Oh goodness, what is Ted doing?"

Ted was standing on a chair, to the alarm of the hotel manager who was standing nearby. He was holding a hand to his lips. Used to the tactic, his and Ian's contemporaries were quietening down. With that diminuendo the remainder of the guests were following suit.

With a grave voice and a sincerity which no one expected to be part of his character, he started.

"I know Miss Armitage wants to get everyone back to school, so this is the only chance I'll have of saying what I want to. Thank you all for coming. Thank you to Uncle Bert for getting us all back here – and thank you to the hotel manager for getting the food for us so quickly. That has really made the day special for us both – for us all."

He bowed in the direction of his honorary aunt and uncle and nearly overbalanced. He recovered and took a deep breath.

"Dad was... was good once. We had a lot of fun in the early days. If we'd known what he was going through perhaps we could have helped him. Perhaps we could have got help from Aunt Amble. But we shall never know. Martin, Ian and I lived through a horrible time. But it can't have been worse than what Dad was going through."

A pause, and a swallow; and in a noticeably tighter voice he continued: "That's it. No, it isn't. If you've still got anything in your cups or glasses please can we toast... toast... our Dad?"

The last effort finished off his reserves of restraint and he crossed the room, at speed, to his aunt. She understood and hugged him.

Unnoticed by most, Ian had taken his brother's place on the chair. With no hesitation he started.

"As Ted asked," he shouted. Heads swivelled. Ted was grateful for the distraction of attention from him.

"I want you – *we* want you – to drink a toast to our Dad. Air Force hero, brother, husband and *Dad*." He emptied his glass and jumped down as the others drank, and joined his family and Miss Armitage at their table.

Martin could hardly see either him or Ted. In a strangled voice he muttered: "I should have done that."

He wiped the water from his eyes and looked at the two, then gave a sigh which he hoped would reduce the tension. Ted looked at him with wet eyes; Ian seemed confident, bullish. Martin offered his hand to be shaken. Ted looked surprised but took it and did so. Ian looked even more astonished but put his own hand into that large paw. And while Miss Armitage was organising the youngsters in a crocodile for the walk back to school the three hugged again.

"I'm proud of you both," Martin told them.

It was not long after that the others started to drift away. Henry and Uncle Bert – as he was now almost universally known – paid the bill and thanked the hotel manager. The car set off for Salcombe and the launch to the Island; they had decided it was too late for a get-together and a meal then, especially as Ted had expressed an interest in returning to school the following day. It was more the social side, seeing his friends again that attracted him; lessons were a necessary adjunct. Ian would have liked more free time but followed his brother's lead anyway.

A sort of normality came over the next few days for the Lofts and for the

Rawles. Angharad, unbidden, started to spend time in the kitchen, and with something approaching magic handmade pies and puddings started to appear. It was as if she were still engaged as a cook-housekeeper and being paid to do so. The others were grateful to her, said so, and over a week or two a smile started appearing on her face.

All those who had been in Chepstow honoured their promise to give statements to the Police the Monday after the funeral, much to the bemusement of Sergeant Franks who hadn't been warned. His expression darkened from jovial to serious when he heard the outline story and arranged for them all to write their own statements in the back room where they would be free of interruptions "except in a dire emergency."

Dolly had to help Angharad with hers as recalling the events brought back the emotions of the day and rendered her tearful and almost unable to complete it. With careful, gentle questioning she completed it for her.

The sergeant read them all, asked one or two questions and added some words. Then they each had to go through the rigmarole of signing each page and initialling all the changes. Finally it was over and they were free. Martin and Mike started climbing the hill to go to work. They had nearly reached Mike's road when there was a thunderous report behind them. They both started, and looked at each other.

"Lifeboat?" asked Martin.

"Think so," came the reply. The final answer was given by a puff of smoke in the air and a second explosion a second later.

"Damn!" said Mike. "I'll have to go. Do what you can. Tell the parents."

"Any use my coming?" Martin asked, keen to be in on the excitement.

"Not yet," Mike called back over his shoulder as he started running. "We'll get you trained up, though." The voice trailed off as he sped down the hill.

The Alexander parents were pleased to see him but naturally worried that Mike had been called out, especially as Martin had no clue about the nature of the emergency. Despite that they made him a coffee and he went up to the office – really a bright bedroom at the top of the house which had been stripped of most furniture so as to make way for drawing boards, desks and wall-mounted pinboards. The phone was ringing as he entered, a phone unofficially quietened by the introduction of a piece of india rubber wedged between the two bells.

Not having been told what to do, Martin was unwilling to answer it, but as it continued ringing he realised he had to.

"Hallo, Mike Alexander… Architects," he announced. The pause was the result of uncertainty over how he should title the business.

"Hallo Alexander," said a voice, "Fortescue here. We need to talk about our little project again. I've received a suggestion from my wife, and if she suggests, it's a command. When might you come tomorrow? Morning or afternoon?"

"Er… I'm sorry, Mr Fortescue, it's not Mr Alexander, it's his new assistant, Martin Rawle. Mike – Mr Alexander isn't here at the moment. He's on a Lifeboat call-out. May I ask him to call you when he returns?"

"Well, yes… Dashed inconvenient, dashed inconvenient. When will he return?"

"I can't tell, sir. He's only just answered the maroons and we don't know what the emergency is. But I promise that the moment he appears I'll tell him you need to speak to him."

"You do that... or... I suppose you can't come and talk over the idea?"

"I only started with him a few days ago, sir, and I don't yet know the project. I would be working from scratch and although I would do what I could it would be quicker and more effective if Mike came."

"So you're not prepared to come?"

Martin thought furiously.

"I wouldn't be prepared, sir; that is the problem. It's different from not being willing. Mike has the details of the project at his fingertips whereas I would have to pick my way through. It would be like starting from scratch again, and neither you nor Mrs Fortescue would welcome that, I'm sure. I want to do the best I can for Mike's clients but I also know my limitations. It would honestly be quicker and more effective for me to get Mike to you as soon as he's back."

"Well, you're honest, I'll say that. Very well, ask him to call me as soon as he possibly can or..." He paused, then said in a quieter voice: "...or I'll set my wife on the pair of you because I don't want it in the neck."

The connection was broken. Martin looked at the receiver in some amazement, wondering what to make of the caller. A tyrant? Married to a tyrant, by the sound of it. But he had a sense of humour too. He smiled uncertainly and wrote on a blank piece of paper: "CALL MR FORTESCUE – URGENT!"

He found a project he had been introduced to and read through it in full, puzzling over some of the notes. He found himself sketching, trying to establish what was in the client's mind from the written specification as subsequently annotated by Mike. With several false starts he thought he had the gist of it and wondered, in the lack of any work he had been given to do, whether he might try some basic drawings to scale. His brow furrowed and he reached for an eraser.

Time passed, and dimly he realised that his name was being called. It wasn't an urgent call, so he put down his pencil and stretched his arms, then looked at the clock.

Two o'clock? How could it be two o'clock? He'd only just got there... surely?

His name was called again, this time with humour in the voice. He made his way down to see what was happening. In the kitchen were Mike's parents standing by a table loaded with food.

"You're as bad as Mike," his father joked. "We have to yell at him when he's working to come and eat. He gets so engrossed with the work that he never hears the first few times. Looks like you're the same!"

"Sorry," said Martin. "You're right, I didn't hear you. But what do you need me to do?"

"Eat some of this," said Mrs Alexander. "We feed Mike, of course, so why shouldn't we feed you too?"

"But... but I wasn't expecting that... it's very kind. I was expecting to nip home for a sandwich, or go and buy a pie or something. There's really no need..."

"Rubbish, Martin. Please, join us. And if Mike isn't back in time we can share his round too."

"Have you heard anything?"

"No – why, have you? We heard the telephone ringing but thought it was a work call."

"It was. I couldn't help, but there's a message for Mike to call Mr Fortescue back urgently."

"Sir Richard? I had no idea Mike was doing work for him."

"*Sir?* Mr Fortescue is a sir? I've put my foot in it – I called him Mr! But how was I to know? He never mentioned it. He won't be happy. Nor will Mike."

"Did he complain on the phone?"

"No... no, he was quite nice really."

"Then he'll realise you haven't heard of him and won't know, so don't worry about it."

"If you're sure... not that there's anything I could do about it now."

"Except apologise if you meet him."

"Oh of course! I rather hope I do meet him."

"Because he's a knight of the realm?"

"No, no; so I can apologise and get to know the work he and his w... Lady Fortescue want done."

Mr Alexander nodded with pleasure. "Glad to hear you're not star-struck. He may be titled but he's a human being like the rest of us."

"You sound like a communist, darling," his wife chided.

"Just a realist. Anyway it's good that Mike and you have a project from him. Getting a client like that will carry a lot of weight in wealthy circles."

"Now who sounds star-struck? But you're right, it will..."

The outside door opened Mr Alexander looked up hopefully, then hurried into the hall. A bedraggled Mike was standing on the mat, taking off wet shoes.

"That wasn't too bad," he said. "Oh good, I'm in time for lunch."

"I'm so glad you're back," said his father with relief. "Yes, we were just about to eat yours."

"Just as well I'm back then.

He smiled when he saw Martin. "Good. I'm glad they're feeding you. We'll need a break and a chat to someone apart from each other in the course of the day, even if it is only my parents."

"Well, that's nice..." his mother exclaimed in mock disgust. "In front of Martin, too."

"Martin understands, don't you?"

"Well, I think so. My Dad was very different, though."

Mike's mouth opened and then closed. He thought hard, then sighed. "It's all so much easier for me," he said quietly. "My father isn't in constant pain so doesn't have that to colour his dealings with family and friends."

Martin nodded, eyes straight ahead, thinking back to the treatment that had caused him to leave home, and further back to happier times when his father had been a proper Dad. He thought to the understated, easy respect and love between Stephen and Henry, and between Mary and Henry. Surely if Mary could become as at ease and casual with a foster parent in that way, he might be able to do the same with the Alexander parents. But they weren't adopted Family as Susan was for Mary.

"I'll be down in a couple of minutes," said Mike. "A quick change and a wash is indicated, I think."

Martin was about to call after him with news of the Fortescues' call but his mother stopped him.

"If he makes a phone call he will be on for ages and will plough straight on with work," she said. "It's urgent, but an hour or so won't make any difference."

So the three of them started eating. Martin joined them only about five minutes later.

"What was the call-out?" Martin asked.

"Lobster fisherman went out to his pots and broke down," Mike told him between mouthfuls. "One of the people at Overbecks saw his flare and phoned us. He was being tossed about like a cork."

"What happened? Did you tow him in?"

"Yes. Edgar took him over from us and towed him the rest of the way. He'll sort him out. Anyway, what did you do? Sit around drinking tea?"

It was said in a teasing tone, so Martin made a pretence of wincing.

"Were you watching from the boat? Twelve cups it was... No, I had a look at that project you introduced me to the other day. I read through it and wondered if I could start making some drawings – sketches, not the finals, of course. So that's what has kept me busy since Sir... er... Richard Fortescue phoned."

"*He* phoned? What did he want?"

"His wife has made a suggestion, he said, so he wants to talk to you."

"What did you say?"

"I told him where you were and that I'd ask you to call him back."

"I bet that didn't please him. He likes everything done yesterday."

"He wanted me to go and deal with it. I said that I didn't have the experience and anyway I'd have to start again from scratch. He sort of accepted that."

"You got away lightly. He's very persistent and his wife's even worse."

"He more or less told me that," said Martin with a smile. "The trouble was, I didn't have a clue who he was and called him Mr Fortescue."

Mike laughed. "What did he say?"

"Nothing. Just carried on as if I'd never said it."

15 – Sir Richard

Before doing anything else, once they had returned to the office, Mike phoned Sir Richard Fortescue. To Martin's relief he spoke to the man in a similarly unfawning manner as he had himself earlier. The two made an arrangement to meet, then Mike listened with a growing smile.

"Very well, sir, I will. He'll be intrigued by the project. And thank you – I'll tell him."

He looked at Martin over the desk. "You made a hit there. He said you were courteous, were honest with him, stood your ground and were helpful. And he wants to see you when I go up there. So read up on the project, would you? Then you'll have some idea of what he's after, when we go and chat.

"And a warning: he's a bluff old boy, used to his way but wants the truth even when it hurts. So don't try and pull the wool over his eyes. If there's something you don't understand or know, say so."

Martin nodded. "While I do, do you want to criticise what I did this morning?"

"I'm not sure about criticise, but I'll have a look and we can discuss it."

The next hour was like a question and answer session. Mike declared he was impressed with the drawings and the ideas that Martin had brought to them but pointed out some faults which were more to do with accepted practice than ideas or neatness. Martin checked his understanding of the Fortescue project and started asking whether they had thought about other additions or tweaks to the details.

"Best ask Sir Richard about that," Mike told him. "It's his project, but if she's there mind you involve Lady Fortescue in the suggestion."

"He said something about having to respond to her command."

"She's a tyrant. Be careful."

The Fortescue pile was a large, attractive house of grey stone on the bluff between North and South Sands. Martin gasped as its full size became obvious. As Mike's car came to a careful halt on the gravel drive the door opened and a figure appeared.

If Martin wanted to imagine a real life Colonel Blimp he would henceforth just describe Sir Richard Fortescue. From the red face with its walrus moustache to the rotund body and the plus-fours, this was the real deal. He was unsure whether to laugh at the apparition or to dread the forthcoming visit.

He made sure to emerge from the car at the same time as Mike and to make his approach slightly behind.

"Alexander, and er... Rawle, I think? Yes. Good to see you. Come in, come in. She's in a good mood at the moment, so we'll strike while the iron's hot, eh?"

In his turn Martin found his hand being squeezed in a vice-like grip whilst an unexpectedly keen pair of eyes bored into his, no doubt looking for a sign of discomfort at the handshake. He made none, just smiled at the old man and knew that he was being tested.

"Er... may I apologise for not giving you your title when we spoke on the phone, sir? And the same for Lady Fortescue. I'm ashamed to say I had never... never seen your name mentioned. Until recently I lived in Kingsbridge, you see."

The hand was released, to his relief, but the eyes remained locked on his and a smile appeared.

"Disgraceful behaviour, m'boy, disgraceful." The smile gave the lie to his words. "And why should you have heard of a couple of superannuated codgers like us? Dashed useful, having a title. Brings out the sycophancy in some and the real men in others. Makes it easy to tell the difference. Hope you're one of the real men, like Alexander here. What did you do in the war?"

"I'm eighteen, sir, so nothing."

"National Service?"

"Never been called up, sir."

"Would you go if you were?"

Martin hesitated. "From what I hear, the training is tedious because everyone knows you're only there for a year or so. But yes, I'd go and do my duty, even if it would count against my course for qualifying to become an architect."

"So you've not qualified yet."

"No, sir. I only started with Mr Alexander a few days ago, so apart from some experience with builders who have been doing up a pair of cottages I hoped to live in, and an ability with technical drawing, I have little to offer."

"Now just one moment, Martin... excuse my interrupting, Sir Richard. You have far more to offer than you are giving away. You have imagination and a natural practical ability which are both refreshing. That's why I wanted you to work with me and you know it. So don't be so modest."

"I've never been good at blowing my own trumpet," Martin said, embarrassed. "I just hope I've got the sort of trumpet worth blowing."

Sir Richard laughed. "I liked your attitude on the telephone, young man, and I like it more now. Come through and beard the dragon in her den, then we can see if you can use your imagination to find a solution to her idea."

"I heard that, Richard. Don't be rude in front of tradesmen. Oh, it's you, Mike. Sorry. And you must be Martin Rawle. Tea is over there, help yourselves, then sit down and I'll tell you what I want."

Lady Fortescue was the physical opposite to her husband, slim and waif-like, but with a pair of grey eyes that darted everywhere, missing nothing. Once they had done her bidding she took the initiative.

"You know we want a... a place where we can sit in the sun rather than just indoors with the lights on. I've seen Richard's ideas and it's a typically male design – no imagination to it at all. He's telling me that my idea can't be done."

They listened, and the more she said the more Mike's spirits sank. Her idea was that the glass of the conservatory – which is what they were commissioning – would slope up from walls of brick, to join with each other with no glazing bars, thus supporting each other's weight. When she had finished there was a silence.

Mike knew it couldn't be done, that it would leak, that it would be dangerously unstable in the strong winds that could attack even this far into the shelter of the hills. Martin saw the same without being told, but wondered how such a design could be adapted to be both practical and safe.

Neither of them knew how to tell Lady Fortescue that she couldn't have what she wanted.

118

Mike was still silent when Martin cleared his throat. Instantly all eyes were on him and he nearly faltered.

"So that I can avoid thinking along a path that would lead to an impractical solution," he started, "can you tell me, Mike, whether anyone has tried gluing glass together like that? In a situation like this it seems to me that it's open to the risk of leaks, damage by the wind which we all know can be strong here, and not strong enough to bear the weight of winter snow. But I have no experience."

Ignoring the look of shock on Lady Fortescue's face Mike said calmly: "No. As far as I know it's been neither done nor tested anywhere."

Martin seized the initiative again. "So if we can't be sure there's no way of avoiding a real danger to life with such an untried method, would stained-glass techniques be strong enough? I think I might know the answer."

"No. Good idea, but the crown joint would be too weak. Lead is good at standing upright in a normal stained-glass window, but at the slant – and certainly at the topmost horizontal – it would very quickly bow and allow the glass to fall."

"I thought that would be the case. So, then, we are back to wooden glazing bars, the sort of thing that Lady Fortescue doesn't want." He stayed silent.

"I see I'm being overruled," admitted their client, "Not by you but by physics. I confess I had failed to consider snow as a problem."

"It can be extremely heavy," Mike agreed. "If you think back to the winter of 1947, the snow inland from here was at the top of the first story of some houses. Even here it lay thickly – and stayed a long time, as you know. If you'd had a conservatory built as you really want it or as Martin was considering, you would have found it a heap of broken glass after the thaw."

She nodded. "So we are having to revert to big, heavy wooden supports."

"Or we could keep them thin, and light in colour and carved, and make a feature out of them." Martin was talking almost to himself. He had absentmindedly reached into a pocket for paper and pencil. Mike was looking at him with almost a frown on his face. The other two, the clients, looked at him hopefully.

Suddenly he looked up, aware of the silence and realising he was once again the centre of attention. Once more he blushed.

"Flash of inspiration, Martin?" his employer asked.

"Not... not exactly, just some ideas, but I'd need to present them to you first so that you can look at them with practical knowledge. We'd need a lot of work even to get them to a stage where we could present them as a possibility."

Martin could see that the Fortescues were intrigued, and worried that they should be so. He was acutely aware that it would be wrong to raise their hopes with even a sketch of his brainstorming if the design was impractical.

"Come on Rawle!" barked Sir Richard. "Out with it!"

"Sir, I don't want to show you something that doesn't have a hope of being practical. At least let Mike tear it to shreds first – if you see what I mean."

Before he could be interrupted he passed his doodlings to Mike who scanned the paper quickly, then at Martin, then back to the sketches. Finally he looked up, first at Martin who quickly looked away, then at the Fortescues.

He pulled a face and sighed. "I'm not sure if I'd have come up with anything like this, but... well, here. It might be made to work." He passed the paper to

Lady Fortescue. She looked for a long time and passed it to her husband who also studied it for a long time.

Finally he looked up at Mike. "Well, Alexander, I think you were right to take this young man on. If he can come up with something like that so quickly, and so completely different from what each of us was thinking. Are you sure you've had no training, young man?" This last was in a bark, aimed directly at Martin, and once again he found those eyes were holding his.

"Absolutely sir," he said. "I did some building work with Stephen Loft over one summer, then left school with 'O' Levels and started work with the building firm. Mr Merryweather gave me a chance and so has Mike. Mr Alexander."

"You have dropped two names at me, boy. Stephen Loft I know by repute along with his father and now his fiancée. Algy Merryweather..." he laughed. "I went to school with him. Marvellous cricketer. Should have taken it up professionally but there was something about his father, I seem to remember. We got up to some scrapes, I can tell you... Least said. But if you know those two, well, you're a worthwhile person. How come you're not in University?"

Martin had no option but to tell him the full tale. Sir Richard left him talk himself to a standstill.

"Brothers all right?" he barked.

"Yes, thank you sir."

"Name of your father's landlord. What was it?"

Martin looked at him, surprised. "Wilson," he said.

"Any other names? Must have had a Christian name for God's sake."

"We just called him Mr Wilson, sir. To his face, at least."

Once again those eyes held his before softening into a smile.

"I can imagine. Especially with a father who was ex RAF. Anyway, I'm a County Councillor and I know quite a few of the Kingsbridge people – councillors too, you know. We might be able to talk to your Mr Wilson – just to ensure that he's not been indulging in any sharp practices, you understand."

Martin thought he did, though was doubtful whether it would be an advantage to him or his brothers.

"And if you decide to go to University, come and see me."

"I think University would be pie in the sky, sir. I would need 'A' levels first. This way I get to study by post and get some experience, and perhaps qualify that way."

"And don't you think, Sir Richard, that a formal course might squash some of that originality?" asked Mike. "I do. But it's Martin's choice now, just as it always has been."

Sir Richard nodded. "Maybe. Wouldn't want to squash that. Bottle it, yes. Preserve it. Offer's there, all the same. No promises, though. Come back to me when you've had a look at that lot and give me the bad news."

Martin looked surprised. The man laughed.

"The bad news about the cost," he said. "We'll make sure the final design is good and give you a quick go-ahead."

"If we can make it work," said Mike.

"If you can make it work," the other agreed.

Mike was monosyllabic during the car journey back home. When they were safely in the office with the door closed he looked at Martin.

"That was uncomfortable," was his first comment. Martin just looked at him.

"It should be me coming up with the ideas. That's what I'm good at. I wouldn't have come up with your solution but that's not to say it won't work. It will. What was uncomfortable was being in the position of having to watch while you put something to a client we hadn't discussed first.

"But that's what I wanted *not* to do and tried my hardest to avoid doing…"

"But you didn't achieve it."

"No, Sir Richard more or less insisted on seeing my sketch – well, scribbles."

"Yes, he did, and I can't blame him. The point is that your idea should have been discussed between the two of us first here, in the office, and then put to the client."

"But I was as shocked as you when I looked up from scribbling and saw everyone looking at me."

"And Fortescue saw what you were doing and made you show it to him. That mustn't happen again. It's not that I don't trust you or your judgement but – well, you have only just started and have only a common sense knowledge of materials to go on. If it were to happen again and the idea turned out not to be practical – for whatever reason – it's me who would look as if he didn't know what he was doing."

"Oh… But then how do I put down things that occur to me when we're talking to clients?"

"I don't know. Perhaps sit further away so they can't see what you're doing. Perhaps say that you're making notes about the things that won't work. But please don't let undiscussed ideas get to the client again. If one of your solutions is the one that's put to the client, we wait until its chosen by him and then I'll give you full credit for it, along with an assurance from me that it will work the way they want it to."

Martin was silent and looked down at the notes in front of him.

Mike continued, in a rather softer tone. "I don't want to stifle your imagination or ideas. That's not it at all. But you have to see that I'm the one with the qualification, the thing clients look for. When you qualify – and I mean 'when' – every project you take on will be your responsibility. Anyway, by then I can see that this practice will be Alexander and Rawle, Architects, and we'll have an expensive office in the town centre. And another in Kingsbridge."

Martin looked up and saw a smile on Mike's face.

"Sorry, Mike."

"Not your fault, really, but we need to take avoiding action for the future. Okay, now let's have a look at that sketch again."

It had been late afternoon when they returned. Ideas and adjustments continued, sketches were done and tidied, and each found that it was becoming more and more difficult to see details on paper. At last Mike looked up and exclaimed.

"Do you realise it's a quarter to seven? You must go – they'll think I've kidnapped you."

Martin looked up from his own drawings and stretched.

"I was enjoying that. But I suppose I'd better get back if you're stopping."

"I'd better, or my parents will be on at me. I may be well over twenty-one but there are times when they treat me like a kid. Well, a teenager. You get off and I'll see you tomorrow. We can carry on with this – shouldn't take long – and then go back and present it. As your idea."

"Despite what you said…"

"That was just… well, it's in the past. And they'll want to see you. We'll both go. Then you can get on with those other drawings you were doing, and then start proper drawings for Loft Island."

Martin looked up, pleased but uncertain.

"But they haven't engaged you to do that, and probably won't be able to until the compensation from the water people has come through."

"Ah, but you're going to do the work in your own time. I'll tell you what to do and then you can do it. Henry told me you'd protested that you wanted to do so as a thank you to them, so I'll hold you to it."

For the first time in her life Dolly had been using the phone without having to ask permission.

Matter-of-factly she made arrangements for an undertaker to move her husband's body from the morgue – she called it "collecting the corpse", much to the shock of the funeral director, to whom she had to explain the circumstances. She and Bronwen discussed their futures and came to the conclusion that they wanted as little as possible to do with the Chepstow house. It held too many unpleasant memories of an increasingly controlled, bullied life for each of them.

Uncle Bert had told them that it was a pleasure to have them share his home but obviously they were free to do as they pleased. He wondered if they should consider offering the Chepstow house for rent.

"It would provide you with an income, if it should transpire that you need one," he had said.

This had set Dolly thinking. Firstly when they had left the house she had left it unlocked, open; secondly they had yet to find a will; and thirdly there were a few items of hers and Bronwen's that they would not want to be lost when some junk shop cleared the house of its dark, Victorian furniture that neither of them had liked. With a sigh of resignation, tempered by not having to ask, she returned to the hall to use the phone again.

Two days later, in response to her questions, a Chepstow solicitor retrieved a large file of documents including the will. His young clerk, pleased to spend time away from their musty office, had also discovered a great deal of money in the house; coins carefully bagged ready for the bank. He reported them to have been still in the deceased's office, the sanctum that had been private to Williams himself except when his wife or, even more rarely, his daughter were allowed to use the telephone. The documents were on their way to Dolly by post.

Whose the money was, no one knew.

"He's done WHAT?" Her brother's exclamation was untypically loud.

"He has appointed a Chapel elder as his executor and to act as a trustee for his estate to ensure that we do not have the duty to look after money." Dolly was also incensed, if quieter.

"Who is the solicitor he has appointed?"

She looked. "It's... oh, it's the same firm that I engaged to send the papers to me."

He looked, read through the paperwork and sighed.

"I think we shall need to visit Chepstow after Easter. Bronwen should come too, I suppose."

"She has a few friends she's in touch with from her schooldays," Dolly remembered. "She'll see them at the funeral, no doubt. Oh – unless she doesn't want to go to the funeral."

"I think she would go just to support you, as I would," he told her. "There is obviously no love lost. It is a tragedy, isn't it, that a human being should go so completely off the rails that no one wants to attend their funeral. I imagine that to be the case, although there might be some die-hards from the Town and Chapel who think they should go out of duty."

Dolly set her face. "If anyone from the Chapel *does* go I shall tell them that his religion may have been Christian but his behaviour towards his wife and daughter, and particularly towards his very young maid-housekeeper most certainly was not."

Angharad was still very straight-faced about life, and seemed to smile only occasionally. The eldest in the household thought that it would take a long time for her to regain normality.

That week had also seen a rush of activity on the Island. The cafe had to be readied for its opening on Easter Saturday. Once again the Loft family had agonised over whether to open it at Easter as they had the previous year, but decided that they should make the most of the opportunities open to them – 'opportunities' being tourists by another name. So the place was cleaned thoroughly and tidied. On the Tuesday afternoon Henry sat himself by the phone to arrange some additional waiter or waitress cover from the pool of people they had amassed over the previous few years. His brow became more and more furrowed as he discovered that many of them were away, were at University, were no longer interested or had jobs elsewhere. As good Friday approached he realised he would have to ask for help from the Williams clan and perhaps even Ted Rawle. He couldn't in all conscience ask Ian, whom he felt was really too young.

The call was made and Bronwen agreed to come ("It'll be boring otherwise," she said). As soon as Martin heard she was going he volunteered, as did Ted, and Ian (despite not being asked) jumped at the opportunity.

After a little drizzle on Good Friday, the weekend weather set itself fine. Visitors flocked onto the ferry and enjoyed their time on the island in the cafe where the star attraction seemed to be an angelic looking eleven-year-old with a serious expression carefully carrying crockery and utensils to and from tables. Henry had seen his pleading expression and weakened, and set everyone else to oversee him and ensure he wasn't overloaded. Ted watched him being talked to and cooed over half in exasperation and half in relief that he himself seemed to be all but immune.

"It's just that they don't realise what a pain in the neck he really can be," he said in the kitchen when anyone would listen.

His feeling of being taken for granted by most of the customers lasted until a girl of about fourteen came in with her family. As he approached the table he could see the back of her head, covered with a cascade of golden curls. He felt eyes burning into the side of his face as he took the order. Turning away he saw her face and immediately went spectacularly red.

It was a miracle their order was completed correctly.

Ian noticed a hesitancy, a muddling on his brother's part, followed the stolen glances back to the table and smiled. He did his best to do all the serving to the table, much to Ted's private fury. She and her fourteen-year-old figure stayed imprinted in the elder boy's mind for a week afterwards.

To everyone's surprise the remainder of the Merryweather household arrived at the island on Easter Sunday after the last customers had left. They were even more astonished when Charlie and Bert appeared too, the boatmen from Edgar's boatyard and crewmen of the Kingsbridge ferry.

"Come over on the ol' ferry, we have," Charlie admitted when the exclamations had died down, "jus' like we was grockels ourselves, look. 'Cept we had to steer the ol' boat usselves. Busman's holiday like."

"I hope Edgar doesn't mind," said Henry in some alarm.

"He doesn't," said another voice. "It was his suggestion." Edgar appeared behind them, next to Mr Merryweather; both of them were smiling widely.

"This is my idea," announced the old solicitor to the assembled multitude. "A year ago this Estuary was graced by the sudden reappearance of my grand-daughter, Mary. Now, being pedantic, it wasn't a calendar year ago but it was on Easter Sunday last year. That's good enough for me. I asked Charlie and Bert to come too because not only did they actually divert to bring Mary back but they have also been good friends to us over the years.

"An awful lot has gone on over this last year, some good, some bad, but I hope we may at least celebrate the good today and particularly the anniversary of Mary's restoration to us. To that end Dolly and Angharad have prepared what they describe as a scratch meal. I'm assured that means a meal from scratch, and has no unpleasant connotations."

After a busy day of preparing and serving food those who had been operating the cafe were delighted to sit and be served by their visitors. Completely by chance Angharad was sitting next to Ted who was chatting to her about his school compared to hers in Chepstow. Very gradually she seemed to become less shy. When the subject switched to the Welsh language, with Ted trying to repeat what he was learning, a smile was seen at the corner of her mouth.

16 – Chepstow and the Will

Uncle Bert, Dolly and Bronwen travelled by train to Chepstow after Easter. They had steeled themselves to stay in the family house, Bronwen in her room and Dolly and Bert in the two guest rooms. It was the first time that her brother had seen Dolly's family home. He wasn't impressed.

"Very tidy, my dear, very clean. But he had absolutely no taste apart from the Victorian."

He was right, on reflection, thought Dolly. Compared with the lightness and tasteful colour of her new Salcombe home, even considering it had until recently been a bachelor establishment, this was dreary in the extreme. Bronwen, listening to the comments, realised how much their environment and the existence of her mother and herself had been controlled by her father – she hardly liked to admit him as being her father. They looked around their own kitchen and decided to go out and eat at one of the local hotels.

Despite the efforts of the young clerk who had rescued the documents, the solicitor presented himself as being as ancient in style as Bert Merryweather tried to be, yet without the Devon man's redeeming features. Indeed, Bert felt almost unseemingly modern when speaking with his counterpart. Dolly and Bronwen sat beside him wonderingly as the dusty phrases slowly emerged into the rarefied air of the office; were carefully weighed and considered; to be followed by counter-phrases slowly enunciated to be similarly dealt with.

After what seemed like just a preamble there was a knock at the door which opened to admit a black-clad frosty-faced lady with a tray of teacups. She announced that 'the other gentleman has arrived, sir' and was asked to show him in.

The new arrival was also black-clad, and seemed horrified to note that none of the Devon party was similarly in mourning. It appeared, though, that he had more life to him than the old solicitor, for his first action was to banish the expression from his face, welcome Mrs and Miss Williams back to Chepstow, mutter condolences which the two felt in duty bound to thank him for, and await an introduction to their companion.

The newcomer's name was Arthur Preece.

"Mr Preece is appointed as the executor and trustee for the Williams' estate in the will, " intoned the solicitor. Dolly felt her hackles rise.

"So we understand," said her brother smoothly. "And even after the circumstances surrounding the death, the behaviour of the deceased immediately prior to it, the behaviour in imprisoning his daughter, and the history of bullying of his wife and daughter within the home, not to mention the surprise presence of a large sum in cash within the deceased's study, you doubtless regard the provisions of the will as sacrosanct?"

The sentence was pronounced in a rising tone of a question.

The solicitor coughed gently. "Mr Merryweather, there is scant proof of any of the – ah – accusations you mention. We are faced, in the simplest terms, with a death and a will, and an executor. It matters little how the death occurred, nor do any accusations change the desires of the deceased."

"I beg to differ, Mr Smythe. The will was written when the mind of the deceased was not disturbed by the sudden realisation that its owner had violated one of God's children. I feel I hardly need to point out to you that neither New nor Old Testament is in any doubt as to the treatment that such a person will receive in whatever afterlife there is for him. Since this is a Police matter, with evidence from the victim, from a doctor and of course from the Police investigation, there is no doubt that the event happened and that, were the deceased in fact still alive, he would be currently in prison awaiting trial. There would be a court case with all the evidence presented and at the end of it the accused would be imprisoned.

"Even more, given the behaviour of the deceased whilst a husband and a father, it is to be noted that both daughter and wife had departed the marital home after so many years of appalling treatment. That is not documented, but a woman of the standing of Mrs Dolly Williams would not dream of deserting her husband unless life with him was intolerable.

"Further, after the rape of a child – and as we both know Angharad Pugh is sixteen years old and therefore legally a minor – no wife of high moral principles would be prepared to stand by the accused as a wife, nor should she be expected to do so.

"I therefore put it to you that the state of mind of the deceased at the time of his death was significantly different from its state when he drafted his will."

The old pendulum clock on the wall ticked many seconds by before the dusty voice grated into life again.

"I have to accept, even without the result of a court case, that the deceased is guilty of rape. I do so unofficially, of course. None of us can know the deceased's state of mind vis-a-vis his will at the time of his death. Therefore I cannot see that there is a legal reason to avoid appointing Mr Preece as the trustee, as the deceased willed. One has to bear in mind that to have a man take over the often confusing and onerous duties of administering property and what is likely to prove a large sum of money as savings is always to the benefit of the widow. A woman cannot be expected to deal with such large matters and the many complications with the clarity of mind that a man would bring to it. If indeed she can at all."

Again there was silence, allowing the clock to clear its throat ready to strike the hour. It was broken by a loud and unladylike snort from Dolly. Her brother looked at her sharply. Bronwen still had her mouth open in shock.

"Mr Smythe," Dolly started. Her brother put a hand on her arm to try to stop her. She shook it off and continued.

"I thought, knowing my brother, that solicitors dealt with facts and not with suppositions or outmoded assumptions. Yet it seems that your view on the abilities of the female sex..." Mr Smythe noticeably winced at the word "...are Pre-Victorian. So I shall correct your suppositions and assumptions: I am an educated woman who has laboured under a tyrant of a husband for the twenty-three years of our blighted marriage. As such I had to beg for allowances to pay for food, fuel and for the occasional day out for my daughter and myself, outings to which at the start he was invited but always refused. I further had to negotiate with him for increases in those allowances so as to cope with increases in the cost of living. Additionally I had to engineer beliefs in my husband that would allow us time away from him in order to enjoy our days out, and to do so without lying. All of which I accomplished.

"In doing so I kept meticulous records of cash spent and saved, and worked out budgets. I was unable to start a bank account since for reasons of history – which are actually the result of male domination rather than having a foundation in necessity – I required my husband's or my father's permission to do so. But the spare money was well hidden from my ex-husband's prying eyes.

"Kindly do not, therefore, regard me, or any other woman, as an incompetent or an ignoramus. There are as many capable-minded women as there are capable-minded men. And we women will wait for the actual *proof* of a person's inability before putting measures in place to help them deal with an amount of money. It would help your clients were you to do the same. I will not – *we* will not accept your biased and unfair comments."

There was a silence. The clock ticked away the seconds again. Mr Merryweather looked up at his opposite number and raised his eyebrows.

The old man spoke again. "And do you intend, Mr Merryweather, to allow a challenge such as that to go uncorrected?"

He could feel his sister tensing again and quickly spoke.

"I do, Mr Smythe, for she is completely correct in everything she says. She is an intelligent woman and very capable of administering money."

"In that case, I will say that I am not prepared to be insulted by someone in my own office. I regard this consultation as being at an end."

Mr Merryweather remained seated.

"I am saddened to hear you say that. For the insult she was indubitably paid by you was just that, an insult to her integrity and intelligence. Her response is a mere clarification of the facts.

"I have to say that in my extensive practice I have many female clients and find that they are intelligent. Many, indeed, are more so than their male counterparts who believe that the law still applies only to the male of the species and that women, as in many cases during the Victorian era, are to be regarded as somehow sub-human.

"I take it, then, that you will not wish to take this case."

"Mr Williams was my client, not his wife or brother-in-law."

"Yet Williams is both deceased and discredited. The executor may feel bound by the will's provisions to pay legal fees for a case you decide not to take, but if guided by me will not do so. We may require another solicitor here, or we may not. That will be my sister's decision, of course, in discussion with the executor. She may well decide to contest the will in view of the harm she and her daughter received over the years, along with the recent conduct of the deceased. I believe she will win. So is that your last word on the subject, or will you apologise to your potential client and allow us to make a fresh start?"

"I shall do no such thing. Good day to you."

"Are you Church or Chapel, Mr Smythe?" This time it was Bronwen.

The man looked at her as if registering her presence for the first time.

"It is none of your business, child, but if you must know I am a member of the same Chapel as Mr Preece."

"That would be the same Chapel that the man who called himself my father was an Elder, I suppose."

He nodded dismissively.

"In that case, as the funeral will be next Friday, *I* will say that my family and I do not wish your presence there. *Good* day."

She led the way from the stuffy office. Her uncle saw that Smythe was about to prevent Preece from leaving, so inserted his figure between the two, ushering Preece out in front of him. Back in the road he looked round and firmly set a course for the nearby Beaufort Hotel where a puzzled receptionist blinked and led them to an unoccupied room off one of the restaurants.

He firmly sat them down and stood in front of the fireplace. Ignoring the previous fifteen minutes of unpleasantness he became businesslike.

"There is, of course, no need to involve a solicitor in the administration of a will. If I act as a solicitor it might cloud the issue if legal action is decided upon. Therefore I shall restrict myself to giving facts on the law rather than leading you. However, the first matter that needs to be discovered is the intention of the executor in dealing with the will. Do you, Mr Preece, intend to engage a solicitor or will you act on information I can provide?"

"One minute, please Bert," Dolly interjected. "I have read the will which is plain enough. Bronwen and I are the main beneficiaries, though there is a small bequest to the Chapel. We are happy to work with the Executor in this simple matter and I hope he will be prepared to do so without the unnecessary assistance of a solicitor. Would you agree, Mr Preece?"

The man appeared dazed by the speed at which things seemed to be going, and by a woman whom he had been led to believe required nursemaiding through her financial situation.

"Er... er... well, if it is really that simple there seems to be no reason to engage legal advice, especially as there is a solicitor in the family. I take it, sir, that you will be able to visit Chepstow when it is necessary to offer that advice to your sister?"

"My sister will be living in Devon, as will my niece. Travelling to Chepstow should hardly be a necessity."

"Ah... I see... so will you intend to sell the property, or return to it in due course?"

"That is a decision for my sister and niece. I am advised that its future will become clear in the fullness of time. So far as I have been told no decision has been made."

"I understand. As an estate agent I would be happy to assist in any way I can, of course."

"I imagine it will be some time before we need your assistance," said Dolly. "But thank you for the offer."

"The other duty the deceased has tried to lumber you with is to act as a trustee for any amounts that remain to their name. You will understand from what was said in Smythe's office concerning my sister's capabilities that the assistance of a trust and a trustee to... To do what? To dole out money? Whatever it may be, it is very far from necessary. Are we actually in duty bound to honour the word of the will? As I intimated I really cannot see why we should under the circumstances." He paused for breath.

Mr Preece looked thoughtful. "Perhaps I may help cut a path through this. Mr Williams was a trusted member of our Chapel for many, many years. He was always very insistent that things were done right, see, and quite a number of our congregation were put off by this insistence which sometimes ignored common sense – or even basic Christianity. My opinion of his behaviour has changed since he asked me to be his executor. Some of his opinions voiced in Chapel committee meetings were becoming extreme. There were more and more occasions when the rest of the other members of committees seemed to have a limited voice to disagree. It was becoming an uncomfortable place to be. He seemed to be taking on more and more responsibility.

"We were also a little concerned about some of the cash collections recently - they seemed not to have been banked. Though I would not like to point the finger at our Elder, deceased or not.

"So in a nutshell, if it is possible for me not to act as executor or a trustee, I would be pleased not to."

A silence, as the information was digested.

"I think we may be able to help with the missing collections, Mr Preece," Dolly volunteered. "We discovered a quantity of change, in cash bags, in one of the cupboards in the house – in the private study." She said the last four words with bitterness. "I imagine that is the money you are concerned about. We can return it at any time." She was glad to have found a home for a discovery which had presented itself as an embarrassment.

"As to your offer to avoid being my dead husband's executor, I am very happy to accept. With my brother's help if necessary the duties of dealing with funds will be no problem for me. After all, I have time available. And it sounds you will have your work cut out to try and reverse some of the changes that have been made at my hus... at the behest of just one man. Oh yes, as a Chapel member at his behest I had noticed too. But in his eyes I was only a woman." She tossed her head. "He is, however, not the only person to think that women are by nature incompetent, as we discovered earlier."

Her brother chimed in. "If that is the case, all you need to do is to sign a formal letter – which I can draft – to record formally that you are legally renouncing the executorship. That is a simple, but necessary, step."

"If it's that simple, I'll sign it immediately," Mr Preece said with some relief.

"I will prepare one immediately we return to Salcombe and post it to you. If you sign it and send it back by return of post we will start the process and inform the Probate Office. And thank you for your understanding and help."

Mr Preece left after thanks and pleasantries, leaving the three of the family together. To thank the hotel Manager they decided to stay for lunch before visiting the undertaker who was almost apoplectic about being unable to contact Dolly in Salcombe.

"We have no form of service," he told them, "no hymns, readings, eulogies... nothing. It's really too bad. And the Mayor has decided on a plot for a burial but we hear from rumour that it was a suicide. And if it was that, neither Church nor Chapel will accept a burial."

"You are right that... that he committed suicide," said Dolly evenly. "If anyone wants to have a service, that's up to them. It may be the Town or the

Chapel will, but I hope not in view of his crimes. I wish the body cremated."

"Does the will state a preference, or is that the executor's wish?"

"The will states he is to be buried, but that is impossible in view of the suicide. I am the executor."

"I beg your pardon. In that case…"

He started describing coffins, funeral cars, plans, and would have continued had not Dolly interrupted.

"I am sorry to interrupt, but the arrangements are to be basic. If it is possible to transport the corpse to the Crematorium and dispose of it, that is what I require. I should explain that before this last few weeks any love in our marriage, and any love felt for him by his daughter, had evaporated. His final act before suicide was to rape our young cook-housekeeper. So far as we are concerned he is beyond the pale. Talk to his Chapel by all means, or to the new Town Clerk if there is one, but make it clear that if they want anything additional to the basic disposal I have outlined it is they who will need to foot the bill. Not I, not his estate, not his relatives."

"I shall put that in writing to you, of course."

Dolly, her brother and daughter, were becoming acclimatised to long silences following explanations.

Finally the man sighed. "Please leave it with us. I will talk to the other Chapel elders and write to you as soon as I have answers."

"Thank you. I shall write to you to summarise what I have said. I realise that we are – the estate is – responsible for storing the corpse all this time."

"Ahh… in fact I am one step ahead of you there. Under the circumstances we have left it at the morgue as there is no contract in place between us. Once there is, we will have it moved, of course."

"No, it's better that it stay there. If possible, please take it directly from there to be cremated."

They returned to the house. Bronwen and Dolly were determined to collect together in one room the items they regarded as theirs, and they wanted to take to Salcombe.

"There isn't a great deal," said Dolly. "Most of the furniture is his choice. I have some smaller things from my parents. How about you, Bron?"

"I have some things, some clothes too. Things that you bought for me, or I bought from my own allowance."

"Is it a car load?" asked Bert Merryweather, "or shall we have a removals company?"

"I don't know yet," said his sister. "Let's just get everything into one room so we can see what there is. If I find what I want, could you and Bron take it downstairs into the dining room? Then we can do the same for Bron's room."

With some struggles, they managed. The dining room's dark furniture became more and more disguised by the more feminine items being placed on and around it. Finally they were finished and ready for a late dinner. Once again the Beaufort Hotel came up trumps and it was a very tired, strangely happy, threesome who approached the old Williams homestead. And as they did so their happiness drained from them.

"The sooner I see the back of this place, the better," said Bronwen savagely as they opened the door.

They saw the back of it the following day as the taxi took them to the station. Arriving at Kingsbridge and being able to walk to the ferry was a delight in contrast to that dark house: dark in furnishing, dark in memories. Several people alighted at Loft Island, and several more joined the boat on its way to Salcombe. They had wondered whether to pay a flying visit, but decided – rightly – that the café would be busy and there would be little time for talk. Their Uncle Bert would have been fascinated to watch the angelic one and the reluctant Romeo at work had they known they were there, but it was not to be.

Home was welcome. Angharad was pleased to see them, and they were all pleased to see her smile occasionally.

The following evening after his office had closed for the day and they had eaten, Uncle Bert called his immediate family in to a meeting.

"I know it's very soon after the event," he started, "but you should know that I have written to Mr Preece. We should hear from him tomorrow. But there are decisions you need to make about the funeral, money, and the house, and if I may steer you a little, the sooner these are done the better. There are two reasons for this: currently the affair is fresh in people's minds in Chepstow, and anyway the sooner matters are finalised the sooner you can forget all the unpleasantness."

"I don't think either of us will be able to forget them," said Dolly. "They will remain a shadow on our lives for ever."

"Perhaps I should have used the expression 'close the door on events'," her brother corrected himself. "Most certainly we need to start obtaining probate, and that can be done quite easily, by post. Preece is in a good position to give us a valuation for the house…"

"But we haven't decided if we want to sell it yet,"

"I do," said Bronwen. "I want nothing more to do with it."

"And you, of course, are the one who will have to deal with it when your mother is no longer able to," came the reply. It was a response that silenced Bronwen. She knew it was so, yet the idea of her mother not being there to deal with it was difficult to take.

"It is not for a possible sale that we need the value, but for probate," the solicitor continued. "We have to state what the value of the estate is. I imagine the deeds to the house will tell us that it is registered in his sole name."

"I had nothing to do with that side of it," said Dolly bitterly. "When we married, he immediately took that sort of thing over. I think every husband did in those days."

"Indeed. Those desperately unfair words in the marriage service…"

Dolly shuddered.

He continued. "Indeed. 'All my worldly goods I thee endow'. Thank goodness more couples are now sharing rather than endowing. So we have to value everything. Or should I say we have to arrange for it to be valued. Perhaps we should ask Mr Preece if he could arrange that too."

"So long as we don't have to go up there again, I'd be happy to do so," Dolly told him. Bronwen nodded emphatically.

"Between you, you need to decide what to do with the house and its contents. You also need to start a bank account, Dolly. And I suggest Bronwen does too. Dolly can now start one on her own cognisance as she is a widow, and either she or I can give Bronwen the permission that a bank will require – iniquitous requirement that it is. Once we have probate we can arrange for funds to be transferred. Having by default taken over as executor you, or perhaps we, need to do what the will requires in administering the money. That will consist of paying it into your account, Dolly, and absolutely nothing else. Unless you need legal advice, of course."

She smiled, for the first time in ages.

"What do I need a bank account for?" asked Bronwen.

"Bron, you are eighteen," said her mother. "You are perfectly capable of looking after money. God knows we are neither of us spendthrifts. We have hardly had the opportunity. So from whatever savings there are in *his* account there will be an amount paid into yours too, to do as you wish with. I might guide you until you are twenty-one, but that is all; after that you are free to do with it as you please. But I do hope that when you marry you choose to share your property, not endow it as I had to."

Bronwen's mind switched immediately to Martin. Surely... but no, her mother was right. What would happen if he died? She shuddered again.

"What do we do with the house?" asked Dolly.

"Once you have probate it will be yours. It can either be sold or rented out, as I think I said. I'm sure Mr Preece will help you with that, whichever you decide."

"I don't want anything to do with it," said Bronwen. "Not even to let it out. It has too many bad memories."

"It should be sold then," said Dolly, "because I agree with Bron."

"Then perhaps you could consider buying a property down here to rent out. Thanks to the return of the water we are experiencing increased tourism, and tourists will always want accommodation."

"Or we could buy a house and live in it," mused Dolly.

"Indeed, though please don't think for one moment I would ever throw you out."

Dolly smiled. "Thank you. But maybe Bronwen and Martin might need a home on their own some time."

"Or maybe, Dolly, you might want to set up a home with someone else. Someone better."

"I think that is pie in the sky at my age, don't you?"

"Not at all. It isn't pie in the sky at any age. I have dealt with many couples who are marrying in their mature years."

Dolly's expression was non-committal.

"Should I write a further letter to Preece, asking him to value the house and contents? And should I seek information about the current state of the bank accounts and tell them of the death? Naturally we have the latest statements from them, but we need a closing value."

"Yes please. We must be in your hands on how best to deal with that. But I, too, can write letters. Please tell me what needs to be written, and to whom, and

132

I will do it."

"I have a list of those who need the information. Some will need a copy of the death certificate so a delay is inevitable until that arrives. But once it does we shall be able to start. I will tomorrow provide a list, including a list of those who can be informed immediately, who do not need a copy of the certificate. If you can write to them it would remove some of the work from my secretary's shoulders."

"Ready?"

"What for?" Mike muttered from his drawings.

"We have an appointment to see Colonel Blimp and Lady Fortescue."

"Oh, blimey... why didn't you remind me?"

"Mike, I just did!"

"I mean before this."

"*You* told *me* earlier. I thought you were ready for it."

"I've been doing the... oh well, it doesn't matter. Have you got your pitch ready?"

"*My* pitch? I thought you would be doing that."

"Your ideas, Martin. As I said, you should be putting your ideas to them."

"But..."

"Well, I'll drive and you can remind yourself as we go. At least they're all costed and so on."

"As far as we can with taking a guess at the cost of carving."

"Quite so. Come on then."

As quickly as he could Martin gathered up his drawings and joined Mike in a rush for the car. They arrived at the Fortescue only a few minutes late, but it didn't stop the old soldier tapping his watch as he answered the door.

They sat round an ornate table. Martin found that all eyes were on him. He swallowed, hoping no one would notice.

"We've examined the original specification in detail," he told the two clients. "The conclusion that I arrived at, guided by Mr Alexander after a lot of research, was that there are no glues or glass cements in existence in 1958 that will allow construction in the style Lady Fortescue really wants; not if the build is to remain safe. That is, I regret to say, what we expected and believed when we last consulted.

"Mike... Mr Alexander has looked at my rough drawings, the doodles that I made when we were last here, and has ensured that the proposal which I believe Lady Fortescue was interested in would be safe. On top of that we... Mike is absolutely certain that it is the least intrusive way of supporting the glass that is technically possible at the moment."

She nodded. So did Sir Richard.

"One moment," she put in. "Are you really saying that if we waited a few years the original design might be possible?"

Martin looked at his employer.

"It's an impossible question to answer, Lady Fortescue. We do our utmost to keep abreast with innovation, not just in building styles but in materials. For example we were looking at an American system which uses two panes of glass so as to reduce heat loss and insulate against noise..."

"Poppycock! Entirely unnecessary! What do they take us for over here? Namby-Pambies?" Sir Richard was on good form.

"I believe, sir, that the idea was to insulate against really strong winds and really low temperatures, particularly in the north of the continent where they are both a real problem."

"Huh!"

"It wouldn't work in the design you are interested in, sir. The weight would be too great if ever we had a really bad snowfall." Martin was back in his stride.

"Then how does it cope in the bloody United States, then? Answer me that!"

"The application they use is only for windows of a normal size, and windows that are perpendicular, sir. The design you are looking at involves angles of forty-five degrees at the least acute, and I... Mr Alexander advises that any major snowfall would add a significant weight to that. A single skin of glass would cope, particularly..."

He paused. On his pad he quickly scribbled the word 'toughened?' and showed it to Mike, who nodded.

"Particularly if we used toughened glass for safety."

"Toughened, eh? How is that made?"

"It's laminated, sir. Two or three sheets of glass are stuck together. If there's an impact or excessive weight, the pane will shatter just like a single sheet of glass, but will hold together."

"So we have the glue that will do that, but not hold the edges of glass together."

"Yes, sir." Mike had taken over. "The area of the glue covers the full face of the glass. In a butt joint there's a limited area for the glue to grip. Resulting in a weaker join"

"So if this additional pane of glass is stuck to the first one, why doesn't it fight the heat loss and noise?"

Martin's turn again. "Because it's the air between the two panes that insulates, sir. An airman wears a leather jacket to stop the wind, but under it he wears layers of woollen and cotton clothing. It's the air trapped in them that insulates and prevents most of the cold attacking the body."

Martin remembered back to his father's lectures when he was on leave, in happier times, from his Squadron. The reference wasn't wasted on Sir Richard.

"Personal experience, boy?"

"My father's flying clothes, sir."

Sir Richard drew in a deep breath. His wife looked daggers at him.

"Martin: I'm so sorry. I had no intention to cause you to bring up the past like that. Please – accept my apologies. I'm an old fool."

"No need for an apology, sir. It's water under the bridge."

"No, young man, it isn't. Never forget your father and what he did for this country. I just wish that his country served him better when he needed help."

"Thank you, sir, but he was always too busy on the farm to look for it."

Sir Richard shook his head. "The independent streak. Admirable in its way, but can be so destructive."

He took a deep breath. "Should we get back to the matter in hand? Are you of a mind to continue?"

"Yes, sir; of course."

"Then I will say that you – and Alexander, of course, have the experience. We have single panes of toughened glass, supported by... what?"

"Carved wooden glazing bars that are adequately wide at the base to bear the weight, but which taper towards the top. Each would be individually carved. I... we... have identified a craftsman who was engaged on Truro Cathedral. He's quite old, but would love a challenge like this, he says. At the apex would be a wooden shape that would stand the weight of the glass as it comes fully inward, but without ever being horizontal. Here is a drawing of what we've planned."

He presented a technical drawing and a an impression of what it might look like. The two clients pored over it, giving him the chance to steal an anxious glance at Mike, who nodded with an encouraging grin.

"How would the wooden bases be fixed to the brickwork?" Sir Richard barked suddenly, making Martin jump.

Mike chimed in. "We would embed stainless steel plates between two courses of bricks below. Stainless rods would emerge from the top and be slightly angled inwards to follow the line of thrust. Where they are mounted, supporting piers would be sunk into the foundations to ensure the outward thrust is supported."

Sir Richard looked up. "That your idea, or young Rawle's?"

"Common practice, sir; taken from ecclesiastical buildings and scaled down."

"Is it now? Used it before?"

"I haven't, sir, but churches have for hundreds of years. We have the advantage nowadays of having good British stainless steel."

He nodded. "How much of this design is yours, Alexander, and how much is Rawle's?"

Martin was about to answer, to say that it was a team effort. Mike put a hand on his arm to stop him.

"The vision is entirely Martin Rawle's. The strength calculations are mainly mine based on my knowledge of materials – he's had limited opportunity to study or experience that when applied to out-of-the-ordinary projects like this. But we worked on it as a team."

Another nod from Sir Richard. "Happy with it, Rawle?"

"*We* are both happy that it has the durability we all want, sir, yourselves as clients and us as arch... and Mike as the architect."

The piercing eyes met his again. "Not what I meant. I take it as read that if Alexander approves, it's strong enough. The question was whether you're happy with how the compromise design will look."

Martin thought, looking for a catch. He could find none.

"Do I think it will look pleasing? Yes, sir, I do. Could I live with it as part of a house of my own? I can't answer that as it would depend on the house. Do I think it would be in keeping with your home? Yes sir, and Lady Fortescue; in my opinion it would. But it's not my opinion that counts, nor even Mike Alexander's. It is entirely yours."

The eyes held his for a moment longer. Then to Martin's surprise he smiled, and winked.

"And what is our opinion, my dear? Do you think it will sit well with the house and its surroundings?"

Lady Fortescue looked up from the drawings. To both Mike's and Martin's relief she was smiling.

"If this man who worked on the cathedral can come up with a batch of designs that echoes the leaves and berries of the seasons, then I would love it. I think you are both artists, as well as architects, and tactful ones at that. I am persuaded. How about you, Richard?"

"Love it, my dear; love it. When can you start, Alexander?"

Mike smiled. "The figures I've jotted down here are based on experience and at this stage a little guesswork. May we approach some builders, sir? We need to obtain accurate quotations and present them to you. And we certainly need to ask our craftsman to come and talk to you about the final designs before we can get a quotation from him."

"Approach away, Alexander, approach away. Get a good builder, mind; not some of these jerry-builder types. Had enough of jerries in the war. Huh!"

"He's quite a character, isn't he?" Martin remarked as they drove away."

"He is. I get the feeling that most of it is acting. He's had to put on a front for so many years in the army that he can't drop it now. He's certainly straightforward and expects everyone else to be. You did well, by the way."

"Thanks. I was trying to make sure he saw we were working as a team."

"You did. No complaints there."

Martin managed to leave work at a reasonable time that night, and walked happily down the hill, pleased with life. Turning the corner to the Merryweather house he was astonished to see a uniformed figure outside it, ramrod stiff. It was not a police uniform but an army one of some sort.

Then he noticed the red top to the cap and his brow furrowed. He approached. The soldier looked at him.

"Martin Rawle?"

"Yes, that's me."

"I have a warrant for your arrest."

"*What*?"

17 – MPs and Lifeboat

"I have a warrant for your arrest. You were instructed to report for National Service a month ago and you have absented yourself."

"What! I've received no instructions! Nobody has mentioned it at all! How was I meant to know?"

"That will be explained to you once in the barracks and you appear on a charge. You need to pack some clothes and come with me. And no attempt to run. We are armed."

Martin's chin dropped. "I am not going to run. If I have to do National Service I'll do it. But nobody has told me anything about reporting anywhere."

The man shrugged. "Can't help that. We're just here to take you in."

"So can I go inside, then?"

"Yes. You need to pack some clothes."

Martin let himself in. The soldier stayed outside, but in the living room he found the rest of his family, looking scared and worried. His honorary grandfather was in the middle of a call. He pointed to a seat. Thankfully, Martin sat in it. The military policeman in the room frowned and would have spoken, but was interrupted before he was able.

"Please say nothing before I have spoken to your commanding officer. You would exceed your authority if you were to do so."

Whether that was the case, Martin had no idea. There was silence in the room for endless minutes. Finally the earpiece made a noise and Mr Algernon Merryweather, solicitor, introduced himself.

The official letter, he discovered, had been sent to the Rawles' Kingsbridge address in March 1957 when Martin had just turned seventeen.

"One moment, please."

He turned to Martin. "He says the letter was sent just after your seventeenth birthday."

"Seventeenth birthday… Well, I never saw it, and Dad never said anything about it. I wonder… I wonder if he just needed me on the farm so much that he ignored it?"

This was explained to the officer, as was the fact that Martin had not lived in Kingsbridge for almost three years.

"We wrote again to request a contact for the boy," said the remote voice, "but there was no response to that either. We had to assume that he had decided to ignore the call-up or had moved. It wasn't until just recently that we were able to visit the address and discover it empty."

The solicitor explained that at the time of the original orders Martin's father was suffering from severe injuries sustained during the war and was unable to deal with correspondence. His son, therefore, remained unaware.

At that point the solicitor took the initiative, pointing out that the entire family at the Kingsbridge address had been involved in farming, which was regarded as a protected occupation by the law. It took a moment, but the officer at the other end of the phone pointed out that if he had left home, Martin was no longer a farmer.

"He was living on a farm and helping there," came the response.

"He is not now. We have traced him to your address, which is why my men have been sent to collect him."

"Indeed he is not now working on a farm. But the fact remains that in the lack of any instructions having been received by him, he is not to blame for failing to appear. That is a matter of law. Therefore, with all due respect, your MPs should be withdrawn immediately. When a letter of instruction to report is received at this address – which you obviously now have – Mr Martin Rawle will react to it as a gentleman of honour.

"However I should point out to you that he is currently in training to become an architect. He is an integral part of a new firm here, a firm which has quickly come to rely on him. If another person has to be employed instead of him, the army will have damaged his opportunity to earn his living, probably so much that he will never recover from the loss of such an opportunity."

The remote voice explained that it was a common problem, and not one they could avoid.

"I should also have mentioned that he is also about to embark on a course of study. That allows National Service to be deferred, at least. However, we shall await the call-up papers at the correct address; this one. In the meantime I will connect you with one of your MPs who is here in the room and I should be grateful if you will recall him and his colleague."

Without any further speech he handed the receiver to the uniformed man.

Five minutes later they had gone.

"You might have to go if they send the papers again... no, not again; for the first time," he told Martin.

He received the news in silence, news that he knew to be true.

"I need to talk to Mike," he said suddenly. "May I use the phone, please?"

Mike, when he answered at last, was horrified. "This has nothing to do with Sir Richard, does it?"

"You think he contacted the army...? No. Impossible. The original was sent just after my seventeenth birthday. I never knew you at that point, so Sir Richard and I had never met."

"Do you want to go?"

"No! I want to work with you and study. Nothing against the army, or even National Service even if it is due to be phased out soon. But my time is better spent learning my career."

"I know what you mean. Look, let me make a phone call."

"You're not going to call the army, are you?"

"No. Well no, not exactly. I'm going to call Sir Richard and ask for his advice."

"He was all for my going, if I was called up."

"Well, no, he wasn't. He asked if you'd go and you said you would even if it would damage your chances. He didn't say anything like "I should hope so too". Let me see what he says. I wonder... what was the name of the officer Mr Merryweather spoke to? And where is he based?"

Martin asked the question and passed the information on.

An hour later the phone rang again.

"Merryweather," said the solicitor.

"Now then, Algy. How is it that we can live three miles from each other and neither of us knows the other is there?"

He looked at the receiver as if it had bitten him.

"Come on, Algy! You remember those girls…" The receiver was clamped to the listener's ear to prevent others hearing. His brow cleared and he started laughing.

"Richard, you old devil! When did they let you out of the Army?"

It became a one-sided conversation so far as the others in the room were concerned. After agreeing to meet his old school friend he beckoned Martin over and handed him the receiver.

"Hallo, sir?" said Martin cautiously.

"Rawle, that officer is a bloody fool. I told him that he was junior to me even if I was retired and he should shut up and listen. Must have some sense, I suppose, because he did.

"Told him you were more use here than in the bloody army… sorry dear, I'm hot under the collar… that wasn't addressed to you Rawle. Told him you were in the Lifeboat crew. You are, more or less, aren't you? If you're not yet, why not? Anyway, the fool agreed with me that you're best left alone here as the RNLI is a recognised, uniformed, official civilian organisation. The notion that you were about to start a university course or something similar helped shut him up too. He agreed to mark the papers accordingly. How are you getting on with my wife's sun room, or whatever it is? Eh?"

Martin took a deep breath.

"Thank you, sir. This has all come as a bit of a shock. As I said when you asked, I would be prepared to do my National Service. But to have a military policeman ready to arrest me was – well, disturbing. And yes, I'll be joining the Lifeboat.

"The other thing that seems unfair is that we've just lost our Dad, and it means that effectively the boys and I could be homeless were it not for their aunt and Mr Merryweather. And for all the army knows I could be the only… the only one old enough to look after them."

"That crossed my mind too. I had it as spare ammunition if he didn't swallow the Lifeboat thing. Never let off your full salvo at once. Sometimes the buggers lift an arm and shoot you anyway… what? Oh, sorry dear. Shouldn't have said 'buggers'. Oh, damn."

Martin was starting to smile.

"I understand, sir, and thank you. And we are writing letters to craftsmen and builders…"

"Just the one craftsman, I hope?"

"Yes sir: craftsman singular and builders plural. We should get replies very soon. If not we'll go and drag the wood carver down to see you."

"I'll lend you some MPs, Rawle. They can be persuasive until their guns are spiked. Good man. Cheerio."

There was a click, and that was the end of the conversation.

"He's a funny old… Chap," said Martin grinning.

"He's an old devil," said his honorary grandad. "Some of the things he had me taking part in when we were at school would make your hair curl. If my parents had heard about them I would have been out of there without a second thought."

"He kept on having to apologise to Lady Fortescue when he swore, just now," Martin told him. "Despite his frightening manner, he seems a really nice man."

"He is. Whenever we were discovered... well, let me just say 'doing things that we shouldn't'... he always took the flak first and tried to keep the rest of us out of it. Yes, I have a lot of time for him. By the way, are you going to tell Mike what he's just said?"

"I imagined that he would have done that himself. But yes, I'll call him."

Martin did so. Mike was intrigued, pleased and relieved all at once. "I think the business about having to look after two little brothers now might have clinched it, you know. And that's even if the little brothers aren't really little at all." Ted and Ian liked the comment when he relayed it later. "The comments made about that side of things when it became public – I should think even the War Office would be embarrassed."

Mike made time next day to take Martin to see the Lifeboat Coxswain. Once again a pair of piercing eyes held his, and seemed to follow his every move and word. It was difficult to read the face that was asking him questions; a weatherbeaten skin, white beard and ruddy complexion combined to hide the expressions and thoughts. It was interesting, Martin thought, to compare the older man's Devon burr, so akin to his own speech, with Mike's more eastern, London-tinged, way of talking.

Martin took it as much as possible in his stride. A fair few of the questions shot at him were beyond his maritime skills and he had either to use his ingenuity or to admit he didn't know. Finally the Coxswain nodded, grinned for the first time, and said "You'll do. Come down next practice and meet the rest of the team. We'll take you out and see what you think. Probably chuck the boat about a bit to see if you get scared, too. It's April, so it should be nice and uncomfortable for you."

Martin made himself grin back, though the prospect of a rough ride at sea on his first outing was not attractive.

His baptism by Lifeboat came the following Wednesday. Apprehension started the moment he woke that morning. The working day with Mike helped, except towards to its early (for Mike) end. Eventually it was Martin who had to remind his employer that they had to arrive at the quay early so that the greenhorn could be equipped with suitable clothing and life jacket. They set off before Mike's parents started the usual round of reminders to their son that he should stop working and go.

"You've taken up the offer, despite what I said, then."

It was an odd greeting from the Coxswain, but Martin grinned and told him that wild horses wouldn't stop him.

"It ain't wild horses you'll see, boy, it's white ones. We've got a Force five, gusting six out there. Once in the bay you'll know it. If you feel sick, find the side with the wind at your back when you're at the rail. Don't, and by God you'll get your own back. And you'll be clearing it off our boat when we get back."

It took Martin a while to understand him. He had felt all right up to then, but the idea made him think again.

The rest of the crew arrived in dribs and drabs. Each was introduced to the kitted-up newcomer and each looked him over and gave either an appraising nod or a grin of welcome once the offered hand had been shaken. The Coxswain called for quiet once they were all present and introduced Martin again. A brief version of his family history was given, and there were approving nods when his honorary grandfather's name was mentioned.

"You can't be too bad if old Merryweather's taken you on," observed one of those who had just nodded to him earlier. Martin was pleased that his sponsor had such a good name in the town, but wasn't really surprised.

They trooped outside and climbed down the steps into the waiting launch.

"No need for a chasing dinghy this time, Martin. I'm here." Mike was typically upbeat and Martin was grateful for it.

It was now excitement that was tingeing his apprehension. The short journey out to the *Samuel and Marie Parkhouse* was uneventful, the same feeling as in the ferry on a choppy day. On board, the rest of the crew melted away to their stations leaving Martin with Andy, the Coxswain, at the helm.

"You're just a passenger. If I ask you to go somewhere, ask yourself if the order 'Safety Lines' has been given. If it has, and you're not already clipped on to one, clip on like this."

He demonstrated how to attach to one of the lines which were securely fixed to the boat's safety rail.

"Otherwise, stay somewhere safe, with someone else. Watch what crew members do. Learn. Get used to the movement. And remember – one hand for yourself, one for the ship. Especially when you're just starting."

He looked at Martin's serious expression. "And one last thing: enjoy it! We're not on exercise as such, just doing some manoeuvres and giving other crew members experience at different tasks."

The Lifeboat slipped her moorings and nosed into the wind-disturbed main estuary. Martin had sailed on this stretch with Mary and Stephen in the summer and in lighter winds. This was different; the Lifeboat was a larger boat although small enough to react to the swell which was evident even there, so far from the bar. As they continued south the black rocks just north of the bar came properly into view. It was obvious that they were doing their best at sheltering the estuary from the sea, as every wave seemed to leave a cloud of spray above them.

Outside them, it seemed to Martin that they were fully exposed to the weather. He held on, white knuckled, until very gradually the motion and he became one. The boat's engines increased their tone and they shot forward into the waves.

They cleared the estuary mouth. To starboard the land vanished to the north west, Bolt Head being its terminator. To port, land continued south east as far as Prawle Point, but beyond it was open sea.

The Lifeboat continued due south. The ride made Martin think of the rare visits to Torquay on bank holidays when the fair would be in town. Rides on the cars which, roundabout-like, nevertheless went up and down on their track. A thrill for a young boy with his even younger brothers, even after fish and chips at one of the fair's stalls. All a long time ago, it seemed to him. It was with this in mind that Martin looked on this ride as an adventure. Gone were the nerves of before, the worries, the apprehension. The motion was one he rode with, that he enjoyed.

"Martin Rawle to the bridge, please."

The order was relayed by Mike, who was stationed next along the port side where Martin was.

Martin looked at him, surprised. Mike grinned. "You okay?"

"Fine," Martin shouted back over the wind. "It's great!"

"Good. Get going. Andy wants to talk to you."

Carefully Martin made his way aft to the bridge, though in his limited experience the word 'cockpit' would have described the boat's nerve centre more accurately. He stood by Andy, who was swaying easily with the boat. Past Andy and inside the tiny cabin he could see the radio operator and navigator, one at either side.

"Sir," called Martin the stern. "You asked me to report to you."

There was no answer. The navigator looked out.

"He's Andy, boy. Not sir."

Martin nodded his thanks.

"Andy – you wanted me?"

"That's better Martin. Christians names here unless we've got two with the same name, then watch out for some suspect nicknames! Come here and tell me what you see."

This sounded like a trick question, but he had no option but to play along.

"Prawle Point on the port... er... quarter, and nothing to the west. Bolt Head..."

"Okay, okay. I meant straight ahead."

Martin looked. He scanned the emptiness ahead, and took some time doing so.

"I don't know if I'm missing seeing something, but my eyesight can see nothing apart from the sea."

"And what's the sea?"

What a weird question, Martin thought.

"Er... well, salt water. We're floating on it."

"Keep thinking. You're doing all right."

"I am right in saying there's nothing visible apart from it, though? No ship or rock that I've missed?"

"You're right. There's nothing else."

"So – the sea. Well, it's... reacting to a wind of – what did you say? Force 6? And it's quite rough..."

"This ain't rough, Martin. This is a walk in the park compared with some of the seas we have to go out in. Wait for a Force 8 or 10. Force 8 is getting uncomfortable, 10 is a switchback. And pray God you never encounter anything greater, even in a self-righting boat, which this one isn't."

That pulled him up. He nodded.

"So what else about the sea?"

"Er..."

"She's a killer, boy, that's what she is. A green, wet, permanently moving killer just waiting for you to make one false move and for your mates here not to be able to drag you out again in time. Sometimes you have to do things with the sea that no sane man would do. That a man who was not intent on saving the lives of other men would do. That's when we really have to bargain with the sea.

"That's best done by being trained. And then trained some more. And then again. Some of that training is bloody uncomfortable, sometimes even dangerous. But we do it so we know the character of the killer we face, and understand ways of beating her. Then we do it again, and again. Because the sea is always different and we need to adapt what we do to beat her, to keep ourselves and each other alive."

He paused for breath.

"Still want to join us?"

"If you'll be training me, Andy, then yes."

"Oh no – you don't get me like that! Lots of people will train you. Your own crewmates, RNLI trainers and officials and so on. Me? I'll just make as sure as I possibly can that you – and all the others – and me – are kept safe. And that we're able to do what we're here for: save lives and save vessels. If I think you're weak in some department or other, you'll be off the active list until I'm happy you're safe. So if I do that, just know that Uncle Andy is looking after you, really. And there are times when it *will* happen. All the crew know it. Some have been told to get training and not come back until they've done it. Others have just been told to get training, and I check that they have. But everyone knows that what I do, I do for their safety – *our* safety."

It was a lot to digest. Martin nodded, thinking hard.

"How long is the training, really, Andy?"

"Depends on you. Depends how interested you are. Depends how much you can take in at once. Depends what new stuff they throw at us to help us. If you get through today and aren't put off, then we'll start with four more practice runs and tell you what you can do and what you can't or shouldn't do. It's difficult to keep to training levels when there's a ship we're trying to help in a Force 9 and the shit hits the fan."

It was the first time Martin had heard the expression and it tickled his imagination.

"Yes, boy, you can grin now, but when the shit is coming your way, sometimes it's instinct and common sense you need, even over training. But we'll start you off gentle. If you decide to stay."

"I've already made that decision."

"Have you? Not put off by ol' Andy and his sermon? Not put off by a moderate sea? Okay. Well, it's getting towards dusk so we'll do a few avoiding actions. You'll hear what's about to happen only just before it does."

Before Martin could say anything, Andy's voice turned to a roar.

"Survivors in the water 2 cables dead ahead. Manoeuvre to avoid. Safety lines."

"What can I do?" asked Martin, shortly.

"Sit down over there. Passenger seat. If you have to get out for any reason, get onto a safety line first."

It was halfway to the nearest seat that the first course change threw Martin off balance. He steadied himself, unfortunately on the throttle control. Andy looked daggers at him.

"Oy! Any of that and you'll bloody know it!"

"Sorry," Martin gasped.

Andy corrected their speed, then almost immediately took the power off and the boat was allowed to drift forward on her own momentum. Martin again regained a vertical position and walked purposefully to the nearest seat.

"One on port side. Ahead, circle and double back."

Martin ended sitting across two seats. Hastily he recovered himself. Andy looked round.

"Good. We're circling. Which side would you need to be to help with a rescue?"

Martin was now in a whirl. What had Andy said? Port side? And they were circling..."

"Starboard side!"

"Wrong. Wind would blow us down on him. We come up against the wind...what's it's direction?"

A pause from Martin.

"No good. That and the tide direction should be imprinted on your mind. Wind's sou'westerly, we're heading straight back to him. What's the helmsman going to do?"

"Head to... to leeward of him."

"Which puts you on which side to be useful?"

He blinked rapidly, trying to visualise.

"Port!"

"Right. Because the boat will be to the east of him. The port side will be nearest him. Good man. Quick on the uptake. Like that. Get to the port side. What's the first thing you'll do?"

At least this was obvious, having been told to him twice so far.

"Put a safety line on."

"Go on, then!"

Outside the comparative peace of the cockpit's shelter the wind seemed to be howling. Martin found a line and clipped himself on. An arm stopped him, another crew member checked what he had done, then pointed to the direction Martin had been intending to go. He went.

There were two men already standing at the side. He made his way to them. They took no notice, just kept staring at the water.

A few moments later, to his complete shock, Martin saw a figure, a human body, face down in the sea. He gasped, recovered and yelled: "There!"

The man nearest him grinned. "Where's 'there' in degrees?"

Martin said something very rude, more to himself than the man.

"F.... Thirty degrees from our course."

"Got the hook, Joe?"

"Aye aye." It was a laconic, casual answer. The hook was lowered to a belt around the figure's waist, twisted to catch it, and a sign was given to the helmsman on the bridge. The engine note changed to idle.

With the boathook, the body was brought nearer.

"Under the armpit nearest you."

Martin realised this was directed at him. Trembling, he approached and, as soon as he could slid a hand under the figure's left armpit and started to lift.

"No! Hold! Now, after three we all lift together. One, two, three..."

Once the figure was on the deck, Joe turned it over. There was no face, just a blank...

...piece of canvas.

Martin's mind was in turmoil. The thing in the water was so lifelike that every hint of this being just a practice, and exercise, a scene maybe for his own benefit, had left him. All he had been able to see was a drowning, maybe drowned, seaman. Passenger. Human being.

His breathing calmed down and he held on to the rail, suddenly reminded that under him the deck was still heaving, the sea was still – what had Andy said? Moderate?

"Martin, may I introduce you to Dead Fred?" This was Joe's voice. "He's one of a very unfortunate family. Dead Freda we see sometimes. But the ones we really hate to see, just as you hated to see Fred, are dead Fredling and dead Fredette. They bring it home to us, even when we know it's an exercise.

"Now, can you help us drag him inboard? We'll have to take him home and wash his clothes, or they'll bleach. Be careful – he's a heavy old sod. About thirteen stone, just as he should be."

Martin, now like a spray-soaked automaton, helped drag the dummy towards the stern, where the three of them dumped it in a stern locker.

"Cheers," said Joe. "That's where he come from when you weren't looking. Best go back to see Andy. Don't tell him he's a bastard to swing that on you. Even if you think it."

Martin did think it was unfair, but said nothing when he came across Andy again. He found him being looked at with something approaching a smile.

"Yes, as Joe said, I'm a bastard to do that to you."

Martin realised the coxswain had very sharp ears.

"You did okay. You saw and you raised the alarm. If you hadn't, the other two wouldn't – under my instructions – and we'd have swung round and picked Fred up again. The only thing you did wrong, and I wouldn't have expected you to do any different, was not to say exactly where the sighting was. That's where the training comes in. It's essential.

"But you worked with the others to hook him out, you didn't drop him, and you watched as the body was turned over. In a real situation that might have been a sight that no man should ever see, yet we do, sometimes.

"You did well. Have a seat now; we're heading for home."

18 – Compensation

He was recounting his experiences to an audience that evening, an audience that included two younger brothers who were hanging onto every word.

"Do you think you will persist with it?" asked his grandfather.

"Yes. Yes I do. It's exciting. And... well, it's a good thing to do as well. I think I can make it fit in with work; after all, Mike does. He's in the same boat."

"Literally," said the old man. Everyone else laughed, joined shortly after by Martin after he realised what he'd said.

"Can I come out on the Lifeboat some time?" asked Ted.

Martin looked at him, amused.

"Not until you're eighteen, I should think."

"It's sixteen, actually."

Ted swung round. Uncle Bert was looking serious.

"That's two years away," he complained, looking dejected.

"Yes, only one and a bit years away," said Martin. "And in those two years you have to build your muscles up so they can lift a fully-grown man from the water – with help. It isn't just lifting your own weight, it's being able to lift other people, other things. I found it hard work, and I'm older. Your turn will come."

Ted almost said 'but it isn't fair' but knew from experience that doing so would have got him nowhere.

The following day the telephone rang. Dolly answered it.

"Mrs Williams? I have news for you. I confirm that the funeral of your late husband can take place on Friday 22nd April, if that is suitable for you and the family."

"Friday 22nd April. I understand," she said. "You'll be aware that we will not be coming up to attend."

"But..."

"I made that very clear when we spoke during my visit and you will have my letter on file summarising what I said."

There was a squawk at the remote end of the line, followed by a stream of words.

"So far as we are concerned it can be a pauper's funeral. If the Town authorities or the Chapel elders want to hold a service over and above that, it is a matter for them to arrange and pay for."

Another outraged squawk came from Chepstow.

"You'll find that we can. On the legal aspect I have confirmed with my brother, a solicitor, that we have no need either to attend or to pay for a ceremony we have no wish for. So kindly confer with the *interested* parties. That does not include us."

Another remote interjection.

"I am perfectly capable of making my own decisions, thank you. I do not need to confer with 'a man' to know what my opinions are and what is best for me. My daughter is of the same mind, *her* mind, without any steering from me. So please do not be condescending."

She brought the call to an end.

"Bron?"

It was the tone of voice Dolly used that startled Bronwen; so different from the usual call asking for her daughter to join her.

"Are you all right, Mum?"

"Angry. I want to know if I'm doing the right thing. Do you want to go to your father's funeral after all?"

There was no hesitation. "No. I don't. I'll go if you do, but it would be to support you, not because I want to remember *him.*"

She would have continued, but Dolly held up her hand.

"I've just had the undertaker assume that we would both be going up, along with 'the family'. Knowing what you have said before I included you in that, but I wanted to ensure that I was right, that you hadn't changed your mind. You're entitled to do so, if you feel you want to or should, and I would go too to support *you.*"

Bronwen was indignant, and showed it. "I still hate him. What he did to me. What he did to us. And particularly what he did to Angharad. Not just now, recently, but for many years before. I used to think that his attitude was normal, then other girls started telling me what their parents thought and did, and allowed and encouraged them to do. It dawned on me over the last three years of school that he was a tyrant, a bully; and that it was right to feel no love for him.

"Oh yes, love went out of the window before then. Well before then."

The thoughts racing through Dolly's mind were of sympathy for her daughter, mixed with envy that she had been able to escape the man while she was at school. For herself it seemed that his presence was constant, even when he had been at work or at his precious Chapel. His aura seemed to hang around the family home like the smell of rancid bacon. She had been unable ever to escape.

"It was no marriage," she said briefly. "It was no daughterhood, either. We were both short-changed; me by an inflexible vow in the marriage service, and you because I felt I had to respect that vow and because a child isn't fitted to make the decision to leave. Until you were a child no longer, and you did just that. At the start I didn't realise what he was like or what he would turn out like, and then it was too late. You had no options.

"It's hardly surprising that neither of us has an iota of love for him."

Dolly was positive. So was Bronwen. There was no desire in her mind to return to Chepstow for whatever reason concerning her hated father.

"Huh!"

It was the third letter that Merryweathers (Solicitors), Salcombe, had received from the Water Board. It contained the second offer they had made following the original decision by the Consortium to refuse the original. At least, he thought, the Board were paying attention. He would need to draft a second courteous letter reminding them that their actions and lack of action had caused three deaths, trauma, a loss of farmland with a consequent loss of business, continuing financial hardship and – this was a new approach – a hardening of attitudes by the local population and their MP concerning their Department.

He drafted the letter carefully and added further large figures for interest on the original, unsatisfied claim, for compensatory interest to recompense those who had had to seek loans. He also increased the main compensation figure.

"It must be stressed," he concluded, "that the figures originally arrived at are not a bargaining position. They were calculated using legal precedent and must be regarded as a minimum. The additional figures I have calculated since then, as each counter offer has been received from the Board, are similarly based on precedent and on the actual hardships and costs that these unfortunate victims have been suffering. It is a suffering that is entirely due to the Board's delays in coming to the obvious conclusion. It is a conclusion with which the Member of Parliament has already stated he concurs. That conclusion is that the families affected have suffered very greatly because of the legally proven failings that occurred and that they must be compensated without further delay." The words were underlined.

"Therefore a daily interest rate will be applied to the claimed amounts, from the receipt of this letter until compensation cheques are received in the full amount of the most recent claims included with this letter. Such compensation cheques must be received by each and every victim, every member of the Salcombe Area Justice Consortium, before this interest figure is regarded as satisfied."

He chuckled again at the observations that Ted had made.

"I must here stress also the word 'Justice'. A word that is an integral part of the Englishman's makeup. It prompts me to consider whether, in the lack of any immediate response from the Board, legal proceedings should be instigated to obtain swift justice for the victims. It is more than likely that the costs involved would be high. Furthermore you already have instructions from Government that compensation is to be paid. We stand no chance of losing such a case. Costs would therefore be awarded against the Board.

"I imagine that would not be what the Board is trying to achieve but, from the Consortium's point of view it will become a necessity if there is no immediate action on the Board's part. In the meantime, as imposed above, the daily interest figure above will continue to be applied."

He read it through once Mrs Damerell had typed it, then added the enclosures and sealed it before he could change his mind.

"Please could you take it to the Post Office immediately, and send it by the quickest means possible? Thank you."

He hoped that he was not making a dreadful mistake. It was a feeling which he, one of the most positive and careful of legal technicians, found disturbing. It occurred to him that what he really needed was an hour in Ted's and Ian's company, time that would always bring him back down to earth.

A week later another letter arrived from the Water Board. It referred firstly to the very real threat of protracted and expensive legal action and their desire to avoid it. It told of their realisation of the pain which those affected most were still suffering.

Merryweathers (Solicitors) started looking for a 'but', a 'however' or a 'nevertheless'. There was none.

It seemed that the dawn of new senior staff appointments, which had resulted from the Kingsbridge and Salcombe events, had brought a sunrise of compassion. The latest demands would be met in full. Final amounts for the cheques being drawn were listed and they hoped this would close the matter. There was the promise that a copy of the letter held by the reader would be sent to the local MP.

Anxiously the amounts were compared with the most recent demands. They tallied. The only missing amount was the daily interest he had stipulated for the delay between his letter and the cheques being received. The fact was noted.

"Henry, have you received a cheque this morning?" he had decided that his friend would be the most logical person to try, so had telephoned him.

"No. But then I've not been to town this morning. Should there be one for me?"

"I rather hope so. When you go in, take a paying-in book with you, and one for whatever account you're using for Mary."

"You're not saying that the Water Board have paid up?"

"I have a letter in front of me to the effect that they are preparing cheques. I was hoping yours might have arrived."

"In that case we will come in right away and check. We'll call in, if that's all right?"

"Please do."

It was only that Susan was expecting that prevented Henry from making the whole journey at top speed. His first encounters with other boats made him slow to a slightly safer rate, and he was almost impatient to get ashore. So much so, in fact, that Susan had to re-tie the painter after his first attempt.

"Sorry," he said. She looked at him accusingly but said nothing.

There was a queue at the post office window, and then the usual wait while the assistant disappeared into the sorting office to fetch their mail.

Given the bundle of envelopes Henry flicked through them and discovered one with the Water Board's name on it. Impatiently he tore it open.

A long letter, and a smaller slip of paper, light blue in colour. Two signatures on the right. He looked at the amount, blinked, shook his head and looked again.

Surely that was too much?

In a husky voice he addressed Susan and told her, sharing the astonishment he had felt.

"We need to check it with your father. Surely it's too much."

"He'll probably say it's only what you deserve, especially going forward, where there will be maintenance bills for boats and jetties, boat fuel, land and a herd to buy. No, I don't think it's too much at all.

"And just think, Mary's is going to be even more. Considerably more. As she deserves. She's going to be a very wealthy young lady."

"But it still won't bring her parents and brother back, will it?" she asked him grimly, trying to bring him back down to earth.

He understood the underlying message. "No. But it will enable her to rebuild a life for herself so she can be independent if she wants."

"I don't think she'll ever want to be independent from Stephen."

"No. And vice versa. But will Stephen think twice about accepting a share in that money? He can be very obstinate, you know."

"Like his father, you mean?"

He grinned. "Something like that. Her letter is here too, you know."

"You can't open it!"

"Susan, darling, what do you take me for? Of course not. But neither am I going to leave it here for Mary to pick up. Come on, let's pay ours in. And Mary's will be waiting for her when she returns from school."

"Should we go and see Dad before we do?"

"Why not? He more or less suggested it."

Her father smiled happily when they were ushered in by Mrs Damerell.

"I take it by your demeanour that you have a cheque and it is in the correct amount."

"We have a cheque, but it seems to be for more than we expected. Is it really correct?"

He looked at the cheque and found the entry on the list of payments enclosed with that morning's letter.

"Yes, that's the correct amount."

"But Dad, it's so much more than we were hoping for. And that's not a complaint, by the way!"

"I confess, my dear, to adding on interest for four years' delay, compensation for interest that individual families have had to pay out and a proportion of the solicitor's fee. I couldn't add a compensation for Henry's time in France..."

The subject of the comment winced.

"...but I've claimed what I thought was ethical. It may have been the mention of a claim in court, or a threat of a daily interest rate to be applied, that hurried them up and made them pay the full amounts – we shall probably never know. But it is an engaging thought that the senior officers of the Board seem to have changed almost entirely over the last few months and we can but hope that the current contingent have a more conciliatory attitude. And that they will maintain their civil works properly.

"Now, the banks are open; are you going to pay that cheque in, or frame it?"

They laughed and went to the Bank, waiting their turn in the queue at one of the tellers' grilles. Slowly, as they moved down toward their target, it became noticeable that they were the only couple who were smiling and talking to each other; other customers were treating the place almost as if it were a church.

The teller took one look at the cheque and poked a piece of paper to them. It was a paying-in slip. Henry looked at him.

"I think you might want to look at the amount on the cheque. Perhaps your manager might be interested."

He received a glare. "All cheques to be paid in have to have a paying in slip."

Henry closed into the grille. "Even those which are for an amount which would buy this bank building and quite a few of the shops on either side?"

This time the man did look at the amount, rose and wordlessly went to an office at the back of the ledger desks that took up the rest of the space.

"Go over there, please," he said, with a very slight lessening of antagonism in his voice. "The Manager will be out to see you in a minute."

Henry smiled at him, wishing he could shout something and waken the man's humanity.

"I think we should advise Mary to choose a different bank, one that has more pleasant staff, don't you?" It was said in a tone loud enough for the teller to hear, although Henry had not intended to do so."

"What about us? Should we?" asked Susan.

"I've been with this lot ever since I started an account," he told her regretfully. "Loyalty counts for something in banking. And the Manager here has been helpful since the flood."

"Let's hope he is today."

Henry gave a bark of laughter. "Today it will be us helping him! Think of the benefit it will be to the bank to have our money to play with. And if Mary was to come here too it would give us a hold over them for a change. Huh! Think of that!" She smiled.

A man was approaching the door at the end of all the tellers' desks and carefully opened it, looking round. Henry approached; he looked alarmed until he recognised his customer. The couple were guided through to the sanctum of the Manager's office, a place where, before, there had been many uncomfortable interviews, some of which had resulted in regretful refusals to offer an advance or a loan.

"I understand there's a problem, Mr Loft," he started.

"I don't think so," replied Henry, surprised. "All I want to do is to pay in a cheque."

"But you were thinking of transferring your account away."

Again a look of surprise crossed Henry's face. "That was a throw-away remark." He thought, slightly annoyed. "Actually, the man I was dealing with was less than helpful, so that's what caused the reaction. Perhaps you should look at the amount of the cheque, and know that my adopted daughter will be receiving an even larger amount which she will need to pay in."

The Manager looked at the cheque and nodded. "I imagine that what he was trying to establish with you was whether you wished to discuss with me the setting up of a deposit account. I'm sure there was no intention to be unhelpful."

"I see. So how does giving me a paying-in slip with no comment fit in with that, please?"

"Then let us start again, may we?" the Manager resumed. "You would like to apply for a deposit account."

"Maybe," Henry told him. "Perhaps you can tell me the types of account there are and what interest they bear. I will also tell my daughter this, so perhaps you could write the information down."

"I will ask one of our people to give you a slip which lists that information and a form to apply for an account. That is the best way forward."

"I wonder why your teller didn't do so at the grille," said Henry, "if that is all that was necessary. But in the meantime I need to pay in this cheque."

"Then if you will complete a paying-in slip, we can ensure that is done."

"I see. Very well, I will take your stationery with me and deal with it."

They completed pleasantries, a little shortly on Henry's part, and left.

"I didn't like his attitude," said Henry as they walked away clutching the paperwork and with the cheque tucked safely into his pocket again.

"I could tell," Susan told him. "So, I should think, could he."

"Do you think I was unfair?"

She hesitated. "Not unfair, just a little abrasive. But it is annoying, knowing that they can't or won't set up an account – a deposit account – immediately so that a large amount can be paid straight into it. If it goes into the current account it will attract no interest to you, but presumably it will do so for the bank."

He nodded. "Indeed. What do you think... and by the way it's *our* money, not mine – about asking in another bank?"

"What about this bank loyalty you were talking about? And it's yours and Stephen's, really. I didn't come into the picture until... later."

He stopped. She looked round in surprise. He walked up to her and put an arm on her shoulder.

"It's *our* money. Yours, Stephen's, mine. We're Family. Mary is a part of that too, but she will be receiving her money separately."

Susan smiled. "I understand. But I wonder what Mary will say about that money."

"You think we should include her in this amount as well?"

"You misunderstand. *I* think she will want us to be included in her compensation amount. She will want to share it with us."

He shook his head. "But that would be wrong. It's hers. Hers and Stephen's – assuming they do actually marry. We should have no part in it."

A smile. "We are at one on that. But Mary might well think differently. In fact I'm almost certain she will."

He pulled a wry face. "I can almost see what you mean, knowing her. We must resist that."

"We must. And don't forget that Stephen and this little chap or girl will be involved as well." She patted her growing bump, despite a scandalised look from an elderly lady who was passing.

"It gets complicated, doesn't it?" he said with a sigh.

"What about this lot?" asked Susan as they approached another bank.

"Why not?"

They entered, to find no queue and a young teller with a smile on his face.

"We're thinking of starting an account, a deposit account of some sort," Susan started, taking the initiative and surprising Henry.

"Certainly, madam. I'll ask our manager to talk to you. May I tell him your name?"

"Henry and Susan Loft," she answered.

"Mr and Mrs Loft. Would that be of Loft Island by any chance?"

"It would," said Henry.

"Then I'm pleased to meet you. I was at school with Stephen. And Mary, though she was in a lower form. So I know your story. And hers, of course. Is she all right now?"

"It's a long story," said Henry warming to him. "But yes, she is. You know..." he hesitated.

"I don't want to intrude," said the young man quickly.

It occurred to Henry that he must be Stephen's age. That he had left school early. If he was a friend of Stephen's, why hadn't he been to visit?

"I'll get Stephen to come in and talk to you," said Henry, wondering if that would be a good idea when the bank was open.

A smile. "After work would be best. Five o'clock any weekday. If you could tell him it's Bob Hannaford, that's me. It'd be good to see him. I'll go and find Mr Selleck."

The Manager turned out to be as Devon as anyone could wish for and had a smile for them both.

Given the cheque, told that Mary's compensation would be even greater and could come his bank's way, and told of the connection between the cafés on Loft Island and in Salcombe, he smiled again.

"I'm really glad that compensation has come your way at last, and more particularly Mary's. Nothing can make up for a loss such as she suffered, but at least now she won't suffer financially. I've heard stories which say that she's a capable young lady and has her own mind, but she will be guided by others into dealing with the money wisely, won't she?"

"My father will make sure of that," said Susan. "He's Mr Merryweather, the solicitor. And we, she, and our son Stephen work as a team."

"And knowing Algy he will do well for her. I wouldn't be surprised if he persuades her to invest. It would be a good idea and should provide a reasonable income."

"I think she and Stephen have their own ideas," Henry told him. "She wants to run a farm, as does he. So I imagine they will be replacing the old Beale farm on dry land, if we can find some available, and building up a business. But it's early days."

"Indeed, and forgive me; it's not my business. But we can certainly help you, and her if she decides, though if she is still a minor there will be the need for someone of age to oversee the account and sign cheques and so on. But you were expecting that, I'm sure."

"It had crossed our minds," said Susan. "As had the possibility of transferring our current accounts – business and personal – over to you so that we have all our eggs in one basket, so to speak."

Selleck smiled. "Normally, as the saying tries to point out, not a good idea. But in terms of banking it's an excellent practice as it gives us an oversight should there ever be the need for a loan, or a mortgage. We shall be happy to help in any way we can."

"Why is your attitude so different from…well, your competitors' down the road?" Henry asked suddenly.

Selleck held his eyes for a moment, then looked out of the window.

"Lovely weather we're having, isn't it?"

His prospective customers laughed.

"So where do we go from here?" asked Henry.

"Let me make a telephone call. That will start the setting up of a deposit account. So long as you're happy with the restrictions of such an account…"

He detailed the one month's notice required to access funds, and certain other conditions, ensured they were content with the 3% interest rate and went into the outside office.

"What a difference," said Susan.

There were forms to complete and sign, which Selleck countersigned, and then he looked at them, smiling.

"There. Not too bad, was it?"

"Not at all," said Henry, returning the smile. "How do we go about transferring our existing accounts, please? If you're happy that we do so, Susan?"

"It seems logical to me. Let's."

"What I suggest is this: you take the forms with you and complete them with details of what Bank stationery you need once you've been able to think about that. Return them a week before you want the transfer to go ahead. And write cheques for, say, half of the credit that's held in any – ahem – other accounts that you want to transfer over. If there are any standing orders, or if you receive standing orders, we can set those up as soon as there's a balance here to set them against.

"Once the accounts are established and running, get balances from the existing bank and write cheques for them. Only then need you write to any other bank and give instructions for account closures.

"How does that sound?"

"If you can guide us when needed, that will be fine," said Henry, and Susan nodded her agreement.

"And if your dau... Mary wants to pay her cheque in to us, starting new accounts, please bring her down and we will make arrangements."

They returned home and laid out Mary's forms with the unopened compensation letter by the side of it to await her return from school.

She, having opened her envelope and read the amount on the cheque, sat down with a bump; fortunately there was a chair behind her.

"It's a fortune," she said faintly.

"Whatever it is, it's no more than you deserve," Henry told her. "You lost more than anyone else."

She was silent. So was Stephen, who looked unhappy. She turned and looked at him.

"What's the matter?"

He shook his head. "It's just so much."

"But we can use it. We can use it to do all the things we want to do. Think of... of our place. Putting a farm there. Maybe buying the land behind it and farming it. As part of Loft's farm, of course, once Henry and Susan have decided what to do about it."

There was a look of hope now. "Is that really what you want? With me?"

She was shocked. "There has never, ever, been any doubt that it'll be with you. Who did you think it would be with? Or have you found someone else?"

He was kneeling by her in a second. "Never. Never. Never. I just thought... it's so much money that you'd want to go travelling, go to London or something, and use some of it on... other things. Without me."

"Without you? Why would I want to do that? Anything I did, I'd want you there too. Travelling?" She laughed. "Not all that long ago I travelled down from Scotland. That was enough travelling for now!

"But going to London and using it on something there? Why? Wouldn't that be wasting it? And wasting it would be – well, somehow insulting Mum, Dad and Greg. They'd be unhappy if I just went and frittered it away on something like... well, like just having a good time. Don't you feel that?"

He was watching her face, and could see that she was sincere. As always.

"Yes," he said, and could feel himself becoming emotional. She was so *nice*, such a good, feeling person. A stab of memory brought back Greg's face to him; not the pale, wet face of a boy dying in his arms from a mortal injury, but the grinning, healthy, ruddy face of his closest childhood friend. "Yes. We need somehow to bring back Beale's farm into existence, and honour them."

She kissed his forehead. "I *love* you, Stephen Loft."

The bank needed the account holder to be present for an account to be started, even if the only signatories on it were to be her guardians until she was no longer considered a minor. Mary had to engineer half an afternoon off school so as to be able to arrive at the bank before it closed at 3.30. Stephen was with her and recognised Bob Hannaford with pleasure, though Bob's eyes were slipping sideways all the time to look at Mary.

"I see you've noticed my fiancée," said Stephen in a tone which held a hint of warning.

"Fiancée? Oh, wow. I thought you were his sister, and was puzzled as I couldn't remember you having one."

Mary laughed. "No, I'm Mary Beale. And now we're engaged."

"Mary Beale... oh, of course. I should have put two and two together. Sorry. But you're... you're..."

"Older?" she teased.

He sighed. "Of course. But...but..."

"Mr Hannaford, are these my visitors? Could you show them in, please?"

"Sorry, Mr Selleck. Just being polite."

"So I see. And you can be polite after we've closed and you can take them for a coffee. But now?"

"Sorry, Mr Selleck. Will you go through, please?" He was back on firmer ground, sure of what to say. He was no longer tongue tied because he wanted to say that Mary was beautiful but didn't want to do so with her fiancé there.

Mr Selleck was pleased to see them again, and particularly pleased to see Mary and to take her cheque so as to be able to set up a deposit account for her.

"She'll need a current account too," Henry told him. "And I think Stephen should have his own account, don't you?"

Very many forms were signed that afternoon.

Whilst Henry and Susan went to pay a visit to Uncle Bert, as he was now known universally by the family, and from there to visit Annabelle, Angharad and the boys, Mary and Stephen waited for Bob to appear when he was released from work.

They went into the Ferry Inn as it was closest. Stephen hesitated.

"It's all right. I had my eighteenth birthday last month," Bob told him. "You're taller than me, so you'll be fine."

Bob was not asked for his guests' ages. The landlord knew him. He felt that the others looked old enough, especially the man with him. The girl, who seemed to be the man's girlfriend, looked younger, but as she was having a soft drink that was all right. Stephen would have been intrigued had he known the landlord's thought processes. Bob had bought pints of bitter for Stephen and himself. Mary had dug in her heels and asked for ginger beer.

There were quite a few early tourists in the pub, despite it being only mid-

May. The island dwellers wondered how many of them would find their way to Loft Island in the next few days.

It was a pleasant session of reminiscing about school life, even if Stephen was still there studying for GCE 'A' levels in June or July; it would be his last school year. Mary was due to sit GCE 'O' levels at about the same time. Bob had left after 'O' levels and found a job.

"Banks are a good bet," he said. "They'll always need people. And if you're any good you can get promoted quickly. You can in our bank, anyway."

"Dad says the bank near you is hopeless."

He grinned. "They're still in the last century. Our lot have decided that banks should serve people, not the other way round. We're even going to stay open later, Mr Selleck says. And Head Office are doing an awful lot of advertising."

"Does that mean working later?" Mary asked.

"Shouldn't do, normally. We've modernised the whole thing, using accounting machines."

"What?"

"Accounting machines. Somehow they let you put information in, then you set it going. Eventually it tells you if what you think you've got in the branch equals the money that's actually there. Interesting things. You press a button, it chunters away to itself for a bit, then comes up with the result on a sheet of paper. Saves all the horrendous adding up of columns of figures when you just want to shut up and go home. Or to the pub."

Mary shook her head. "Beats me. It sounds like a conjuring trick."

Conversation turned to Loft Island and the happenings of the last few years. Bob was interested to hear about Martin, whom he knew, and Bronwen. He was horrified to hear of the reasons why she, her mother and maid came to Salcombe.

"It must have been bad enough for Bronwen and her mother," he said thoughtfully, "but for Angharad it must be the most ghastly experience imaginable. Imagine being raped, then torn away from your family. Poor girl."

Although the other two had had sympathy for Angharad, it was the first time anyone had really spoken of her experiences in that vein. Being caring types they each felt guilty that they had left her to Dolly, Bronwen and their joint grandfather to look after.

"I know," said Mary suddenly. "Why don't we make up a party and go out somewhere? We three, Martin and Bron, and Angharad? Even if it's just a night out in a pub."

"Would she come?" wondered Stephen. "Has she recovered yet?"

"I don't think you ever recover, really recover, from something like that," Mary told them. "I was lucky in Scotland, but it could have happened to me. It took some time to get over that, though you helped by taking me on."

This was to Stephen, who smiled and then grew serious. "If he had... had done anything like that I'd have... I'd have half killed him. And Grandad would by now be defending me in court."

"Excuse me?" Bob asked. "What is this about Scotland, and who is Grandad?"

Mary explained her encounter with the temporary teacher. Stephen explained how Mr Merryweather had been adopted by them both.

156

He was shocked into silence, then just said "Phew! You have been through it, Mary."

"Not as much as Angharad though."

"No," he said thoughtfully, "not as much as Angharad. Yes. I'd like to meet her – meet with you all. It'd have to be a Friday evening or over the weekend, for me."

"We probably can't manage weekends because the café's so busy," said Mary. "And Martin can't do… well, we'll just have to persuade him to leave work early on a Friday night."

"What does he do?" Bob asked.

"He's just started with an independent architect. We think he's very clever – he's designed an extension for our house on Loft's so as to get the café into it, provide toilets and make life easier."

"But he's our age."

"Yes. He's not qualified, but he just seems to have the knack."

"I remember him making a fuss about doing technical drawing. He must have got on a bit from there." Bob was impressed. "Anyway, how about next Friday?"

"Er…" Mary dropped her voice. "…Stephen's eighteen on the thirteenth. That's the Tuesday after. Could it be the week after that?"

"Fine by me," Bob responded. "And happy birthday for next Tuesday."

"What are you doing for your birthday?" Mary asked.

Stephen shrugged. "No one's made any comment about it. It's not like I'm still eight. Birthdays don't mean as much now."

"*I* think they do. And you deserve something."

He shrugged again.

At last they left.

"Should we have asked him to come to the Island, do you think?" asked Stephen.

"In time. It's early days."

They visited the Merryweather house to collect Susan and Henry and to ask the other three out after Stephen's birthday. It was Angharad who answered the door and she smiled shyly at them.

"Hallo Angharad. It's you we want to see, actually. We want you, Bron and Martin to come and have a drink with us in a couple of weeks. It'd be a Friday night. We've met up with one of Stephen and Martin's friends from school – Bob Hannaford – who works in a local bank."

Dolly appeared in the background before she could answer.

"Oh, hallo, you two. Good to see you. Come in."

They did. Angharad was about to slip back into the kitchen but Dolly firmly steered her into the front room with the others.

"I heard the last part of what you said. Your place is in here with us, Angharad. You're not a maid. Not here."

Angharad stopped herself from bobbing in a sort of curtsey and smiled faintly.

"It's just that we've met up with an old school friend of Martin's and mine, and arranged an evening in a pub so that we can chat. Friday week."

Stephen was almost asking for Dolly's permission.

"You're under eighteen, aren't you, Stephen? Is it a good idea?"

"I'm eighteen next Tuesday. Bron, Martin and Bob Hannaford are already over eighteen. So it's only Mary and Angharad who are below, and they can drink soft drinks, can't they? Can't you?"

Mary smiled; Angharad blinked.

"I'm going," said Mary to the Welsh girl, "and I'd really like you to be there so we can just relax and chat. And Bron is a friend of yours, isn't she?"

Angharad nodded, still too shy to speak in a large group.

"Then you'll come? Please?"

She looked hopelessly around the eager group. It was the first time that this had happened to her, ever. She was used to one, or at the most two, people talking to her, but she'd never had a group inviting her to be with them. All of them seemed really to want her to come. And if Bronwen was there, and Martin; and Stephen had been with her on that journey from Chepstow, and Mary had been through a horror herself, and she must know what it was like.

Slowly her mind cleared, and cautiously she nodded.

"Yes, please. I'll come."

She hardly expected the chorus of pleasure that greeted those four words.

19 – Planning starts

"You'll be around this weekend, Stephen, won't you?"

"The café's open, so yes, of course."

"No plans when it's shut?"

"No... Why?"

Susan hesitated.

"Will you just trust me, and be here?"

"Is this to do with a birthday?"

She closed her eyes tightly. "I asked you to trust me."

"Ok, ok... I'll be here. Short of haring over to Salcombe or somewhere there's not a lot else to do."

Her eyes opened wide. "You're not getting bored with the Island, are you?"

"No, no of course not. But it's nice to go and be somewhere else occasionally."

"Where, particularly?"

"I don't know. It doesn't matter where. Just somewhere different. For a change. What do they say? A change is as good as a rest? Well, after the exams I think I'm going to need a rest. A change. I don't want to leave the Island, as I said, but just something completely different from school and the café would be nice. For a week. Or for two. Mary and I never seem to do anything but pass like ships in the night."

"So how about taking her somewhere else?"

"What, this weekend?"

"No! After the exams."

It dawned on him, like a stab of sunlight from under a cloud-laden sky, that this could mean being together. Spending evenings together.

Sharing a hotel room?

Unbidden, a shiver ran down his spine.

With difficulty he dragged his libido back from the brink, knowing that Mary would probably not accept what he was yearning for, that it wouldn't be fair, that she had another two years of school ahead of her, and then maybe University. He had declined the idea of University for himself, knowing that even with the family's new wealth it would be a cost they could do without if the farm was to be revitalised.

And anyway, what about Mary? Was she intending to continue studying? To follow a University course? They had never discussed it, for the simple reason that they never had enough leisure time together to do so. Long gone were the days of sharing a room, a bed, in the far away days of their innocent childhood. He pulled a face, uselessly wishing himself back there, but realising that at the time he would never had known about their intended future together, never have even dreamed about University and its application to either or both of them.

Or should they both go to University? And if they did, would they see each other? No. Probably not. Different Colleges. Maybe different towns. Too much money, anyway.

But would it be, for Mary? She had much more compensation than they had. And she had no impending baby to think of.

Which though, unaccountably, brought him back to the idea of spending time in a hotel room with her. He pulled another face.

"Sorry. I need to... to... I'll be back in a minute."

Susan had a dim idea of the attraction of being on their own somewhere different, but had she known of his more explicit thoughts she would have been surprised at first, then understanding, then worried.

Mary and Henry joined her, it having been their turn to feed the few animals left on the Island. She had been banned from helping, as the baby was due in five months.

Mary detected the air of puzzlement.

"What's up? He hasn't planned something for this weekend, has he?"

"No, my dear. I mentioned the possibility of a break for you both after the exams were finished, he'd left school for the last time, and you had started your holiday. He seemed to be – well – quiet for some time. Then he rushed upstairs."

She smiled. "I was thinking about doing something in the holidays, even if it *is* the café's busiest time. If we did, could you get someone else in? Would that be too much to ask?"

"We have the boys now, if they want to help still," Henry said. "And Ted's old enough to do an adult's work, more or less. But we can easily hire help at that time. There are plenty of students about!"

"So you wouldn't mind?"

"No. Not at all. But what about you two?"

"I'd... I'd love it. Stephen would too. But where we'd go, and what we'd do, I really don't know."

"Have you asked him?"

"No – you've only just suggested it."

"I didn't," Henry reminded her. "Susan said that Stephen wanted to."

"Best you talk about it. Together," Susan put in.

Mary wondered what the others were thinking about. The idea of being on their own for a long period – say a week, maybe two – attracted her. What would they do? Where would they go? Would they camp? Would they... would they share a tent? After all this time would they actually be sleeping together as they had when they were kids?

But they weren't kids. Not really. And would Stephen want...? They couldn't. they shouldn't. Should they? What would happen?

She stopped herself, hoping the sudden heat she felt rising to her cheeks wasn't visible as a blush.

"Excuse me," she said. "I'll be back in a minute."

Susan and Henry were left looking at each other in surprise. Why should a break, a simple break away, cause so much apparent mental turmoil? Surely they weren't contemplating an actual liaison? A physical one?

"Are you sure... Do you think that we are letting them get too close together?" Susan wondered.

"The thought had occurred to me. But no hotel would allow kids of their age to book a hotel where they were together. Not in Britain."

"I hope you're right."

"I'll talk to Stephen, shall I? And you talk to Mary?"

That seemed wrong to her. Stephen was too close to his father to take it seriously. If he took Mary and she took Stephen, it might come over with more immediacy.

As Mary walked slowly up the stairs she saw Stephen at the top. He was looking at her in a wide-eyed way she couldn't remember having seen before. A finger went up to his lips. His head inclined to the direction of his room. Hesitantly she followed him in. He sat on the bed, the bed she had once shared with him as a child. There wouldn't be enough room for that now. Not to sleep. Not really. Not without being too close to him for comfort. But then...

He patted the bed beside him. Obediently she sat.

"How do you feel about going somewhere in the school holidays? Just us two?"

So this was it, she thought. Do I risk... it?

The long look, the doubt that started on her face and then vanished, unsettled him. "If you'd rather not, just say, and we can stay here and sail. And perhaps think about what you want to do about Beales' farm."

A sudden smile. "I'd love to go away. But where?"

"I was thinking. Did you and Greg ever read any Arthur Ransome? I can't remember seeing the books in his room."

"I did. He wasn't really much of a reader – apart from the *Eagle* every week. But I know you've got some of the books."

"Yes. And I was thinking about going up to the Lake District and sailing on the lakes where the books are set. How do you like the idea?"

She thought for all of a second.

"Can we camp on Wild Cat Island?"

"If we're allowed to," he laughed. "That would really be something! Maybe in better tents than theirs. Or just one tent."

He cursed himself. He shouldn't have added that. It would make a choice awkward. I would scare her off.

So this was it, she thought. Not a hotel. Not a double room. Not even a choice of two single rooms or two beds in the same room. But a tent. Sleeping alongside him, as they had in that very room all those years ago, when neither of them were aware of what people thought, or what might have happened had they been only a little older.

The memory of *that* day came to her mind, that hot day when they had both forgotten their swimming things, when they had been – what? Twelve and thirteen? When they both threw caution to the winds and stripped off completely. And she saw, for the first time...

The boy. A real, older boy. In all his innocent glory. And how, then, they just swam and dived and played and dried on the sand next to each other, unashamed but, in her case, fiercely proud of their more-than-friendship. Maybe he had felt the same.

And now that more-than-friendship had somehow become an equally fierce attraction, and had become love (the two are different); so much so that they were engaged to spend the rest of their lives together as a married couple.

"Yes," she whispered. "Just one tent."

He looked her straight in the eyes, for a moment unsure. His expectation had been that she would somehow quietly insist on the sleeping being separate. For a moment he faltered. Could he... would it be possible to...

Would anything come out of this holiday that they didn't want?

"We'll have to be careful," she said.

As his arm raised to circle her shoulders as so often before, he could feel himself trembling.

They made their way downstairs again and broke the news of the decision to Susan and Henry, but without any details of the sleeping arrangements.

"Well, at least we can afford it now," said Henry.

"We have enough between us," said Mary, without thinking.

"Have you?"

"We've each been keeping the café money. And Stephen saved most of his from last year."

"And you have enough, yourself," Henry said quietly.

She looked uncomfortable. "That's for reinstating the farm. Not for... for having fun."

"Don't you think they would have wanted you to have a break? A holiday? I think it's only right that you should, after what you went through. They would have agreed. And by now I should think Greg would have found himself a girlfriend, and would have wanted to come with you, or go somewhere else with her. No parent would try and stop that, so long as the people were sensible."

The thought occurred to them simultaneously: was that a warning shot?

"How do we go about booking it?" asked Stephen. "We travel up by train to Bristol, then from there to... where?"

"The Lakes. Where's the nearest place?"

"No, Dad. I meant where is Wild Cat Island"

"What?"

"Wild Cat Island. Where the Swallows and Amazons camped. That's where we want to go."

"Good heavens. I should get some maps from somewhere. See if you can identify it from the books, though it'll be a needle in a haystack, I imagine."

"The books have maps," Mary told him. "So all we have to do is look at maps in the library and match them up."

"When do we get a chance of doing that?"

"Does the school have maps of the Lake District?" asked Stephen.

"I know they produced a map of Corfe Castle for a practice GCE," Mary told him. "Maybe they do. At least they could tell us where to find one."

Susan cleared her throat. "This all started with my checking that Stephen would be around this weekend. He is. Good. You two get planning. It's only May, so you have some time. Just don't leave it too long."

"What's this weekend, then?" asked Stephen. "Isn't anyone going to tell me?"

Glances were exchanged around the room, looks that even he noticed.

"No," they said in chorus, and then laughed.

Maps were indeed sought out at the school the following day and Stephen – who had less on his academic plate than Mary, formally speaking, discovered that they had all those covering the Lake District.

"Why do you want them?" asked the English teacher, who was also the

Librarian. Stephen told her their plans.

"Oh, that's simple. The lake's based on Windermere – you know not to call it 'Lake Windermere', I hope – and the Island is on Coniston."

"Oh… it's not an actual place, then?"

"It's a combination of two real places, so you should visit both if you want to get the full feeling for the books."

He thought.

"May I have a look at the maps, please? Or better still, may I borrow them overnight?"

It was prime sailing weather, so Mary and Stephen had elected to start very early and sail on the morning's rising tide to Kingsbridge. Ian Rawle, the younger brother, had befriended Stephen – and Mary – after being scared of him for so many years. Stephen noticed his infectious grin as they turned away from the bus that evening on their way back to the boat. Mary saw his face fall.

"Should we let him come with us?"

Stephen thought, looked back and shrugged his shoulders.

"Suppose we could. That means that Ted could take the maps, stop them falling into the water."

"Are you criticising my sailing?"

He grinned. "Wouldn't dream of it, Captain."

They changed course towards the bus.

"Hallo, Stan, good to see you. We're sailing home tonight and we wondered if we could borrow a crew from you."

"You want me, boy? Who's going to drive the bus, then?"

He laughed. "One day, maybe…"

The rest of the conversation was drowned out by young voices shouting "Me! Me!" He laughed again.

"We need someone who's got a brother on board. Ian? Are you there?"

The lad jumped up, hit his head on the luggage rack, sat down again hard, and then rose more cautiously, grinning again.

"If you give these to Ted for safe keeping, you can sail home with us, if you want to."

There was a scurrying, a snatching of maps and a throw, and he was on the road with them, looking like a Cheshire cat.

"Can you look after the maps, please Ted? We'll collect them at the Hard. And it'll be your turn next time."

A incomprehensible answer came from the middle of the bus.

Although Ian was by then quite adept at handling the launch and smaller motor boats, he had never sailed before. So it was the same baptism of fire for him on the journey down the Estuary as it had been for his tutors four or so years previously. After the flood the dinghy, this dinghy, had been offered back to Mary from Susan's home where it had been kept.

Now, the wind, though not strong, was enough to have them heeling over from time to time, as much as a clinker-built, broad beamed dinghy can heel. Ian was again beaming like a Cheshire cat by the time they reached Salcombe's Hard.

"Can I do that again?" he said in a wheedling voice. "That was blinking marvellous!"

"Depends on the weather, really," Stephen told him. "Sometimes it's too rough, and frequently the tide's wrong. I think you'd always be welcome, though. Mary? What do you think?"

She thought that he'd had a pretty dreadful life so far, and the more they could make up for it, the better. "Yes. Good idea. We'll need to be fair to Ted as well, though."

He jumped in the air. Fortunately by this time he was out of the boat but slipped on the weedy surface of the Hard and fell on his bottom. He shook his head as if to dismiss it and jumped back to his feet.

"Oops. Thanks. Thanks a lot. See you tomorrow."

He was about to run off, blissfully unaware of the green slime on the back of his shorts, when Stephen called him back.

"What about our maps, Ian?"

"These maps?" said a voice nearby. Ted, also grinning at his brother's fall.

"Thanks, Ted Have you been waiting long? You'll get your chance soon. Maybe we can have a go at the weekend, if it's not too blowy."

"I'd like that," he said. "I've sailed before, but it was a long time ago, when... Dad was better."

Mary felt a sudden stab of sorrow for him, but just nodded.

"We'll soon get you back to it," she told him.

Susan and Henry had taken the plunge and visited the estate agents who were handling the sale of land that he had been told about when prospecting for land prices. The agent told them where it was.

"That rings a bell," said Henry. "That abuts Beale land, doesn't it?"

"Er..."

The agent examined the drawing.

"It certainly has some land between it and the banks," he said, "and I think that may have been Beale land, yes."

"It still is, surely."

"I suppose so. But I don't know who owns the estuary bed now. Has it been taken over by the water board?"

"Not as far as I know," Henry told him with some spirit. "They would have had to buy it if that was the case. And there has been no contact from the Land Registry. I suppose I had better check with the Post Office again to see if more letters have arrived for Mary, addressed to the old farm."

"If it still belongs to the Beales, and you are looking after Mary Beale, it should become yours. That makes this parcel of land more valuable."

"It wouldn't be ours, but Mary's. So actually it only makes the land more valuable to her and Stephen, if they marry and inherit the farm."

"But we don't know what this little chap or girl will want," Susan reminded him.

He looked at her aghast. "All these months, and I still can't get used to the idea. Sorry. I think a family conference is required."

Mary and Stephen, full of plans for the Lake District, were pulled up short by the details of the land. Seeing where it was, they looked at each other.

"Just up from… well, you know."

"From where?" Henry asked.

Stephen sighed. "It's a place we used to play when we were younger." He hesitated. "It has special memories."

Mary nodded.

"Well, wherever the boundary is, that's where this land starts. It goes up to the top of the hill and over that headland, between the estuary itself and Frogmore creek."

"I suppose it's not the old Manor lands, is it?" asked Susan. "Charlton Court?"

Henry looked again.

"By gum yes it is. I hadn't realised the scale of this or where the village was. It's a big area, bigger than I expected. And there's a lot of good land there, too. I don't know if the old rifle range is still used, but if not we might be able to do something with the marshy bit between the fields too."

"Watercress," said Mary.

"Wha… Good grief, I'd not have thought of that. Why not? And anything else that likes running water."

"Henry…"

Mary again, sounding thoughtful and hopeful in equal measures.

He looked at her, wondering.

"How would it be if Stephen and I, and Susan and you, bought the land between us?"

He looked at her in wonder. Why had he not thought of that as a possibility?

"That way," she continued, "we could farm it together. We could keep the part that's near 'our' bit, the Beale land, but the rest of it we could look after between us. You know, manage it as a business and do what's best for each of us. Then, if any other land comes up for sale we could buy it, and adjust who pays for what, so that your new arrival will have a farm of his or her own if they want."

"They?" asked Susan in alarm.

"He or she!" Mary exclaimed. "And if not we could continue to farm it so as to provide an income for the two parts of the family."

There was silence when she stopped, as everyone thought furiously, looking for drawbacks.

At length Henry let out a long sigh. "I've been so worried about what we do, what you do, with all this money. I could see circumstances where it could come between us, because there's not a lot of land to be had in the area, especially after the estuary flooded. But what you suggest overcomes any unpleasantness before it starts. Thank you, Mary.

"What does Susan think? What does Stephen think?" she asked.

"It sounds extremely sensible to me," said Susan. "But what we don't know is what Stephen has decided to do after his 'A' Levels. Is University on your horizon, Stephen?"

He pulled a wry face. "I think Mary's idea is great. And if we do as Mary suggested I want to be involved on the farm. With the farm. As I think she would be, too. We'll need some help, because there's a lot to do to get it right, I should

165

think. As to University, I suppose it has its attractions. But then I was helping Dad for years before the flood, just as Mary and Greg helped their parents on Beales'. That's what I want to do. Maybe I could do a course on farming somewhere, if there is one, but other than that I just want to be here. Farming. And with Mary."

He looked at her. She touched his hand.

"I think the same," she said. "I'm not even sure about 'A' Levels. I'd rather be here and if necessary study farm book-keeping or some other specialist part of farming. And I don't mean watercress growing!"

They laughed, but Henry became serious again quickly.

"I suppose that if you change your mind, or if there's a course that will help you or attract you, you could still follow it. If Martin can follow a correspondence course, so can you. But don't forget that if you *do* decide to go for 'A' Levels or any other qualification at any time, we're on your side. We'll do everything we can to make it possible."

She smiled. "Thank you. All of you."

Susan looked at her. "Mary, once again, you're family. We're not being kind, we're just doing what families do."

Susan and Henry visited the estate agent the following day and started the ball rolling to buy the land. They also visited Merryweathers to tell Uncle Bert and to thank him.

The first impression of his outer office was that it had reopened as a florist. Mrs Damerell seemed dazed, as were they, at the bowls of flowers and profusion of plants around the walls.

"His office has rather fewer of them," she said. "He said he needed to keep his decorum, though I'm not sure what he means in this context."

"Where are they all from?" asked Susan, amused.

"They're compliments from the farmers and their wives who have received their cheques from the Water Board. Everyone seemed to have latched on to the idea that flowers are the best way of saying 'thank you'. He was really embarrassed to read some of the cards and letters that accompanied them, they were so fulsome. And some of them were written by these hard-bitten old farmers themselves, people you'd have never imagined could do such a thing."

"I think he deserves them," said Susan. "He's not a bad old stick."

"You have a vested interest, my dear," said Mrs Damerell, smiling. "But you're right. He's not. He's a lovely man and I shall be sorry, in many ways, when I retire."

"You aren't thinking of retiring, surely?"

"Well yes. Didn't I mention it? Hasn't he mentioned it? I shall be of an age to retire by the end of the summer."

"But you can't... I mean, you're such a part of his work. You're a fixture. Whatever will he do without you?"

She smiled. "Thank you, my dear, for the implied compliment. I'm sure there are many younger models available who will fill my shoes."

"I think my father would say that they are impressive shoes to fill, Mrs Damerell," Susan said quietly.

The lady blushed. "You'd better go in before I become too big for them; all

166

these compliments," she said with a smile.

He was in a good mood. "What do you think of my conservatory?" he asked with a happy smile. "People have been really nice, don't you think?"

"No more than you deserve," said Henry. "We haven't thanked you enough, but I hope we'll be able to do so at Stephen's get-together this Saturday. You are still able to come, I hope?"

"Of course I will. I wouldn't dream of missing my grandson's birthday party, nor would any of the others in my new, large household whom you've invited."

"Angharad as well?"

"She was a little reluctant – no, that's not the word. She was surprised that you would want her there too."

Henry smiled. "That young lass needs to realise that she's wanted in the world."

"If I may promote an opinion, it is not in the world that she needs help. It is in the more immediate circumstances of where she is. Here, and with us, rather than with her parents at home.

"The matter has been concerning Dolly, too. She is now horrified that it became so easy for her family to come to regard her as a part of the household in Wales, yet part of neither their nor her own family. She quickly became just "The Maid", and as we know she was treated by Mr Williams as merely a possession. As a result, for reasons I confess I'm unable to fathom, her mother declines to welcome her back, though her father is more accepting.

"She is only sixteen or so, and has as good an education as a small school could give. I see, at home, that when she can forget her immediate past she is bright, and on the rare occasions when she can bring herself to talk to me she shows a perhaps surprising intelligence. Though why it should be surprising I don't know. We all have an intelligence, after all; some more than others. Not all are recognised. I should be ashamed of myself for being surprised at the level of hers. She has as much right to an intelligence as anyone else."

"How has she been getting on?" asked Susan.

"She is still very quiet and self-effacing. Left to herself she would volunteer no conversation. We talk to her as much as we can to bring her into family matters, though it is difficult. The people to whom she talks most freely are Ted and Ian, particularly Ted. It's difficult to realise that the two are only two years apart, although Martin is becoming quite surprised that his child brother is so much less of a child nowadays."

"How old *is* Ted?" asked Susan.

"Fourteen. His birthday was in October so I suppose he's halfway to fifteen."

Henry remembered the tragedy of four years previously when his thirteen-year-old son's attitude and abilities had been tested so severely. He recalled also the boy's actions and maturity in the months that followed, the months during which he had subtly changed from being a boy to a young man.

"Perhaps he and Ian are the best tonic for her," he said.

"They are. Up to a point. That point is that we have no real idea how much of an adult Ted is in her eyes, and how much she is encouraged by his interest in her to talk to older people."

"Ted's interest in her?" prompted Susan.

"Perhaps that was not the phrase I should have used. Certainly the two talk, but so do she and Ian. No, I gave the wrong impression there."

Susan nodded. "But two or three years' difference..."

"No. Read nothing into it, please. I doubt it is a possibility that he would be attracted to her in that way, not at fourteen. And she, no doubt, would be horrified if someone thought that a boy, not even yet a man, should be the object of her affections."

But Henry's mind returned to the near-invisible, yet budding, attraction that had existed between Stephen and Mary, almost fourteen and barely twelve respectively. Even if in that case the genders had been reversed. No, he told himself. He must not jump to conclusions.

"But the reason for your coming to visit me was not just social, I'm sure. Has something happened? Do you need my help, professional or otherwise?"

The couple looked at each other. Susan nodded.

"We have decided, before it's too late, to tell the nearest estate agent that we want to buy the land that is on their books. Happily, its south-eastern boundary marches with the remnants of the Beales' land. The rest of it is quite extensive. We think it's partially the remnants of the old Charlton Court lands."

"I know more or less where you mean, and as you say it will do what you wish. But what does Mary – I suppose I should include Stephen in that – think of the idea? She – they – wanted to resume farming too, I believe. Stephen has a foot in both camps, as it were."

"We've had a family conference," Susan told him. "The only person we couldn't ask was this little person." She patted her belly gently. Her father, from a different generation, winced.

"Sorry, my dear. I should move more with the times. It's just that... Well, please continue."

"What we want to do is to buy the land jointly between Mary and the Lofts and farm it between us, as a partnership. Stephen is more than happy with that; Mary is as well, and so are we. Stephen has decided in favour of farming from now on, and Mary has decided against continuing at school for the same reason. We have made it plain that any further study she decides on later will receive our absolute blessing."

"May I see the details, please?" her father asked. His tone was non-committal.

Henry passed it to him. It was scanned with great care. The only sounds in the office were the ticking of the clock and muted voices from Fore Street. The window was open.

"Is there a problem?" asked Henry eventually.

The solicitor met his eyes, and smiled.

"I have been wondering what the end of the saga of the compensation would turn out to be," he said. "It seems you are very lucky indeed to have found that particular parcel of land. It seems ideally situated for each branch of the family. Your idea of joint ownership is not a new one, and it is a course of action that will keep the Beale and Loft contingents on the best possible terms."

He sighed. "I have to admit to you now that I was worried. I was all but certain that Mary would be blessed with a large amount of compensation and was confident that she would want to reinstate Beales Farm in some way or another.

168

Also I knew that you would want to reinstate Loft Farm with your and Stephen's compensation. My worry was that money has a dreadful way of driving wedges, both between people and into families. Poverty seems to bring them together."

Another sigh, and this time they could tell it was a sigh of relief. "None of us knows yet how the farm will work alongside the café, and who will ultimately be responsible for what. But this arrangement seems to give you all, including the member of the family still to be born, the best possible chance of making a long-term, profitable business. Or should I say a combination of businesses? Because inevitably your milk will be used for the cafés – don't forget the Salcombe café! – and if that, why not cream and butter too? And if that, why not cheese? Maybe even ice cream; that seems to be the up and coming treat. Perhaps that is where Mary could gain expertise, not just in the farming but in the processing afterwards."

There was another silence, shorter this time, as Susan and Henry looked at each other, surprised.

"We never thought of that, Dad," said Susan.

"Sometimes it takes a third party to offer something to the pot, just as seasoning, and then only if accepted by the cooks."

"I think we like your seasoning! Please always offer advice."

He smiled. "Shall I start the ball rolling with the purchase? Who is the vendor?"

They admitted that they didn't know.

20 – Boatyard

"Let's get going, then." Henry was trying to chivvy up Stephen to make the journey into Salcombe with them.

"Why the rush, Dad? What are you planning?"

"Planning? Me? What makes you think that? We just want to get going."

"There's still washing up to do! The last lot have only just left."

"For once that can wait. We don't get out for social time very often. Your birthday gives us an excuse."

"Ok, ok… I'm ready now."

The thing with Stephen was he looked acceptable in whatever he was wearing, thought Henry. The slacks and shirt he had worn for four hours in the café still seemed pristine and tidy. How did he do it?

They used the launch for the voyage to the town. With the boat moored at The Hard Henry said nothing but just led them along Fore Street, turning left up Market Street. Stephen assumed they were visiting Uncle Bert but was surprised when they continued up the hill. He was even more surprised when Henry led Mary and him into the Knoll Hotel. There was a hum of voices from behind a door. Henry opened it and ushered the two inside, following them in with a widely smiling Susan at his side.

It was like entering a village pub. As they appeared there was a near-immediate silence before people started with a mixture of "Happy Birthday", "About time!", "You're late", and some more general pleased exclamations.

Stephen was dazed. The nearest people to him were Martin and Bronwen, the latter having Angharad's hand firmly in hers.

"Thank goodness," said Martin. "Now we can have something to eat. My brothers are nearly dead of famine over there. Angharad, Bron and I are weakening, too."

"Idiot," Stephen responded, automatically. "Whose idea was this, anyway?"

"A general one, I think. Your Dad and Susan said that they needed to surprise you, we all agreed, and it just grew out of that."

'This' was a gathering, not just of the local friends, but those who had touched their lives over the previous few years. Friends from school, those who had attended Mary's family's and Simon Rawle's funerals; Edgar Mustchin and Charlie from the boatyard; the younger Rawles, their aunt and, naturally, Uncle Bert whose smiling face was the next he saw.

"Are you sure you weren't responsible for all this, Grandad?" asked Stephen.

"Not guilty, though if someone hadn't suggested a get-together I should have done."

"Why would anyone bother so much?"

He couldn't understand the look he received. All he got, apart from a smile was: "Decline to comment, as apparently they said in the Navy when asked awkward questions."

He grinned back, still wondering.

Ted's and Ian's eyes kept wandering to the laden table of food the hotel had provided. Quietly their brother crossed to them.

"For goodness sake, you two. Leave it alone. It's only food. You see it every day."

He had started speaking in a fairly loud voice to be heard over the conversation. Simultaneously, Henry had shushed everyone. His last two sentences were heard by everyone.

Angharad looked at him, her mouth open, clapped a hand to her face and roared with laughter, followed a moment afterwards by everyone else. Even the intended subjects grinned. It didn't stop them looking at the table, though.

Through the meal, conversation flowed naturally. Most of them were at least acquainted with each other. Mary and Bronwen ensured Angharad was included in conversations, especially with their and Stephen's friends. Angharad kept noticing looks, sometimes frankly appreciative looks, in her direction, and kept blushing.

In her mirror all she was ever able to see was a thin girl with dark hair and dark, unhappy eyes. The young bloods, many of whom were just about to leave school for ever, saw an attractively dressed, really good looking girl of their age, with shoulder length, naturally wavy near-black hair, a most attractive face, and those eyes which looked as if you could lose yourself in them. And a voice which, shy and occasionally used though it was, sounded mellow and tinged with that enticing accent from the mysterious land of Wales.

Gradually she found that the young bloods were to be found hovering near her. Some even managed to pluck up the courage to try and start a conversation. But she was wary, cautious, unwilling to become even remotely close to any male who seemed remotely 'interested' in her. She had spiritual scars which were still too raw.

Ted and Ian, the incident of the compass still in their minds, sought out Edgar Mustchin, who listened gravely to the story and made some pertinent comments. He had to admit that had no idea why boxing the compass was so called either. Ian was watching his twinkling eyes and hearing the way he treated them with seriousness and decided he liked him.

"Can I come to your boatyard some time, Mr Mustchin? Have a look round? Maybe help? Please?"

Ted was surprised and was about to stop him, but Edgar looked at the eleven year old seriously.

"Interested in boats, are you? Come down and welcome. Who knows, if you're not put off we might find something you can do. Are you good at making tea? Sweeping the floor?"

Ian reacted to the smile in the voice with a smile on his face. It was the same smile that charmed the customers in the café when he was there.

"Next Saturday, if your people agree," Edgar continued. "We'll see what you think after the first morning. You'll need to be there at eight in the morning, though."

Ian, eyes blazing, shot him a look that made him smile more, then tore off to seek out his aunt.

"Are you sure, sir?" Ted asked. "He can be a pain sometimes."

"We all were, Ted. Even me, even you. But if he's interested enough to ask then I'm interested enough to take him up on it. If he doesn't like it, no hard feelings. If he does, well, we'll see. Ah, it looks like the answer may be 'yes'."

171

Ian was almost hauling Annabelle behind him as if she was a dinghy he was taking out to her moorings.

"Hallo Mr Mustchin," she started. "Ian's telling me he had the cheek to ask if he could come and help next Saturday."

"Told you so," Ted muttered to his brother.

"Hallo, Miss Rawle. Ian asked very politely if he could come and visit so I asked if he was any good at making tea or sweeping the floor. He wasn't put off, so I asked if he'd like to come on Saturday next at eight in the morning and see what he thought of us all. So no cheek at all."

"But he's only 11…"

"Aunt Amble!" came the shrill protest.

Edgar laughed. "And I was only eight when I started sweeping the boatyard floor after school for my Dad. Did me the world of good. Got me a clip round the ear when I broke things, though."

Ian looked surprised. "How many times did that happen?"

"Twice. Once when I broke his mug when I jogged the table and once when I didn't let a plank steam long enough and it broke when the boatbuilder tried to bend it. Learned both times, I did."

"I promise I won't do that."

"Wouldn't be surprised if you did. But things have changed a bit since those days so you might just get a talking to, but not a clip round the ear unless you've been really careless. Can he come, Miss Rawle?"

A moment later Ian jumped in the air, nearly jogging Angharad's arm as he did so. Ted went to apologise to her. Soon after she was smiling again.

"What about that brother of yours, Ian? Doesn't he want to come down too?"

"I dunno. I think he prefers farming still."

Stephen was passing at the time and registered the remark, storing it away for future use.

It was one of those evenings which turned out to be memorable for all the right reasons. Apart from the food nothing had been planned; there was no band, no music, no 'entertainment'. Stephen found himself buoyed up by the goodwill of all his friends and was sorry when, late in the evening, they started to drift away.

As the launch picked its way cautiously up the estuary Mary heard him sigh heavily.

"I'm so lucky to have so many friends. Good friends. And you, of course."

"Aren't I a friend too?"

He just looked at her. Seconds later she was being unmercifully tickled and Henry had to tell them both to sit still or risk capsizing the laden launch.

After a busy week at the café in which neither Mary nor Stephen could take part because of exam revision, school and the exams themselves, their parents were pleased to remember that there would be no one on the island apart from themselves and the dogs the following Friday evening. The two younger ones took their dinghy down to Salcombe, met with Bronwen and Martin who had almost to drag a suddenly shy Angharad out of the house to meet with Bob Hannaford at the Ferry Inn. When he saw them his face broke into a smile; a smile which seemed to focus itself on Bronwen after the initial greetings and an introduction.

Only Stephen and Bob drank beer. The girls and Martin settled on Corona fizzy juice and shandy respectively. Conversation revolved round antics at school in Bob's and Stephen's younger days. Mary knew many, not all, of them and found herself laughing at some of the pranks that had been acted out on unsuspecting teachers and other pupils. Bronwen said little, but laughed a lot; her school had offered a much more sedate way of life. She looked across at Angharad and was pleased to see, too, that she was enjoying the stories and also laughing, uproariously at times. When there was a lull in the others' conversation she told a story of her own school which had the others laughing with her. Mary was pleased, feeling that some of her barriers were possibly being broken down. She noticed that Bob was playing special attention to her, realising Angharad would often turn to look at him, to see how he was reacting to stories, and always his patient eyes were on her, encouraging her.

At last Mary and Stephen had to retell the story of Mary's rescue from the storm and the death of her parents and brother. Although Angharad had picked up parts of it over the weeks she had been with them, she was hearing the full details for the first time. The two tellers of the tale found her eyes on them constantly, and it was noticeable that tears came when Greg's death was haltingly described.

There was a silence after the description of the funerals.

"I said, back at the Bank, that you'd had a time of it, didn't I?" said Bob slowly, in a quiet voice. The telling of the tale had brought emotions back to the tellers as well, and they just smiled at him shakily.

"It's sorry I am not to have known before," said Angharad, in her quiet, musical voice, "or perhaps I could have said something, done something to help."

It was unusual for her to volunteer a comment unless as the result of a direct question. Mary smiled at her.

"It all started four years ago, Angharad, and we've come through it now. When we think of it, it brings back sadness but we are past the hurt. But thank you for saying that. I appreciate it and I'm sure Stephen does."

He nodded.

"And you, Angharad?" asked Bob. "Surely you haven't been through such a time as that?"

Silence. Then hesitantly: "It is a time I have been through, but not one like that. My time was in Wales, in Chepstow where my family had moved to be close to work. To help out, I took a job too, see. But it did not work out well, even if the mother and daughter of the family were lovely."

He nodded. "Not every job works out well. Was it a big family?"

Angharad was looking directly at Bronwen, who didn't know what to do or say.

"No," she said slowly, "it was not a big family. I think... I think it would be best if I said no more."

"As you want, of course," said Bob. "But Bronwen has told me that, like her mother and her, you decided to come to Salcombe to live. It's difficult, perhaps?"

"Difficult it is indeed," said Bronwen.

Another pause.

"Angharad, tell him if you want. Or would you rather I did?"

Bob's eyes swivelled to Bronwen.

"I don't want to offend," said Angharad.

"You won't offend me," Bronwen assured her. "He did that himself. He caused the most offence to his family that anyone could have done."

Bob was looking at them alternately, as if at a tennis match.

"I'm so sorry. I didn't want to open old wounds..."

"Old wounds they are not," said Angharad, stung a little at the sympathy being offered to Bronwen. "This happened two months ago only, and it happened to me. I was... I was maid to their family; Bronwen, her mother and... and *him*. He was horrible to me, but always had his eyes on me. Every time I was in the room with him. Even when the others were there. And he was treating them very badly too. At last Bronwen escaped from his cruelty and came here. Then Mrs Williams escaped from him and came here. And then... and then..."

She stopped, unable to say the words. To her surprise a hand came gently to rest on hers. It was Bob's.

"And then he mistreated you. I can see the hurt in you."

"He – raped – me," she said, from between closed teeth.

He was shocked into silence. His hand stayed on hers, something she noticed. Something she allowed.

There was another long silence, broken by Bob.

"I wish I had known you then. I would have... destroyed him." It was said so vehemently that even in her misery at having to tell the story again she felt grateful.

"He did a good job of that on his own," Bronwen said angrily. "Angharad's Newport friends called us in Devon and we came up. Before we had a chance to get the Police to arrest him he had jumped into the Wye and was swept away and drowned." She paused. "My own father, and he did that! I had hated him for years, once I had realised what he was like and how Mum feared and hated him.

"After he'd proved what sort of person, what sort of coward he was, Mum and I did our best to make sure everyone realised what had happened. He was an elder at the Chapel and the Town Clerk, and we left both Chapel and Town in no doubt about what he had done. But still there seem to have been people who wanted him to have a Christian burial."

The hand that was not covering Angharad's was balled into a fist on the table. There was another long silence.

"And now, I suppose, you hate all men," Bob said thoughtfully. "You feel... somehow... different. You feel a lot of things, but very few of them will be true. Most of them are things you are thinking onto yourself. They cannot change that you are beautiful inside and out, and worthwhile, and the sooner you realise it the better you will feel."

The others looked at him in astonishment. Angharad's emotions were in a whirl. What sort of a man was this? What did he know of it? What made him think he could tell her about herself?

But he was continuing. "I can say this and know it to be true. You see, my sister was... well; attacked... in Exeter when she was my age. She kept it hidden

174

for months. When Mum and Dad started asking why she was so quiet nowadays, really kept on at her, she let it all come out. By then it was too late for the Police. They wouldn't have believed her anyway. The boy who did it was the son of a foreign politician. He ran away back home afterwards and never returned, as far as we know.

"Once my parents had the story they were horrified and had no idea what to do. My sister and I were inseparable, although I was two years younger. She told me how she felt. At sixteen I could hardly comprehend what she was describing, but from her I could catch the horror and the hurt and the frustration at being powerless."

He paused.

"So you see, I do have something to go on. And what I said to you was what she was told – by someone else who had been raped, but who had got over most of the effects."

"Is...is your sister all right now?" Angharad asked in a voice that quavered.

"We write to each other. She won't come home whilst I live with my parents. They weren't so accepting. You see, she became pregnant. Mum and Dad wanted her to have an abortion, but she refused saying that a decision on the life or death of a baby wasn't hers or theirs to make. She called in some favours and went to live in London with some old school friends.

"I've never met the baby – I don't qualify for holidays this year and can't afford to travel to London. I can't travel after work on Saturdays and be back in time to start on a Monday. Our parents aren't interested. So that's that. But the baby is fine. One day I'll meet my niece."

He stopped. The hand not on Angharad's was used to dig out a handkerchief from his pocket. Once he'd blown his nose and replaced the handkerchief, Mary and Stephen noticed a hand cover his. Angharad's. Now she was looking into his eyes, straight faced. He smiled.

"Perhaps you could meet her one day. I think she'd like you. We always seemed to like the same people."

Why, after her so-recent experiences with an old man, should she feel attracted to another man? Even a man so much younger than her attacker? But a man who had a sister who had endured an experience similar to hers? And why did she really not object too much to the challenge he had set her, the challenge of thinking she was more worthwhile than she had felt for months? Was he right? His sister's recovery showed, perhaps, that he knew what he was talking about.

Conversation shifted gradually to other, more palatable subjects. She shifted her hand from Bob's but left hers on the table. He looked at her and immediately put his back on top of it.

It was not lost on the other four. Bronwen was glad for her. It seemed that there was someone apart from young Ted to whom she could relate.

Ian left the house early the next Saturday, thinking how peculiar it felt not to have his brother with him. Except at school it seemed the two had been inseparable, particularly since their father's death. Being alone was strange; strange but exciting. He felt older.

His arrival at Edgar's boatyard was early, but he still found the place open and sounds of hammering coming from inside. Nervously he entered and immediately stopped.

Two men were concentrating on an upturned hull that was being built. The hammering, as Mary and Stephen had discovered years ago, was the nailing down of a plank that had been bent and roughly fixed the previous day. Neither men noticed him, so he edged his way down the side of the workshop to a glass partitioned room, inside which was a figure he recognised.

At the soft, nervous knock at the door, Edgar looked up, saw the short, serious faced figure, and smiled. He beckoned, and Ian came in.

"You're early," he said, offering a large and work-worn hand to be shaken. "Good. It show's you're keen. How good are you at adding up?"

Surprised, and a little nervous, Ian said "Not too bad, I think."

"Add those up, would you? See if you get the same answer as me. I always like to be right before I pay money in." He pointed to a chair at a table opposite, on which was a paying-in slip. Ian looked at it, hoping it would make sense to him. It did. It was just adding up the £5 notes, £1 and 10/- notes, and the various denominations of coinage. Adding those few lines was something he did at school every day.

He was in the middle of it when something made him think, pause, look again, worry and eventually look up.

"Mr Mustchin…"

The man looked up.

"I think there's a mistake. I know there's a mistake."

"Oh? Show me."

He took the book round. "Here, sir. You've written down 8 £5 notes but the total is only £30. It should be £40."

He looked, as if it hadn't been a deliberate mistake.

"You're right, Ian. Very well spotted. That would have made me look a real fool in the bank, wouldn't it? Should I alter it, do you think? Or would you prefer to write it out again?"

Ian thought. Was this a test? It sounded as if it might be.

"It'd be neater if I wrote it out again. If I was careful."

"I think you're right. Do that, would you? It'd be a great help."

Fifteen minutes later, when Edgar was wondering if he'd asked too much, the pen was put down. They both looked up.

"Done?" he asked.

"Yes. I've checked the other sums and they seem to be all right, and I've put the right total at the bottom."

"You've checked the other cross-calculations?"

"Yes."

"So that was why you were taking your time. Thank you. And well done again. May I see?"

The book was handed over. It may have been evidently in a very young hand, but Ian had reverted to the copy-book practice of his early school career and had ensured that the figures were all the same size and correctly spaced. It was legible, and it was correct.

Edgar looked up. "That is extremely tidy, Ian. Thank you. Now then, I'm going to see what's going on out there, and you wanted a look round. Best if you come too, I think."

That was an good hour's tour that Ian was to remember for the rest of his life. All the boatbuilders were friendly, local men with children and grandchildren of their own, and the idea of a boy so young having asked to see how things were done tickled them. When he had seen all the work that was going on it was 9.30. One of them looked at the clock.

"Time we got that kettle on, I reckon."

"Ah, we've got a trainee to do that today," Edgar told him. "You can show him where everything is, though."

The man looked at Ian, who met his gaze with a pair of solemn eyes.

"Come on then, ol' son. Let's see how you do. Tea making's an art, you know…"

Living in a large household, Ian was on firm ground in a kitchen making tea, even with as large and heavy a kettle as was on display there. Once full he could hardly lift it to the single gas ring, and spent a long time working out how he could fill the teapot without lifting it off when boiling.

"Pete!" The man with him was being hailed by Edgar. They both looked round.

"While it's heating, can you get one of the Bermudas in, please? We've got a customer. Best take your trainee with you."

Pete grinned and beckoned Ian with an inclination of his head. He led out of the building and down to the slippery steps to the water. A little rowing dinghy lay there.

"Row, do you?" Ian was asked.

"No," he said regretfully. "I've steered a launch, though."

"That'll be the Lofts', will it?"

He nodded.

"Tell you what. Watch me on the way to the Bermuda, then I'll row that back and you can come behind me. Don't try for a record, though, and if you get into too much trouble we've got a little motor boat here to come and tow you back."

His rowing was watched like a hawk all the way out, and a stream of instructions given. Their target was a sailing boat moored to a chain attached to a buoy about forty yards out.

"There. Think you can do that?"

"I'll try."

"Tides coming in, so it'll take you up Batson if anywhere. I'll keep an eye on you. Keep looking round, though, so you can see where you're going."

"Why don't you row forwards?"

"What?"

"You face the wrong way."

He laughed. "Always been done that way. You get more power to the oars when you're pulling them. Anyways, you face the other way and everyone in Salcombe'll laugh at you. And at us, for letting you do it. So don't."

As Pete was fitting the dinghy's rowlocks and readying the oars, Ian readied himself and found that he was drifting with the tide. He looked round with alarm. Pete was busy. Cautiously he put the oars into the water and pushed.

To his alarm the little boat went the wrong way, putting distance between Pete and himself.

He was about to yell, then remembered that he was being watched by the people of Salcombe. He thought, then pulled on the oars instead of pushing.

It worked. He was heading back, but slowly. He took another pull, and another. What was happening? Why was he turning? He looked round. Now he was heading out into the creek and again nearly panicked. In time he remembered what Pete had told him as they had rowed out. "Pull harder on the side you want to turn away from."

He pulled on the right oar so as to turn the other way, and the boat spun round almost in its own length.

He stopped again, thinking. If Pete had done it, so could he. Pulling first at one side, then the other, he ended up facing more or less the right way. Checking over his shoulder showed him that Pete had dropped the buoy and its chain back onto the water and was watching him. He had a clear run to get near the boat which Pete was just starting to row towards the shore.

As carefully as possible he dug both oars in at the same time and pulled, making sure he was giving the same effort to both sides. To his surprise the boat surged forward. He did it again with the same result. This was easy! A third time, and his left oar missed the water completely and he almost fell off the thwart. He could feel his face reddening, quickly readied it again and tried to resume.

The error had resulted in his heading out again. He could see Pete in the sailing dinghy off to his left, still watching him, so he composed himself and cautiously pulled with both oars, giving slightly more power to the right one so as to turn more gently that way.

By continually checking, thinking, correcting and pulling he made a zig-zag course after Pete whose strokes were seemingly effortless. Had he known it, the man was worried lest the boy made such a complete mess of it that he would have to turn and rescue him. That would have delayed getting the dinghy ready and Edgar would have cursed him for a bloody fool to let the boy row for the first time on his own.

But no, the boy did all right. He even seemed to be settling down. Pete, in a manoeuvre that was effortless because of long practice, swung his dinghy and caught the hanging chain, made the painter fast to another one, then turned to look for his protégé. He was glancing anxiously round, wondering what to do.

"Stop worrying, look, and think," Pete called to him. Ian stopped rowing, looked, and found he was nearly heading in the right direction. Thinking of the way the Lofts approached the Hard, and how he had nearly seen what they had done, he tried to do the same. Oars make close manoeuvring tricky, but he did his best, ending just a little too far away to cling onto the sailing dinghy.

"Hold an oar up!" Pete called.

Immediately he saw what the man meant, worked an oar free and held it towards him. Pete caught it and held on.

"Now pull, and work the boat alongside," he said. Ian did, and Pete was soon fishing for the dinghy's painter which he made fast.

"Careful now, step into this boat, then onto the steps. Don't fall in – it looks bad."

Ian made it onto the slippery steps and, with legs that for some reason felt like jelly, made himself climb. There was a knot of people at the top, including Edgar, who shot a glance at him, then at Pete.

"All yours, Guv'nor," said the latter, and made his way into the building without another word. Ian thought it best to follow.

Someone had made the tea.

Neither of them had noticed the ferry had berthed for fuel. The first that Ian knew was that Charlie was greeting him as an old friend.

"Soon get that right, that coming into the side," he said. "Took me a month of Sundays with a rowboat, that did. Didn't know you'd have got a chance at rowing, being a farmer and all."

"I didn't," Ian explained. "That was the first time."

"First time rowing? *First* time rowing? Well, that's how they taught me – put me in a boat and set me adrift. I had to be rescued twice before I got the hang of it. By the looks, a few more weeks' practice and you'll be fit to go anywhere. Mind the blisters, though!"

Ian smiled at him and thankfully took a pull at the mug of tea that had been thrust into his hand.

Edgar saw him and Pete later. "I've told Pete he was a fool to set you off on your own, but he tells me that's how he learnt and that he never took his eyes off you. He says you did very well for a first attempt."

Ian said nothing, but smiled happily.

"You'd better get those friends of yours to give you some practice. Though a sailing boat is a clumsy thing to row. Best not to, except in an emergency. No. We'll have to do better than that."

Ian waited for him to say something else, but nothing was forthcoming.

"Anyway, you can do me a real service, and that's get the broom and sweep up in the other room where they've been using the planes. Stick the sweepings in the tank with the rest of the shavings, then we'll have another look."

Ian did, found it boring apart from being able to look at the launch that was being built at close quarters and to compare it with the Lofts' boat. It looked very similar.

He reported back to Edgar afterwards, and his work was inspected. He received a pat on the back and a smile from the man, and took it to be the equivalent of a ten-out-of-ten. A hand beckoned him to see Pete again who was waiting by the quayside.

"Reckon you need to know what you're doing with the oars, young man, so Pete's going to give you a proper lesson or two. Then we'll see if you can beat him in a race."

Ian knew that was impossible, but he wasn't about to turn down such an opportunity. For the next hour he was put through his paces, with Pete cajoling him, teasing him, demonstrating to him, and just letting him row. By the end he was exhausted, his arms and legs ached and he had blisters on his hands. But he could row in a straight line, turn when he needed to, and wasn't catching crabs any more.

Pete rowed him back to the quay. Ian staggered after him up the slippery steps.

"Thought you might be shattered, boy. But you never gave up, and it's done you a lot of good. Practice – when you can."

Edgar saw them approaching, read Ian's face and directed him to a chair in his office.

"We'll be shutting for lunch soon," he said. "Probably best if you start on half days. If you – no, *when* you're more used to it, we'll think again. I can't employ you as such, 'cause I'm not allowed to, but there will be something in it for you, quietly, if you come back next Saturday. If we haven't put you off too much, that is."

Ian smiled at him, feeling physically tired but mentally more keyed up than he had for ages.

"I'll be back," he promised.

"Good for you. Make sure they're all right about it at home, though."

Ian promised he would and swayed to his feet. He walked with a rolling gate to the door and turned to leave, then looked to where Pete was grinning at him.

"Coming back next week, then?" he asked.

"You bet," called Ian, then walked down to him and offered his hand. Pete shook it.

"You'll do, I reckon."

"Thanks, Pete."

When he arrived home, tired even more by the hills between Island Quay and his home, he was bullied into a bath by Martin, who knew about using young muscles on unfamiliar jobs.

True to his word, and to his elder brothers' surprise, he appeared the next week, and the week after. Each time he was given a little rowing dinghy and asked to visit some of the hire boats moored in deeper water to check on them and bail them out if necessary. Once or twice baling was needed, particularly on his third week after there had been some considerable rain. He spent such a long time attending to the fleet that Pete rowed out after him to check he was all right. He was; wet but happy, yet pleased to be told that tea was ready.

After the morning's work he was about to go when Edgar called him back.

"Not walking up that hill again are you, Ian?"

"Yes. That's where home is."

"But why walk from here when you can row?"

Ian looked at him, head on one side. "I don't have a boat."

"Ah, well. You see last week we had a look round the back and we found a little old ship's boat that needed a new plank and some tar, and we thought that it'd be good to see her got back into shape. Pete worked on her this week and we think we've got her watertight, but she needs a test, really. Would you like to take her on?"

"What, me?"

"Can't see anyone else in the room, boy."

"But what do I do with her?"

"Take her round to the place nearest home, moor her properly, tuck the oars under the thwarts. Unship the rowlocks, of course. Then you can go and have a look at her when you want, take her on the water – maybe you can teach that brother of yours how to row if he never has. Just make sure she doesn't leak.

Then we'll see you back with her next Saturday, eh? Unless she's seen to be leaking in the meantime. If she does you tell me immediately, please."

For a quite young child, Ian had a face that was capable of a wide range of expressions, several of which passed over it in the following seconds. Then it fell.

"I'll have to ask Aunt Amble."

"P'raps I phoned her earlier. P'raps she said 'yes'."

"Perhaps?"

"All right, I did. And she did."

Yet another expression found its way on the face, a half smile with an accusing look that quickly softened.

"Thank you, Mr Mustchin."

"Go on with you. Go and see Pete and he'll show her to you."

He needed no second telling, but ran to see a smiling Pete who turned his back and led, once more, to the quay.

She may have been an old, black, battered, well tarred praam dinghy with a thick, worn cable-laid hawser round her as a fender, but to Pete she was the Queen Elizabeth. Once more he turned to Pete, who by now had a radiant smile, and just said 'thank you' in a voice of absolute sincerity, before almost running down the steps.

He found that not only were there oars and rowlocks, but a small anchor, along with a painter that was long enough to moor her at low tide. He had been warned about tying with a short rope at high tide and returning to find the boat hanging down the quay wall!

Sitting in her, thinking the boat into his life, he was suddenly, deliriously happy and looked up with a wide, excited grin to see Pete still there, watching.

"Don't forget to untie her," came his voice, quiet for a change, and sounding odd. He did so, quickly shipped the oars, set a course and rowed away.

Pete fished out his handkerchief and blew his nose.

21 – Angharad and Bob

It was on the Monday that Angharad felt most peculiar. Unsettled. Almost as if she had the start of indigestion, yet not the same. She didn't feel like breakfast. Although she had been told she didn't have to, she made tea and got things ready for the household, then cleared away afterwards. The burst of activity made her feel worse. She paused at the kitchen sink, waiting for the feeling to pass. It *would* pass, wouldn't it?

She was still there five minutes later when Dolly bustled in, looking to help wash up as always. The cheerful comment she had on her lips froze there when she saw the girl.

"What's the matter, Angharad?"

"Nothing, Ma'am."

"Nonsense. You look dreadful. Come and sit down. No, not in here; somewhere comfortable. Come on. No excuses."

"But I haven't washed up!"

"Blow the washing up. It can wait. You matter. Come on. Please."

Sitting comfortably in the living room, which everyone else had left for tooth brushing, readying for work or school or, in Bronwen's case, a morning looking for a correspondence course that would interest her, she cajoled the girl into speech but was immediately interrupted by the ringing of the telephone.

It turned out to be completely unimportant. She dealt with it and put the receiver down.

"Sorry," she said to Angharad. "Now then... Why, what's the matter?"

Tears were streaming down Angharad's face. Dolly went to put her arms around her.

"It's all my fault," Angharad sobbed. "If I hadn't let him... you and Bronwen would still have been there and none of this would be happening."

"Absolute nonsense," Dolly said in as firm a tone as she knew how. "Most importantly, he... forced himself on you, not the other way round. And he is no weakling, I know that, so you had no chance. How can it be your fault?"

"I should have let him, and kept quiet."

Dolly almost shook her. "You did *exactly* the right thing. *Exactly.* You have a right not to be treated like that by anybody. *Anybody.* And any man who can't control his urges deserves everything that he gets. You did what was absolutely right. Never, ever doubt it.

"In any case, do you think that Bron and I wanted to be there any more? He was an appalling husband almost from the wedding day. He was a love-less father, treating Bron as a chattel, not as a child. It was a relief to escape from him. If anything, it's my fault. I should never have left you alone in the house with him, and had I known what sort of animal he really was I would absolutely not have done so.

"So it should be me apologising to you, going down on my knees to beg forgiveness. Not the other way round."

The tears were now tears of near-belief, and near-relief. No emotion so strong as Angharad's can be halted in its tracks by words, except over many months or years. But she was comforted all the same.

182

"I think... I'm scared... that he has left me with a baby."

This was the thunderbolt to Dolly that she had been dreading all along.

"You think that this feeling, this illness, is the start of it? Have you – may I be personal? – missed a period?"

She nodded. "I have. I missed the second one last week. I can't say for sure, but this feeling of illness is what I understand can happen."

Dolly thought furiously for a moment, and made a decision.

"The doctor for you, Angharad. And we will stand by you no matter what. Have no doubts about that either. We will be there to sit with, to cry with, to be quiet with, to talk with. No: I will. You ask anyone you want, whenever you want. But I am here for you all the time. That is a promise."

"Wh... what am I going to do?"

"First, we find out whether you are, or not. Then you have to decide what to do."

"But what can I do, apart from have the baby?"

She has no idea, no knowledge, thought Dolly. And she was not going to be the one to plant ideas into the girl's mind.

"Let's take one step at a time. I'm going to phone the doctor for an appointment."

Angharad nodded.

It may have been the phrase "sister of the Solicitor, Mr Merryweather", but Dolly found herself offered an appointment that morning. Poor Angharad had to agree once again to an intimate examination though the Salcombe doctor was more understanding of the circumstances, once they had been explained, than her experiences at Chepstow had led her to fear.

"It's very difficult to say without a test," the doctor told them, Dolly having been present behind a screen. "Physically everything is entirely normal. Even the feeling of being unwell is normal if you are expecting. This was not your choice. Have you been to the Police about the man who did it?"

Dolly took over. "The man who did it was my husband, who then took his own life. Yes, the Police have been given statements, not just about his taking advantage of Angharad but his suicide too."

"And when did this happen, please?"

"Thursday the twenty-seventh of March," Angharad responded slowly. "The date is written on my mind."

The doctor made some calculations.

"Then that is about the right time for matters to – well – make themselves felt. I have taken a sample and will send it away. It should take about a week to be returned so please will you make an appointment for about that time?

"You also need to keep a record of what happens and how you feel over the next week. Bring that along when you see me again, would you? Lastly, for the moment, you have an important decision to make. If you feel that you cannot accept what has happened to you, that you feel disgust at the idea of carrying the baby, then unofficially, to maintain your well-being, it might be possible to arrange an abortion. There are advantages and disadvantages in that. It may be that the feeling of horror at carrying a child conceived after rape is less than the feeling of guilt that many girls and women experience after an abortion.

"A second possibility is that the baby may be adopted immediately after birth.
"You will need to make a decision on these possibilities."

There was a silence in the consulting room. It was broken by Dolly.

"There is the third possibility, of course. Angharad could accept the baby and raise him or her."

Once home, the two sat down over a cup of tea in the comfortable living room. Angharad was in deep thought and Dolly let the comfortable silence continue. At last the girl looked up.

"Please, Ma'am; what *is* an abortion?"

Dolly explained. The more she said, the more horrified the girl's face became.

"But that's murder!"

This time Dolly could say little, apart from explaining that sometimes the prospective mother's feelings, wellbeing and future had to be considered, and maybe she should come first.

Angharad was silent.

The sale of land to the formally established legal farming and produce partnership of Beale and Loft continued. To Mary and Stephen it seemed that 'dragged on' would be a better description, but their solicitor, Grandad, friend and confidant smiled and told them that this was a normal speed and that there were many safeguards to their eventual ownership status that were being investigated. It didn't stop the two from walking the land that would be theirs, the land that abutted Mary's old farm lands. It didn't stop Henry and, on the shorter expeditions Susan, from walking around and weighing up the merits of the land they would farm. It would be mid-June before he was called in to Merryweathers (Solicitors) to be told the end of the searches was in sight, that all was well, and that there were signatures needed.

"So are you going to start building a new farmhouse straight away?" Henry asked Mary.

It was a brutal way of focussing minds on the development of the farm now that the land was all but theirs. She and Stephen had taken little part in the process of buying the land as each was a minor and their signatures made whilst younger than twenty-one would have counted for nothing in legal terms. There was a document they *had* all signed which set out the joint rights of each of them; a document binding all the signatories by honour rather than by law.

She looked up from her book, trying not to lose the thread of the revision she was forcing herself to finish before the following day's 'O' level GCE exam.

"We've not had time to think about it yet, Henry. We've not even talked about it, have we Steve?"

His turn to look up. "Hmm?"

"We've not talked about building a new farmhouse on the new land yet, have we?"

"No. Why?"

"Didn't you hear? Henry wants to know if we're starting to build one now."

"Not until the exams are over, that's for sure. You know, I'm sure they must have done this bit in class, but I'm damned if I can remember it. Must have been asleep."

"I've been having the same problem with something else," Mary complained. "Perhaps it was something they didn't do at the Scotland school, so I missed it."

"You need to think about what's happening next, now we've got the land," Henry said.

Stephen looked up. "What's happening next is that Mary and I have exams ahead in the next two weeks. We need to get through those, then we can start thinking about the details of what's happening to the farm. You wouldn't want it any other way, would you, Dad?"

"I know, I know. But I'm impatient to use this land, to get our stock onto it."

"Yes. But you'll need to build a milking parlour first. You can't ship an entire herd to the island twice a day. And that means thinking about... oh. I see what you mean."

"Yes. So much depends on what, where and when. That's why we need to start thinking."

"But we've just waited for a month whilst the land was bought," said Mary. Surely another fortnight or so's delay won't make a difference?"

"No, maybe not. But I wanted to give you two something to talk about when you have some respite from studying."

"I don't know when we're going to be able to have a rest from studying, at this rate," Mary said with a grimace. "It seems never ending."

"A fortnight, that's all," Stephen told her. "And that's it for ever. Until you start studying at home for cheese making or something. And talking of studying, Dad, have you decided what you want to have in a new milking shed? Things have come on a lot since the Island one was built. If the herd is going to increase we won't have time for hand milking anyway, not with a cafe to run and all the other things we want to do."

"And a new baby to look after," said a placid voice.

Her husband swung round to look at her.

"You're right," he said. "Priorities."

"But there's nothing to stop you looking at how we could set up a modern system, Dad. Its location could come later. And we need to think what other animals we could usefully rear. Like pigs."

"One thing at a time, old son, one thing at a time."

"Yes, Dad. And my one thing at the moment is to get past the A-Levels. Then I can leave school and start work. As can Mary when she's finished with her exams, as I said."

Henry held up his hands in surrender and went to look at some farming magazines.

"The results of the test are now in and I can tell you now that you are expecting a baby..."

They were the words that Angharad was hoping not to hear, despite being almost certain in her own mind that she was pregnant. Her decision for herself, her decision for the baby's future – and indeed whether it had one – had been put off until this moment. She slumped in the chair, now too defeated to say anything. The doctor was droning on about how important it was to make the right decision and how there were always couples waiting to adopt newborn babies.

"... but the decision is yours, of course. Or your parents'."

She knew that. She knew it only too well. And if she had – what was it? An abortion? – she knew she would find the weight of guilt unbearable. And if the baby was to be born she knew it would be part *his*. But it would also be part hers. And it would be a half-sister or brother to Bronwen, as Dolly had pointed out. Would she be letting Dolly and Bronwen down if she didn't go through with it? Should that come into her decision? Could she bring up a baby on her own? Would it matter that she was still sixteen – seventeen when the baby arrived? And *her* parents? What was it to do with them? They weren't even here, even if she longed for her Mum to accept her and offer... what? But they knew nothing about all this. She didn't want them to know anything until it was all over. She knew what her mother would say. She would be banished for ever.

She put her hands in front of her face and squeezed her eyes shut. Why her? Why did *he* have to choose *her*? Because she had been there. In the house and female. That was the only reason. Once again a wave of hate flowed through her, and immediately she felt it was a pointless emotion: he was dead.

The room was quiet. Why? Was someone expecting her to speak?

Dolly asked again, her voice was a gentle one that she had come to trust.

"Angharad? You need make no decision now. There are still many weeks before the first decision has to be made, and many months before any others have to be made. Why not come home now? I will be there to answer questions at any time. Never forget that."

Numbly, she nodded. Dolly rose. She automatically did the same. Blindly she followed her ex-employer back home.

At the home of Bob Hannaford an official letter fell to the mat. Across the top were the words 'On Her Majesty's Service' In place of the stamp was what looked like a franking mark but it just said 'Official Paid'.

Bob picked it up, his hands suddenly shaking. He tore it open. Ten seconds later he was talking to his parents more animatedly than he'd done for a year, then swore as he saw the time. He rushed out of the door and down to Fore Street to work.

"Sorry, Mr Selleck, but I've just had my draft papers for National Service. They say that I'll be required to serve for a year, but I don't know what to do about the job... the career." He had asked to talk to Mr Selleck as soon as he had arrived at work that day. His announcement was greeted by an exclamation of shock and a look of dismay.

"Well that is a problem. Bother. A problem for both you and the Bank. I thought that as you'd had no call-up papers before you were eighteen and nothing for the two months since, they weren't going to bother you. Oh, dear. I will have to talk to Divisional Office to see what they advise. Not that they can do anything about the call-up, of course. But how we deal with your absence."

Bob put the question that was bothering him the most. "Will I still have a job when it's over, sir?"

The man grimaced. "That's what I want to know too, Bob. It's a new one on me."

After work Bob found that he was drawn to visit Stephen to chat about his problems, but realised that to pop in to see someone who lives on an island is impractical. Instead, he found himself being drawn to talk to Martin Rawle and Bronwen, and maybe Angharad. He smiled as he thought of her.

It was Bronwen who answered the door. She looked preoccupied and he wondered why. He asked if Martin was there.

"He's not back from work yet," she told him. "He's often like this. He and Mike get deep into some problem or other and before they know it half the evening has gone. I imagine that's what's happening tonight."

"Oh... oh well. It was only for a quick chat to pick his brains, really."

"How about my brains? Will they do?"

He smiled at her. "I imagine they would, and very well. But then girls don't get called up for National Service."

She thought of Martin's near-miss.

"Come in. Martin has some history there."

She invited him into the sitting room where Annabelle was sitting, trying to follow a knitting pattern.

"Will you forgive me if I'm not social for the moment? I'm trying to fathom out this pattern I've been given and it's like a wartime code."

He smiled at her. Bronwen and he sat; she quietly explained to him what had happened to Martin. He was shocked.

"Poor old Martin. What a thing to happen. But I'm glad he was able to get out of it."

"I think Martin's a feeling a bit guilty. He feels he should have gone, but if he had it would have affected his career. If he'd received the call-up papers when they had been sent to Kingsbridge he'd have gone. There would have been no choice. And then he wouldn't have met me, his brothers would have been taken into care when his father died, and Mum, Angharad and I would still be living in misery in Wales. Though of course Angharad..."

She tailed off. Should she tell Bob? He seemed a steady chap. But he was finishing her sentence.

"Angharad would not have been attacked."

She grimaced. "More than that. She wouldn't be pregnant. But don't tell anyone else, please."

The look he gave her was one of complete shock. Over the several seconds it took him to recover, the expression changed through sadness to a look of determination.

"When did you find that out?"

"She went to the doctor for the test results this morning."

Another silence. He nodded slowly.

"May I see her, please?"

Bronwen looked at him. He seemed genuine, but she wasn't certain.

"What would you say to her?"

"I... I'd want that to be between her and me. You see, I like her. Even after just one meeting I knew there was something about her... And she's had a dreadful start to an adult life, hasn't she?"

"She's not an adult. Not any more than you are, or Martin and I, or Stephen and Mary are. Not legally. We're old enough to work. We're old enough to do National Service and risk getting killed, but we're not old enough to make our own decisions legally, or even vote. But yes, she's had misfortune and a bad start. And she's more intelligent than you'd think..."

He interrupted. "I know she is. I could see and hear that when we met."

Bronwen nodded. "And I want – Mum wants too – to protect her against more misfortune. As much as we can."

He sighed. "Would it surprise you to know that I want that too? That's why I want to talk to her."

Bronwen weighed him up as best she could and decided that he was honest, and honourable. He had his wish. When Angharad saw him she was at first horrified. But when he had explained the reason he wanted to see her, to support her, to help in any way possible, she was silent and, oddly, almost excited.

"What should I do about the baby?" she asked out of the blue, throwing him completely. His mind raced.

"That's... that's too early to say, surely? Are you going to keep him or her? Would you rather look at adoption?"

It was her turn to hesitate, though deep inside her she was glad he had not mentioned stopping the pregnancy.

"That's what I have to decide. And I just don't know. It depends what I feel like later, I suppose."

"And looking after a baby on your own must be hard... if you are still on your own by then."

"No one wants to marry a girl who's pregnant, who's been raped." She sounded so bitter as she forced herself to say the words that he almost jumped.

"It depends on the girl. It depends on the boy, too. Don't rule it out."

She couldn't read him. Surely he didn't mean, after one evening out, that he would consider her? She decided to raise the question that had been scaring her, horrifying her, since talking to the doctor.

"There is another choice. That I have an... that they end the pregnancy."

At that he was still. Still and silent for so long she wondered if he had heard. But he cannot have missed hearing her, she thought.

At last, cautiously, he spoke. "Some men – some boys – might prefer there to be no child, no history, no past, no problems. Some might be able to shut their minds to... to all that. But for me..."

He stopped talking again. There was another long silence before he stood up. "I might as well make ready to go now, because I think that if I say what I know to be true for me, you will want me to go. You will probably need to get Bronwen in for comfort, or her mother. Because I have to tell you what I feel. If you want me to."

She nodded, dumbly.

"Then I will say that at the moment, I have a – a respect for you and for how you are facing this. You know that my sister had to go through the same sort of decisions as you're having to make. You know what she decided. I respected her decision. Absolutely.

"If you decided to have an abortion..." He gulped. "Most of my respect for you would... would waver. Might well even disappear.

"There. I've said what I believe. Now I'd better go and ask Bronwen to come and sit with you and be a shoulder you *can* cry on."

The door handle was in his grasp, but he looked back.

She was looking at him with an intensity he didn't understand.

"Please stay. Because we agree."

He felt as though a light had come on.

"I can't face stopping the child from growing inside me. It would be... wrong. I will be pregnant, and I will bring the child to the light, and take my chances. More than that I cannot see at the moment."

Now by her side, kneeling, he felt overcome. But his hand went to cover hers again, and again she didn't remove it.

"Am I being a fool, do you think?" Bob asked Martin. Bronwen had joined him in Angharad's room and could see that the girl looked less strained, almost happier, than she had all day. Dolly, too, had come in and had been shocked to find a strange man there, but still noticed the changes to the girl's face and demeanour. Bronwen had introduced her, but it was obvious that Dolly was still concerned that Angharad should have been left alone with someone she didn't know. Bob had taken the hint, said his farewells and left with Bronwen in tow. She had offered him some tea. Whilst she was making it Martin returned from work and joined him in the front room where he explained the situation.

"Not a fool, I imagine; just a little too quick, perhaps. You've only known her for the few hours we were in the pub. Indeed, I've only really known her since we brought her back here, and I feel I hardly know her at all."

"I know, I know," came the answer. "But what I meant was: am I being stupid to want to get together with a girl who's about to have a baby. Someone else's baby. It's a big step."

"I *think*... I think if you are attracted to the girl, then that's what matters. In fact, if eventually you get to *know* you're in love, it's *all* that matters. And the baby... well, he or she will have half Angharad's character and you can train him or her out of any of the father's. I've been wondering, imagining, that the man's attitudes could have been the result of how he was brought up. And Bronwen's nothing like him, is she? I don't think you need worry."

Words of wisdom, maybe, even if from another eighteen year old who was yet to become a father.

"I hope you're right," Bob told him. "And as to not knowing her very well; you're right. But having met her, and having heard her story and how she told it, and how it runs parallel with my sister's experiences... well, it really got to me. And you must admit she's a beautiful looking girl. And yes, I know that's not everything, by any means, but... well..." He trailed off.

Martin was looking thoughtful. "I suppose... well, Bron and I met at a party and hit it off within a few hours, then there was another party – blame the Lofts! And after that, of course, there was the visit to Chepstow... and we all knew where that led." He winced. "Really, we're still just at boyfriend and girlfriend stage, but I've not met anyone else who attracts me so much. Not ever. Why am I telling you all this?!"

Bob was thinking. "I need to invite her out, spend some time with her and get to know her better. More particularly, I need *her* to get to know *me*, and realise that I'm not an ogre or just after... after... well, you know. And then we can see how we go. And all this is happening just as I get the damn call-up papers. I don't even know when I have to go yet."

Martin smiled. "Better get busy, Bob. Maybe you'll find she'd welcome the distraction from everything else."

She did welcome the distraction. At first she was cautious, and nervous, and almost asked Bronwen to come with her for support and as a chaperone. But Bronwen persuaded her, and was satisfied when Angharad first met Bob at the door, smiled at him, and quite willingly left the house with him.

Dolly and the other adults, having heard of the exchanges and having asked some pertinent questions, were at last reasonably happy with the liaison. The only person who went about looking like a kicked puppy for some days was Ted Rawle. But even he eventually came round to realising that there was too big a gap between his fourteen years and Angharad's nearly seventeen, and the prospect of a baby in the equation in a few months' time really made him think twice and more about it. It didn't stop him watching her, making sure in his own way that she was as happy as she could be, and thinking about her at other times. The excitement of Ian's dinghy helped him as well, especially as his brother was being generous with sharing it.

For the month between receiving his papers and Bob's having to report for training the two spent some increasingly happy times in each other's company. Twice they had invitations to visit Loft Island and chat casually to Mary and Stephen. Once she had acclimatised herself again to their ready acceptance and cheerful good humour she became more relaxed. She was shown the work that was already starting on marking out the boundaries for the extended house and to provide for the café.

She met Susan and Henry and was at first shy, but Susan put her at her ease. They were pleased to see Angharad looking more lively – and saw how comfortable she appeared to be with Bob.

The island entranced her. The café in its present state entranced her. She asked what the plans were and was talked through them.

"Mam used to make some wonderful *bara brith*," she told them wistfully. "So easy to make, it is. You could try it."

"Or you could come and make it for us," said Susan with a smile. "Then it would be really authentic."

The look of pleasure she received made them all notice. Once on their own again the Lofts asked each other why they'd never asked Angharad to come and work there before.

"That'd be something you could do while I'm away," said Bob.

"It's just that they were being nice," said Angharad. "They don't want me, really."

"Didn't you hear what Susan said?" he asked. "She was being genuine. Talk it over with the others and see how it could work. I don't want you to be some galley slave... Sorry. I meant that I imagine you wouldn't want to work like a galley slave but if you can earn something..."

"Earn money, is it?"

"Well, yes. If you're doing something for their business then they would expect to pay you. I know Bronwen has worked there when they needed help and she is paid. You would be too."

Her expression told him that it had never occurred to her.

As the day of Bob's departure for training drew closer Angharad became noticeably quieter. She was still unsure about being hugged by him, and would shake her head if he tried to kiss her, but when it was so close to the end of their last outing she became emotional.

"It's so good, these last weeks," she told him, looking up into his eyes. "And you have shown me what a real gentleman should be. I will never forget."

"But I'll be back on leave, I'm sure, and we'll see each other then. It's only Exeter I'm going to."

"But you will meet someone else. Someone better..."

"I may see other girls, but only see them. Not go out with them. And as for 'better', I doubt very much if I could find someone better than you if I looked for the rest of my life. And I don't intend to look. But you may find someone here who sweeps you off your feet."

She shuddered, and looked away.

"A man swept my feet from under me once. Once was enough. And he raped me."

He was brought back down to earth with a bump.

"I'm sorry," he said, full of contrition. "It was just a way of speaking. A saying, if you like. But I will always be there for you to talk to, and to be with if you want, every time I'm back home. That's a promise. And in the meantime I'll write to you. Whenever I can. That's a promise, too."

She looked into his eyes, something that itself would have been impossible for her a few weeks previously. She saw honesty, and warmth, and concern. No guile. No attempt to control. No hidden, unspoken persuasion to go any further. Nor even to kiss her after the many times she had shaken her head at his clumsy attempts to give or receive a 'social' kiss.

She gave in, closed on him and laid her head against his chest. As if acting on a will of their own, her arms met at the centre of his back.

Cautiously he gently put his arms around her. Felt her stiffen with shock as she felt them there. Felt her relax again, so slowly, as her instinct realised that this was different. This was pure. This was real.

They stayed like that for a period that could have been measured in minutes. He didn't want to do anything, say anything, that would make her think back to *that* time. She didn't want to lose her instinctive realisation that this was what a man *should* feel like. And that innocent embrace was the very early start of a process of healing. A process which would in time exorcise some of the effects of that thirty minutes of intimate force from her mind.

At last she looked up. The word 'sorry' almost formed itself on her lips. His eyes were still looking into hers, gravely, gentleness shining from them. Instead of 'sorry' she found herself smiling, smiling wider than she had felt like doing since *it* happened.

"Will you want to do that again when you come back on leave?" she asked.

"If you would accept my doing so, I would be honoured," he said fervently, hoping he wasn't sounding too formal.

"Comforting, it is."

He made ready to encircle her again.

"No. Not your arms, but your face. It is a kind face, and honest and gentle. A gentleman's face in a boy. That is what I like." She smiled again. "As well as the arms."

This time he laughed quietly and just offered his arms again. She snuggled into them. But this time the eyes were still looking into his. Cautiously he closed the distance. And for the first time, for a moment or two, they kissed.

22 – The End of School

"Well, that went better than I thought," said Stephen as he met with Mary on the bus from the Kingsbridge school to Salcombe.

"I wish mine had," his fiancée complained. "The first one wasn't too bad, but history... I just can't remember things. And two exams in one day where each needs a lot of writing is really unfair. My hand feels as if I'd just milked an entire herd of cows – and a big herd at that."

He had to smile at that. "Let's hope the next one is better. I've got nothing tomorrow. It seems they don't want us in, either. That's nearly a first – apart from the floods."

The days of the floods, yes. When Mary had lost the rest of her family and Stephen had lost one best friend and nearly another. The other who was sitting next to him and was secretly (so far as the school was concerned) his fiancée. He must ask her if they should announce it before they left the school properly.

During all the uncertainty of the period after the flood, when it had caused all its devastation and death, the school hadn't tried to persuade them to attend, not least because there were so many other things they had to deal with. And then there had been the dreadful business of the funerals, when volunteers came from the school to carry Greg's coffin; boys who were the same age as their dead friend. All the tears of that day...

His hand found hers as his throat contracted. For a moment he felt as if he was about to cry. It was one of those emotions that creeps up and surprises us in unguarded moments. She was watching him, surprised.

"Thinking of *that* night?" she asked quietly.

He nodded. "Happens, sometimes. Usually when I'm not expecting it."

"Me too."

They decided later that if there was to be the usual school assembly on the day of Mary's last O-Level exam, they would tell everyone their news.

"Had we better ask Miss Armitage first?" asked Mary.

Stephen gave a sudden laugh, having recovered quickly from his memories. "I suppose we'd better, although we would get quite a reception if we both just marched up in front of teachers and everyone and announced it!"

"I couldn't do that," she said, horrified at the thought of such disobedience. "And Miss Armitage has been very good to us both. No, we should ask her."

And so they did, and found her reluctant. "It's not that I don't wish you well. Of course I do, with all my heart. But I have this feeling that others might want to jump on the bandwagon. You know, announce engagements that have no substance – unlike yours, of course, which is as solid as a rock."

She thought. They waited.

"Oh, go on, then. You'll make it public as a matter of course, and it'll be all round the school soon after anyway. But please, go through the whole story and what finding each other again really meant to you. That might just show that there were special circumstances which led to it. Which of course there were."

On the last day of O-Level exams the school entered the assembly hall as usual. The routine had been part of their lives for as long as they had been there and was a matter to be endured except on a few special occasions. They failed to

193

notice, as they wandered into the hall as usual in a state of semi-somnolence, that two of the elder members of their number were standing at the front, just next to the stage.

Miss Armitage was on good form. After the hymn – a rousing number that got many of them to pay attention for a change – she paid tribute to those who were leaving, since the day would be their last ever at the school "unless or until they decided to visit us again, of course," she said. "But I've been asked to announce something special concerning two of them. In fact it's only right that they make their own announcement."

She stepped back and motioned to Mary and Stephen.

It was quite a long talk they gave. There was a lot to tell. Some of the younger ones would have only a basic remembrance of that dreadful autumn that had started their story. There were many silences. Whichever of the two who was talking at the time gave time for the horror of the events to sink in. But when they came to the return of Mary there was a small cheer which made her smile.

"You can't go through a friendship and events like that, sometimes together, sometimes apart, and not develop feelings for each other," said Stephen slowly and deliberately. "So before her sixteenth birthday I felt – no, I knew – that there was no one else I wanted to spend the rest of my life with. On her sixteenth birthday last January I proposed to her."

He paused again for it to sink in. There was excited muttering in the hall.

"And I accepted," said Mary in a loud and clear voice. "So we shall be married at some point soon, but we had been asked..."

The rest of her speech was drowned out by applause – and some cat-calls which they ignored. Miss Armitage didn't, however, and looked round with the all-seeing, discipline-mode, accusing gaze that they all knew so well. She was about to say something when Mary continued, oblivious to all around her except Stephen.

"So, if you want to wish us well, please do. If you think we're too young, you can tell us but we are now entitled to ignore you as today is our last exam and our last day at the school. And... while I'm here, may I thank all my teachers, and particularly Miss Armitage, for teaching me and supporting me over some incredibly difficult times."

Stephen was about to add to that but was prevented by more applause. No cat-calls this time. He never did get an opportunity to add his thanks as Miss Armitage took over again.

Finally the last exams, one 'A' Level and one 'O' Level GCE, were over. Mary was first out, blinking in the sudden welcome sunshine after the nervousness and dimness of the exam hall. She ambled aimlessly around the playing fields for ages, unaware that she was in full view of her old classroom to which the pupils of the year below her had just been promoted. Attention inside it wandered from the teacher's efforts to keep their concentration on a new year's lessons. It was noticed and a member of the class was sent out to tell Mary to report to the school secretary.

Surprised and put out, she did so, then discovered that the secretary knew nothing about why she should be there. After explaining in an unaccustomed fit of independence that she'd just taken her last ever exam, and that she was 'allowed' out she was released and went to sit on the school wall until Stephen appeared.

"Too late for anyone to try and give us a detention," he crowed. "We're free now. That's school, over! For ever! We've got all this afternoon before we get the bus back to Salcombe, and then we can start farming. Together."

"We should have come up by boat," Mary said, smiling at and sharing his fit of freedom.

"We'd have needed to get up earlier with the wind and tide as it is."

"True." It had been a north-easterly wind and the tide was at full ebb when they started.

"What shall we do this afternoon, then?"

Mary thought. Nothing run-of-the-mill seemed appropriate. But there was little out of the ordinary to do in Kingsbridge.

"I want to do something adult," said Stephen. "I know. Where's that hotel? The one where you bought some pies when you came back from Scotland, and that Mr Rawle's wake was held at? We could go there and...and have a beer, or something."

Mary looked at him, shocked.

"On a school day?"

He laughed. "No more school days, Mary! Not unless you want to go back and do another two years' studying for 'A' Levels."

It was an odd feeling. There were so many years behind her when she had been a schoolgirl and life had been organised for her. A pub or hotel had been almost out of her experience until the previous few months of her life. Even then visits had been a rarity, occurring at weekends or for special occasions only. She was still conditioned, that day and at that point in her life, to be a schoolgirl. And here was Stephen telling her that school was out of the equation now – unless she decided otherwise. She stopped walking. He looked at her, still smiling, but she was looking back at the building which had been her second home since the age of five – apart from the three years away after the kidnap.

The security of a known environment and routine, versus the excitement, the risk, the adulthood of a pub. On a school day. With Stephen.

Into adulthood.

It turned out to be less of a dice with the future than she feared, than she expected. He quailed at the bar at the last moment and asked for a ginger beer. She followed suit and they found a table.

"What about that beer?" she asked, almost accusingly.

He screwed up his face. "I'm... I'm just not used to ordering beer. Not yet. I don't know why. For the first time for ages I was too nervous to do something." His voice had become ashamed. Or was it just annoyed with himself?

"I can't drink in a pub legally," she reminded him, "but still it seems – well, wrong. Wrong to be in here when we've just come from school."

"Is that it? Perhaps that's why I ordered... Oh well. We're here now and I'm thirsty after that hot exam hall. Aren't you?"

She nodded, relaxing at the shared truth. And she was thirsty. They drank.

Later, walking back to board the school bus, they looked at the building as it disgorged its young pupils. It almost seemed a different place, as if a barrier had been erected between them and it. But there, still, was the old bus with Stan at its wheel, and they were expected on it. And the small children – who had been their schoolfellows until earlier in the day – accepted their presence in the changeless way that they were used to, yet with an attitude that had been altering at a snail's pace ever since their own nervous first day.

Everything had changed as they left after their final exams: yet nothing had changed.

"We should buy old Stan something," Mary whispered as the bus climbed a hill. "He was so good to us when we came back after the flood – and he's such an old dear."

"I should have thought of that too," Stephen whispered back. "What to get him, though?"

Others whose exams had finally ended were on the bus as well. Whispered consultations took place. One suggested a pewter tankard, inscribed with the date, and thanks from the 1958 leavers. It seemed a good idea, appropriate. Stephen promised to arrange it and that they would meet the bus at Kingsbridge on the last day of term.

"That would be a better end to it," said one of the others. "Today's been just a damp squib for us, hasn't it?"

Mary and Stephen agreed. Apart from the visit to the pub, which they kept quiet about.

Stephen had his chance to thank Miss Armitage on the first Friday in July when the school broke up for the summer. They had gone in early to say their farewells as they were to visit an agricultural store with Susan and Henry later in the morning.

"It's lovely of you to say so, Stephen," she said. "I only wish we had been more aware and had been able to save Mary three years of absence. If she had blamed me for that I wouldn't have been surprised."

"But once she had returned, you supported me to the hilt – if that's not mixing metaphors!" Mary said with a laugh.

"Mary! That's dreadful! 'Supported to the hilt...' Whatever next. We'd better have you back for English, I think." It was said with a laugh. "Do you know, I've been teaching all these years and it still feels peculiar to talk to people who suddenly appear as adults in front of me. A few days of knowing that they're Old Boys and Old Girls and I feel as if we're on the same side of school. And you'll know what I mean, because each of you is far from stupid."

"Does that mean we use your Christian name, Miss Armitage?" asked Stephen.

The silence made him wonder if he'd actually gone too far. But there was a sudden laugh.

"You are a mischievous little boy, Stephen Loft. And it's refreshing to hear cheek come from someone who's a foot taller than me and as broad-shouldered as a Devon ox. No, you may not. Not today. Perhaps next month if you come and visit."

"Will you come and visit us, please?" asked Mary.

"I will most certainly be doing that over the summer, as a customer..."

"I meant as a guest."

"In that case, I would be glad to. And when I do, perhaps we can arrange some school visits to help some of the townies to understand where their milk bottles come from."

The Loft-Beale partners met for their appointment with a representative who would guide them through the design of modern milking parlours and their requirements. In consequence Mary's and Stephen's heads were spinning by the time they reached the school again for the bus's departure early at two-thirty. The plan was that Henry would take the boat back to Lincombe. The others would travel on the bus to Blanksmill where the little ceremony would be held, and they would walk together down the hill to the shoreline. It was the route they had taken to and from school since starting there, except in later years when journeying by boat. Travelling it for the last ever time seemed a fitting end to their long school careers.

Stan was open-mouthed when, at Blanksmill, six young men and women marched down the bus and all but dragged him from his seat. They marshalled the other passengers into a semi-circle which included the bus, the bus stop and him. Even Mrs Luscombe emerged from her store to watch the proceedings.

"I'll never forget how you dolled this old girl up when we came back to school that time," said Mary, indicating the old bus with a flourish. "And you've kept us safe on these wonderful, hilly, narrow roads since we started in the junior school. This is just to say thank you and give you something to remember us all by."

She handed over the box. Stan started to say something but decided to open it. Amongst all the silk protection and cotton wool he found a good, solid pewter tankard. With hands that shook he read the inscription:

> For our good friend Stan
> who kept us safe on our
> way to and from school.
> With thanks from the
> Kingsbridge leavers, 1958.

"You silly, lovely lot," He exclaimed when the cheers had died down, he'd wiped his eyes and recovered a little. "Thass a lovely thing to do. Be christened tonight, that, and I'll use it all the time. An' if ever you're in the Fortescue at night, you come and have a drink – when it's legal, that is!"

"Did he approve?" asked Henry when they appeared at the Lincombe 'jetty', the old road that had once extended across the dry valley to the island.

"Very much, I think, Dad. He says he's going to christen it tonight and we can go and have a pint with him in the Fortescue when we want to."

"What time is he going?" Henry asked. "I probably owe him a few for keeping you two safe. Especially the night when... well, you know."

"We could all go down. We could get Martin as well. I wonder if Susan knows him too?"

"Not fair on Susan – she's expecting. But get any other friends down, certainly. And Bob of course."

The old Fortescue was becoming busier now the visitors had started to appear. It was even busier that night. Stan's face as they all appeared had a look of permanent amazement. He produced the tankard, already full.

"But you've christened it already, Stan!" Stephen complained.

"No, not at all. 'Tis only christened when you drink from it, see? And you're just in time. I wish you and all your friends every success and… and it's been a pleasure knowing you and ferrying you to and from that ol' school."

He drank deeply as they watched, then stopped with a sigh and a bright-eyed look round at them.

"Yew lot going to sit and watch me drink all night? Or do I buy you one?"

"I think, Stan, that we buy you one," Henry laughed. "More than one, in fact. That's as a thank you for keeping these two safe all these years, and for just being there for them on occasion. There'll be another waiting in the pipeline for you when that's empty with my very sincere thanks."

"And ours." There was an unexpected chorus from young and older people around him. Stan swung round to look at them.

"Whoi blast… You really come to town for me?"

It was a memorable night. Bob eventually decided he should go home and once the cold air hit him was seen to start weaving his way along Fore Street. The Lofts, slightly unsteadily, regained their boat and Mary insisted on steering her back to the Island.

The following morning there were tears in Angharad's eyes as Bob left for the start of his training. She felt that he was in danger, that he might never return, that if he did return he would be a different man, a man trained to kill and maim, a rough man, maybe even the sort of man that her tormentor had been. But now the eyes that watched her as the train left Kingsbridge station were gentle; troubled, but gentle. They told of the character she had so quickly come to see as attractive, and to love, even after such a short time.

Would that character be changed by the army?

"So what do we do first?"

By the middle of the same Saturday evening the Lofts were discussing what steps they needed to take for the future. That was not just for the new land, but for the café too.

"I can't help but wonder what Bronwen and Dolly do with their time," Susan said wistfully. "And Annabelle, come to that."

"And Angharad," Mary reminded her.

"But she's expecting."

"So are you!"

She laughed. "I know, but after me. And she did say she'd like to come up and make *bara brith*. We really need someone who'll manage the café properly whilst we concentrate on the cooking as much as we can, and get rest when we need it. You three aren't going to be much use there if you're sorting land and milking parlours and creameries out, are you?"

Henry, Stephen and Mary looked at each other.

"How about Dolly?" Henry mused.

"Do you think she would?"

"I'd imagine she's not content to be sitting at home doing nothing," said Henry. "I get the impression that part of her feeling of dissatisfaction with life in Chepstow was that she was expected be a housewife – and one who had a maid to do much of the work. Now she's free, who knows?

"And maybe Aunt Amble would be prepared to do some of the paperwork. What did she do when she was in Kingsbridge?"

"Don't forget me," Mary reminded him. "I'd like to learn some of that too."

"But wouldn't you rather be busy on the practical side of things with me?" Stephen put in. "You always used to be."

She thought for a moment. "I think I want to be a part of everything. Farming, paperwork, café – in fact cafés – the dairy and - well, everything."

"If I can suggest something," Susan said. "Whilst I'm – expecting, and then looking after him or her, there's going to be work here in the café. While Angharad is in the same condition there will be cooking here too – assuming we offer her a position. But these will be seasonal. In fact thinking about it, her baby is due in December so it won't matter if she's out of the picture then. But we need staff here whilst I'm – otherwise engaged."

"But we need help sorting out the farm, and that needs people like Mary with experience," Henry objected. "We need you two particularly, to think about it, and anyone else in the family who knows their milking parlour work."

Susan looked up. "What about young Ted? He's worked hard on his family's farm in less than ideal conditions. He could help when he's not at school. He'd love to see what a modern set-up could offer. After all, he said he wanted to farm."

"Is that fair on him? He's only a schoolboy," Henry said.

"I was at school..." The protest came simultaneously from Mary and Stephen, who then stopped to avoid interrupting each other.

"We were at school when we were helping on the farm," Mary continued. "It worked for us."

"It was my life," said Stephen. "Apart from you two." He meant the younger Beales, his closest friends almost since birth. It was a bittersweet reminder of that terrible night.

The memory stopped the conversation for a few moments. Memory honours those who were our friends, whom we have lost. It does so in such unlooked-for silences.

"So it would mean a lot to Ted if we could continue his involvement in farming," said Mary gently, to restart the discussion. "Specially as Ian seems to have started work at the boatyard already."

That caused a smile. Not only was Ian still attending on Saturdays but had even offered to go in the holidays if they were short of people. The little rowing dinghy had had something to do with that.

"Not just that, but he'd feel he was continuing what his father started, I imagine." Henry was thinking of when he took over Lofts Farm from his own parents.

"You'd need to pay him," Susan told him.

"Of course!"

"Why don't we sound these people out, and see what they'd like to do?"

Stephen posed. "It's pointless making plans involving people if they aren't interested. What we should be doing is to design a good, modern milking parlour and decide on a size of herd we can manage."

"And that depends on how much of it we can sell." Henry put in.

"The Milk Marketing Board will take up what we can't sell to our own dairy – after using a lot of it for the café," said his son.

"How about my cheese?" Mary asked.

"Are you serious about that?" Henry sounded hopeful.

"I am. I've had a look at some books and it's a challenge, but one I can rise to."

"In that case we're looking at a milking parlour, a shed for cooling and storing the milk, and a cheese dairy. How about clotted cream as well, Mary? And what about ice cream? We mentioned them before."

She thought for a moment. "It'd take a lot of learning, and I'd need help, but yes. The trouble is that ice cream and cream are summer only things – ice cream particularly. At least cheese can be made all year round."

"We could…" Henry stopped, and laughed at himself. "I was going to say that we could start a stall up on the main road. But then someone would have to sit there all day and sell the few bits and pieces we produce."

"But we could have a shop in Kingsbridge, and another in Salcombe," Susan put in. "There's my café, of course. That could sell a lot of our produce, especially in summer. And there's nothing to stop us opening another in Kingsbridge. Maybe even in Bridge Street or Fore Street."

"At this rate you'll want to expand the Salcombe café into the next door shop!" Henry joked.

"That's not such a bad idea, if ever it comes onto the market," she responded, surprising him.

Talk switched to new designs of milking parlour, and laying out a new farm from scratch. Henry, Mary and Stephen knew that what they were planning was a very different business from the traditional hand-milking they were used to.

"Where's all this going?" asked Mary suddenly.

"If we're going to build a house in our special place…"

"No!"

"What?"

"Not in it. Near it."

"Oh, yes. Near it, but leave that natural."

"Yes. Please. Not even have a landing stage in it."

"So the house would be nearby, and it makes sense to have the dairy near. And if the dairy's there, the milking parlour needs to be there too."

"Other animals? Sheep? Pigs? How about arable?"

"If we're going to be concentrating on cows, should we look at the land we've got and decide how many cows it's viable for?" Henry was thinking hard. "There has to be such a thing as the right size of herd for – what – two people to manage?"

"Don't forget Ted," said Mary.

"Ahh – Ted. Do you think he'd work for us?"

"What's he said about it?"

"Just that he wants to be in farming."

"I think…" Henry said slowly, "…that we need to have an extended family conference. We need all the people we've been talking about. We need Martin, for designs. We need to talk to Ted, and to Angharad, and to any others who might feel left out; and we need to do that separately so that they know they can voice opinions from the start.

"Then we need to earmark a place for a house and the other things but get the milking parlour built urgently. Then we can take over our own herd again, and give the Rawles' cows a permanent home too."

Angharad knew that the only person who would have written to her was Bob. She opened the envelope with shaking hands.

It was a chatty letter, telling her that the barracks were okay, the men he was with were a mixed bag, and that one was from her family's old town of Llandeilo (which he had spelled with one L). She smiled.

'He speaks Welsh,' the letter continued, 'so if you get something that's in Welsh you'll know he's translated it for me. I don't think I'll be asking him, though, in case he puts in something else!'

It finished by telling her that training so far consisted of marching and drill, inspections and being sworn at, and a route march which he described as having 'half killed my feet'. His last sentence, in carefully written letters, were '*Rwy'n dy garu di*' [I love you]. It made her smile, but tearfully. He wasn't there. She missed his attentive company, his level and honest way of expressing himself.

Bronwen found her in the kitchen, wiping her eyes. She looked at the letter, guessed who had written it and was alarmed.

"Is he all right?"

Angharad nodded. "He is. But he's not here."

"But he would be if he could. And he'll be given leave soon. *Peidiwch a pheini* [Don't worry]. He's given you his address, hasn't he?"

"Yes. I will write. Tonight."

"Why not now? You aren't a maid any more. Remember?"

She smiled through the tears. "Good to me, you are. They all are."

Bronwen was indignant. "We have both disowned my father, Angharad. You know that. Nevertheless, he it was who wronged you, and we it is who want to put it right, as far as we can. Also…" She gulped. "…we like you. For who you are. For just being you. You know I always have and I know that Mum respects you too. You are one of us, not a maid. It was not Mum or I who employed you – remember? – it was *him*.

"And now – come into the front room, please? You belong there now. Never forget. Oh, we all need to do some cooking, and that's just because it's what women do. Though why, I don't know."

She was conscious of a long, measuring stare from Angharad and knew that her sincerity was being judged. She returned the gaze levelly, knowing that she meant every word.

The phone rang in the hall, interrupting the moment but causing both to smile. Angharad felt that she may have crossed a boundary.

"We'd love to come," Bronwen heard her mother say from the hall. "I'll ask

Bert and the others… I beg your pardon?"

One-sided phone conversations were annoying, Bronwen decided.

"*All* of us? Oh… well, yes. Look, you'll have been running the café all day. Why don't we bring everything with us and save you all having to start cooking again?"

Another gap.

"Oh, I'm sure they'd love to. In fact, let me talk to everyone and make sure, then I can call you back."

Bronwen motioned Angharad ahead of her and they went into the living room. Dolly, Annabelle and Bert were there and smiled at them. Martin was still at work, to her slight annoyance, and the boys were out somewhere.

"Good," Dolly started. "That saves my having to fetch you. We've all been asked to visit Loft Island tomorrow. If Annabelle agrees, Ted and Ian can go back with the Lofts after the early church service, with Angharad if she'd like. Susan would love it if Angharad could show her some Welsh recipes and the boys can take it in turns between working in the café and sailing practice. The rest of us can be fetched later.

"Is their Grandad not good enough to go and help in the café in the morning?" Bert asked in a mock-aggrieved voice.

"Bert, they're going to be busy. They don't want you there getting in the way."

"I wasn't thinking about me, I was thinking about us."

"But that would be more inconvenient for them."

"Not if we helped. We could wash up."

She looked at him sharply. "Bert, the idea of you washing up all day is a strange one. Incompatible with your character, I would say."

"My dear, I rather like the idea of our doing the drudgery whilst Angharad performs like a star with her baking."

Angharad was startled. She was very much in awe of this old gentleman who spoke at times as if he had been written by Dickens. Glimpses of a very different character showed at times, like sparks in the night; his agreeing to offer her a home in the first place, his gentle appreciation of what she was doing, his occasional bursts of humour. She liked him. To have him compliment her in that way was a shock. A pleasant shock. Having seen him react to others over the months since she had arrived, she thought she would try something. Turning in his direction, and with a smile, she bowed.

"Angharad, you are getting to know me too well!" Bert chuckled. "I take that as a turning of the tables. Thank you and you are welcome. There is no need for you to be a drudge in this house or anywhere. You do a lot for everyone. Within the atmosphere of working as a team in this house to feed and clean, you are ever present. And, may I say, always appreciated even if the words are not said often enough. I shall be pleased to see you doing things that you enjoy, as will Aunt Amble. You always sing when you are baking, so I would imagine that it gives you pleasure. Would that be a good guess?"

She hesitated. "It is… it is in making things that create delight that… that I find pleasure."

"And what you have made for us since you came has certainly done that,"

Dolly told her. "Especially when it has been a surprise. In case you don't realise, you really are wanted at Loft Island this afternoon with all of us."

Bronwen nodded her agreement. They were rewarded by a rare, full smile from Angharad, a smile that lingered.

Dolly lifted the receiver and agreed that the boys, her brother, Annabelle and Angharad would come over in the morning to help and in the boys' case, have sailing lessons.

They set to cooking and preparing.

23 – Decisions

At the Hard next morning, Susan found an excited Ian jumping up and down and pointing to an old, black-tarred, disreputable looking dinghy moored at the jetty. Deducing it was something to do with him, she moored next to it.

"Can you tow it to the Island? Please? It's the boatyard's – Mustchins – but they've asked me to check it over to see it doesn't leak. I really, *really* want to row her round the Island."

Susan had heard some of the story and knew there was a boat in it somewhere. So this was it. Well, it was afloat, and dry. She remembered the excitement that discovering a sailing dinghy had caused Mary and Stephen.

The others of the first batch of islanders appeared, and his Uncle Bert looked down at the dinghy, then at Ian.

"I understand you're going to row to Loft Island, Ian, and tow the launch to save petrol. Is that right?"

Ian knew him by now. The two had teased each other frequently on a regular basis.

"You said you'd row, Uncle Bert, and that I could steer the launch to save my muscles."

"Ah, did you now. And who told you that, pray?"

"The same person who told you I was going to tow the launch."

Bert roared with laughter. "Touché, Ian, touché. So are you going to steer her?"

"No, if we shorten the painter, she'll tow behind the launch. Though I could ride in her."

"If it's anything like my first bicycle was to me, you'd have had difficulty removing me from it. So you sit in it if you want. Do you want Ted for company? And does Ted want to ride in her?"

"I'd rather steer the launch, if that's all right."

"You shall, Ted. But just remember you're towing your brother and it'd be rude to drown him."

"I think it'd be a good idea,.."

They laughed at Ian's mock-horrified expression and clambered in.

"Yesterday was as near chaos as we have ever been," Henry said by way of greeting once the launch had been moored at the Island's slipway. Despite his earlier comments Ted was helping Ian hop from dinghy, to launch and to terra firma but heard the comment.

"You needed us!" he called.

"You're actually right. We did. You two would have made a lot of difference."

"I could have come," said Ted. "Ian was at Edgar's but I could have come."

"We'd have had to fetch you," Susan told him, "and that would have meant one fewer to serve here."

"We need a boat," he replied.

"You forgot there's a ferry, Susan," her father pointed out.

Both the Lofts gaped at him, then at each other.

"We're stupid," said Henry. "All of us. Just one phone call…"

Mary and Stephen were cleaning in the café and greeted them all effusively. Angharad was looking round curiously. It was only her second time on the Island and she was still intrigued.

"But where do you cook?" she asked Mary.

It was rare for her to start a conversation. Mary smiled.

"In the house, until all the alterations are finished, and they won't be started until we close. We can't have the house surrounded by a building site when we're trying to run a café."

"No, indeed."

"Come in to the house," Stephen said, and led the way. They gave her a tour, starting and ending with the kitchen where she was drawn to the new, large cooker.

"Wonderful, it is," she sighed. "And all the cakes and scones are made here? You buy nothing from the shops?"

"Only bread," Susan said as she joined them. "And that comes from a real bakers. None of the packaged bread for us! And now, really, we should start cooking."

"Please – may I help?"

"Very gladly, my dear. I have to start with scones, as people seem to latch onto them, but I really want to see how you make *bara brith*. And are there any other specialities of yours you'd like to try?"

"Cheese scones have always been good," she offered.

"Cheese scones! We've never tried them and I don't know why. It just never occurred… Have you a recipe?"

"Scone mix, it is, with grated cheese rubbed in. A lot of cheese gives a proper taste. Shall I… may I try?"

"With the greatest of pleasure," Susan told her. "Here's Mary; we usually help each other but we can all work together today. But if you get tired, you just say."

"But you, too are… expecting."

"Yes. And occasionally I need to sit down for a while. But we have good waiting staff today, and some very good washers up, so we should be able to take it a little easier."

Salcombe was full of visitors. The ferry was also busy and even more people were seeing the neat notices by the ferry piers telling of a Café on an Island. At one point in the afternoon there were so many in the Ferry queue that Charlie, in charge of it, had to call Edgar from the pub and ask if he could send another boat. Edgar dug out two of his staff, gave them the biggest hire launch he had available and sent them to help.

The Island was throbbing with people. The café was full and Mary was having to ask people to go for a walk round until they had some space. Ted and Ian were busy serving and charming customers, especially Ian who caused so many comments of "Ahhh… isn't he sweet?" from the grandmothers that he would have been really embarrassed had he heard. Ted was looking around everyone and hoping that the girl he had seen when he was last there might return.

"If we thought it was chaos yesterday, this beats it," Henry muttered to Susan as she, Mary and Angharad made yet another batch of scones.

The end of the afternoon loomed and they were thankful when the last visitor had left. Henry called everyone out to the café and told them to sit down with the last lot of dirty plates and cutlery still on the tables.

"We've never been that busy before," he said, relieved that it was over, "and I'm so grateful to you people for coming and pitching in. For Aunt Amble and Uncle Bert it was a baptism of fire and I apologise to you both, as well as to Angharad, Ted and Ian. Angharad because all she was expecting to teach how to make *bara brith* – which was very popular, by the way, as were the cheese scones this morning – and to the boys for forgoing their sailing. We will do something about that, won't we? Tomorrow, if we're spared another onslaught and Mary and Stephen can make time."

"I'll have to ask Mr Mustchin," said Ian cautiously. "He might be busy and need me."

Henry knew that the Yard had managed very well before Ian and would do so again when he had eventually tired of it, but said nothing.

"You're there mornings, aren't you?" Ted asked. "How would it be if I went out in the morning, and you in the afternoon? Mary, could we fetch him from the Hard once he's moored Black Beauty?"

Ian was about to protest at the name, but as he'd never thought to provide the dinghy with one of his own he couldn't really complain. And as names went it could have been worse. He wondered if he could ask for some white paint from the Yard to try writing it on her bow.

Henry cleared his throat to attract attention. "We didn't actually ask you all here to help us out. We asked you if you could help us think through the plans we've been making for the farm, its new land and some prospective new buildings."

Martin's ears pricked up.

"All of you are either family or extended family. We know you and know we can work with you. Whatever we do, we need people to look after things. Our plans are getting towards being finalised, detailed design and planning is the next step. And yes, Martin, that means you and Mike, who I need to talk to as soon as I can."

"We can," chipped in a quiet voice. Susan.

"We can. Sorry. I've done it again. 'We' in this case means Susan, Mary, Stephen and me. Before we do, and when planning is being done, we really want your views. Everybody's views. We'd appreciate comments from all of you, please, even on the most minute details."

Henry outlined the basic ideas for milking parlour, dairy for butter, clotted cream and cheese production. He mentioned watercress, he mentioned grazing. He mentioned pigs (to Stephen's slight horror). He mentioned shops.

"Stephen and I will have our work cut out looking after the milking herd for a good part of the day. Mary is interested in starting and developing the making of cheese, cream and ice cream. Susan will be out of the picture for a while, as will Angharad from next winter."

Angharad's wandering attention focussed on him. What did any of this have to do with her?

"Uncle Bert is obviously out of the equation, as is Martin – except that he will be here with or without Mike working on the architecture side of things.

"But we are going to need help; management help and expertise. We wanted you here so we could think about whether any one of you would be interested in coming in with us.

"We shall need someone to do the book-keeping, gathering in all the figures from the various parts of the farm. We need someone to look after the staffing of the cafes and maybe helping to start up or take over other cafes around the area – like Kingsbridge, for example. Other help we need, not so managerial, will be to do with the dairy and its activities under Mary's management, with the pigs, the watercress – yes, really! – and any other new farming activities we introduce.

"The Salcombe café will become very important as it will double as an outlet for the farm's products. And if it can expand in size, so much the better.

"So, Dolly, Bronwen, Annabelle, Angharad, Ted and Ian: what do you think? And yes, Ted, I did mention you particularly. We need a part-time helper for general farming jobs. From what you've let slip we thought you might be interested in doing the sort of things that Stephen used to do before the flood. You know, out of school time."

There was a look of amazement on Ted's face. He was nodding furiously. "I really, *really* want to do that. I miss farming so much."

"Even the early morning starts?" Henry asked with a smile.

"Cows don't wait," was his only answer.

"Then we'll talk to Aunt Amble and come to some sort of arrangement. It won't be for some time yet. We have to have the buildings ready first."

"Who's planning the milking shed?" Ted asked. "Martin?"

"Not likely," said Martin. "I have no experience. Nor has Mike. It's the job of specialists, I should think."

Ted nodded, looking thoughtful. "Mr Loft," he started in a hopeful voice that seemed not to have the childish wheedling note in it any more, "would it be all right if I looked at the plans when they're ready, just in case I can add anything?" He thought. "Even if it's only a name…"

Henry grinned, knowing what he meant. "Everyone involved can look at them. Knowledge and common sense are welcomed anywhere, and from everyone, the more so if they have experience and know what *not* to plan."

"It strikes me…" Annabelle had spoken, but now paused. She was looking a little worried. "It's going to be quite a lot of work for you, Ted, with school as well. I suppose for Stephen it was different: this was his home. But how would you be able to get here, come back for school, then travel back?"

Ted had not thought that far ahead, and hesitated. "I… I could live here," he said uncertainly, looking at Henry and then, with a sudden shock, at his younger brother who appeared very straight-faced.

"We need to think that through and come to a decision once you've discussed it, I think," said Henry soothingly. "Mornings would be the main rush for you, even if you joined the school bus at Lincombe direct from here. But if you wanted to come here after school in the afternoons, and perhaps do a Saturday or Sunday – anything to work in with you, really."

Ted nodded, smiling widely. "Thank you, Mr Loft."

Annabelle cleared her throat again. "I used to do some accounts and administration work when I was in Kingsbridge. If I could help with anything like that, I'd be happy to."

"That sounds like a very good offer. Thank you, Annabelle. These are all salaried posts, by the way. Just as we want to be able to live off the businesses, so should anyone else working with us."

"I'd just like to be farming again," Ted said. "I don't need paying, but it would be nice, I suppose."

"You'll be paid," Henry assured him.

"May I ask something before anyone else does?" Uncle Bert was looking thoughtful. "You know that Mrs Damerell retires at the end of the summer and I shall need someone to replace her. I was wondering whether any of my own extended family would be interested in becoming a secretary-cum-assistant. Maybe, if the person wanted, they would take up an even more important role, as there will come a time when I shall seek to retire. So please. Annabelle, Dolly, would you think about that? And Bronwen: if you feel you could work with me before attending University and qualifying with a degree, please may we talk? For you have a good brain, one that was wasted doing so little in Chepstow.

"Another thing, Henry; have you talked to Peter and Dot about your plans? Are you sure neither of them would like to be involved?"

Henry hesitated. "I did wonder about them. But when we last spoke Peter was still happy where he was and seemed to have no interest in farming..."

"Ah, but that was when it was farming - the practicalities of farming. Given the organisational side of the business as you plan it, might he be interested, I wonder? I suppose what I'm trying to say is that it would help to avoid any bad feeling if he was offered a chance."

Henry grimaced. "I have been worried about that, but we've not discussed it here – or with Peter of course. We should. In fact, he and Dot should be here." The Loft family looked at each other guiltily.

In the natural pause that followed, Angharad cleared her throat. "I... I would love to do some real cooking. Cooking for a café, I mean. Or even, cooking for however many cafes you have."

This was more Susan and Henry's province. "We would really value that, Angharad. But you will have a little one to look after, don't forget."

Susan was also thinking. "But really, Angharad and I could help each other look after each other's babies, if she agrees – and I'm not looking for an agreement now. Or even an agreement at all. It's a very personal thing. But we can both still supervise others to do the work, particularly in the summer. It will be too much for one person to do."

Angharad was taken aback. She had only worked with Susan for a day, yet she had been accepted readily as someone who knew what they were doing. And now she was being asked, almost, if she could boss other girls around, other cooks. And she only sixteen!

"But... but Ma'am... they would take no notice of me, other girls you employ. It's older than me they'd be, surely."

"It makes no difference, Angharad. Anyone we employed, and by "we" I mean you and me, would realise that they take direction from both of us. They

208

will know that I know the cafes, we both know the cooking. And we shall each of us be learning from the other. We can agree between us what we want to offer and what we then produce in our kitchens, then we instruct the staff.

"No: we're not a big firm with managers who are self-important. We're here to contribute to a business that we want to see grow and provide us all with an income. That would include you if you accept and if, most importantly, it all works. With the growing tourist trade that's already coming it our ideas won't let us down, I'm sure. You and I have a particular interest in making it work as we shall both have very dependent babies to care for."

Once more Angharad was astonished. She found herself smiling at Susan.

"Thank you, Ma'am."

"And Angharad – please use my Christian name. I really would appreciate it."

The smile grew wider and the girl nodded.

"Well, that's the cafés sorted out, it seems," said Henry. "Anyone else want to come forward and take on a project? Or should I phone Peter and Dot first? Maybe they would want to be involved in that side too."

"I think *we* should," Susan said, accenting the pronoun. Henry winced.

"Sorry. Will you, or shall I?"

"I will," she said. "That'll surprise him. It's almost always you who ends up talking to him!"

Peter's first words once Susan had told him who it was were "There's not been an accident, has there?"

Susan laughed. "No. Why would you think there might have been?"

"It's always Dad who phones and talks first." He paused, then added quickly "Not that it's not nice to talk to you, obviously. But…"

Susan laughed. "Peter, it's all right, really. You don't have to try and dig yourself out of a hole – there isn't one, so far as I'm concerned. Everything all right, that end?"

"It's fine, thanks. In fact we were wondering why we'd not heard from you for some time, with the news about the Water Board coughing up and everything. Have you got what you deserve? And has Mary?"

"We should have told you. Yes, we have, and so has Mary. Really, it's what we want to talk to you about."

"Er… right; I see, I think; but we don't come into it, really. I'm not a part of the farm now. I made my choice years ago."

"But you are a part of something bigger: the family. So is Dot. We've been talking about what we want to do with the farm, and it's very exciting. We want you to have a chance of joining in with the parts of the business that aren't farming and which might interest you, if you want to."

She let that sink in for a few seconds.

"But I'm on to motors now, not farming. But then – what are the parts of the farm that aren't farming?" Peter asked cautiously.

"We're just thinking now about the various possibilities. It wasn't possible to get you here as well because we've had an incredibly busy few days in the café and just haven't had the chance. But I'll put your Dad on and he can tell you what we've been discussing."

Henry took the receiver and was soon in full spate with plans and hopes. When he came to a halt, Peter's first words were "If you can fund that lot, the compensation cheque must have been immense."

The phone, of course, was in the farm house. The extended discussions had been taking place in the café, so Henry was free to remind his elder son that Mary's compensation took into account three lives, a home and farm buildings as well as the land lost, and was being pooled with the lesser Loft Island farm compensation.

Peter was silenced.

Henry continued gently. "What we want to do is to tell you what the ideas are so far, which I've done, and ask for any thoughts you've got. I imagine that you won't want to go back into farming, but if there is anything else that interests you in what I've said, I'd love you and Dot to consider it. To consider joining us. But only if you want to."

There was another long silence.

"I think Dot and I need to talk. You see, where I am in the garage we're doing a lot of work, and more's coming in all the time. It's something I enjoy and I'm being looked after really well by this guv'nor. That's how we knew we could afford the payments on the cottages – they're ready, by the way, so we could move in. But my work's here in Torquay so it's going to mean a lot of travelling when we do. It's no good saying we'll sell those two cottages and buy something here. It's just too expensive. But I can either travel or…"

He paused. "Or, I suppose, look for a job in Kingsbridge that's as good as this one."

"Or, of course, start up on your own in Kingsbridge," Henry mused.

"I couldn't afford that! And it takes a long time to win customers in this game."

"Then how would it be if you developed the garage side? Dot, with help, could look after a café and shop, selling the family's ice creams and cakes and all sorts from the farm and its other activities? Or maybe your guv'nor might look at setting up a branch in Kingsbridge if the work is increasing. You could come to an agreement with him that you'd manage it and that the café would be run by Dot as a business separate from the garage.

"I'm thinking as I go here, Peter, so I have no idea if there's anywhere in the town it could be made to work. But a café and store combined – well, it's the sort of thing we've been talking about doing in Kingsbridge. Not the garage, but a shop and café."

"I wonder if she would, Dad," Peter said slowly. "And I wonder if the guv'nor has even thought about starting up somewhere else. And if he did, I wonder if he'd trust me enough to look after it. I think we have some talking to do Dot and me, then Paul and me."

"Paul?"

"The Guv'nor."

"Ah. Yes. I should. You never know what he might say. And Peter – never forget that you are a part of this family. If I can – if we can help you start up a business, we will."

"You've had enough expenses with buying all that land, and you're going to have more before this really gets started. And Mary put down the deposit on those cottages for us... no, you've done enough and I'm grateful. We can't accept any more."

"Peter, this is a business proposition, not a sort of gift. If you and Dot are interested in a place which is part garage, part café, part shop, then it could fit in with all the rest of what we're trying to plan. The café is something we've been talking about, and I can't think of anyone I'd rather see run it than you two. But only if it's what you want and are happy with. And if that includes a garage – well, why not? Talk about it. Think about it. Please. We're not short of time, because it can't happen before autumn. Though we can at least make plans and look for a prospective place for it."

"You're serious, aren't you?"

"I am, Peter. I miss you."

Where that came from, Henry wasn't sure. It wasn't something he had planned on saying but he knew as soon as the words were out that it was true. There was silence at the other end of the line, though, and he wondered if he'd said too much.

Finally there was a sigh. "Hell, Dad. You got to me just then. Really. Look, let me talk to Dot. We'll come and see you next weekend. May we?"

"Peter, you know the answer to that. We'll need to get some people in to help to give ourselves a rest after this weekend. And that would release us to talk too. And you can stay the night – we'll work something out."

Henry returned to the café, stopping just inside the doorway to listen to the eager talk still flowing as his extended family discussed the possible future. He smiled to himself. If that enthusiasm could only be bottled! Talk petered out as he re-entered.

"How is he?" Susan asked.

"They're well. He's going to talk to Dot and to his boss, to put forward an idea that came to me as we were talking. He enjoys his job and wants to continue with it, so I suggested he looks for a garage in Kingsbridge which could double as a café and shop for us. Whether his boss would start it or whether he takes the risk of making it work on his own – their own – is what they have to discuss."

Stephen whistled in surprise. "What did he say to that?"

"He didn't turn it down out of hand."

There was an impressed and hopeful pause in the chat. Bert Merryweather was smiling.

As they left the island Mary turned to Ted and Ian.

"You're coming up tomorrow for sailing?" It was more of a statement, even if her voice lifted at the end of the sentence.

"Please," said Ted immediately. "If I come in the morning, we could pick Ian up in the afternoon.

"I'll pick you up after church, shall I?"

"Oh... Yes, okay. Thanks." Since their mother's funeral and, more recently their father's, Church had not been a part of the younger Rawles' calendar.

"Or come with us, if you like," Mary added, wondering if she was going too far.

"I need to be at the boatyard in the morning," said Ian doubtfully.

"We go to the early Service," Mary said. "Edgar's there too."

"I will if you will," said Ted.

It was later, in Salcombe, that discussions were held, individual hopes calculated. Bronwen was thinking that her schooling had demonstrated that she was capable. The occupations that women were expected to take up held little interest for her and she knew she wanted something more challenging. She had also known that her father would hear of nothing for her but marriage to a suitable husband, the running of a home and the bearing of children. It would have been anathema to him to see her attempting to qualify for a University place. He would have refused to finance it, and she would have been bullied well and truly into what he saw as her place..

But now he was out of the question. Her future was hers to decide; hers and her mother's, perhaps. She felt a growing need to kick against the traces, even if the traces probably no longer existed. Dolly was in deep conversation with her brother. Uncle Algy. She smiled. Uncle *Bert*. After all this time she really should get used to that.

Was Dolly thinking of asking if she could take over from Mrs Damerell? Did she need a job? If she had been stifled by *him* for so long, surely she deserved freedom too?

Her name was being called. Uncle Bert. She crossed to where he had been talking quietly to Dolly and was welcomed with a smile.

"Well, Bronwen. Where do you want to fit into all this? Have you been thinking?"

She hesitated. "I'm not sure how I fit into it. Apart from you no one has suggested anything. And I really don't know."

Her uncle would had continued, but Dolly held up her hand to stop him. "We've been talking about you, I'm afraid. We all know that your future had been planned out for you. And it was as bleak a future as my life with my father had been bleak, in those far off days. I was given no choice. Neither was Bert. We were told what to do, and in minute detail. But I know that you have a good brain and that you can make more of yourself than I have ever been able to do. You must realise that."

She waited, and Bronwen realised that for the first time in her life she might be able to have an input into her own future.

"I... want to think so. The school thought I should continue with an education. They mentioned College. But he would have none of it."

"Did you know that your school wrote to him and suggested university? I found the letter. He had ignored it, as you might imagine. That was only a year ago. But..."

She smiled and looked her daughter square in the eyes.

"...it's still not too late to act on it."

Bronwen blinked. That was sudden. Was it what she wanted? Her first thought was that it would mean her having to live away from home. She had never experienced any such thing, and had no certainty she was capable of it. Even less was she sure of her confidence to follow lectures and gain from them.

"I don't know. I hadn't thought. And what would I study?"

Her uncle cleared his throat. "May I?" he asked. "Bronwen, the last thing I want to do is to steer you into anything you don't want to do. You might want to study architecture with Martin, but you might not.

"There is a law practice here in Salcombe whose owner will want to retire at some point and would like to be sure of his successor. If you were to consider law as an area of study and if you think you could work with me for a short time, as I said when we were on the Island, there is no reason why you shouldn't take the firm over."

Surprise after surprise. She almost stammered her next words. "But... but solicitors are men. Always. Aren't they?"

"Most girls who study law at university are there because they kicked against the traces and insisted. Their path into legal practice once they qualify is usually to approach a law firm for almost any job. Generally, law firms are so traditional that they will keep the new applicant busy making the tea or sorting papers. A girl graduating from university would normally have no ready-made practice to join, since places in family firms normally go to the sons of the family.

"I know from Martin that there is one thing that your father successfully taught you, even if he never dreamed he was doing so: to argue and stand your ground when at the end of your tether..." He paused, then laughed at himself. "That is a mixed metaphor. I really should be more careful. He told me of the exchanges between you and your father in Chepstow. It shows that, *in extremis*, you will stand up against someone trying to browbeat you. In law, your client is almost always *in extremis*, and relies on you for representation against the powerful bully or the Law. If you can build on that ability to argue when necessary then you might have what it takes to become a solicitor. Apart from the legal knowledge, of course; and that is what University would give you."

Bronwen had a tremendous feeling of being buoyed up by the compliments implied by her school, given by her mother and particularly by this uncle whom she instinctively regarded as the fount of wisdom. And he was so obviously sincere because it would be his practice she might be taking over.

Taking over! Her! She who had never been allowed by her father to make a decision for herself in her life! And she would potentially be making decisions for other people which would alter their lives, or at the very least allow their lives to continue as normal.

"It's a lot to take in," she said hesitantly.

"Yes," her uncle replied, "it is and it should be. You should sleep on it, then talk it over with... with anyone you want. But the decision has to be yours. There is no compulsion. But..." he stopped and smiled warmly at her. "... If I didn't think you could do it, I wouldn't have suggested it. And that's all I'm going to say tonight."

24 – Sailing lessons

"It's a very small boat," Ted remarked.

"She," Mary instructed. "A boat is always a she."

"Even a dinghy?"

"Especially a dinghy," Stephen told him, "because you're never really certain what she's going to do next...OW!"

Mary smiled at him sweetly as he held his arm in mock pain.

"Push off," she commanded.

"Me? Or the boat?" he asked, giving a good shove against the edge of the hardstanding.

"Both, if you're not careful," she said, pulling the tiller round to bring the sail into play.

Ted grinned at the two. So being in love wasn't all holding hands and kissing. It was treating each other like he did his schoolfriends, with mock-insults and teasing. Yet he had seen them being close and personal, when they had thought no one was watching. Perhaps it was both. Perhaps it was like a good friendship that somehow went beyond that. And maybe, all the time, with the sudden feeling he had experienced with the girl in the café once.

Is that what awaited him? And who would it be? Angharad? No she would never... What? What was Stephen saying? More by instinct than having heard the warning he ducked. The boom swung over his head, missing it by inches.

"You've got to be quicker than that, Ted. We can't teach you to sail if your mind's elsewhere. And you'll need to keep your head where it belongs to be able to use your brain anyway. "

"Sorry," he mumbled. "I was thinking."

"Good, but you need to make sure it's about the boat and what we're saying."

"Okay, sorry, sorry. I'm listening."

The wind took them away from the Hard and into the narrow, mud-banked channel. The tide was low and had there not been a beam wind they would have had to row as there was little room for tacking. Ted watched Mary like a hawk as Stephen gave a running commentary. Once in the main estuary, and with a reasonable breeze, he was shown the principles of sailing.

Come his first attempt at the tiller he proved himself a competent, if unexceptional, trainee. They put him through his paces until he begged for a rest and a cup of tea. Stephen, at the tiller, headed into North Cove at the south west of the estuary, in sight of the sinister-looking Black Stone Rocks near the Bar.

"It's quieter than South Sands," Said Mary.

Ted looked at the swimmers hording near the café and wondered what South Sands' crowds would be like.

"We should get them to come up to the Island," he observed.

"Oh, they will soon," Stephen laughed. "Tourists love going anywhere unusual. It's a pity in a way we don't own another island so we can open a café on that too."

With a start, Mary's mind switched to her first home, now long drowned along with the rest of her family. Why, oh why had her ancestors decided to live there and not on higher ground? Stephen saw her expression change as the dinghy grounded lightly and Ted jumped ashore.

"Is something wrong?" he asked anxiously as he finished lowering the mainsail.

She shook her head to chase the thought away. "Just thinking back to my old home and wishing it had been on an island, or on any higher ground."

The sail was left untidy as he took two steps down the boat to her and enveloped her in a hug. There was no need for words between them on this subject; he had been there. Quite literally he had been there. He shared her sudden pangs of pain and knew that, along with his own emotions, the first words that sprang to mind were "if only…"

Ted, holding the painter, was watching them gravely.

"Have I upset you?" he asked when they had released each other and completed stowing the sails.

Stephen smiled. "No. It's just that Mary had one of those flashback memories of her old home. You know, her parents and her brother. I was there when we found them all that night."

Ted knew the story. He remained grave.

Tea and a bun each was a relief. The three found plenty to compare with their own café, and were happy that the service they offered on Loft Island was far better, that the buns were fresher, and that even at their busiest their café seemed quieter.

"It's the take-away service that makes it so noisy," Stephen commented after two spectacularly noisy infants and their parents had been served at high volume. "We aren't offering that, and I really don't like people wandering round the island with our plates and things, though they do. Even now we keep finding them in all sorts of places."

"Some people are just untidy," said Ted, himself one who mostly left plates on a table for others to collect – except in the island café when clearing tables was part of the job.

He was given the helm again on the return journey up the Estuary and acquitted himself quite well, slowly acclimatising to giving orders to the other two, as befits the helmsman. Just as Mary and Stephen had when learning, he had a close shave with an unintended gybe whilst taking avoiding action to miss a hired motor boat. The man steering it laughed at the exclamation and the sailing dinghy's sudden lurch to leeward, and was about to say something when Stephen shouted at him that it was his job to give way to unpowered craft.

The retort was sharp and unpleasant. Ted was about to swing the dinghy round so as to be able to retaliate, but Stephen crisply told him to ignore him.

"We'll tell Edgar when we go and pick up Ian," he said. "That's one of his boats, so he'll be able to say something."

"I could get Ian to get him to fall into the water," Ted replied, still angry.

"Best left to Edgar, really," Mary said soothingly. "He's quite capable of crushing people when he needs to."

Ted settled down again. The lesson continued past Salcombe's Ferry Steps, across the main fairway and into Southpool Creek. Here, the wind was chancy; and coupled with the narrow, mud-edged channel, it made sailing more difficult. Despite his best efforts, and with direction from his mentors, Ted ran the boat aground. He couldn't be blamed as there was rippled water on every side of them. The mud at that point had only just been covered by the rising tide.

There was immediate action as the mainsail was lowered. Mary stowed it loosely, ready for hoisting again.

"Why not the front one?" Ted asked.

"It's called the jib. We'll leave that up so that when the tide has risen and we're afloat, it'll take us forward."

"But if it's shallow ahead, is that what we want?"

"Ah – we're going to use a bit of estuary seamanship," Stephen told him. "Take an oar up for'ard and gently dig about a bit to find where the deep water is. Then we'll know for sure."

With a quizzical look at his mentor he manoeuvred an oar from its stowage under a thwart and cautiously headed forward. Standing to windward of the flapping jib he dug into the mud. Two feet. Even he knew the dinghy should float on that. Dripping water and mud over the bows he dug the oar into the water on the port side.

Still two feet. He looked round with a puzzled frown.

Stephen smiled at him, pulled a rope clear from its cleat, and pulled. The centreboard came up on its pivot and the dinghy slowly moved ahead. Mary steered to windward and the jib flapped.

"That's estuary seamanship," Mary explained. "If you run aground gently, think where the deep water should be, free your centreboard and sail into it."

She hauled up the mainsail again whilst Stephen took the tiller. Ted struggled back with the oar, looking sheepish. He stowed it again, having washed it over the side.

"Don't worry," said Stephen. "We were taught the same way. It's a good lesson to learn. You have some flexibility if you remember the centreboard, but don't do what we did."

"What was that?" Ted was feeling better.

"We were running before the wind – like you were earlier – and when we started tacking we forgot to lower the centreboard again. Worse, old Charlie forgot too, and we nearly came to grief. Okay, we're sailing again. Probably best head out of the creek and go to find that brother of yours."

"Okay. What do you want me to do?"

"We're going to be doing short tacks so as to keep in the channel. If you and Mary don't mind keeping an eye out for shallows in case I miss anything, and you each look after the jib sheet your side, I'll helm. Then if we run aground again it'll be my fault."

"Would you like me to lower the centreboard again?" Ted asked innocently.

The other two laughed. "Touché!" Mary laughed. "Yes please."

Ted took over again as they cleared the last of the long creek's shallows. He was doing well until a ferry, no doubt returning people from Loft Island, appeared to be on a collision course with his reach across to the town. He hesitated.

"Keep going," said Mary quietly.

He did. Their wake straightened again. A figure appeared outside the ferry's wheelhouse, carrying something. He put it on the thwart and was seen to say something. The passengers either side of it moved away and hands were seen to raise to cover their ears. There were two blasts, causing even those protecting their hearing to flinch.

Mary and Stephen laughed.

"That must be Charlie," Mary told Ted. "He's telling us he's altering course to port."

She waved, and received an answering wave. True to the signal, the ferry veered a little so as to avoid them.

"Thanks, Charlie!" bellowed Stephen without warning. It was Ted's turn to flinch.

"Steam gives away to sail!" came the response. "And we do, even if we're petrol!"

Stephen waved again as the ferry cleared their stern by a comfortable margin. Ted smiled. "Good of him."

"Rule of the road at sea, like we told that motor boat steerer," Mary told him. "He wouldn't want to run us down, would he? He's been a seaman too long for that. And he'd never hear the last of it if he did."

The ferry had moored at the Ferry Steps well before Ted sailed past on the way to the boatyard. It was at Edgar's that Ian was to be collected. They almost expected him to be sitting on the edge of the wall, waving, but he wasn't. There was no sign of him there, but as they headed in with Mary now at the tiller, a small rowing boat was seen returning from a moored sailing lugger, a familiar, small figure rowing fast, with two adults sitting in the stern. It seemed to be heading to the steps far too fast, but at the last minute the rower backwatered. The contact with the wall was light, and immediately the small figure had caught one of the hanging chains to allow his passengers off.

"Is that really my kid brother?" Ted asked no one in particular.

"Looks like it," Stephen said with a laugh. "I think he's been practising."

"A bit more than that," Ted muttered, "He's showing off!"

Having attached the painter to his arm, Ian scampered up the steps after his two customers, catching them up before they reached the boatyard's flat stone-flagged deck. They turned and were seen to hand him something which he promptly pocketed.

Stephen and Mary executed a similarly impressive manoeuvre. Mary lowered the mainsail and started furling it. Before the mast, Ted did the same with the jib, but found he had to grab the chain first to keep the boat alongside. Stephen headed for the steps with the long painter and was met by Ted once the sail was furled. They met Ian at the top.

"You took a tip!" Ted accused.

"Yeah...well? Anyway, Mr Mustchin says I can. Lots of people give them."

"What's Dad going to say..." The words were out of Ted's mouth before he realised.

Ian's face straightened, then a softer smile returned. "He'd say he was glad I was earning money for the farm."

"But it's not for... Oh well. Never mind."

"Should I give it to Uncle Bert?"

"I don't think he needs it. Maybe save it - put it in the Post Office."

"Oh."

Edgar emerged from the workshop, blinking in the sunshine, and smiled when he saw the group.

"He's going to learn to sail now, is he? Well, he can row well enough, so I suppose that's the next step. Be careful now, young man. I need you. And others might as well."

Ian grinned at him, then scuttled down into the boat. The others joined him.

"You've not coiled the sheets!" he exclaimed accusingly.

"Your job," Ted told him. "Anyway, we're just starting again. And I'm at the helm still. Aren't I?"

"It's only fair," said Mary. "You can finish at the Island, we'll have a bite to eat and then it's Ian's turn.

Without mishap they continued to the Island, avoided the crowd around the café went to the house. Lunch was created and eaten despite Ian's protestations that he wasn't hungry and wanted to start immediately. It was noticed that he ate everything in front of him and asked for more, however.

Ted was planning on talking seriously to Henry about the farm that afternoon, and was looking forward to a time when he became free from the café. He knew that he wouldn't be bored. The other three made their way back to the dinghy, Ian was hopping about like a demented ant until they reached her. At that point he calmed down suddenly and became businesslike. So businesslike that he had started hoisting the jib before being told what to do, and then set himself at the mainsail too.

"Have you done this before?" Stephen asked, surprised.

"I've ... hoisted ... sails ... to dry them," the boy panted. "Is there enough water to lower the centreboard?"

"Not yet," Mary told him. "But well remembered."

"I do it for hirers," he explained.

"Do you teach them how to sail as well?"

He grinned. "I've read books, so I think I know."

"But...?"

"But – well, doing it's different."

It wasn't long before they were beating across the estuary, heading down towards the town. With the benefit of his work tidying boats, readying boats, rowing his loaned dinghy and reading about sailing, it wasn't surprising that Ian was a good pupil and learned quicker than had his brother.

"Can we go into Batson? At least past the boatyard?" he asked with a broad smile.

"You want to show off, don't you? All right then. See if you can work out what the wind's going to do when you get out of the main estuary."

"Won't it blow the same way?"

"It's coming straight up from the sea at the moment. What's going to happen when the hill's in the way?"

He thought for a moment. "No idea."

"Nor have I. So be prepared for anything."

'Anything' turned out to be a flukey wind that really didn't have much of an idea what it was doing either. He made the best of it, but his passing the boatyard was hardly the triumphant roaring through the water that he'd hoped for. He looked carefully, but there was no one outside to see him anyway.

"Do you want to sail down to Batson?" Stephen asked.

"Not in this wind," he said, just as a gust was funnelled down to him from the hills past Shadycombe Creek.

"So how are you going to turn round?"

"Head into the wind, go about, and reach back the other way."

Stephen just nodded and let him get on with it.

They put him through his paces, retracing their voyage of the morning and stopping again at North Sands. On jumping ashore with the anchor he wobbled and nearly fell, but regained his feet to plant its flukes into the sand.

"Are you all right?" asked Mary, seeing his face was not pale, just surprised.

"I – I think so," he said cautiously. "I think I've been sitting concentrating for such a long time that my legs had got weak."

"Sea legs on land," Stephen laughed. "Come on, let's go and get another tea."

"Sea legs? But I've only just come down the Estuary."

"But you're doing something you've never done before and, as you said, concentrating really hard. It's surprisingly hard work at first, and there's a lot to do and think about."

"Can we go and get a drink, please?" he asked, feeling in his pocket. "Oh... where's my money gone?"

Stephen looked at him questioningly.

"I had five shillings."

"Has it fallen out of your pocket?"

He thrust his hands back into his shorts' pocket.

"Oh..." A finger appeared at the bottom of his shorts by the side of his leg. "There's a hole."

"Look in the boat?" Mary suggested, "though you'd have felt it, surely?"

He shook his head and went to look. There was a shout of triumph as his top half disappeared over the gunwale, making the dinghy rock. After a good deal of scrabbling about he pushed himself upright, his left hand clenched and a grin back on his face.

"Found four and six! That'll buy the tea."

He saw surprised grins on the faces of the other two.

"We never expected you to buy tea!" Mary said, "but it's a kind offer."

"Only fair," Ian muttered, suddenly shy. "You're teaching me to sail and... and you could be together somewhere."

Stephen and Mary looked at each other. There seemed to be no useful response to that, so Stephen just clapped Ian on the back and steered him towards the crowded café. Used to café life on Loft Island the boy ordered teas and was surprised to hear the man behind the counter ask Stephen whether Ian had enough money to pay for them.

"Of course I have!" he said indignantly, "I wouldn't have asked for them otherwise!"

"Some do," said the man darkly. "You'd be surprised."

"Never had that in our café," Stephen spoke for the first time.

"Oh yeah?" the man almost sneered. "Where's that, then?"

"Them," Stephen told him. "Salcombe Fore Street and Loft Island."

▸ "The competition, then. Come to see how it should be done, have you?"

"Wouldn't dream of it. Don't need to." Stephen wondered why he was allowing the man to annoy him. "Two with sugar and one without, please."

"Sugar's on the table." The man turned away, muttering to himself, poured out the teas and put them on the counter. "Two and thruppence, please."

Wordlessly Ian handed over a shilling and three sixpences and was just as silently handed the three coppers as change. They turned away.

"Who owns this?" asked Mary when they were sitting at a rickety table as far away from the café itself as possible.

"Don't know," Stephen responded, "but it could be a goldmine if it was dealt with properly. No wonder the South Sands café is busier."

"He's got what my parents would have called 'The London Disease'," said Mary with a half-smile. "They have no trust in anyone and no idea how to treat them either."

"Didn't sound Devon either," said Ian, still smarting.

"Should we try and take it over?" asked Stephen. "Then Ian can come and work here and show him how it *should* be done."

The lad's head swivelled round. Once again he was surprised.

"He'd not work with me! And I wouldn't work with him."

Stephen grinned at him. "If we did take it over he wouldn't be working here! We get better people than that – as you know. You've met them. You're one of them. If they treated people like that in our cafes they'd be back on the mainland by the next ferry."

"What about Susan's in Fore Street?" Ian asked with a sudden grin. "You couldn't send them to the mainland from there!"

"We'd shove them out of the back. You know what I mean. And I say, this tea's stewed, isn't it?"

"Probably the same brew they made this morning," Mary offered. "They may be quieter in the afternoon, but there's no need to skimp. And they're charging the same as we do."

"Perhaps we're better see if it's up for sale at the end of the season," Stephen mused.

"Why not now?"

"It's the middle of the season. Wait until it goes quiet and the takings are low, then we'll find out who owns it. It only needs redecorating, new staff and higher standards, and a bit of advertising from our friends on the ferry."

"You're serious, aren't you?" asked Mary.

"Why not? It's worth while investigating."

With ever-increasing confidence, and an aptitude in feeling the wind's direction which astonished his tutors, Ian reached and gybed his way up the Estuary. As he gybed for what he thought would be the last time, by the entrance to Southpool Creek he opened his mouth tentatively.

"Centreboard, please!"

Mary and Stephen looked at each other with raised eyebrows.

"Should I have done it?" he asked, concerned lest he'd gone too far.

"No," said Stephen, "you're the helmsman and it's your place to command.

When we were learning we forgot. In fact old Charlie forgot at one point and we nearly drifted onto the slipway at Portlemouth."

"Good," Ian said, then added swiftly: "not good that you nearly hit the slipway; good that I was doing the right thing."

"Still enjoying sailing?"

The beaming, full on expression that was turned on him was enough to answer that.

"By the way," said Mary, "if ever you go down one of the creeks, make sure it's on a rising tide and you know the time of high tide. Six hours is a long time to be marooned on mud in a listing dinghy."

"You haven't done that, have you?" he asked with a grin.

"No. Charlie impressed it on us when he was teaching us. That's why I'm telling you. We don't want to have to find you in the launch, worried sick that you've drowned, only to find you bored and uncomfortable with mud all round."

"And hungry," said the student.

"And hungry. I suppose we'd better get back, hadn't we? Then we can talk about South Sands to Dad."

They made their way back to the Island, where Ian was taught as best they could to read the wind and to come in to the family's mooring without fuss. The last of the afternoon's customers were leaving from the main slipway. At the house they ran into the task of washing up and groaned when asked to take drying-up cloths.

Once there was an opportunity, the idea of the North Sands café was mentioned to Henry and Susan. The former made comments about not running before they could walk, but Ian was indignant enough about the treatment they'd received that Susan ended up thinking quite seriously about it.

"There's nothing to stop us finding out who owns it," she said. "Just maybe it's someone new who can't make a go of it. We know *we* can."

Ted declared that he had enjoyed his day tremendously. He had been given the plans of the new milking parlour to look at. His questions had been hesitant as he did his best to understand them, but gradually more searching as the plans became clearer in his mind. Henry had taken him to the mainland so they could look at the proposed site for it. They had found Martin and Mike already there, looking and thinking.

"Come to look at the site for the house? Best to wait until Mary and Stephen are here for that. They have very definite ideas." Henry knew the resistance there was to a building overlooking the shore, though not the reasons why.

"I wasn't certain who would be clearing the plans for it," Mike had told him. "Really it's going to depend on how many cottages for staff you want to think about. That will almost dictate the spacing of it all. I understand they won't touch the foreshore for some reason, although in my view it'd be best to have the main house there. It'd give a really good view across the Estuary and we could make a better landing stage for the Island."

"Will you need to ferry animals to and from the Island?" Ted had posed the question cautiously, aware that the planning was a Loft prerogative, not his. "A landing stage with a ramp, perhaps, if you are."

Henry couldn't think what was in his mind, and had asked.

"I just wondered if you would want to have any animals there for people to look at while they were on the Island. Maybe even milk some there in the afternoons as a demonstration."

The incredulous stare Henry had given him had almost made him want to start apologising.

"That's the second time you've really surprised me, Ted. I don't think any of the others would have thought of that. It would need a special boat, and as you say, a ramped landing stage. The island one is easy – we already have the old road. Let's talk to the others later. I'll leave you to introduce the idea."

Ted had acknowledged the implied compliment, pleased but slightly embarrassed at the praise. Years of living with a father who rarely if ever even said 'thank you' had rendered him unused to having his efforts rewarded.

"If you're building cottages for farm staff, Mr Loft, perhaps I could stay in one sometimes." It was a tentative comment, but it cemented his sincerity about working on the farm into Henry's mind.

"What about Ian?" Henry had asked. "What about your Aunt? What would they think?"

"I know. That's the problem. We could all live in one but if Aunt Amble and Uncle Bert are…" he had tailed off, remembering that he had been all but spying when he'd seen them holding hands the previous evening. Henry waited, wordlessly.

"Oh well. I suppose it won't happen. And Ian's got mad keen about boats. So I suppose I'd better just live in Salcombe and come here for the afternoon milking and stuff. And weekends."

"But don't forget to have fun as well, Ted. Life isn't all work, you know."

"Oh, farming isn't work. It's just… just how you live."

Henry had been reminded of his son's very similar words from years previously. Farming was in Stephen's blood. Because of Mary's background it was also in hers. Ted's background was similar, if harder. It sounded as if he was from the same mould, although there was always the possibility that his mind might change as the teenage years progressed.

They were a considerable time walking around the site, visualising how all the new buildings would fit in. So engrossed had they been they that they were surprised to find their popularity had diminished in the very busy café, which had only Susan and Mary with one member of paid staff staffing it. Glances were exchanged and they immediately started taking on the tasks of washing up and table clearing.

Equilibrium had been regained by the time the last visitors were leaving and the dinghy sailors had returned, which was when Henry felt safe to enter the conversation about North Sands café, even if he was partly, and gently, overruled by Susan.

Aunt Amble had a lot of young talk to listen to in Salcombe that evening, followed by long discussions with Dolly, Bert and to a lesser extent Bronwen and Angharad.

"I know Ted badly needs to be farming," she started, "but my own view is that for him to live on or near the island just cannot be made to work. He and Ian need a period where there is a stable family around them, a foundation that has

222

been lacking for at least two years while Simon's injuries were increasingly telling on him. I know Ted won't thank me, now; but when he's an adult on a farm somewhere he will have at least the knowledge of having had a family and love around him.

"The other consideration is more practical, and we can all see it: to arrive at the farm for morning milking would need such an early start from here that his sleep patterns would suffer; and as a result, his education. Evenings and weekends would be fine, except maybe in the winter when travel back here could be dangerous. During holiday times I think we have to ask the Lofts to maintain at least one day off a week, maybe two. I can't remember what the law dictates, but that only applies when the child applies for a formal job, I believe."

"It does," Bert confirmed. "And I do not want to hear of any payment being made – to either of them. It would rebound on the farm, the boatyard and our Practice should there be any suspicion of payment to a minor."

"We need to tell Henry, then," Bronwen put in. "He was determined that anyone working for him should be paid."

"Wages are most certainly not allowed. Regular payments are not allowed for they amount to the same thing. But a gift occasionally, as one might give a gift to a nephew or the son of a friend, would not be covered by that particular law."

They each digested his meaning. Bronwen looked up first.

"But if a regular amount each week was paid into a separate bank account in the Lofts' name, as if it were a regular savings amount, that is not being paid to anyone. Most importantly, if neither Ted's name nor anyone's name from the Rawle family were ever connected with it, that amount would not constitute either wages or a regular gift. Therefore it would not be illegal."

"Technically speaking you are entirely correct," her uncle confirmed. "Ted would not benefit from such a savings scheme."

"Is there anything to stop Henry giving a large gift to Ted on, say, his twenty-first birthday? Maybe at Christmases, too."

"Gifts, freely given and received, are not in the sphere of the law appertaining to child labour. They may be liable to tax, as are all large gifts. But properly advised, crossing the tax threshold would be a matter of legal advice."

"And their legal adviser would be aware of such a threshold," Bronwen concluded.

"In years to come, Bronwen, after you have qualified, that might be you, so I suggest you include such an accountancy matter in your learning."

The two smiled at each other.

"May I interrupt you two legal eagles?" Annabelle broke in. "I was hoping to be able to come to a decision tonight, not just about the boys but about me. It looks as though my reason for being here is still the nurture of those two, and I'm relieved about that. With that in mind I would like to do more in the house here as it seems really unfair that Angharad just defaults to the kitchen every time."

She turned to where the girl was sitting.

"I know we keep telling you that you're not a cook, or a maid, but you have to be almost dragged in here so as to be a proper part of this household. Nevertheless what I'd really like is for you to teach me more about cooking, as my experience is only with the plain meals I cooked for myself from necessity.

"But you will be at Loft Island much of the time if you are going to take over producing cakes and scones and heaven knows what for the cafes. I shall be cooking for two hungry schoolboys, a hungry Solicitor, his secretary and her daughter when she's here. And there's the cleaning of the house to do as well..."

There was a clamour at that and she held up her hand, determined to hear nothing until she had completed her comment.

"... and although I know that you'll all take part in that, and maybe we take on someone to help, it still needs to be managed. If I am to help with Loft Farm's accounts and maybe knit some ganseys for sale in town, I think that might be my dream job and I'd be very happy."

Of all the people who were looking at her as she finished, she found the twinkle in Bert's eye the most noticeable. It accompanied his half smile so well that she almost felt herself starting to blush.

Dolly was also smiling. "And here was I thinking that I should offer to take over the house, and wonder what would happen with those two upstairs. I have no experience of boys..."

"They're just humans, like everyone else," murmured Annabelle.

"I beg your pardon? I missed that," asked Bert.

"It's just they still have a few funny ideas. Oh, and quite a lot of mischief. But it's usually funny mischief."

He laughed. "We see a lot of the funny mischief here."

"It's not too bad, is it?" asked Annabelle anxiously.

"Not at all, not at all. They are a tonic, as I've said all along. I'd be very glad if they continued to live here and be that tonic and, more importantly, not split up. If Ian is intent on a seafaring career of some sort, with Ted farming, they will split up eventually. No, let them enjoy each other while they can. And you, Annabelle, of course."

"Bert, you're incorrigible," accused Dolly. "But I do agree with you. If we have now agreed on a course of action that pleases you two, and if Angharad is intent on taking over the food side at Lofts with Susan, and Bronwen is going to University..."

"Mum! I don't know yet. I have had no chance to think about it or even look for a course..."

"But I have," said her uncle. "I hope to have some information from three Universities very soon."

Bronwen's expression was comical.

"Speaking of education..." Dolly was determined to make her point. "I started a secretarial course soon after moving here, because I was both becoming bored and was determined not to be a wallflower any longer. I wanted to start doing something. It might be nowhere near as grand as Bron's being at University but I've had a later start. It's a correspondence course, naturally. I may be of little use to my brother to start with but I hope that as time goes on I could become efficient. I hope he doesn't mind, but when the house was empty once, I bought a secondhand typewriter and am picking up speed in copy typing."

This time all eyes, surprised eyes, were on her. She smiled.

"I have never heard a typewriter in the house," her brother exclaimed. "And it is a difficult sound to ignore, as I know with Mrs Damerell at work in the reception office."

"I only practise when everyone else apart from Angharad is out of the house. It is our secret, Angharad, isn't it? And she has been teaching herself too during the times when my wrists start to hurt with unaccustomed exercise!"

"I admire you, Angharad, "said Bert admiringly. "It is a useful skill to have even if you choose to follow the baking and supervising role at Lofts. And you must do what is right for you, of course. But as for you, Dolly, do you really think you could put up with working for me? I profess to being a tyrant at work, as you would expect."

She smiled. "I think that after what I've been through since marriage…" she shuddered "… a little tyranny from someone whose character I trust would be very welcome. And you forget that I can give as good as I get, my dear brother!"

"You always could, Dolly. Even if you are my child sister! And I never was really able to lead you. Working with you will be enjoyable for me too."

25 – Rescue

"So you can sail now too, then boy? Didn' take long, did it?"

Ian, knowing he was being teased, grinned back at Pete. "I picked it up quite easily, I think. It just seems I know what to do."

"If you're a natural you're very lucky," Edgar told him. They were awaiting orders for the day in his office. "How would it be if you showed him how our hire boats are rigged, Pete? With one thing and another it's a quieter day today and we can get one of the others to take your place in the ferry to give you a break. And you can check on how this lad's really doing. You could take one of the una rigs out once he's used rigging the yawls."

"Will do, guv'nor."

That was Ian's morning planned, to his surprise and great delight. There was a lot to for him learn with the yawls as they had a mizzen mast and sail to deal with as well as the mainsail and jib. And when at last Pete firmly installed himself in the forward thwart of one of the small gaff-rigged dinghies and told Ian to get on with it, he was in his element. Even with the class of boat being known for being safe and solid rather than speedy, Ian made good use of the freshening wind and had the dinghy moving quite swiftly. Pete even had to help trim the boat at times by shifting his weight.

"You'll do, I reckon, " he said at last. "But this is the most wind you're to handle on your own. Even then, be careful and steer up into the wind when the water gets too close up to that gunwale. I don't want you drowned, nor does the guv'nor. You're too useful."

"Aye-aye sir!" Ian chirped happily as he carefully hauled in the mainsail to gybe as safely as he knew how.

With farm work for Ted and boatyard work for Ian, interspersed with sailing when Mary's dinghy was available, work in the café and the kitchen sometimes, and the occasional errand to Salcombe for deliveries or collections, the month sped by. Susan and Henry, Mary and Stephen spent a good deal of time planning for the new buildings when not dealing with the café and its continuing success. At last there came the day when civil engineers started to dig a trench for water and other services from the main road down the field boundaries to the site of the dairy and house. Building anything couldn't proceed without it.

"Whoever you use as a builder, insist that they never make use of Estuary water," Martin told them. "I thought, and Mike confirms, that salt water in cement and mortar will attract damp. That's the last thing you want."

The other four took this on board.

"I almost wish we weren't going away next weekend," Stephen said, causing such a look of shock from Mary that he had to laugh.

"Don't you dare, Stephen Loft! Or I'll go without you. Maybe I'd invite Martin instead."

It was Stephen's turn to look shocked.

"I'd go like a shot," Martin said gravely, then found himself unable to keep a straight face. "If Bron would come too. It's a pity that Mike and I are too busy for holidays this year."

"I could take Ted and Ian, I suppose," Mary mused.

Stephen just gave her a hug and squeezed until she squeaked.

"All right, all right! But you'd better not back out now."

"I can't," he said casually. "We've paid the hotel and hired a dinghy."

"No other reason?"

"Well…"

She put her tongue out at him.

The following Saturday saw their departure to Kingsbridge station for the start of their long journey to the Lake District. Mary couldn't help thinking of the time four years previously when she had boarded a train there, unaware that she was being kidnapped and would be away for three long years.

From the slow, local train from Kingsbridge to South Brent they were happy when the express reached its top speed and felt that the journey had really started. With confusion born of unfamiliarity they managed to change at Bristol and Birmingham, but then were able to sit back knowing that the next change would not be until Carnforth.

"Don't get any smuts in your eye there," Stephen told Mary, "I'm not a doctor."

"I really wouldn't want to have one anywhere, but why particularly not at Carnforth?" asked Mary.

"*Brief Encounter*?" said Stephen with a question in his voice.

"I've heard of it, but never seen it. My school didn't take us to the pictures."

He thought back. "No, I suppose not. It's really a rather good film. And Carnforth station was where they filmed most of it."

"Oh. And someone got a smut in their eye?"

"Yes. She did. I'll take you to see the film if ever they repeat it. It's very romantic. And naughty."

"Naughty?"

"They're both married, but to different people."

Her eyes grew round. "I say…"

"First lunch sitting….First lunch sitting please…"

The steward's voice faded as he announced his way down the carriage. The two raised their eyebrows. Breakfast had been early and there had been no option to eat or drink anything apart from the sandwiches which had vanished as elevenses. They made their way to the buffet car. Lunch on the move with attentive stewards was a novelty for Stephen, and Mary was delighted to tease him that she was a seasoned train journey diner, having had breakfast on her only other long train journey when southbound from Scotland.

They pulled in to Carnforth eventually and asked for directions to the platform for the stopping train, only to find that one had just left. The next would need almost an hour's wait.

"Cup of tea?" asked Stephen.

They found themselves in surroundings that looked so familiar to Stephen that he frowned. At last it came to him; this was the very refreshment room used in *Brief Encounter*. He explained to Mary as they stood at the counter waiting to be served.

"It's not very romantic," she said. Turning, he caught her in his arms and kissed her, careless of the disapproving glances from some of the older customers.

"Better now?" he asked.

"Stephen! Behave!" she laughed. "We'll be thrown out."

They sat with a pot of tea between them and a Bath bun each, happily chatting about plans for the farm and branching out from farming.

They had only one station to pass through on the stopping train, and arrived at Oxenholme in time to make their last change.

"Remember *Pigeon Post*?" asked Mary. "This must have been the station where Roger released the pigeon."

"Wasn't that Strickland Junction?"

"Was it? I don't know where that is."

"Perhaps it's on another line, then. But this fits the bill."

Their last ride was behind an ancient steam engine that had them both thinking of their own Kingsbridge line. It arrived with much fuss at Windermere Station some thirty slow minutes later.

"Now all we have to do is get ourselves and our luggage to Bowness" said Stephen. "How do you feel about a taxi?"

"Can we aff..." Mary broke off. She knew very well that they could afford it. She had been persuaded that with the work coming up in Devon they should have two weeks away, in peace, even if it meant spending some of that money.

"Yes," said Stephen, laying a hand on her arm. "We can, and after travelling all day, we should."

They found one, and if the driver was dubious about two obviously quite young passengers he said nothing when they had named their highly rated hotel. It was a short ride and the driver brought Mary's case into the foyer. Stephen paid him.

With formalities completed they were taken upstairs and shown first one, then the adjoining, single rooms. When they had booked they had considered sharing a room but knew that the hotel would object to two young people with different surnames doing so. If Susan and Henry had heard about it they would have had something to say too.

"It's fine," each of them said in turn. "Thank you."

"The other luggage will be up in a moment," they were told.

Each of them examined their room properly and were interested in the door half way along the party wall. Mary cautiously tried its doorknob. It opened and she found that she was facing Stephen, who had raised his hand to knock on his side of it. Mary looked at him with a half smile.

"Sorry," he said, unnecessarily.

"Are the rooms the same?" she asked, thinking it best not to comment about the interconnecting doors. With one or two exceptions, they were. Quite high ceilings, decorated with diagonally patterned, light wallpaper, and well lit by the window that gave onto the lake. Then added: "We could leave the door open so it's easier to say goodnight."

Stephen found he was unable to speak, or was it just that he didn't know what to say?

"We used to share, all those years ago," she said, amazing him still further.

When she had been rescued from the flood there had been little option but to share; besides, she had been twelve and he a young fourteen. They had found mutual comfort then, each having suffered great losses in their lives. In Mary's case the loss had been so great that it had taken many months to come fully to terms with it.

"But that was different," he said huskily.

"It can be different now," she told him, and kissed him.

There was a knock at Mary's door and he retreated into his own room. The remaining cases and bags were delivered to each. The porter was about to leave Mary's room when he paused. He seemed about Stephen's age, though not as tall or as broad.

"Should I lock the door, ma'am?" He indicated the connecting door.

Mary smiled at him, unaware of the effect this would have.

"It's fine as it is, thank you. We can manage."

His face dropped, he nodded and turned away.

Once he had gone she went through the unlocked door and found Stephen looking at the extensive view past Belle Isle and down the Lake.

"He wanted to know if we wanted the connecting door locked," she said.

"What did you tell him?"

"Oh, I asked if there was some way of putting bars in as well."

They set about unpacking. Stephen was still aware that he was effectively in a hotel room with his fiancée, alone, with no bothersome interruptions to ask for help in the café, and that each room had what seemed a double bed. He was still disorientated when Mary spoke again.

"Come on! We need to go out and look at everything before the evening meal, and we've been sitting all day in stuffy trains. I need fresh air!"

He pulled himself together and followed her downstairs to walk around Bowness. They visited a pub. With just the two of them together it still felt like devilment. The visits to various Salcombe pubs with friends and with parents had been different. This was just the two of them alone, and it felt as if they had played truant from school.

Entering the hotel's dining room later made them feel under-dressed. Neither possessed much in the way of smart and "suitable" clothing. The impression given by the dress standard of the other diners was that Mary would almost be expected to wear something expensive and different each night. It was a matter of some slightly worried discussion between them which was interrupted by the waiter coming for their order. They were both unused to hotel life; the menu was aimed at the older generation who were. Their joint reticence and confusion caused the waiter to smile, to unbend and to talk to them as ordinary people. He left them smiling, and with an order which had been largely based on his own suggestions.

Afterwards, as they left, they thanked him, engaging in some friendly chat as they did

"Should I try and keep up with everyone else's dress standards?" Mary asked suddenly.

He smiled at her. "Not really my place to judge, madam..."

"Mary."

"Er... well, between us only then: Mary. And I shouldn't try to compete. None of the people who have been through the war bother too much now. It's only the...er..."

"Older generation?" Mary prompted.

"If you put it that way, then yes. All of them still have clothes from before, or are rich enough to have bought expensive clothes since rationing came off. And that's only six years ago."

"So really, we're all right like this?"

"You are fine like that. And – " he lowered his voice " – manners maketh man. Not clothes. Not everyone treats waiters as human beings and you do. Thank you."

They moved to the residents' lounge for coffee. His remarks encouraged them to feel they could relax and talk, and to make plans. Sunday... they knew there would be few bus services and wondered how easy it would be to explore. Or would the day have to be spent at the hotel and around the town?

"We're stupid," said Stephen at last. "We're worrying about buses and trains and not having cycles when there's a place almost outside the hotel where we can hire a sailing dinghy."

Her face was almost comical.

"Why didn't I think of that? Isn't that why we're here?"

They relaxed again. The evening was spent talking about developments in Devon and the people they would have around them to help make everything happen. It pleased Stephen greatly that Mary was so engaged and particularly that she was so excited about the plans for using the milk that he, his father and Ted would be producing. From her point of view it was wonderful that he was as natural a farmer as she, and that they could work happily together.

"Pies!" she exclaimed suddenly, startling him. "If you're getting into pigs, one of the things the dairy could also do is to make really good pies."

He blinked for a moment. "We need to make sure it would work, that the meat wouldn't be better sold as joints."

"I'm not talking about the best meat. I'm talking seconds, and sausage meat. We could make sausages as well. But lattice-topped pies. They look good and we can certainly experiment until we have a really good recipe."

"Should we wait until the cheese and ice cream and, I suppose, butter making has settled down first? There's going to be a lot of work there, particularly at first."

"I forgot butter! Of course we should make it. Yes, I suppose you're right, but we need to make sure there's enough room to do sausages and pies. Or enough space to add on to the buildings when we need to. And don't forget pies can be sold through the winter, when ice-cream sales drop."

"Or we could take the raw materials to the town and manufacture them there."

She thought. "Or take over the shop next to Susan's café and turn that into a bakery."

"Whoah! You're moving too fast again!"

"There's no harm in planning ahead. I can't imagine that any shops would be available in Fore Street in the near future in any case. But it's worth bearing in mind."

"And we've got to start with the pigs first in any case."

Discussion continued until eventually Stephen started wriggling.

"Should we go for a walk? Are you getting restless too?"

"I am," Mary smiled, "and I was about to ask you the same thing. Where shall we go?"

"Out. Anywhere. Preferably by the lake, though."

'By the lake' led them down to the boatbuilders' sheds. Immediately they were transported back to Edgar's yard in Salcombe.

"Really, though, we should be thinking of the Swallows visiting, or Captain Flint and John bringing Swallow in under jury rig," Mary remarked. After the last of the boathouses there was a gate into a field and they followed a path along the shore. They paused to take in the peace, with the moon peeking from the high clouds, transforming the scene and rendering puny the lights from Belle Isle.

"The last time we stood like this by the shore with the moon shining, you proposed to me," Mary said suddenly.

Stephen was well aware, had already made the connection. "You're not regretting saying yes, I hope?"

The kiss was long, and gave him the answer.

Almost ashamed of himself he thought back to those hotel rooms and to that communicating door. What if...

He shook his head. No. Yes, but no. It must never happen. Not until they were ready. But when would that be? When they were older, and sensible?

A circular walk complete they regained the hotel. Despite his resolve, he found his heart beating faster than normal as they climbed the stairs to their rooms. Mary stopped at hers, the first of the two along the corridor, and paused, turning.

"Are you coming in to say goodnight?"

Wordlessly he followed her in. They found that the bed had been turned down, but that the connecting door had been closed. He looked at Mary and smiled.

"I don't seem to be able to get to my room."

"Does that mean you need to stay in here?"

He found that the question almost left him speechless.

"I could do."

Their embrace may have started by the door but soon they were sitting on the bed and then slowly reclining on it until they were side by side and still together, as one, showing their love for each other.

It was half an hour later Stephen found he was trembling and knew that decisions had to be made. Mary was aware of him, of a change, and pushed herself away a little.

"We daren't."

Only two words, but he knew she was right.

"I wish..."

Her hand came up and a finger touched his lips to top the rest of the sentence."

"I wish too. But think. Think of what... think of everything."

"I want you with me so much. All the time."

"I am."

"I mean *all* the time.

"We have so much to do."

"But we can... look at Susan and Dad."

"I know, but they're older."

"And they have so much to do too."

"It's not that simple."

He sighed. "I know, I know. But we... but I just wish..."

"The time will come."

"Soon." It wasn't a question from him, a seeking of permission. It was a statement.

"And we need to get married."

He nodded, once again with that half smile on his face that made her realise part of him was far away. She loved seeing that, and almost weakened.

"Stephen?"

"Yes?" he said. There was still a note of hope in his voice.

"We need to sleep, or we'll be late for breakfast."

His body slumped. She meant it. Reluctantly he pushed himself to a sitting position, hoping his body wasn't letting him down.

"Will you come in and kiss me goodnight?" he asked hopefully.

"I might."

The door between the rooms hadn't been locked. He went through, leaving it open.

"And no peeking!"

"No, Mum."

"And don't be cheeky."

"Yes, Mum."

"Are you decent?" she asked five minutes later.

"Fairly."

"What does that mean?"

"You'll have to find out."

He was decent, at least from the waist down. It was too hot for a pyjama top. Her nightie was attractive and he almost weakened again. But there was a kiss, and a hug, and she was walking back to her room.

The door stayed open.

It was the day after the passing-out parade. Bob Hannaford was relieved to have finished with the tedious business of endless drills, forced marches, boot cleaning, being sworn at and shouted down by sergeants, learning to clean, to cook, to polish... To date no information had come to any of his intake about what was due to happen next. Another intake was due later the same day – they had at least been told that.

After the usual morning parade they were told to stand down. Still no information came about their next duties. Some just milled around, unaccustomed to the freedom, whilst others headed back to their hut to relax or write letters. Bob chose the latter, and was at last able to take his time composing a long screed to Angharad and a much shorter one to his parents. So engrossed was he that the stentorian yell at the door made him physically jump. The pen made a line across the page and fell to the floor. He cursed it.

"What was that, Hannaford?"

"Nothing Sarge. Just cursing my pen for falling on the floor."

Had it been a month earlier he would have found himself on fatigues.

"Lecture Room 3 at the double! Come on. Get that tunic back on and look tidy, damn yer eyes. You may have passed out, you lot, but you're not going to look scruffy while I'm in charge."

They all knew better than to object and were soon running to one of the large, block-built halls where instruction had been pounded into their heads for four weeks. Bursting in, they discovered that there were so many stripes and stars on the miscellany of uniforms at the front of them that any conversation died on their lips.

A major introduced himself, his attitude and accent calm in comparison with their instructors' ungentle tones.

They were presented with a shock. Unlike most other recruits who would have been offered training in trades or some field of engineering, they were to be sent abroad. Not only that, but they were to leave the following day.

"The situation in Malaya has become slightly more difficult," they were told. "Reinforcements are needed there. You and the previous intake will be going to help. Firstly you will help look after the base, releasing our people to go on patrol. After a while it may be necessary for you to go on patrol yourselves. The first few weeks will allow you to acclimatise and train, then we shall see what is needed.

"Your Sergeant Major has all the details and will brief you further, and then you need to stow your gear as the fleet of coaches will collect you for the airport at 4.30 tomorrow morning."

From a leisurely morning to a frenetic afternoon and early evening: Bob's feet hardly stopped. Finally they were despatched to get some sleep, though the noises from other platoons in the camp made it impossible for most. Bob hurriedly completed his letters, telling them all where he was going. He was able to beg a favour from their sergeant, who would be remaining in England to train the next recruits, and who agreed to post his letters. Finally he managed to rest.

If the shock of the major's announcement was disturbing, so was a wake-up call at four a.m. In a daze they all scurried round, tripping over each other and everything, and finally being pushed into an array of olive green army coaches. Bob tried to doze, even to sleep, but even on decent roads the motion was so unpleasant that he found it impossible.

They arrived at a base and were herded into a stores where lightweight rig was handed out, then given a chance to grab food before being herded, 45 at a time, onto several large transit aircraft which Bob identified as Hastings'.

None of them had counted on the journey having to stop and refuel, or for the flight to be staged overnight. Their first stop was in Germany, and at last, there, they managed to collapse into beds at a reasonable hour.

For three more interminable, boring days they flew, landed, slept and flew until at last the immense cargo doors of the aircraft opened and hot, humid air streamed in.

"All change, please, all change. And welcome to Butterworth, Penang!"

Stiffly they climbed from the plane and spread out, stretching cramped muscles. The usual fusillade of shouting brought them back into a phalanx and they were marched away to a nearby barracks.

They installed themselves there, hating the heat and stuffiness. The next spate of training, jungle training, took place in this heat, interspersed with insects, frequent brief thunderstorms and brief, torrential showers. It was uncomfortable. Lectures told them of the Malayan National Liberation Army, and the more they learnt of its previous conduct the more concerned they became. It was pointed out to them that Australian and New Zealand detachments were present too, and that the current skirmishes would likely be the last gasp of the conflict; all of which comforted them a little.

They settled down as well as the mosquitoes and the training would allow.

"There's a tin in the cupboard," called Susan. Henry had rushed in from the café asking for stocks of strawberry jam.

"Which one?" he asked after a flurry of door opening and the sight of empty shelves.

"The one you've just looked in – oh, don't say that we've run out? I'm sure there was a tin in there yesterday."

"I opened one yesterday afternoon. Was that it?"

"It's the only one we had."

"Then we've run out. I'd better rush down to Salcombe to get some, but it'll have to be in jars."

"Better to get Ian to go. He knows everyone and can handle the launch."

"He's a bit young for that, surely?"

"He'll be fine. There's scarcely a ripple on the water and he's as good a boatman as any local lad. He'll be quicker than me, and I'm quicker than him in the café."

At Henry's request, Ian's head snapped up with a smile. "Cor… yes. I'll be there and back before you know it."

"Know how the launch works? Sure you can start her?"

He looked scornful. "I do it often enough at work. Yes, I know about the petrol tap as well."

He was as good as his word and stormed away from the family's mooring in double quick time at a speed that would have caused Edgar to frown and the Harbourmaster to have some stiff words.

Being a boatman, albeit a trainee boatman still, he noticed that the tide was just past the turn. It would just help him speed down the estuary to the town but would hamper his return. The engine was good and powerful, and well maintained. He throttled back as he approached the cluster of boats moored off the town, and noted from the corner of an eye a small sailing dinghy with two boys in it, weaving its way through them and a little too close for comfort to some. He recognised it as one of Mustchins' dinghies and made a mental note to check on its progress later.

There was a space at one of the pontoons, fortunately, and he swiftly moored the launch and ran off into the town on his errand.

In the grocer's shop he tried to hurry the assistant along, but she was not one of those to be hurried, especially when a full case of twelve pots of jam is being requested by a young-ish boy whom she thought she recognised but wasn't sure. Eventually she became sure and asked how his aunt was and wasn't he lucky to have been taken in by that Mr Merryweather and given a home with her and his brothers and all those other lovely people. It took at least ten minutes to complete the purchase before he could escape. He made slower progress back to the launch; a cardboard case of jam jars is heavy when you're eleven.

With the case firmly sheltered on the bottom-boards for'ard he started the engine and set off. Remembering the likelihood of moving boats he made his way cautiously parallel with the shore, thinking to turn just before the Ferry Steps. As he was about to do so a large, important looking, seagoing launch rounded the point and headed to the north of him, slowing down as the helmsman encountered the confusion of moored craft. He had no option but to head further out into the main estuary to make the turn.

That dinghy! He remembered it now. Where had they got to with it? He glanced down toward South Sands and there was a boat there which he thought might have been them. It appeared even to his inexperienced eye that there was something wrong. The single sail seemed to be flapping in the breeze, doing nothing, and was it at right angles to the hull? Was it listing? And was there only one head visible?

He hesitated a moment, wondering what he should do. Or should he leave it to adults to deal with? But it was one of Edgar's dinghies, and they were his to deal with – in his mind, at least. He made a snap decision, opened the throttle and once again started creating a wake which would have caused official heads to shake.

He passed the Marine Hotel, still flat out, and heard a loud report from behind him. The Lifeboat. More trouble, but at sea, he supposed. And yes, there was the second maroon. He sped after the troubled dinghy, all thoughts of jam and Lifeboat forgotten.

As he bore down on the dinghy his eyes were all for the boat itself. Certainly there was no one at the tiller and the sail was as he had noticed. The ebb tide was taking her south down the estuary, out of control. The only head he could see was kneeling by the side, and appeared to be shouting, though not at him.

Ian frowned, looking away from the boat. There was something there, a head, and arms were moving, but...

He altered course and carefully allowed the boat to drift nearer, propeller now at rest. He ran to the bow and gathered the painter in his arms, then threw it as near as possible the near-submerged head as he could. Then he remembered the boathook, freed it with a struggle, and as carefully as he could touched the shoulder nearest to him.

A pair of hands made a grab at it. He pulled in as carefully as he knew how. Now the waterlogged figure was close to the boat.

"Hang on to the gunwale!" he shouted. "I'll have to help you in."

He had to guide first one, then the other hand onto the launch's edge. The boathook rolled away, fortunately falling inboard. Ian hauled at the arms but only succeeded in getting them over the edge. How could he...?

He reached down. There was a belt on the trousers. He gripped it and tried to lift. Too heavy.

He stole a glance at the little sailing dinghy. Too far away to help. The agonised look on the boy's face staring over at him pulled some sort of trigger inside him. He knew it was him, or nothing. And if nothing the boy would drown.

"Grab that rib – no, there –" he made sure both hands were on one of the launch's horizontal ribs. "When I say 'three', pull like fury!" He renewed his grip on the belt.

"One...two...THREE!"

The waist was on the gunwale. Water sluiced around. He pulled the legs in.

"You all right?"

The head shook.

"What's the matter?"

"Lost my brother."

"Is he the one on the dinghy still?"

The head swivelled and eyes looked at his, round as saucers.

"Is he... is he all right?"

Ian looked over to the dinghy the occupant was now sitting inside, facing the other way, shoulders heaving.

"He's alive. Now all I've got to do is take him in tow."

He coiled the painter and returned to the controls. Using every instinct he had he cautiously closed the gap between the two boats, then called out.

"Oy! Get up for'ard – the front – and throw me the painter. The mooring rope."

It was his voice that startled the figure into action. The face looked round.

"Is my sister all right?"

Sister? Oh well. Good thing she was wearing shorts with a belt, then.

"Yes. But hurry with that rope. Look, I'll bring up the stern of mine and you can hand it to me. Don't try throwing it."

He grabbed it, then made it fast to the centre thwart so it would be close at hand. There were two fairleads on the transom for use with running moorings, to his relief, so the tow rope would stay in one place.

"You need to get that sail down as soon as the boom is central," Ian instructed. "Otherwise it'll swing about all over the place. I'll get going and tell you when. But lower it slowly or you'll get a cracked head."

Back at the controls he pulled the throttle back enough to take up the slack in the tow line, then slowly brought the dinghy's head round to face the north. The sail strained at the sheet, trying now to power the dinghy northwards. Increasing the revs a little more put on more speed for them both and at last the boom was blown into line with the hull.

"Lower away!" he bellowed.

It was with considerable relief that he saw the sail diminish into the boat and was able to reduce speed again and start the homeward voyage.

A sigh of relief escaped him, and he felt oddly trembly.

26 – Swallows

The girl who had been lying on the launch's bottom-boards slowly hauled herself to a sitting position and looked at him gravely. She looked about a year or so older than him.

"You're very young, but you saved my life."

Ian glanced down, immediately embarrassed, and glad he had to keep his eyes open, not just for'ard as Charlie had drilled into him, but now behind as well to ensure the dinghy was still following. He shrugged.

"Couldn't leave you there, could I?"

He stiffened, looking forward again. The unmistakable shape of Salcombe's Lifeboat, *Samuel and Marie Parkhouse*, had appeared shortly before, but now seemed to have altered course and was heading straight for him. Brow furrowed, he watched as she seemed to be heading to intercept them. His hand hovered at the speed lever, undecided.

Now she seemed to be slowing; at least the wash had diminished, but she was still on her intercept course. She came closer and he reduced speed.

"Do you need help? Suggest you maintain speed." The loud hailer message made him jump.

He sped up again. The *Parkhouse* completed a manoeuvre that brought her within hailing distance of the sailing dinghy.

"Are you all right? Do you need us to board?"

There was nothing but a shrug from the boy in the boat. She came closer to Ian and the launch. "Do you need us to take over the tow. Or shall I put someone aboard you to help?"

He faced the low, blue hulled craft and yelled back. "If you want, or I can make it to The Hard."

There was a pause and some clicks.

"*Ian?* Is that you?"

He just recognised the voice of his brother, Martin. An odd sensation came over him. He was at once totally relieved, aware he was doing the right thing, and fiercely proud of his brother's membership of the Lifeboat crew.

"Yes," he almost screamed back.

More clicks, and another pause. Then an amused sounding voice.

"All right, boy. Take her to The Hard. But we'll come alongside as you get there and take your tow rope and moor her. Acknowledge, please."

"Aye aye, sir!" Ian yelled.

It was an odd sensation, to be at the helm of a launch, towing a boat he felt responsible for which was in turn being followed by a fully crewed Lifeboat. He was nearing the ferry now and watched for the departing boat for East Portlemouth. But, oddly, although it had cast off it seemed to be waiting, almost motionless. Hand near the throttle again, he was about to pause but realised in time that would make his tow try to overhaul him.

He watched carefully, making sure the skipper was aware of what was happening, when he heard three short blasts and saw the passengers cover their ears. That made him grin: "I am going astern" it meant, and he could see the disturbed water under the ferry's stern as confirmation.

He continued, waiting for the moment when he should alter course. Would the idiot on the dinghy steer, or would he let the dinghy swing in a wide arc and foul moored boats? He looked behind and yelled again.

"When I say, steer to port – to the left. Keep her pointing at my stern." Remembering the Lifeboat skipper earlier he added "Acknowledge, please."

There was no response. The figure was just sitting on the thwart, unaware of what was happening. He thought. This is where the Lifeboat could be useful and take over except that she was behind them both.

If he slowed, he could haul the dinghy towards him. He did so, then pulled on the tow rope. He didn't have the strength. Damn. He slowed more and pulled hard. This time, very slowly, she came towards the launch. He hauled in, kicking the speed lever to tickover. That eased the strain and she started coming closer.

But what was the Lifeboat doing? She was almost alongside now.

Martin and, he thought, Mike, were standing at the side.

"Coil the towrope, Ian, and throw it to us. We can take over now. You've done enough. Go and moor at a pontoon and we'll come and get your patient once we've got the dinghy moored."

He released his knot, released the rope from the fairlead and was about to make the throw when Mike shouted.

"No! Keep hold of the rope until we've got it!"

He cursed himself for not realising. It took two goes, but he made it, then thankfully released the tow and headed into the shore.

What? Why were there people clapping? He looked around. Did they always clap the Lifeboat when she returned? But the crew – those who weren't busy with coming alongside – were also clapping.

Ian felt his face heat up as he realised.

He helped the girl ashore into the arms of an ambulanceman, aware of a crying woman by his side. Mother? Probably. He wondered what to say but decided that silence was the best thing. At least the two with the girl were keeping the clapping crowd away. The Lifeboat had also docked and the crew were seeing to the dinghy and its occupant. A figure dressed in navy blue with a white-topped hat pushed his way down the pontoon towards him. He recognised the Harbourmaster, who stopped a few feet away.

"Bit fast down there, weren't you?"

Ian knew he had been going at the engine's limit and was ready to nod guiltily but saw, at the last moment, the smile. The gap was closed and his hand was shaken so heartily that his whole body shook.

"If your Dad ent proud of you now, boy, I'll make sure I tell him what for when I see him in Heaven."

Ian looked astonished, then everything went misty for a moment. When he next looked up he was aware of a wetness in his eyes. His hand was still in that large, calloused paw.

"You all right, boy?"

He nodded. The man helped him onto the pontoon and he nearly stumbled.

"Come on, folks, make a space. I need to get this lad a cuppa. If he were a bit older I'd buy him a beer and I reckon there aren't many here who wouldn't. Come on, lad, let's get you some peace."

238

Ian was half way up the hard towards the office when he remembered.

"I can't!" he said, looking up at the official face that was currently looking anything but official. "They've run out of jam and I've got to get it to them."

As the Harbourmaster halted suddenly Ian almost ran in to him.

"Jam? Jam? You've just saved two lives and all you can think about is jam? Boy, get your priorities right."

"But they won't be able to do cream teas without jam."

"Loft Island, is it?"

Ian nodded.

"Come with me. We'll get them their jam."

In the office he found Edgar, to his surprise and pleasure. With him was his old friend Pete from the boatyard.

"Eggar, can you spare Pete to run a pot of jam to Lofts? They're waiting for it, 'parently."

Both of them looked shocked. Pete recovered first. "I'll take their launch, guv'nor, shall I? I'll deliver it and come back here."

Edgar nodded, still looking at his young charge. Ian found his shoulder squeezed none too gently as Pete passed him on the way to make his delivery.

Edgar and the Harbourmaster exchanged glances.

"What were those two idiots doing, Ian?" Edgar asked as the blue uniform moved away to the kettle.

Ian thought. "I don't know. When I came into The Hard they were getting very close to moored boats. It didn't look as if they were really in control. But I was in a hurry so I just left them to it."

"Ah yes," said Edgar, "the jam."

Ian nodded seriously. "Yes. And when I was coming away again I remembered them and looked down the estuary and saw what I thought was them. It didn't look right. The sail wasn't doing anything, the boat was broadside on to the wind and looked as if she was listing. I knew she was one of ours..."

Edgar put his finger to his lips and indicated that the Harbourmaster shouldn't hear that sort of thing.

"...so I chased after her. The girl was in the water and the boy didn't know what to do. Or that's what it looked like."

He stopped. Edgar waited. "So what did you do?"

"Pulled her out of the water and took the dinghy in tow."

The Harbourmaster returned to the desk in front of him. "Didn't you hear the maroons? Didn't you realise the Lifeboat had been called?"

"Oh yes, I heard. But I thought they'd have been called to a ship at sea, not something like a dinghy."

The two adults exchanged glances again.

"A life is a life, Ian, no matter whether it's in an ocean liner or on a dinghy. A Lifeboat will save either." The Harbourmaster spoke as slowly and as deliberately as he knew how.

"Oh," said Ian, deflated. "So I should have waited for them."

"No. Because if you had, maybe that extra ten minutes would have meant the girl could have drowned. We all have to save lives where we can. I mentioned the Lifeboat because I didn't want you to think that they wouldn't go to 'just' a dinghy. You saved her life. There is no doubt about that. Maybe you saved her brother's life too, because they would have eventually drifted down onto Black Stone and maybe foundered, or out to sea, and God knows what could have happened then."

"But then the Lifeboat would have gone out."

"If someone noticed. If someone called them. It was someone in the Marine Hotel who made the call, but if they hadn't had sailing experience they probably wouldn't have thought twice. Then nobody would have wondered until Edgar didn't get his boat back, or the parents wondered where their children were.

"It takes someone who knew what they were doing to notice. A seaman. Fortunately there was someone."

"The man in the Marine Hotel."

"No, Ian: you. Here's your tea."

The boy blinked, and sat down. He had never been complimented before to such an extent, and by Salcombe's Harbourmaster, no less. A seaman. Him. Wow.

There was a knock at the door; it opened to reveal two Lifeboatmen. Ian smiled, looked more carefully and sprang to his feet. Martin.

"You all right, kid?" his brother asked. "They say you're a hero but I told them you're just my brother."

Ian grinned and was astonished when Martin enveloped him in a big, oilskin-smelling hug.

"You're really something, you know?" His voice sounded husky, thought Ian. Must be too long breathing sea spray. He wondered if his own voice sounded husky too. Martin turned away, revealing the Coxswain who offered a rare smile.

"Reckon there's a place on the Crew for you when you're sixteen if you want it, lad. You did all right today. Pity the RNLI can't take credit for two more lives saved, but saved they were. Now then, Willum. You going to brew more tea or shall we take this lad home?"

Was the launch back already? Surely not. And why would the Coxswain ask a question like that? Ian's head snapped up, half hopeful.

"You'd best call 'em, Willum. Get a reception committee and stop the launch coming back. We'll bring back your man. Come along, you. Finished yer tea?"

Ian looked at the untouched mug, still too hot to start, shook his head but stood up anyway.

The crowds had almost melted away. Just a few holidaymakers were standing around looking at the Lifeboat. Two Lifeboatmen and a boy marched down to her, Ian almost unable to believe what was happening. He climbed aboard when asked and was told to stand with the Helmsman in the cockpit. Someone draped an outsize oilskin round his shoulders and he knew with a stab of pride that he now looked like a Lifeboatman too.

"And you hang on to those rails."

They eased away from the pontoon and headed along to the Ferry. Once there the Coxswain looked up and down the estuary.

"Push that button twice. Two long pushes."

Ian did, wondering what was going to happen. Two loud blasts of a horn rang out, and one of the crew members looked round reproachfully, but the Coxswain took no notice. He swung the wheel to port, the Lifeboat swung round in response to point towards Snapes Point. Ian was almost pulled off his feet as the throttles were opened and she surged forward.

They stormed up the estuary. The familiar landmarks sped by, Ian hanging on to the rails for dear life. It took him a few minutes but he learnt how to sway with the motion like everyone else was and then started to enjoy himself.

They were at the island in about half the time the launch would have managed it. A party was standing on the shore, and Ian noticed Susan and Henry there, Ted, Angharad, Bronwen and even Aunt Amble. Behind them was a crowd of what he thought must be customers.

With a flourish of good seamanship the Lifeboat landed at the slipway, to the excited mutterings of the crowd. Ian turned to the Coxswain.

"Thank you sir."

"I told your brother that I'm not a sir, and the same goes for you. You can't be proper crew yet, like I said. But I'm Andy to them that are crew and that includes you. Hope you enjoyed the trip but don't tell old Willum how fast we were going. Geroff with you, and well done."

Ian nearly saluted him, decided just in time that wouldn't be right and just grinned. He looked doubtfully at the oilskin and handed it back to Andy before jumping off. Martin was one of those holding the mooring lines and so grinned at him too.

"I'm still proud of you," he said quietly as Ian was passing on his way to find his other brother. The broad and genuine smile that was returned from the boy melted Martin's heart.

He found he wanted to hug his brother, something that never happened. So shocked was Ted that he found he had to respond, and the two were embarrassed when a joint "Awwww…" came from the surrounding crowd. They looked round, found that they were the centre of attention, and walked up to the house to escape, followed by the rest of the family.

"It's a heck of a way to deliver jam," Henry said, smiling. "We wondered what was happening when the launch came in with someone else at the helm, and astonished when he came ashore with a box of jam jars. Then when he told us what you'd done – well, you can imagine. And very well done, hero of the hour."

Annabelle was seen to wipe her eyes.

Ian didn't know what to say, so just grinned and shrugged his shoulders.

"You'd have done the same."

Henry shook his head. "Farmer, me. I wouldn't have had a clue when I was eleven. You've really learnt some seamanship, Ian, and you have my respect for it."

"So, Ian, are you going to charge me salvage on that dinghy you towed back?" Edgar had puzzled him, and he showed it.

"I'd have thought that honorary uncle of yours would have told you what to do. You saved a boat and her crew, and you're not a Lifeboat, so you're entitled to a good percentage of the value of the boat."

"Am I? Why?"

"Law of salvage. Simple. So how much are you going for?"

"I wasn't going to. I don't want any money for doing what I knew I had to do."

Now Edgar let his smile show. "Legally you would really be entitled. But I never really thought you would, and I know Mr Merryweather well enough that he wouldn't advise you to claim it. Despite that I'm in your debt and the parents of those two are even more so. Did you know what happened?"

Ian shook his head. "The girl was in the water and the boy was just hanging over the side, doing nothing."

"We got the truth out of them after they'd been looked over and the parents had stopped..."

He paused.

"You've never lost a son or a daughter. You don't know what it's like. Those two might well have done."

"I've lost my Mum and Dad," said Ian, uncharacteristically quietly.

"I know, boy, I know. So have I. And I lost a son. And I tell you, it's a thousand times worse."

Ian's memories and emotions made some important connections.

His thoughts strayed from the rescue and focussed on the man in front of him, so easy to like, whom he regarded as a friend as well as a sort of unofficial benevolent employer. He suddenly found that he was horrified by what the man had endured and was genuinely sad for him. He remembered what people normally said to each other in cases like this.

"I'm sorry..." And as the words found voice he knew that he meant it, with all his heart, and sat, eyes lowered, finding himself shocked almost to tears.

Each found that they could add nothing for several moments.

"He was in the war, lost at sea. His brother was on another ship and survived, thank God."

The silence was about to be broken by a knock on the door. Pete, two mugs in his immense paw, could see that now was not the time and turned away.

"Thought I'd got over that," Edgar said, looking up. "But you stopped a couple of parents having to face a hell like that – sorry – and they know it. When those two had been looked over by the lifeboat first aiders and then the doctor, old Willum – he's really William, but everyone in the town calls him Willum – talked to them.

"Seems they didn't get permission from the parents to hire the boat, then told lies about being able to sail well – and it was a stiff old breeze yesterday – so off they went. Down the estuary they were more drifting than sailing, it seems. When they got scared the boy tried to turn and then got worried that they were heeling over. He set off up the estuary again and the first thing that happened was that they gybed. The sail must have gone over with a bang and the girl fell backwards to avoid the boom."

Ian nodded. He and Ted had endured one or two unplanned gybes.

"Then the girl was in the water. He let go of everything and just sat there watching her. The boat stayed broadside on the waves, for some reason. Normally she'd end up head to wind, but – well; don't know what happened. And that's when you came haring onto the scene, and thank God that you did."

242

"Are they all right? And is the boat all right?"

"Well, that's what we've got to find out this morning, about the boat, that is. Pete thought she was sound, but I want to get the sail and mast out of her and check everything before she gets hired to anyone else. Do you feel as if you could help? That'd be some proper boatbuilding for you. About the kids, the father asked for your address, but I told him that he'd better talk to me and I'll talk to you or your Aunt."

Ian nodded. "I'd like to help check the boat over."

"Pete's hovering outside the door with tea, so when we've sunk that you can go with him and bring her up the slipway. There shouldn't be too much wrong. We build them strong here, so they withstand the treatment hirers give them."

For the second time in two days Ian was presented with a mug of tea that was too hot to drink. Edgar and Pete finished theirs quickly and Ian suspected they had throats of asbestos.

At last they brought the boat and hauled her up, three of them propping her up on improvised legs. With Ian trying to help, the mast was unshipped, the sail unlaced from the boom, the spars, stays and sheets laid out for inspection.

Ian was talked through what they were looking for and told to feel in certain places for wear and damage. He found none, nor did the expert hands and eyes of Pete. When it came to the mainsheet, Ian found what he described as a lump in the rope. He told Pete, who looked, and announced that one of the three yarns that made up the rope was parting and that a replacement was needed. Since knotting was a skill of which Ian had only touched the surface, he was given a proper lesson.

"And if it isn't tight, boy, it'll come undone and maybe all your efforts of yesterday will be wasted."

That struck home.

"Can't we camp on Peel Island?" asked Mary. Peel Island on Coniston Water had been Arthur Ransome's basis for Wild Cat Island in the Swallows and Amazons books.

"I've looked, and It's National Trust now. We've got the dinghy hired here, so we can at least have a look."

It was the second week. Their time at the Bowness hotel had ended and they had just arrived at a guest house on the shores of Coniston. This time they were sharing a room – to the unspoken amazement of both of them sharing had been suggested by the owner. The atmosphere in the place, immediately friendly and informal, was far more relaxed and to their taste. Not that there had been a problem with the Bowness hotel, but it was designed to cater for a clientele that had undergone different experiences from theirs, and whose expectations of holiday accommodation were very different.

They acclimatised themselves to the dinghy and set off to investigate Peel Island. Once on land, and having laughed at each other for mooring with the tide's ebb in mind, they looked round. Trees by the landing place showed them that the style of tents used by the Swallows could be made to work, so long as there was little wind. There was an obvious camp fire spot there and they wondered if it had ever really been used by Arthur Ransome and friends.

243

Tarpaulins and ropes were readily lent by their host and hostess, and Stephen asked about an old kettle and saucepans too. Amazingly they were provided, accompanied by a twinkle in her eye.

The weather forecast was fair, with light winds, and they loaded the boat. Setting off under the shadow of the 'Peak of Darien' seemed a privilege, and they made their way slowly to the Island.

"Is it safe to leave everything here?" Mary asked once they had unloaded again and Stephen had mentioned taking her to the hidden harbour.

"There's nobody here at the moment. We'll soon see if anyone else lands, wherever we are. They'll be the Amazons."

Mary laughed. They stowed everything out of sight of the shore and boarded the dinghy again. Mary grabbed the oars. Heading south the instructions in Swallows and Amazons were followed and they found the narrow, rocky inlet. The only missing parts were the leading marks to guide them into the famous, deeply inset anchorage.

Two hours later the tarpaulins had been suspended from trees to resemble the special tents Mrs Walker had made for her children. It looked similar to the drawings in the book and they felt they could be comfortable for a night there. A fire was started and tea brewed. They had lunch.

It took very little time to explore the island.

"I'm sure it was bigger in the books," Stephen complained.

"I'm sure the undergrowth was thicker too."

"People visit it too much nowadays."

Eventually they gave up and went sailing, looking for – and finding – a few of the places recognisable from the books.

"It's freezing," Mary said much later when they had crept into the makeshift tarpaulin tents and snuggled into the blankets.

Stephen had been wishing his feet would warm up and had to agree.

"You asleep?" he asked in a whisper thirty chilly minutes later.

"No," came the unhappy reply. "I'm too cold."

He thought. "Mountaineers, when they're cold, pair up."

"Stephen…"

"I was being practical. Honest."

Silence. Then some rustling. Mary appeared at the open end of the tent, blanket draped and looking as if she would be at home in a ghost movie.

"I just can't get warm."

They woke late the following morning. No sun could appear early over the rim of the hills or percolate through the trees to their shelter. Stephen, gradually awake, felt that his arm could belong to someone else. It was partly without feeling from where Mary had been lying on it. He cautiously moved to try and send some blood down to his fingers.

Mary's eyes flickered open, showed a momentary astonishment, then relaxed into acceptance and happiness as she looked, unashamedly, into his more worried gaze. His own furrowed brow smoothed though, quickly, and a smile was shared. They moved to ease stiff muscles and Stephen's numb arm, and kissed once more.

It was not until much later when a fire had been started and a kettle set to boil that the question was asked.

"Were we silly last night and this morning?"

Mary paused for a split second. "No. I don't think we were. I love you." She swallowed, then looked up at him. "I think – no, I know – you love me. You've said so, often. And we're going to be married. We've both left school now, so we could get married at any time."

"But weren't we going to wait? And… and if anything – well, happens – what will our parents think?"

A smile, and her arm came round his shoulders.

"They'll think we're impatient. Maybe they won't like the idea. But we won't be the first, nor the last."

"'Just in time, or born in the vestry', you mean?"

She shuddered. "We can do better than that."

"I know we can," he said quietly. "And I promise you this, that whatever happens I will be yours forever and face life with you forever. I can't make how I feel plainer than that. You are all that I have ever wanted. That I shall ever want."

She stood, almost in tears at his conviction and his earnest promise. He looked surprised and stood too, wondering what was going to be said next.

"And I will promise you the same thing. You have no idea how much I missed you when I was a prisoner in Scotland, and how much the need to be with you grew over those years. Yes, I will promise to you that I will want you with me always, and we shall grow old together, and still in love when we're old and grey and fifty."

The long embrace and that time of emotional union was interrupted by a shout from the water's edge. A family had just arrived and youngsters were milling about excitedly.

"Look!" shouted a young girl, "there's even tents there like the Swallows!"

Mary and Stephen regained the guest house late that afternoon and asked where they could clean the fire-blackened kettle and saucepans.

"Weren't you cold last night?" asked their host.

"Freezing, to start with," Mary admitted, then blushed as she wondered about the next question.

"Well, if you need a fire in your room I can get you coal and start it for you. Just don't build it up too high or you'll set the tree alight. Maybe the house too."

"It'll be all right, I'm sure; but thank you."

"Will it be cold later?" asked Mary when they were at last ready to go to bed.

"It feels warmer here than it was on the island. Why?"

"I wondered if we should – well – make sure we were warm enough. To start with."

Only one bed was slept in that night. The other remained lonely that night, and cold and unruffled for every night until they left.

27 – Mrs Damerell

Watching the two returning holidaymakers as they heaved their luggage from the launch and walked up to the house, Susan thought that they looked subtly different. Not different in appearance, but in the way they reacted to each other. They seemed more mutually attentive and in an undefinable way more close. Not that they had exactly been distant ever since the announcement of their engagement. There was just something, a nuance of difference. She was afraid she might know what it might be, had privately feared it and hoped she was wrong. Should she now show that she was shocked if later they admitted it? Would they do so? They were both minors, so should be guided by Henry and her. Yet to look and to listen to them now, particularly having watched their maturity increase over the months, and more markedly since they had left school, they seemed almost adult. They had each attained an easy grace, in movement and in attitude; a grace that came from being well placed in their surroundings.

It was later, once the last vestiges of the café's and domestic washing up had been completed and the Town contingent had returned to Salcombe, they could relax. Stephen cleared his throat and announced that they had come to a decision. The room quietened.

"Yes, before anyone asks again, Mary and I have had a wonderful time. We've done all the things we wanted to do – and thank goodness for having learnt to sail here. If we hadn't been able to we wouldn't have been able to explore nearly as much as we have.

There came the inevitable comments of congratulations.

"We have also done a lot of talking." His tone was now more measured, more deliberate. "We've thought long and hard about it and have decided that we want to marry now. Sooner rather than later. We've both left school now, so there is no awkwardness to endure by being a married couple in the same school.

"In any case we'll both be at work as soon as the farm buildings are complete. We shall have a house on the mainland near the farm but still be near enough to the Island to help when needed. There is nothing standing in our way."

It was said with a courteous gentleness that was still firm in its delivery.

The announcement was received in silence. Susan asked herself if the arguments Stephen had given were the sole reason and or whether they knew that something else was in the air. Sense told her that it was far too early for Mary to know if that was the case, unless they had been together before heading north without anyone else realising.

Henry took Susan's hand. "You've rather caught us unawares, old son. Don't you think that you're still very young? Too young? I do."

"We've talked about that, Henry," said Mary. "We know that we want to be together, for life, and we've already made promises to each other."

Susan gave a start. "You don't mean you've already got married?"

Mary smiled. "I doubt if that would be possible to arrange in two weeks, and without permission. No. We mean promises made between us."

Henry looked helplessly at Susan, who raised her eyebrows. He lifted his shoulders in a slight shrug.

"I think we need to sleep on it," said Susan slowly. "We've all had a long day and you've had a long journey. We'll see how we all feel in the morning."

Mary looked at her, almost indignant. "But a night's sleep won't change the way we feel, or the promises we made to each other. We've made that decision between us and nothing will change it."

"There's something else to think about," Stephen added, nodding in agreement with his fiancée. "When the house is built we shall need to move into it straight away. We wouldn't want to be living together and not be man and wife, and you wouldn't want us to, I'm sure."

"But you're still so young… especially Mary. She's only just sixteen…"

"No, Susan; not 'just'. I'm nearer seventeen by now."

"But it's still young to embark on married life. You should be enjoying your childhood still."

Mary looked shocked. "Being seventeen isn't being a child! A child is an eight year old, or Ted and Ian. I am enjoying being seventeen and no longer a child, particularly because of Stephen."

"In the eyes of the law you're still a child."

"Then so am I, Susan," said Stephen quietly, "but I think you mean 'minor'. We are both minors, yet the law also says we can marry if our parents agree."

Another silence.

"Let us digest it overnight, please," said Henry at last. "It's a big step and we all need to think of all the positives and negatives. Don't forget that as you *are* both still minors, if anything happens the responsibility will fall on us, the parents. We need to have time to think it through. You've had two weeks to talk about it all and arrive at a decision. We need time too. It all needs to settle into our minds, then we can discuss it levelly."

Angharad knew it was a letter from Bob. Carefully dropping all the other letters on the kitchen table – she still gravitated there in the mornings – she opened the thin envelope with his writing on the outside. Dolly found her in a chair, weeping, when she came to find her and help with the breakfast.

"What on earth is the matter, my dear? Bob's not hurt, is he?"

Angharad handed her the letter. Dolly read it. It had been delayed in the post by a week and she understood Angharad's shock. Bob was by then either already in Malaya or would be well on his way.

"*Dwi byth yn mynd i'w weld eto*" [I'm never going to see him again] she sobbed.

Dolly didn't have a clue what she was saying and her expression told Angharad so. She repeated it, haltingly, in English.

"Of course you will," Dolly told her. "They wouldn't send him somewhere dangerous after only a month's training. He'll come back soon when whatever it is has been sorted out, looking strong and bronzed. You'll see."

"It's not strong and bronzed I want," Angharad sniffed. "It's him, by here, now."

"I know. I can see that, and you've had a shock. But really, it will be all right."

She spent another ten minutes comforting her before Ted came in, wondering if there was anything to eat. He took one look, and sat himself beside the two of them, tea forgotten. Dolly told him what the letter said.

He found he didn't know what to say, so just held her hand. She smiled shakily at him.

"Good for me, you are," she said, and his heart melted.

Over the next hour the news spread. Ian took it to the boatyard, Ted to Loft Island. Merryweather (Solicitors, Commissioners for Oaths) made some cautious enquiries with friends. Martin told Mike.

"You could try asking old Fortescue. His wretched Solarium is almost finished at last, and he's written to ask us up to see it. It's quite a placid letter, if letters can be placid, so I think they must be pleased.

They found themselves at the Fortescue estate that afternoon and were welcomed in by Sir Richard almost as old friends. He seemed pleased with himself.

"I'm in her good books," he announced happily. "The old boy's got the last few inches on the last upright to carve, and that's it. You didn't tell me he's be so expensive on tea, Alexander."

"Drink a lot does he, sir? I suppose these old boys do. Probably trained by the Army."

A bark of laughter. "You're not wrong there, Armstrong. He was in the first lot and bloody lucky to get out with his life. Good man, you know. Very good man. We've swapped some yarns, I can tell you. Ah, here she is, and looking radiant as always."

Lady Fortescue's lifted eyebrows made them all laugh, but she did look happy. "Come and see," she said. "He is just the sort of craftsman you hear about but never meet, much less employ. Look at what he's done for us."

The slim, pale oak glazing bars were covered with carvings of leaves, flowers and small birds from the heel bar on the stonework up to a lightweight boss where the glass panels came together. The boss itself was a stylised sun, its rays slimming down to finish almost as pen-nib thinness. Even Martin, whose idea it had been, was silenced at the craftsmanship. Without thinking he let out a sigh.

"I hope you're satisfied, Rawle."

Martin's mind moved swiftly. "The answer should really be that if you and Lady Fortescue are happy with it, and Mike Alexander is satisfied, then that's enough." He paused. Before anyone had a chance to break in, he carried on. "I know that I said I would have to be careful before thinking of using such a design in a house of my own, but having seen this result I can say with all honesty that I would be very, very happy with it."

"I'm glad you said that. And if you did have that sort of design you'd like to work with the same carver, too, I imagine."

"Very much, sir, and I'd like to meet him."

"You shall. You shall. He's not here this week. He needs time to relax after such intricate work, but when he comes back I shall phone Alexander and ask you both back up here. How's that?"

"We'd love to come, Sir Richard," Mike chimed in. "Thank you."

"Now then, I imagine you have your invoice with you, Alexander. What?"

"No, Sir Richard. That will only be presented when the job is actually complete and you and Lady Fortescue have formally signed it off as satisfactory."

"Will it, b'God? Well, you'll just have to accept what's in these envelopes on account, then. Yours is to go against the invoice, Alexander, and yours isn't, Rawle. That's just a small gift to say thank you. And nothing to be said by you on that score, Alexander, or I'll find another way of saying thank you."

Martin's jaw dropped. "But, I can't..."

"You can, and you will. Be frivolous with it. Just don't do anything dangerous and kill yourself, that's all. Those brothers of yours need you and so does that girl of yours."

Martin was even more astounded.

"How...?"

"In the war I was in intelligence, young man. Playing the daft old bugger...sorry, dear: buffer... stood me in good stead. It still does. Information comes my way easily. So just enjoy what little that is and no more said unless you're silly enough to come up against me in court. But then I suppose Algy would defend you..."

Martin was brave enough to interrupt. "If I'd been that silly, sir, I hope he wouldn't defend me."

The gimlet eyes bored into him, then softened. "You seem to have principles too. Good. Just enjoy it, then."

Martin looked carefully at Mike and was reassured by a wink and his smile.

"I saw that, Alexander. You can take that to be permission from your employer, Rawle. I look forward to seeing you when old Gardner's back here so that we can have a slap up tea the day he finishes. You can inspect it, present your billet-doux, I'll sign the release papers and we can pig out... I mean enjoy our tea together. Is that a deal?"

They took their leave. In the car Martin was about to open his envelope.

"No. Do that at home. I don't need to see what he's given you. But don't expect that to happen with every job!"

Martin laughed, now confidently at ease. "I won't!"

On his arrival at the boatyard next day to start work, Ian noticed that Edgar's office door was shut and he was talking earnestly to someone who was so smartly dressed that it looked too formal to interrupt. He hoped it was nothing serious. After half an hour the Suit had left in a laden car that Ian hadn't noticed. Edgar put a piece of paper into a drawer.

After a busy morning with plentiful hirers needing to be ferried out to their boats, Edgar coincided with Ian as the lad climbed the steps from the rowing boat.

"Everything all right?"

"Yes thanks, guv'nor." Ian had followed the lead of the yard's staff.

"How's that boat of yours? The old rowing dinghy? Letting in water anywhere?"

"Don't think so. I've had to bale her out once or twice, but that's been rainwater."

He nodded. "Can't help that. But I've been wondering about something, now we're getting so many leisure sailors and are hiring motor boats out. What do *you* think is the sort of boat people would want if they're here for two weeks or longer?"

"Sailing or motor?"

"Well, that's the question I'm asking. Or should it be one that could do both?"

"But that's a sailing dinghy with an outboard, surely, guv'nor."

"Could be, could be. But what sort of boat would *you* hire if you had a long time on the Estuary?"

Ian thought hard. He loved sailing, but knew that the wind had to be strong enough but not too strong. Rowing was all right, but slow and hard work.

"Really, I'd like something with an engine but which would sail like a dinghy when I could," he said slowly. "That means I could get up to Lofts quickly if I needed to, and go sailing at other times."

"So an outboard, then?"

Ian had already seen too many people trying to start reluctant outboard engines in his short time on the water. He knew how much strength it took to pull the starting cord, and even more to lift the engine to and from the boat.

"Well, no. Not really. I'd rather have an inboard engine."

"But that'd get in the way of the centreboard if she's a sailor."

Ian frowned and thought some more.

"I suppose there's no engine small enough to go under the stern thwart?"

"You'd need a long tiller. But I suppose it could be a hinged one like they're starting to fit to racing dinghies."

"That'd do it."

Edgar nodded. "Food for thought, that. I'll have to have a look."

The door slammed. Dolly thought it was one of the boys, yet surely they were both still on the Island? Puzzled, she went to reconnoitre and found her brother standing in the hallway with an expression on his face that had been strange to her since their childhood, when he would show his frustration with his father's overbearing attitude.

"Bert?"

"What make it ten times worse is that it is entirely my own fault."

It was not the explanation she had hoped for.

"Bert, what on earth has happened?"

"It's Mrs Damerell. She had a heart attack." His voice dropped at the end of the sentence and Dolly knew that her near-indestructible brother was near tears. The thought shocked her, and it was only after a hesitation that she took his hand and led him into the kitchen. Annabelle looked round, took stock and went to help Dolly lower him into a chair. Instinctively she filled the kettle. Dolly told her what had happened.

"How is she?" Annabelle asked.

He shook his head. "I don't know. The ambulance came and took her to hospital. I was so disturbed all I could do was come away and walk home."

"They would have taken her to Kingsbridge, I suppose. We can telephone them later to find out. But in the meantime you need to rest."

"I can't rest," he exclaimed, almost savagely. "She's been my Secretary for… for decades. I owe her more than just to rest while she goes through… through whatever it is she has to face. I need to go to the hospital."

He stood up. "Please will one of you come with me? Annabelle?"

"Should you be driving, Bert?" she asked gently. "I think it would be better if someone else did. What about Mike Alexander?" What about a taxi?"

"If one of them can get here quickly, I don't mind. Otherwise I shall drive myself."

Dolly went to the hall to make a call to Mike. Used to dropping everything when the Lifeboat maroons sounded he just said crisply: "Yes. Of course. From Martin's home? He can come too to support you. I'll get my parents' car. Give me five minutes."

Martin looked up.

"We're needed. Come on. I'll explain on the way."

Martin understood what had happened from the disjointed information gleaned as they drove down to the waiting party. Only Dolly and Bronwen were staying behind so as to be present should the boys return. It was the second time that Mike had driven at high speed to Kingsbridge, but at least this time he had no need to continue to Chepstow.

As soon as they had parked Bert had climbed from the car, and with a brief "excuse me if I run" he was, if not running, walking very fast toward the hospital entrance. Annabelle followed.

Even as she hurried after him she was aware of a sting of jealousy, a thought that astonished her. It was not in her character, she thought, to worry that the man she was so comfortable with should have feelings for another woman.

He was talking to whoever was on reception – she couldn't see who it was. Hearing footsteps, Bert looked round.

"Thank goodness… please, would you come with me?"

So he did still realise she was there. "Of course, Bert; why do you think I'm here?"

They walked through what seemed like miles of corridors. The hospital was actually quite small; it was the strain of not knowing that added to the distance. At last: "Emergency Ward" was the sign over the door. They pushed it open.

"Amelie Damerell?" Bert's voice sounded quavery, a tone Annabelle had never heard from him.

The nurse was young, brown haired and tired, but had a smile as she acknowledged him. She looked at a list. "She's in treatment at the moment. The doctors are doing what they can."

"Can we wait?" This time there was a definite sob in the phrase.

"Family?"

"No. Employer. It was in my office it… happened."

"Should be relatives only. But as you're here. And who are you, please?"

Annabelle looked at her and back at Bert. This was no good.

"His girlfriend," she said firmly.

The look on the nurse's face was almost comical, but Annabelle hardly noticed. The shock from Bert was almost tangible and his head snapped round, the eyes wide.

For a moment there was no sound. "Good God, Amble. So you are. Thank goodness."

For the first time in decades he felt confused. Mrs Damerell had been a constant presence in his life for as many decades. He knew she was a friend as well as an employee. There had never been any other feeling for her. When the heart attack happened his natural first concern was for her, that she would be well looked after, that if anything were to happen, then at least he would be there. Up to that moment his focus was solely on her.

Yet he had wanted Annabelle to come with him to the hospital. She had been out of the car immediately after him. She was there now. He was supporting Mrs Damerell; she was supporting him. To hear her words had been a clarion call, a call he knew but had only half learnt.

With a fierceness that surprised them both he grasped her hand.

The door opened behind them. Mike.

"Is she all right?" he asked quietly.

The nurse frowned. "Really, no more, please, or you'll all have to go."

"No news yet," said Annabelle quietly. "She's still being treated."

"Has anyone phoned Mr Damerell?" asked Mike.

"Yes, Bron and Dolly were going to try from home."

"I'll leave you to it," said Mike. "We're in the foyer if we're needed."

"Sorry, Mike. Thank you. If you need to return, we can get a taxi."

"We can wait, sir. Martin wouldn't forgive me if we left his grandad to find his own way back."

Bert smiled. "Not completely incapable yet, young Mike Alexander, but thank you."

Mike disappeared. Bert and Annabelle waited in silence.

It was fully twenty minutes later that doors in the centre of the ward swung open and a trolley appeared, pushed by a porter and attended by two nurses. It made its way to the side of a bed. The nurse at the table stood.

"Wait there, please."

The four of them lifted a recumbent figure from the trolley to the bed and drew the curtains round. Movements of the curtain and the occasional bumps appearing in it showed that there was work going on, but nothing else happened until the porter emerged with the trolley and wheeled it away.

"Is that her, do you think?" Annabelle whispered.

"I think it may be, but we dare not interrupt."

They waited in silence again, a silence that was broken by a crescendo of running feet outside the door until it swung open with a bang. A man stood, looking round wildly as the swing doors flapped themselves to a halt. He was breathing heavily.

"I suppose you don't know if there's a lady with a heart attack... no, you wouldn't."

"Mr Damerell?"

He swung round, hopeful. "Yes. Do you know?"

"We're not sure, but we think she may be just out of treatment. I'm Merryweather. She is my secretary."

"Oh... yes, sorry I recognise you... what happened? And is that her?"

"We suppose so, but don't know. She stood up, looked peculiar, then sat again and- well, slid off the chair onto the floor. I called the ambulance, of course, and tried to do what I could."

"She's dead, isn't she." It was more of a statement than a question.

"Well, they whisked her up here in an ambulance, so I don't think so. And if that is her in there, then no."

Mr Damerell looked a little easier. The curtains opened and the nurse the had originally seen came to them, looking disapproving.

"I really must ask…"

"This is Mr Damerell," said Bert shortly. "Is that his wife?"

She nodded. "It is. And she's asleep. You may go and see her for a few minutes, Mr Damerell, but it must be a very short visit. I'm afraid you two may not, that is for the relatives only. But I can tell you she is alive, and as well as can be expected, and we'll see if we can get her to make a full recovery."

"How long do you think…?"

She held up her hand. "Your guess is as good as mine, I'm afraid. A heart attack is a serious matter and it depends on all sorts of things. She has done well to get through the first part of it, which is to keep breathing all the way here. Now it's down to the doctors and us to get her slowly better again."

Still he hovered there. Annabelle put a hand on his arm.

"We should go. Leave her husband with her."

He nodded and spoke to the nurse. "May we call… would you call me if there's anything we can do, or… any change?"

"Best if Mr Damerell does. We would tell him first. He could tell you."

"Then please could you give him my phone numbers? This is my card. Let me write my home number on the back – damn. Have you a pen, please?"

He wrote the number and was about to pocket the pen had not the nurse held out her hand with a tired smile.

"I'm so sorry, nurse." He was able to smile for the first time for hours. "And please, could you tell Mr Damerell that her salary will continue to be paid, so not to worry about that."

She smiled back at him. "Best if you did, really. I'll ask him to phone you."

But Mr Damerell was walking up towards them, looking dazed. They waited.

"She's asleep," he said. "They say that's a good thing. I just wish I knew. Or could do something."

"That is exactly what I feel," Bert said, holding out a hand to be shaken. "Please may we keep in touch? I would really appreciate daily updates if you feel you can. And if there's anything I or my extended family can do to help – transport, maybe – you must let me know."

"Oh, I couldn't…"

"Yes, you could, and please do. And I know your wife is due to retire soon; please rest assured that her salary will continue to that point."

"But you'll be out of pocket."

"Your wife has been my assistant and friend, as well as my secretary, for more years than I care to remember. She's worth her weight in gold to me. So let's hear no more about being out of pocket, please. *I'm* in *her* debt. It's about time I made up for that."

He found his hand being shaken again before the worried man turned back towards his sleeping wife.

"We managed to do something, at least," said Bert when they were walking back to the car. "It's just not what I expected. But then I didn't know what I expected to be able to do."

"There is nothing else you could have done, you know that. But what you did was no less than I would expect of you."

He turned to her. "You sound as if you know more of me than I do myself."

"Perhaps I do, perhaps I do. And that would be because I see you from the outside, something you are unable to do. And because I'm interested and I care."

The face softened, and he smiled. "Yes… my girlfriend. That startled me!"

She laughed. "It was meant to cause some astonishment, both for you and for that nurse. I believe it worked."

They were nearly at the car. "We must talk about it later," he said quietly. "If you would like to."

"I think we should, and yes, I should like to."

The state of play was described to the others once they had started the journey, but apart from that the journey was completed in near-silence.

Dolly and Bronwen heard the news with sympathy. They both knew how serious a heart attack was, and how a proper recovery was quite rare.

The boys and Angharad returned from a day partly spent on the water and partly helping in the café – Angharad and Ian, and talking farming to Henry – Ted. Henry was still pleased with the boy's knowledge and the attitude he'd noticed from the start. Ted was unworried about the responsibilities that Henry had mentioned might become his. If anything his smile had just grown wider.

Back at their home they were quietened to hear of Mrs Damerell's heart attack, and naturally worried that none of the adults could tell them of the likely outcome.

"Will she die?" It was Ian who asked the question everyone had been avoiding.

"No one can say, Ian," his Uncle Bert told him honestly. "I suppose it depends how bad it was, and we can't see inside the heart to find out. Her husband will tell us each day what's happening, and that's all we can say."

It was a quietened group that night. Bert, particularly, seemed worried. Bronwen noticed.

"There's nothing you could have done, Uncle. You do realise that, don't you?"

He smiled. "I suppose so. I can't help feeling that I should have noticed something, something that wasn't as it had been for the last thirty years, but I don't know what I should have been looking for."

"There. You said it yourself. You have no idea what a heart attack looks like until it's happening; nor has any of the rest of us. I doubt if even a doctor would notice. If she never complained of any pain or looked different, then there's nothing to see. But if you're in doubt, ask our doctor."

"You are very wise, Bron. That is exactly what I'll do tomorrow. Ah, here is your friend, back from work at last. He works as long hours as I used to when I was starting the practice."

A tired Martin looked into the room. After a smile at Bronwen his first words were "How is she?"

"No news, I'm afraid, Martin," Bert told him. "We'll only hear tomorrow when her husband has telephoned. Bother. I should have offered him a lift to Kingsbridge in the car if he ever needed one. I could do that now."

"If you telephone him now, Uncle," Bronwen said, "you'll alarm him. He'll think it's the hospital. Wouldn't it be better to wait until he calls here tomorrow?"

"You have logic, my dear. You're quite right, of course. I shall do so."

"I'm going to make a sandwich, if that's all right. I've had nothing since lunch." Martin dodged back into the passageway. Bronwen followed him.

"Do you think I should go and man the office?" Dolly asked the room at large.

"I don't know who's going to do the typing and show the people in unless it's one of us," said Annabelle. "And you've done some typing, so it would be a start."

Dolly sighed. "I know, but I have no shorthand. He needs a real shorthand typist. Oh, I could write it out longhand from dictation and then type it, but it'd take ages. I could just go with the sense of what he's saying, but if I get a few words wrong in a legal letter it could be disastrous."

Bert chuckled. "Do I have a say in this? I was hoping Dolly might be prepared to help. In fact if Bronwen wanted to come as well it would be an experience and she could perhaps see if it was the sort of vocation she would want to follow."

"But I shan't be able to keep up with the typing!"

"No, and it may be that we need a part time help. Unless we try, we shall never know. And to serve those for whom I'm acting we need to ensure there is as much continuity as we can manage."

28 – The Presentation

With the end of the school holidays came a decrease in visitor numbers, much to Susan's relief as what little work she was then able to do was starting to tire her considerably.

"There's only a few weeks to go," Henry reminded her when he found her sitting, exhausted, in the kitchen one day. "Please – just take it easier? We can still get help in, don't forget."

Ted and Ian had pleaded to be allowed to return to school a week later "just in case they were needed" in the café but neither was surprised when they were denied. From that point on their routine was set. School bus in the morning; and while it was still running, the ferry from Kingsbridge in the evenings. Ted would alight at Loft Island and start his few farming jobs; Ian, who was often seen illicitly at the wheel of the Ferry, would travel to Salcombe, either to the Ferry Steps or, if there was time, to the boatyard where he would greet his friends. Once the ferry stopped for the season Ted would be put off by the school bus at Lincombe, relying on someone from the Island to fetch him. Ian would continue despondently to Salcombe knowing that even if he went to the boatyard it would be about to close.

Bronwen was readying herself to start at Exeter University. She was due to leave in early October, probably immediately after the birth of Susan and Henry's baby. Her departure had been one of the main topics of discussion between her and Martin ever since she had enrolled.

"It will decide whether or not we're going to make a go of it. Of us," she said.

"What – if you go, or if you don't?"

"If I go and we're still together."

"I know the answer to that already, and I hope you do too."

"I do."

Bulletins about Mrs Damerell's health were regular. She was slowly recovering, but they said that it would be a long road and that she needed regular, but gentle, exercise, increasing a very little each day.

In the Solicitor's office there was at first desperation and sometimes panic as Dolly struggled to speed up her typing and take notes more quickly. Bert was always patient, and endured many calls of "please slow down!"

Dolly had been offered the chance of typing in the storage room. That meant fewer interruptions as Bronwen could receive people in the outer office. Most visitors were taken aback to see a young girl acting as Receptionist. Some were inclined to be dismissive at first until they were treated with courtesy and firmness, followed by pertinent questions to the best of Bronwen's ability, on which the start point for the Solicitor himself could be based.

"I must try and get a record cut to play to people who ask about Mrs Damerell," she complained after the third day. Bert suggested the best solution was to print out weekly updates and pin them beside the door. It helped a little but she was still asked by many.

One afternoon the phone in Loft Farmhouse rang.

"May we come over, Henry?" asked Martin. There was a muttering in the background. "Oh... er... I should call you Mr Loft as you're a client."

"Don't you dare," Henry told him. "This isn't with some drawings for the mainland farmhouse, is it?"

"It is," Martin told him happily. "We'd like to talk you all through them, please."

"Should I fetch you from the Hard?"

"Please. Mike didn't think much of the idea of bringing his car over."

There was more background muttering and Martin laughed.

"About half an hour?" asked Henry. "Are you staying for a meal?"

"That'd be lovely."

What Mike had admitted to being drawings were really halfway between technical sketches and an artist's impression of the proposed appearance of the new farmhouse. It would be quite substantial. After the smallness of the old farmhouse Stephen and Mary found it quite astonishingly large.

"Do we need all those many rooms?" she asked.

"I believe so," Mike answered. "I hope you don't mind but I looked at the plans of the Beale farmhouse. It had four bedrooms, and as there is space to build a similar sized house, it seemed logical."

"But Stephen and I won't know what to do with all that room..."

"Your family may well grow," Martin said quietly, having beckoned them away from the table. "And there's Ted to think of to start with, when he starts working full time in the holidays. And you want a spare room for friends. Besides..." He paused and grinned. "Your family seems to make a habit of rescuing waifs and strays. First it was Mary, then me, then Bron, Ted and Ian. Who knows what you're going to do next? Should I add another floor?"

They could see he was joking and Stephen cuffed him lightly round the ear.

"Four's enough," he said, "and if we employ more staff who need accommodation we'll have to build cottages for them. We're not going to cook for *them*!"

They looked at the plans, asked questions, made comments which, usually, Mike had already foreseen, and eventually pronounced they were very happy with the proposals and the siting.

"...Though really you should have it on the other corner so as to get that view over the Estuary," Mike finished.

"No!" The two voices rang out in unison. His idea would have given a view not just over the Estuary but of their special bathing site, a piece of land they were determined should remain unchanged.

"Well, it'll be your house," Mike said with a smile as he packed up the drawings. "Now we've just got to draw these up properly and get them round to some companies for quotations. Work on the café starts at the beginning of October, so it's going to be mayhem on the island for a while."

"When can work on the house start?" asked Stephen.

"If you and Henry sign off the access road today, we can get that built. The time that takes will depend on the weather. Once that's in – or maybe before if we can get heavy stuff down here safely on a temporary road – work can start on the house."

"And when will that be ready if it is?"

"Oh... I suppose about 6 months if we really push it. More if we find problems."

"Problems?"

"Constitution of the ground for the foundations, that sort of thing."

"It's a long time," said Mary.

"It can be done quicker, but the standard of the work will suffer. And don't forget the farm buildings will be in build at the same time."

"Would they be finished sooner?" asked Stephen.

"I'd hope so. There's only one storey for most of them, and the build quality doesn't have to be so high."

"I hope it stays up, then!"

"Oh, It'll do that. Actually, one good thing in its being ready well before the house is that the water and electricity has to be laid on first. And while we're digging for that we can dig for the septic tank."

"Just a minute, Mike," put in Henry, "can't it be connected to the main sewerage?"

"Well, no, it's too far away, and uphill anyway."

"But the Island's on the main sewer. It's a complex set-up and has to be pumped from our own tank to Lincombe. We only had that put in because the water board's idea of maintaining the pump is hit and miss."

Mike didn't know whether to look ashamed or astonished. "But I assumed... So the Victorians installed a sewer... where?"

"Lincombe."

"But that's... huh! That *was* just a pipe under the grazings. Easy. That's where the pump is, I suppose? And now, of course, it'll be just Lofts on the system. But why isn't it flooding?"

"Why should it?"

"Because it would have been shared by Beales," said Mike quietly.

This was talk of Mary's old home which would have shared the sewer. Often her emotions would be triggered by such a sudden reminder, but this was so basic and down to earth – and she had an answer – that she piped in quite cheerfully.

"That's because the system had a valve in it. Dad used to say it was an airtight ball which seated on a rim to stop it flooding."

"I imagine our 'friends' at the water board would like to be reminded about that so they can seal it off properly," Stephen put in. "We can use that to persuade them that an extra property on the system isn't actually any additional burden."

Two weeks later the first major work on the new farm buildings started, much to the relief of all of them. Holes and trenches were being dug, ground prepared and the whole area at the base of the hill started to resemble a bomb site. Stephen and Henry, with Mary and Ted when they could, made daily visits so as to ensure their carefully drawn plans were being observed. All seemed well, though they were dismayed at how much mud had covered a large swathe of good grass.

"It'll come back," They were told. "We'll leave it beautiful for you. We'll even put in some potted plants for the cows, shall we?"

This, addressed to Ted, pulled him up short until he realised he was being teased.

As if that hadn't been enough, deliveries of building materials were starting to arrive for the alterations to Lofts Farmhouse. Postponed by the need to keep the café open for the season, this was long awaited, but Susan was finding it all too much. Her baby was due the following week, and she was anxious for some peace.

Angharad was aware of her mood. She mentioned it to Dolly and Bert when she returned there after the café had closed for the season.

"She must come here," said Bert, "and I'm ashamed not to have thought of it before."

"I'll vacate my room on the ground floor," said Dolly. "It's big enough for her and the baby to start with."

"It's not what I think she would want," Angharad put in suddenly. "It's her husband and her own home she'll want when the baby's born. But here she could be until the birth. Please."

They were becoming used to her increasing confidence. It seemed to have stemmed from the realisation that she was needed, that her opinions mattered, that her abilities were being discovered and that, after all, she was the same age as Mary. Mary whose word was, if not law, then respected. Who had been orphaned and who was therefore not as fortunate as she, who had not. And Mary was self-assured... why should she not be the same?

"Do you think so, Angharad?" asked Bert. "I just want what is best for her, and should have thought that the peace of this house would give her what she needs."

Angharad was still in awe of him, and bit her lip. But no... "I think she should decide, sir, don't you? Please?"

Bert knew by now that when Angharad started calling him sir she was feeling cautious but was holding her ground. He smiled and took the pressure off her.

"You are quite right, my dear. I will ask now."

Susan was overjoyed at the suggestion, but worried about taking Dolly's room.

"I'm not having you traipsing up and down stairs, Susan, and you're most certainly not sleeping in the kitchen. You come here tomorrow, if Henry agrees, and stay as long as you want. It's absolutely no hardship."

Henry agreed, and with some relief. It meant that he would have no need to keep checking on Susan where she was either sitting, looking exhausted; or attempting to work, at which point his hidden annoyance would require him to chivvy her back to a chair or a bed. Bert was about to end the call when Angharad raised her hand as if she was still in class.

"Just a minute, Henry, Angharad wants to says something."

"I should go to live on the Island, maybe, whilst Susan is here? Then I can make sure they all get fed."

She got a smile in return. Bert relayed her offer to Henry, who laughed.

"Doesn't she trust us to feed ourselves? Not even with Mary here? And Angharad's expecting, too."

Bert relayed this to Angharad, feeling like a secretary to both of them.

"I would like to," Angharad said simply. "Mary and I have often cooked together."

"Then yes, Henry. That seems like a good idea. At least for the moment. But I suspect there will come a time when all except maybe you, Mary and Stephen will need to take refuge here whilst the building work proceeds around your ears. There will not be a room left untouched, I believe, except for the main bedroom. And you must come if you need to. We have the space."

It stirred a memory, a thought of what he needed to do. His mind returned to that moment at the hospital: "I am his girlfriend..." His eyes sought Annabelle, but she was carefully knitting the fourth of Salcombe-ganseys for local fishermen; the first having been bought readily by a boat owner who had enjoyed a good tourist season, and the second and third having been quietly made when the boys were at school.

By devious means he managed to delay her going to bed until everyone else had said their good-nights. They stayed there on their own until each of them started yawning and simultaneously exclaimed at the time.

"You are a bad influence on me, Bert," Annabelle said, laughing, "but my heart is as light as it has ever been."

Susan's arrival by car from the Hard the following morning found her looking more than a little white. It caused concern.

"It was unexpectedly choppy out there this morning," she told them, "and I think it affected me a little." She was certainly grateful for a comfortable chair.

They fussed around her for a while, but all she really wanted was a cup of tea and some peace. By mid-afternoon she looked better, with a good colour. Henry felt it was safe for him to return to the Island where he could check on progress, even though he trusted Martin's ex-employers' work completely.

The next day was Saturday. Ian slipped out early having had a breakfast of tea and cereal made by a very tired-looking Aunt Amble. He was heading, as always on a Saturday, for the boatyard. The dinghy hire season may have all but ended but Edgar was finding him work to do inside, and recently he had been employed helping with the building of a motorised sailing dinghy which was the result, said Edgar, of their chat some six weeks earlier. That had given him a great interest in the result and the only criticism he had with the design was it had been impossible to fit a small, reliable engine with adequate power under the stern thwart.

"They just don't make 'em," Edgar had told him. "So we're going to try our usual engine in the usual place, with the centreboard case just for'ard.

The result, Ian had to admit, was attractive and workmanlike, and he looked forward to seeing her and her sisters in the hire fleet the following year.

As soon as he was clear of the house everyone else except Susan started preparing themselves. Susan and Angharad, as quietly arranged, would stay behind – to Susan's regret, because she liked Ian, but she realised that she mustn't put herself at risk when she was so near the birth. It was just before ten o'clock that the remainder set off.

Ian had been tasked first with helping to ready the new dinghy so she could be swung out over the estuary on davits and lowered to her launching.

"Why don't we just go ahead?" he asked, impatient to see how she would float.

"She's a new class for Salcombe, lad, so we've invited a few come to see her first. A celebration, like. It'll happen. all in good time."

He was set to sweeping up in the part of the yard where she had been built, tidying up after some of that day's efforts to complete the final touches. It was when he had lifted the last few ends of the remaining new rope from a table that his eyes hit on what he thought might be the drawings for her. Ignoring a call of "Tea, Ian" he looked, closer. Yes, there was the distinctively shaped casing which combined the engine housing with centreboard case. Yes, there was the hinged tiller – still needed now to allow the helmsman to reach the centreboard if necessary. His eyes wandered to the heading of the plan, and he found he had to look twice, his eyes widening. In Edgar's rounded script, that he used only on boat plans, were the words

Rawle Class

He looked round, then back. There was a noise at the entrance and he looked up again. Pete, with the inevitable mugs of tea in his hand.

"Ah, found it, have you? Well, best come out anyway, or you'll miss her launch and you'd not want that, I can tell you."

There seemed to be a lot of people by the boat. Locals, he thought, come to criticise his ideas. Rawle Class, indeed. Then he noticed his brother. And his Aunt. And, it seemed, the rest of his family. A voice rang out from the quay edge and a short, red-faced man stood there, wearing an important looking army uniform, and looking fierce. Ian stood, wondering, then found the man was marching towards him. He took a step back.

"Stay there, boy, or I'll have further to walk. And this damn uniform's too damn tight nowadays." It was said quietly, but in such a human voice that Ian had to smile. The apparition stopped six feet away from him and drew a breath, winced at the tightness of his tunic, and barked out as if addressing a passing-out parade:

"Ian Rawle: this town salutes you for your courageous actions and good seamanship when saving two lives and a sailing dinghy from the Estuary last August. If there were more youngsters like you, the world would be a better place."

He closed the distance between them and gripped Ian's hand, shaking it. "Your brother's a good, principled lad too," he continued quietly. "You're a credit to each other. Stay where you are a minute."

As if Ian wasn't surprised enough he found himself being saluted, automatically felt he should salute back, but didn't. Another two figures separated themselves from the crowd; Lifeboatmen. *Was* that his brother? The one with the suspiciously shiny eyes? And the coxswain... he mustn't be called 'sir'. What was his name? Andy. They were carrying something, something blue.

Andy grinned at him. Martin dashed something away from his eye. Ian felt more at ease. At least *he* wasn't in tears... but then why was Martin?

"Get that ol' jumper off, Ian. Got something better for you." Andy stood, waiting. What was going on? He looked at Martin, who just nodded. He hauled his old, work-worn jumper over his head. Now what? Drop it? He looked behind him. Ted, standing near, also smiling. He threw it to him.

261

"Best put this on, lad."

Andy held out a navy blue jumper. Ian knew that pattern. He had seen it around the town enough, and more recently he had seen another jumper with that pattern grow at his Aunt's hands. "For sale", she had told him. Oh well.

He hauled it over his head and worked his arms into it. It felt good. Fitted well too. *Was* it his Aunt's work?

"And now you'd best look at the front, old son."

Why? What for? He knew the pattern. He looked down.

Four capitals, in red, across the chest.

And underneath... what was that? He couldn't read it upside down.

"It says Honorary Member, Ian" Martin said, seeing his puzzlement. "Welcome to the team."

But now Ian found that now his own eyes were becoming misty, and him nearly twelve, too. He shook his brother's hand, looking down, then found another being offered to shake. Andy's. He met a smile.

"My idea," said Andy, "but the rest of the crew agreed. Very unofficial, but Salcombe knows why. And by the time you've grown out of it you'll be able to have one with just the initials. Though I guess that by then, this one'll be as tight as the old soldier's uniform."

"I heard that, Cox'n, damn yer ears. That'll cost you a scotch."

Andy looked round, grinning. Martin and Ian were both astounded that anyone should talk to Sir Richard in that way.

"He and I understand each other," said Andy with a grin. "Now, I'm told that you have another brother, apart from my new crew member here..." He nodded at Martin "...and it seems only fair he should get a jumper to label him part of Salcombe's seamen, even if his real interest is farming, as I'm told."

He beckoned to Ted, who looked astonished, but came forward anyway. This time both of the old jumpers were dropped to the ground so that Ted could wear his own new gansey.

"It's got no R N L I on the front, son, because you didn't have the opportunity of beating us at our own game like your brother did. But the Rawle family is respected round here, so it's right you should have one."

Ted managed to stammer his thanks in a voice suddenly higher than usual.

There was another clearing of a throat. Edgar, this time.

"It's lovely to have so many customers here, past, present and I hope future. But we have a boat to launch too, and to pass on to her new owner. She's the first of a class of dinghy based on our designs but with ideas from, believe it or not, the lad who's now sporting a very traditional Salcombe gansey with some important writing on it. He thought that a combined motor and sailing dinghy would be a good idea, so we built one as a trial on the instructions of one of our new clients. The client can't be with us today, because he said he and his family would find it too embarrassing. But we'll launch her, anyway.

There was a bustle by the water's edge, and for once Ian hung back with the others. Slowly the falls were let slip and the dinghy – the first of the Rawle Class – was lowered into the water to clapping and sounds of approval.

Once she was there, suddenly looking smaller, Edgar regained everyone's attention.

"Now I have a letter to read out," he announced. "This is from the family who commissioned this build. It says this:

'I said that I would be too embarrassed to attend the events today. That is because it was my two children whom Ian rescued. Over the weeks since then our blood has run cold many times at the idea of how nearly we lost them, and what that loss would have done to my wife and myself.

So many times, it seems, a rescuer is heaped with praise and given a medal, and then forgotten. We are lucky to be in a position to be able to do a little more, to show our immeasurable gratitude to our children's amazingly young rescuer, in a way which will last him into adulthood and maybe middle age.

The dinghy that has just been launched is therefore now his; to own and to use – safely, please – as he wants, under guidance from his brother and the adults round him if necessary. Though given his seamanship skills which have impressed even the Lifeboatmen, I imagine that will be rare.

God bless you, Ian Rawle.'"

There were a few seconds of silence before the quayside erupted into applause. Ian was as a statue, stunned into silence, looking out over Batson Creek, seeing just the top of the gleaming mast of what seemed now to be his boat.

His boat.

His emotions didn't know whether to make him cry, shout, laugh or look around for support. As it was he chose the last, and jerked his head to where his brothers were standing to beckon them over. They were still applauding and he wished they would stop. Annabelle joined them as well.

"Is it real?" he whispered.

She nodded. "Edgar told us some time ago what they wanted to do. They had asked him as they knew no one else in town, and he felt this would be what you'd want most."

He nodded, still almost unbelieving.

"Come with me?" he asked the other three, and led them down the steps. Looking at the boat now he was seeing her as if for the first time, yet with a prescience of every rib, every plank, every fitting. He had witnessed her building; her long, slow birth. At last tears came, tears of happiness, tears of a fierce pride. He sat, suddenly needing to be out of sight, and buried his head in his Aunt's shoulder for a minute.

Recovering, he said shakily: "I can't take her out now, not with everyone watching. Can we just sit here for a while, 'til they've all gone?"

"You three sit there for a bit, and I'll go and face them," said Martin. "I'll come back when it's all clear."

He clambered up the steps again and to their surprise they heard him speak, once he had achieved silence.

"I think anyone would have been overcome by what's happened today, so Ian won't be making a speech. I know him well enough to say that he can't express how much this means to him – in fact I don't think I could either in his position. His family is proud of him, and I'll include our father in that, if only he'd lived to see it." He paused, emotions threatening again. "As if it wasn't enough to receive such a thing as the dinghy of his dreams, then to receive the appreciation and acceptance of the Lifeboat crew – my crew..."

There were some raucous comments from the blue-clad gathering and he turned and grinned at them.

"...who are also my friends..."

"Okay, lad, you win!" Andy called, and this time there was applause.

"...was the icing on the cake. And thank you also to Sir Richard whose arrival, and in uniform, was a surprise to all of us."

"And bloody uncomfortable it is too... Oh, sorry dear."

Sir Richard waited for the laughter to subside. "When a youngster does something like that, he and all his ilk should be encouraged. And who best to give that encouragement than an old... buffer... from a different era who can add a bit of ceremony, eh? Got to use the rank and title for something good.

Then to Martin: "Better bring him to tea with you and Mike – you know when – and get him to criticise my carver's creation. And mind he wears that jumper, you hear?"

Martin smiled, knowing the man by now. "I'd love to, Sir Richard. We can use it as his birthday party, perhaps."

"Birthday? When? How old will he be?"

"Twelve, sir," and Martin named the date.

"If you think we're going to have a load of screaming kids up there, Rawle, running around and making a nuisance of themselves, well...."

He paused for effect.

"...you're absolutely right. Just his friends though, eh? We've got enough grounds for them all to play in - they could probably start a fire and brew their own tea if they've got the nouse? How about it?"

"If we can persuade the school to release them, sir, I'm sure he and they will love it."

"And his brother, of course. Leave that side of it to me. Still Miss Armitage up there, is it?"

"Yes, sir." He wanted to enquire whether the old Colonel had been taught by her as well, but thought he had better not.

"That went well, I think," said Bert, walking up to them. "Hallo Richard. It's been a long time."

"Algy Merryweather, by all that's holy! Or should it be Bert nowadays, as young Martin tells me? Darling, come and meet the other half of an unholy duo who raised merry hell at times at school. Bert – sounds strange to call you that, but I suppose I'll get used to it – this is my wife Isabel."

The correct things were said. "I would like to introduce you to my fiancée, but she's currently sitting in a dinghy."

Martin started, wondering if he'd heard right. He ran the previous sentence through his mind again and gaped stupidly.

"Algy, you old devil! Congratulations! This is all very new."

"It is to me too, sir. To all of us." Martin may have been interrupting, but his brain gave him no choice.

"Sorry, Martin. It only happened last night and there has been no chance to tell anyone yet. Yes, I asked Annabelle to marry me and she agreed."

"And is this the attractive lady who ventured down those stops just now as if

264

she were going to be taken off into the distance looking like Britannia?"

"The very same, Richard."

"Good God, but you always knew how to choose them... sorry, dear. No, it wasn't polite but it was no insult to you, believe me. Algy - we really must meet and go over old times. Isabel, Algy... Bert... is one of my oldest friends and until we spoke on the telephone when young Rawle was in danger of wasting a year of his life on National Service I thought he must be at the other end of the country by now. I've told you enough about him, God knows. It was young Martin here who mentioned his name and told me the old devil was just a few miles away from us. For once my grapevine had let me down. Bad business. Have to growl at a few people. Said then that I should make contact with you, Algy. Never did."

Martin escaped eventually to find Pete in the boat, quietly making sure Ian knew where everything was and how to deal with the engine. Being retold how to do something he had done so many times in a week, not only in the boatyard but on the water and at the Island, brought Ian more or less back to an even keel. He was about to exclaim indignantly that he knew, when Pete grinned and interrupted.

"Bet you didn't know about this, then."

He showed Ian the new site for the fuel tank, and where it was filled.

"That's for safety, that is. And there's one other thing. We want to see this boat once a month and that there engine needs to be sparkling, the drip tray clean and dry, and the planking under it dry before we do. Edgar doesn't know about that 'cos we haven't asked him. But ol' Charlie and me, we want to see you keep this boat not in Bristol fashion, but Salcombe fashion. And that's even higher standard.

"An' why? 'Cos we like you and want you to be safe, and we don't want to have to get that Lifeboat out to you when your boat's ablaze in the middle of the fairway 'cos you let fuel and rubbish accumulate under the engine. Got it?"

Ian looked up at an uncharacteristically sombre face and found himself nodding his agreement.

"Should I have been doing that when I've taken a motor out?"

"No, 'cos one of us always does it. And when we check over Lofts' boats, we do that as well. But this one's yours, and you need to do it."

A broad smile from Ian this time. If Pete said that the boat was his, it really was. He knew he'd just been presented with it, of course, but sometimes adults said and did things for kids just to make them feel good. He knew that. But Pete had always been as down to earth as the grass.

"Shall I start it?" he asked no one in particular.

"Your boat, boy. If you reckon it's safe to go, you go."

"Shouldn't it be?"

"Your decision. If you can't make a decision, yes or no, you shouldn't be on the water, much less own a boat. I knew a couple o' kids last August who didn't really make a decision and someone younger than them had to go and tow 'em back." He caused a smile all round.

Ian glanced all around him, judged the seaway running, felt the wind; and started the engine.

29 – Next generation

Susan knew she really should have gone to the Service with the others. Her not being able to go meant that Henry had stayed behind too. Ian was most anxious to go, suddenly. No one was sure if it was an urge to show off his new, unique jumper, or whether he felt he should just say thank you to someone. He was unsure if he would be allowed to wear a jumper to church, and wasn't surprised when his Aunt quietly told him that he should wear school uniform, but with a plain tie, as usual.

News of Annabelle and Bert's engagement had quickly circulated around the family and around the town itself, so their progress to the church was interrupted with having to stop and acknowledge congratulations and well wishes. Mary, thinking back to hearing Peter Loft's banns read in Kingsbridge, wondered if she would hear her adopted grandad's at the Service. She didn't.

Once again she tried to make herself feel that what had happened between Stephen and her in the Lake District and, quietly, at home since, was a sin. It was impossible. It felt so right; it made them both so happy. How can any expression of love between two people who have vowed to spend their lives together be seen as wrong, as dirty, as a sin? Even if they had not actually gone through a marriage ceremony?

There was still this feeling of unease to her, though; one that she knew would only be cured by that marriage service. But they were always so busy, and Susan was near her time, and Henry was torn between the building work and Susan.

"Henry… Oh."

It was not so much the volume or pitch of the call, but the tone. Henry came running.

"I think it's starting."

Half past eight on a Sunday morning is as good a time as any for a birth to start, and better than many. For a moment he stood, statue-like.

"Are you all right?"

"No. Could you call an ambulance?" A hospital birth had been arranged in view of Susan's age and because it was to be her first child.

He vanished, panicking, into the hall and to the phone.

"The door's unlocked!" called Ian in alarm as they returned to the house from church.

Martin was at the front in an instant. "I'll go in first." Bert, whose mind was thinking along lines of labour rather than burglary, nevertheless let him do so. He called out; the lack of an answer worried him. Briefly looking round all the ground floor rooms he finally noticed the scrawled note on the kitchen table: *Hospital – baby.*

Rushing back to the others he gasped out the reasons.

"I think it may be my turn to drive fast to Kingsbridge, don't you?" Bert said calmly. "I confess that I guessed as much. And I want to be there; I suggest that Mary and Stephen should too. Any more, and we shall swamp them. Indeed, even those few may be too many. I will fetch the car."

266

Bert turned out not to be the best driver, especially on Salcombe's narrow streets, and they all breathed a sigh of relief when the main road was reached. The car was left at the side of the nearest road to the hospital and Bert would have left the keys in the ignition had Stephen not asked if it was wise. Bert looked impatient for a minute but was told that he wouldn't want to lose the car, especially if there was a chance of bringing a new grandchild home in it.

They found Henry sitting in a bare waiting room with his head in his hands. He looked up at three horrified faces.

"She had to have a Caesarean," he said. "The babies were in a difficult position."

"Is she all right... *Babies*?" Mary was shocked.

"Twins. One of each. I'm as shocked as you are."

"Is she all right?" Bert butted in. "For God's sake say she is."

"The operation was a success. She's still recovering, of course. We were so lucky the specialist was at home, or she could have been in real trouble."

Bert sat down suddenly.

"I can't lose her."

"We're not going to, Dad. She's in the best hands."

"When shall we know if she is?"

"They've not said. A nurse came in and told me about the Caesarean and then a bit later about the twins. That's all I know."

Stephen went to his father. "Are you all right, Dad?"

"No, not really. But I can't do anything, so I might just as well sit here. I hate feeling powerless."

Mary had sat herself by Bert and put an arm round his shoulders. He looked at her and smiled.

"Thank you, Mary. She's very special to me."

Mary nodded. "She is to all of us."

Time and cups of tea came and went. When Henry had almost reached the point of exploding with worry the door opened and a midwife appeared. She was smiling.

"She is in recovery. It was not easy for her, nor for the surgeon. It's often the case when an older lady has her first baby that complications might arise; and of course none of us was expecting twins. They are doing well too. It will be a little while before the mother can see them, I'm afraid, because we need to keep her sedated for a while once she recovers from the anaesthetic.

"You're the father, I believe? You could see the babies now, if you like."

Henry rose quickly and looked apologetically at the others.

"Your turn will come," he said, and followed the midwife.

His feelings as he walked along the corridors were mixed: excitement at the prospect of meeting his second and third children; deep concern for Susan; the memory of seeing Stephen as a baby all those years ago and his feelings then; and the responsibility of having not one, but two extra human beings to look after.

The room had about fourteen cots. Henry felt as if he was looking at something approaching a baby farm, with one stall for each animal. The midwife indicated two next to each other, half way up the room.

In each, he saw a tiny creature, human, asleep. The two were facing each other. They were his tiny creatures; Susan's and his; it came to him as a bolt from the blue. Amazed, humbled, suddenly emotional, he walked up to them.

He was allowed to stroke each tender head as if each owner was a pet. He had been told he could not hold them, cuddle them; to make them his by being as close to them as possible. He craved that with all the strength of his being.

They were perfect. He looked at them; from the balled fists to the closed eyes, to the slightly open mouths: he took them in. The emotions strengthened. He never even thought to ask which was which, or what their birth weight was, or even exactly when they had been born. To see them and understand that these were Susan's and his, that was enough. Standing by the head of each cot, finding his eyes misting, glistening, was enough.

"We don't like people to stay too long, in case they've got some infection," the midwife said in a matter-of-fact voice, so destroying the moment. "You'd better come away now. You can see the mother, if you like, though she's still asleep."

"I intend to," said Henry, stung. Reluctantly he left the two – his two – and followed her, pausing at the door to look back to check.

More corridors, through the waiting room where all he had time to say was "They're wonderful. Going to see Susan now."

Susan was in a ward of four occupied beds, lying still, deeply asleep, the anaesthetic not having yet worn off. He sat beside her, holding her hand and was hardly surprised when the door opened again and her father cautiously came in.

Henry smiled. "I had to come," said Bert. "I couldn't just stay there. How is she?"

"Still under the anaesthetic, as the midwife said."

He would have stood to let the older man sit, but to do so would have meant releasing Susan's hand. Bert quietly walked to the other side and took her other hand. The tableau lasted for some few minutes, each man trying to will the patient to recover, to be strong.

Once again the midwife's return to the ward interrupted the mood.

"Really! One visitor only, please. Who are you, may I ask?"

"I'm her father. We both need to be here."

"But there's nothing you can do. She won't be conscious until tomorrow morning some time, so you might as well go home and come back then. We allow the *father* in for a quick visit, but this is a recovery ward and these mothers may wake at any time, so finding a strange man in the room would not be right. I think you both need to leave now, please, and we'll see you tomorrow."

"But..."

"Really. I'm afraid I must insist."

"Do you have my telephone number?" Henry asked, standing, carefully letting go of his wife's hand. "I want to be told if there is any change during the night, please."

"Yes, we have all your details from well before she was brought in. You will be called if there is anything for us to call you about."

"May I see my grandchildren, please?" Bert asked suddenly as they were being led back to the waiting room.

268

"I'm sorry, we allow a quick visit by the father only. Not others. It's for their safety as we don't want them open to infection, do we?"

He couldn't argue. Neither of them could. There seemed little point, anyway. Tails between their legs they collected Mary and Stephen and returned to the car. Once in it, Bert sat for a still for a moment, hands gripping the wheel, immobile.

"You know they're right to want to protect the mother and the babies. But it's the way it's done, with the father allowed so little contact and the grandfather none. Yet we know that only a few years ago babies were born in homes with very little in the way of intervention except by a midwife. And as soon as she had gone, the father, siblings and relatives would be all over the baby."

"But she had to be in a hospital, Grandad. We were all told that, and it's as well she was."

"I know, I know. Perhaps it just hurts to be treated like an unnecessary adjunct to the baby – and in my case to the mother as well. But we will return tomorrow and beard the dragons again. I doubt if any attempt to be a solicitor will have any effect on them but I shall be tempted to try."

The reception committee in Salcombe was clamouring for news as soon as they spotted the car's return. They were silenced firstly by the news of twins, secondly by the news of a caesarean... "I'll explain later, boys", said Henry ...and thirdly by the lack of any real information about their weights and the time of birth.

Henry, exhausted beyond his comprehension by the nervous wait and by emotion, accepted Annabelle's offer of dinner, but made his excuses almost immediately afterwards claiming the need to be close to a phone. The three island dwellers set off for the night.

"Right, you 'orrible lot. You've 'ad your time at ease here and you're friends with the base now, aren't you? Well now you're going to be friends with the jungle, 'cos you're going to a base camp in the mountains tomorrow. It's a nice little excursion and your luxury coach picks you up at five in the morning."

Bob had received no letter from Angharad since his hurried scrawl as he was about to leave Britain. He wondered if the Sergeant had remembered to post it after all. Or had Angharad changed her mind?

He spent the rest of the evening writing again, though had no confidence that the flimsy envelope would ever reach his home, the only address he could be sure of, having lost Annabelle's Salcombe address in a muddy ditch during training. He knew *where* she lived, of course, but the number escaped him. Writing to his own home was the only answer as a copy of her address had been left with his parents.

The promised luxury coach was naturally the usual Army bone-shaker, and in it forty soldiers sweated their bored way upwards through the never-ending jungle. After many hours, when they felt they could bear it no longer, they were greeted by the usual ugly Army huts and even more tents, this being only a semi-permanent site. As they were higher the heat was less oppressive, though the humidity and regular downpours were unrelenting. Shown to their barracks – tents – they made themselves as comfortable as they could, and for once the powers that be were kind to them and allowed them the evening off.

The next morning, summoned to a drill hall, they learnt that they would be going out on patrol with some of the more seasoned men. It came as a shock, since the impression they had been given was that their job would be to look after the base. But no, they were now expected to act up to the training and flush out the remaining communist fighters of the MNLA where they could.

Inevitably they found none. After the first ten or so halts when they had piled out of the bus, formed platoons and fanned out into the jungle, they were fed up with it and were glad to be told they were heading back for the night. It proved to be the pattern for many days following, though the time they spent searching through the jungle lengthened each time. It may have resulted in fewer such sorties in a day but increased their exposure to bites and stings, and the revolting leeches that had to be removed with a burning cigarette.

It was on one of these longer sorties that Bob almost fell into a booby trap that had been left either by local villagers needing to catch food, or the communist fighters trying to catch soldiers. He and the other six in his group stopped just in time, having been trained on what to look for. It was a simple, deep hole with smooth near vertical sides.

Bob swore. So did the others. "That wouldn't have done us much good," Bob said.

He found his arm being grabbed by the nearest man; Sean, who not only had been made corporal but had become a friend during their training in Malaya. There was a look of intensity on his face. "Hear that?" he asked quietly.

Thinking there was an enemy near, Bob's eyes opened wide. He listened.

A whimper. Human. From below them.

Shocked, they looked at each other, then into the hole.

Almost invisible, there was a small brown body curled up at the edge of the hole's bottom.

"It's a child," whispered Bob. "What do we do?"

"How do we get it out, you mean." Sean was one of the good ones. That was one of the reasons each was glad they had paired up. They turned.

"There's a child down there. We've got to get it out. But how?"

"Cut some creepers, like they told us?" another of them suggested. "Climb down, then we can haul him up."

Bob just nodded, thinking back to recent tricks they had been taught about survival. It was meant to be for their own survival, or to rescue a soldier from just such a predicament as this. Nowhere in the training had rescuing local people from a pit trap been mentioned. But common decency said that leaving a child to die in a pit was not to be countenanced. Besides which it had been drummed into them that they were there to win the hearts and minds of the local people, not kill them.

The four set to and started cutting thinner lianas that could be used as a makeshift rope. Once it had been tested on the ground as best they could they let it down into the hole. Bob was the lightest of the group, though not by much. He grasped it and once again tested its strength. It held his weight.

It was an easier climb than a conventional rope would have provided. Protuberances for twigs and branches saw to that. He found himself at the bottom and was being watched by a pair of scared eyes, eyes that were also watering in pain.

"Hallo," said Bob quietly, as if he was talking to a scared dog. "What's the matter with you then? Are you all right?"

No answer, except for a gulp and an attempt to put distance between himself and this white man who was dressed in the dangerous colour of khaki. The attempt caused an involuntary cry. Bob could see why. The boy's left forearm was forming an unnatural angle half way along itself.

Bob held the boy's gaze, moving no closer. He tapped his own left forearm and made a face as if he was in pain.

The boy stopped, watching for signs of a trick, saw nothing but concern in the white man's face and nodded.

Bob thought, and looked around. Good. A fairly straight stick. He took it and held it to his arm, then raised his eyebrows.

Puzzlement.

Looking up he said in as gentle, unsoldierly voice as he could: "Throw down the field kit, would you?"

Sean's face appeared over the edge. "Injury?"

"Left forearm. Both bones."

"Ow. Here's the kit."

Bob caught it, put it down with a grin at the boy, and searched around in it. Five triangular bandages; they would do. He got the stick and made a show of tying it above and below where the fracture was, knowing how agonising it would be when the arm was straightened. Then he pointed at the boy and raised his eyebrows again in a question.

Soldiers medicine. the boy knew a bit about it. He had seen white men in khaki who had been attacked by the Malayan soldiers whom they had come to take prisoner. These were the bad men he had been warned about, and who left the white soldiers to die if they hadn't already been killed. He had seen the white soldiers' friends return with more soldiers, many more, some of whom had chased after the rebels and others who had put the white cloth things on their wounded friends to make them better.

He wanted to be made better.

He knew it would hurt. The soldiers always yelled when the white things went on. But he was hurting already.

He nodded. The white skinned man in the dangerous khaki was coming nearer. But the look on his strange white face wasn't fierce. He looked like his father did sometimes when he was looking after a burn his son had suffered when he'd forgotten that a cooking pot on the fire would bite him if he touched it.

He was near. In fear his lower lip went between his teeth. The man looked and smiled, and said something in that quiet voice. He tried to move his arm, and yelped again. The man looked around and found a short stick and made to put it in his own mouth, then handed it over. He looked at it and put it in his mouth, releasing the lower lip.

What was the man doing? A big white cloth thing was being held against the man's khaki chest, between it and the arm. Then he was leaning over to put it in the same place, between the agonised arm and the bare chest. Why? An end went round the back of his neck. The man made a sign that he should use the good arm

271

to hold it.

Two more white cloths, narrower. The sign came that he should hold the injured arm still. He hesitated. The stick was being tied around the arm above the elbow. It brought tears to his eyes and his voice raised in a keening sound. Then...

Ah... the pain! More than he'd ever known. He screamed. He couldn't help it. But the arm was straight, and being held, and two more of the white cloths were being tied on the injured end, the end that had been flopping around uselessly, making a horrible noise and hurting, biting, when it did.

There was a voice from above. His father. "It's all right. We will come and kill him."

"No!" cried the boy, between sobs. "He is making me better. I fell and my arm broke. He is curing me like a white soldier does."

Bob gave a start when he heard the exchange and realised there were local people there now. But he could not stop what he was doing.

The other soldiers at ground level had not heard the villagers approach either, being more concerned about Bob, the boy, and how the two of them would get out of the hole without getting hurt. It wasn't very soldierly behaviour, Sean was aware, but they had different priorities. The first he knew was when his arms were grabbed from behind and a blade was being held at his neck. The other two were in a similar predicament.

Bob looked up, saw the father, and did the best thing he could have done. He gave a smile. "Nearly there now," he said in that calm voice again, and looked back to the patient, still smiling.

The boy was still in pain, holding his arm by gripping the stick. Bob took the end of the triangular bandage and lifted gently so it supported the arm. Next thing, the boy felt the man close to him and a fumbling at the side of his neck. Then the solider sat back and smiled again.

"Better?"

The boy didn't know what the word meant, but he put the rest of the weight of his arm on the sling and felt that it was whole again, even if it still hurt a lot. He smiled as best he could through tears of pain.

There was a noise behind Bob and he swung round in alarm, back to being a soldier now that the boy stood a chance at life. A tough looking villager stood looking from him to the boy and then back again.

"English?" asked Bob. The man shook his head.

The man pointed to the boy, then upwards. Bob nodded.

"Sean, let down more of that rope thing. And have we got a real rope? I have to tie a knot and I need to keep the boy away from the side." He didn't know that Sean was being held.

"Can't," came Sean's strained voice. "I'm a prisoner."

Bob was annoyed. "Well, really..." He knew it was no use, so stopped himself and thought.

He pointed to the rope, made signs that it should be paid out, and threw out his arms to show how much – fortunately they had cut it long.

He was the subject of a searching look, so pointed at the boy and up the cliff, then made pulling movements.

272

There was a call from beside him, some muttering from above, and Sean's face reappeared.

"I've still got a knife at my back but I can let some more down. We've got some cordage here too. Okay?"

"Yes, please," Bob called back.

Movements above, a wriggling of the rope, and it came down, followed by a hank of thin cord. Bob grabbed it and, remembering his training again, tied a knot that gave three loops. He looked at the father and son and acted out wriggling into the loops, then pointed to the boy.

Both of them understood. The boy came over, whimpering as the arm was jogged. Obediently he wriggled himself in, Bob adjusting the cord around him, then removed his shirt to pad between the cord and the body. It all had to be done so carefully so as to avoid moving the arm. The end of the cord was tied as carefully as Bob knew how to the 'rope' of creepers..

"Okay, Sean," he called at last, "take in, gently."

The rope tightened, lifted and stopped, taking the strain on the cordage. Bob checked the knot and where the boy was being supported by it.

Satisfied, he called again: "Haul away, slowly."

The boy, still moaning sometimes, was hauled up to the top of the pit with Bob holding the remainder of the liana rope to keep him from bumping against the side. At last he was up, and Bob gave a sigh of relief. The man looked at him; this time it was his turn to smile. He held out a hand. Bob, trembling now it was all over, shook it.

Once the rope had reappeared the man indicated that Bob should go up first. He did, rolled over the edge onto flat ground, stood and looked around. The other six of his group were being looked at with something like respect by this time. All were free. As Bob appeared there were excited Malay words. Bob turned to help the father over the edge of the pit; he too stood and grinned at Bob again before turning to face the others. And to Bob's surprise he pulled Bob's arm up in an international gesture of congratulations and victory. There was a shout from them all.

"Anyone speak English?" asked one of Bob's colleagues.

There was a movement from the back of the villagers and a younger man come forward.

He had just about enough English to understand that the boy should go to a hospital to have the arm plastered, and repeated that to the father and the boy, who looked somehow hopeful at the idea of more soldiers' white cloths but hoped it wouldn't hurt so much. The father shook his head.

"Tell him that the arm will always be weak if he doesn't. But that if he does he will be able to take the plaster off after..." A quick calculation: "...forty two days. Then he needs to be careful with it for another forty days, then it should be back to full strength."

There was considerable conversation, the boy standing there holding his arm and blinking back the tears of pain.

At last the interpreter said that he could go, if the father went too, but they would take four days to walk.

This time there was talk between the soldiers.

"Doesn't this come under the heading of showing that we're on their side, winning over hearts and minds so that they oppose the MNLA?" asked one of them.

"We're due to radio back soon," said another. "Best not to ask the Sergeant over the air. Let's just ask them both to come with us, with the interpreter, and argue it out when we get there." They knew that their new sergeant was more mellow than their training sergeant back in England.

"It won't go well if he doesn't let them," said Bob.

"We'll explain it to them now, so they know we have to ask the Sergeant."

Two of them retreated into the jungle a short way to try and raise the temporary base, leaving Bob and Sean to explain to the boy and his father.

It was a quiet exodus from the camp. The villagers kept looking at their khaki-clad visitors and holding their fingers to their lips. Apparently there was a chance that MNLA soldiers might be near. The road seemed to be reached a lot quicker than the soldiers expected. The locals knew the nearly imperceptible paths far better than the blundering foreign soldiers. After a discussion with the interpreter they sat quietly, out of sight, getting bitten by the inevitable insects, until the unmistakeable sound of a lorry could be heard. As they jumped out onto the road there was a squeal of brakes, the driver having been spooked by the sudden appearance of people in this apparently uninhabited area. Having seen and identified the khaki he moved up towards them.

"Nothing to report, Sarge, no contact. Except..."

Sean explained.

It was a very full bus that returned to the camp that night, with the Sergeant saying that he hoped he was doing the right thing.

"It's all very well that we're told to win them over," he grumbled, "But how looking after one native kid who's life's not in danger helps do that I don't know."

"Perhaps the boy'll learn to be a doctor, Sarge, and help us in the next lot."

"Don't be a twit, Hannaford. He's a native from the jungle. How can that happen?"

Bob shrugged his shoulders.

30 – Mary and Stephen and Bob

The phone rang in Lofts' Farmhouse. Henry, startled out of his wits and scared of what he might hear, rushed to it.

"Hallo?"

Stephen was shocked to hear the fear in his father's voice.

"Oh…Peter… I thought it was the hospital…"

"Susan?"

"Yes, it started when the others were in Church. We were rushed up in an ambulance."

"How is she? Ok? And the baby?"

"She's okay… Well, I think so. You see it was a caesarean and… well that's why I'm worried."

"You've been to see them?"

"Yes of course we've been. And the babies are fine. Oh, I didn't say: it's twins. You're a half-brother to a boy and a girl."

"Dad! Oh good heavens… Are they all right?"

"Yes, they're fine. Before you ask, no, I don't know how much they weighed or exactly what time they arrived. I'm more concerned about Susan. She was fine when I last saw her about three hours ago. I was worried unless it was the hospital calling. And yes, I know I said that before."

"Give her my love, Dad. No – give them all three my love. Twins! I can't get over that. Look, I won't keep you a minute but the guv'nor has just put down a deposit on a place in Kingsbridge that used to be a commercial vehicle garage. It's got a pit and everything. And there's an office by the side with stores and all sorts that we can make into a café and shop. There's a bit of work to do before we can start but I've got to make it work. It's in a good position so it should be profitable for him and you. He's open to you paying rent for the café and shop, or we could organise it a different way."

A long pause.

"Oh, Peter, that's wonderful," said Henry. "You're going to run it, I hope? Is Dot happy to run the shop and café side of things? And it's not whether it's profitable for me, it's for us. You, Dot, and us as well."

Peter chuckled. "I stand corrected; no, reassured. Dot said she'd love to run it and make her own decisions, if that fits in with what you want. She thinks she might be able to make a few other bits and pieces for sale in the shop, but it's early days. Look, let's talk more about it when things have calmed down a bit and we can come and see my new brother and sister. I'll get off the line now. The hospital won't need to phone, I'm sure, but it's better if the line is free."

"Thank you, Peter. And I'm so glad to hear your news. It's wonderful. We'll be in touch once everyone's safe, all right?"

"Of course, Dad. Give them all my love, please. Bye."

"Good," Stephen said when he heard the news. "It's yet something else to get our teeth into, but we can cope. We can look forward to getting it going early next year when we're producing enough from the farm."

"I'm not sure it's going to be that quick," Henry told him. "It'll take some time to build up the herd and for Mary to sort out her side of things."

"And there's a lot to learn," she added. "I've only just started looking at courses."

Daily visits were made to Kingsbridge. Susan, at first groggy, then delighted with the twins, grew gradually more comfortable – and increasingly bored. The babies were coo-ed over by the family and admired by all. As far as the babies were concerned, the visitors deserved scant attention. Their focus seemed to be most on each other except at occasions when the demand for feeding took over.

Often Bert accompanied the others. The limit of two visitors per patient had to be observed, so when he could he visited Mrs Damerell, who seemed to be getting stronger. Her view seemed to be that he was wasting time visiting her and should be busy at work or seeing to his family. He often had to remind her that it was half past six, that he had finished work for the day and that it was the official visiting time. At that she would worry about how he was coping, which he countered by saying that Dolly was gradually becoming faster and was wrestling with the learning of shorthand.

"Poor girl," was her usual comment.

When Susan was fully recovered mentally, she broached the subject of names.

"We chatted about what to Christen them," she said, "but never came to a conclusion."

"Have you any ideas?" Henry asked tactfully.

"How about Algernon for the boy?" she asked with a mischievous smile.

Henry winced, then laughed. "Now I know you're feeling better."

"And bored. About the girl, then: Mum's name was Alice."

He thought. Then "Alice Loft has a good ring to it. And Bert would be delighted."

He smiled and nodded. "How about a middle name?"

"Your turn!"

"My mother was Anne. I don't think two initial 'A's would work, though." They discussed several. At last Henry mentioned 'Jennifer'.

"I like that. Alice Jennifer Loft. Yes. How about him?"

"I thought you wanted Algernon?"

She looked round. Nobody else was looking. She put her tongue out.

He chuckled. "Well, my father was Thomas."

"Thomas Loft. Tom Loft. Yes, I like that. And should he have Beale as the middle name?"

He hesitated. "I wondered about that, I must admit. Isn't that best left to Mary and Stephen, though? Her parents and his best friend? They might even want to call him Greg if it's a boy. Maybe Beale could be a family middle name."

"But could we start the tradition going? Could we add that as a second middle name? They were your friends too, and it seems that the family tie was there before."

His mind whirred.

"Alice Jennifer Beale Loft and Thomas Beale Loft. I really like that idea. Should we consult the other two before we make it official?"

She smiled. "Of course we should. I imagine Mary would be emotional about it. In fact they both would be. And I have another idea for another middle name for him: Henry."

This time he was unable to speak for some time.

"Thomas Henry Beale Loft," he finally said in a husky voice.

"May I talk?" he said, after they had eaten yet another late meal. Stephen looked up, smiling. Mary's hand came up to the word she was reading in her book about the making of cheese, then she looked up too.

"Susan and I were talking about names for your new brother and sister," he told them, "and we want to ask you something. You see, we've never had a family name, one that is passed down the generations. So we wondered if we might be allowed by you two, especially Mary, if we could start a tradition in the hope that you might use it and so on."

"But isn't that your decision, Dad?"

"I suppose so, but in this case not really. We've decided to call them Alice Jennifer and Thomas Henry. Alice was Susan's mother's name, and she wanted him to share my name..." He swallowed, and paused. But what we want to introduce is a third Christian name. and this is where we want... permission." He swallowed again. "The name we want them to share is... is Beale."

He had expected emotion from Mary. He hadn't expected a sudden flashback to *that* night, a flash of memory which would penetrate the chinks in his own emotional armour. He knew that he had to jump and leave the room.

The younger couple were astonished. Mary, as Henry expected, was emotional, but smiling at the same time. Stephen found that his eyesight had blurred too. They hugged.

He looked at her with raised eyebrows, finding words unnecessary. She nodded.

She recovered her equilibrium. "And when we have a son, we can call him Greg." It was not a question.

He nodded. "Greg, or Gregory. Either way he'll be called Greg. Gregory Beale Loft."

"Gregory... what about a second name? Henry?"

Stephen hesitated. "It's a good idea. But it doesn't sound right... How about Albert?"

"Albert?"

"Can't use Herbert, or Algernon. But Albert is... well..."

They talked about it until Henry returned with a cup of tea. There was silence while he passed the cups around.

"We think it's a lovely idea," said Mary, rising to hug him, "and we've already decided to continue it too."

After a fortnight of visits they found that Susan was sitting in a chair.

"I've been helped into it for some days now," she told them, "but today was the first time I got up and sat here by myself. It was uncomfortable, and I told the nurse that I wasn't going to return to bed until you'd all gone. But they'll make me do more and more now, so I may as well get used to it."

A week later she, Alice and Thomas arrived at Salcombe. Susan looked tired – it had been her first time in the open air, her first road journey, since the birth and the operation. She sat thankfully in what had been Bert's comfortable study but which now seemed to be on its way to becoming a nursery. The babies were in cots provided by Bert without having to be asked, and with Annabelle, Angharad and Henry fussing around them all. She accepted a cup of tea and begged them to sit down and join her.

"You have no idea how boring it is, doing nothing. Even reading palls after a while. There's no intelligent conversation, and what talk there is concerns babies and, worse, the birth process. I'll be glad to talk about mundane things and gradually get to do more and more. What is happening on the island?"

"The mud bath, you mean?" asked Henry. "It's been raining so much that much of the building site has no grass left at all. I hope it'll return by next year, or customers will wonder what we've been doing."

"Turf it?" asked Susan tiredly.

"We may have to. And that's outside my experience. Grass grows, is eaten by cows, and grows again. Turf is a foreign thing to me. But Mike and Martin are happy everything is going to plan, though getting bigger stuff from the mainland when it's needed is a challenge. And on the new land, well, the shell of the dairy is nearly complete, so before long we can start on phase two."

"Phase two?"

"Installing machinery and getting our cows back. That'll give Mary and Stephen something to do!"

She nodded, her eyes closing.

"You should be in bed."

The eyes reopened. "No. Please not. Let me just drowse here for a while. These two will need feeding soon, and they'll make sure I'm awake!"

"I can't help you with that," said Henry, with a smile.

"Not without some severe modifications, no," she said, eyelids drooping. "Unless we switch to bottles," she mumbled slowly, "and...I... don't..."

Henry kissed her, wondered if she should be on the bed, and followed the others into the nearby living room.

So began a time when Henry, Mary and Stephen were shuttling between Loft Island and Salcombe as if they were still attending school – albeit irregularly. Work on the milking parlour and dairy on the mainland, and on the building extension on the Island, continued.

It was at the end of October, just as the dairy was nearing readiness for machinery to be installed, that Mary started feeling ill. Putting it down to overwork, and excitement at the impending realisation of the first part of their dreams, she continued until one morning Stephen found her rushing upstairs to the lavatory.

Later she returned slowly, looking white and holding on to the handrail.

"What's the matter?" he asked, alarmed, ushering her to a chair.

She just shook her head. He sat beside her. This was just not Mary. She was never ill.

"Is it 'flu?" he asked, holding her hand. They had been worried lest the Asian Flu should travel as far south-west as Salcombe, and even more worried that Susan might suffer while she was expecting.

"I suppose so," she said. "I've been feeling off colour all week, but this was...

278

well, different. I wonder if I should see a doctor?"

He looked at her, glanced at the clock, then jumped up.

"Come on. We'll go now. We might catch the morning surgery. If you're all right to go?"

She nodded. "I feel better now. I think."

"If you go down to the boat, I'll meet you there when I've told Dad."

"Don't be too long. We need to get back."

Henry was concerned, and asked if he should go too, but was told that he was needed on site with the builders on Island and mainland. Stephen found Mary readying the launch and was in time to stop her wielding the starting handle.

To his disgust, he wasn't allowed in the surgery when Mary was called. She went in.

Fifteen minutes later there was a bustling as the receptionist was called into the room, then returned and spoke quietly to him.

"Could you come in, please? You're the fiancé, we understand?"

"Yes," he said wondering. Then a coldness clutched at his stomach.

That night on Peel Island. Those nights in the guest house. Surely... No... it couldn't be. But common sense told him that it could be, and he cursed himself roundly as he approached the door, knocked and was told to come in.

"Well, young man, it looks as if you may have given your fiancée a baby. How do you feel about that?"

It was the tone of voice. The condescending nature. The unspoken disapproval. Stephen felt as if he had been hauled in to see Miss Armitage at school. Despite his usual good behaviour throughout his school career it *had* happened. This was far more serious than a schoolboy misdemeanour, but the sense of accusation was the same.

He thought of all the things he could say to respond but could find nothing useful.

"Is she all right?" was the obvious question.

"We still await tests before it's definite. But you need to know what you are letting yourself in for. I hope that you *are* going to be letting yourself in for it, and aren't just going to abandon her."

That stung Stephen into indignation. "Most certainly *not*. We are engaged, We will be getting married. That we have already agreed, committed ourselves to. All it means is that we will be married sooner rather than later."

"Rather more than that, young man. You will start your married life with a screaming baby and a wife who is constantly tired. In fact you will be constantly tired too, dealing with the baby at night so your wife can get some rest. It is no sinecure, being a parent, especially as young as you two are."

It was not so much what was said, but the critical and condescending way it was said that made Stephen's brow furrow. Before he could say anything else the doctor carried on.

"Ah – having second thoughts now, are you? If you leave this girl alone to give birth and to look after the baby on her own then your name will be mud in your family and hers, and probably in the rest of the town too."

There was silence after this outburst. Mary was looking at the doctor in disbelief. Stephen was now roused and looking him in the eye.

"I think you're fairly new in Salcombe, aren't you?"

"I have been here six months," came the surprised reply.

"Then you don't know that Mary's brother and parents were killed in a flood four years ago, and that my father and I have adopted Mary, so that she is one of our family. You don't know the history of the Beales and the Lofts, and you have no idea of our standards – of how we behave as a family.

"I said just now that Mary and I have committed to each other, alone, and with… with absolute meaning. Neither of us will go against those commitments, and once we are married our wedding vows will be equally meaningful. Not more, not less. Because a commitment made because two people love each other is as valid in church as when it was first made. If it isn't, then it was never a vow. If you like to look at it this way, the same God oversees both. When will the results be back?"

The question was almost barked.

"In about a week. But I must say…"

"Are you feeling all right?" Stephen interrupted, talking to Mary.

She nodded.

"Then we will return in a week and fetch them. Be assured we *shall* be together."

In the street he turned to her, and was surprised by a kiss, and a smile.

"I'm marrying the right man," she said.

The wind was taken out of his sails.

"I'm… I'm glad you think so," he said apologetically. "I know I'm marrying the right girl. So… Was I rude to him?"

"No. He was being… I don't know if rude is the right word."

"I felt as if I was in front of Miss Armitage at first," he told her, causing a smile. "But look… I'm…I'm sorry. I don't really know what to say. We shouldn't have… But…"

She heaved a sigh. "I'm only just getting used to the idea. I think if it hadn't been for Angharad accepting her situation, and Susan having just had her twins, I should feel different. But although I feel shocked, I'm really…" She gulped … "Happy."

He looked straight ahead as they walked down the road, his mind in a whirl. He was going to be a father. Eighteen, and he was about to become a father. Father to a child who would grow up with them both. Would they have that easy relationship Henry, Mary and he had? Absolutely, if he had anything to do with it. And Mary, still sixteen, but seventeen when the baby would be born. Wow. Could she cope? Could they both cope? And Mary had said she was happy. Oh wow. He stopped, enveloped her in a hug. "We're going to be parents!" he said. "We're going to be *parents!*"

When the euphoria had died down it was Mary who broke the spell.

"Yes, but everyone else is going to be furious."

He came back down to earth with a bump.

"We're going to get married. Please? And soon."

Henry sat down suddenly.

"Oh."

It wasn't what either of them expected. There was an uncomfortable silence. He broke it after what seemed like ages.

"I think you've both been bloody fools. And not fair on Susan and me. And what your mother would have said, I don't know."

That stung. Two hands sought each other and held.

Another silence.

"What are you going to do about it?"

Stephen gave a start. "*Do* about it? We're going to get married. We're going to see the house built and bring the baby up there, properly." He sounded hurt, indignant.

"You needn't sound so pleased about it, Stephen. It's shameful. Don't you see that?"

Stephen could feel Mary tensing. She drew a deep breath.

"No child of mine will be shameful. No child of Stephen's will be shameful. We love each other, you know that. And we have made vows together, even if we haven't done so in church yet." She paused.

"And when we did mention getting married all you said was 'wait until we've slept on it," said Stephen, now angry. "You've slept on it, and no more has been said. But now we are going to get married, as we've wanted to all along. And I hope you and Susan will be there. In fact I hope you will give permission because otherwise we will have to... to go to Gretna Green."

He almost pulled Mary with him as he swept out of the room.

Alone, Henry held his head, wondering how all this mess would end, and amazed that his young son had spoken the way he had. And that Mary had done nearly the same. Had he been incautious in what he had said? Had he used the wrong words? It was a lot for them to take on, to take in. But then it was a lot for him to take in, too. He stood, thinking to follow them, to ask them back to talk about it. On his way down to the landing place he was stopped by Martin with a question, and uncharacteristically brushed him off. Reaching the shore he could see that the launch was already pulling away, gaining the benefit of the ebbing tide.

He returned slowly to the house. Martin, now worried as well as taken back by his brusqueness, turned away, thinking that this was not the time.

The launch arrived at the Hard, much to the surprise of the Harbourmaster who was sure he'd only seen her head north an hour or so previously. The two made their way to see Susan, who was still living in the town because of the disruption to the Island farmhouse. They entered to a happy looking scene with Susan looking fondly at the two babies as they lay facing each others. They were now starting to take an interest in life around them as well as each other. Mary and Stephen were calmed by their quietness and the haphazard movements as they looked at their mother.

She smiled at them, seeing beyond their expressions to a strain.

"Is everything all right?" she asked.

"Yes and no," said Stephen, sitting beside his baby brother and, at a nod from Susan, picking him up. Mary sat the other side and picked up her adopted sister.

"I'm glad there's a 'yes' to it, anyway," Susan smiled. "Would you like some help with the 'no'?"

"I think… I think it's me that may need the help as time goes on," said Mary slowly.

Susan, now free of the babies, paused and looked at her. Really looked at her. She sighed. "I thought something had changed between you when you came into the house first, back from the Lakes. The feeling between you was different. And I think I may know what it is. But you must tell me."

Silence. Alice Jennifer and Thomas Henry examined the faces of the people holding them and seemed to like what they saw. They made no sound.

"I think… the doctor thinks… I'm going to have a baby."

"We're going to have a baby," Stephen corrected.

Another silence.

"I wondered if it was that. It was that – that difference. Maybe it's because I was expecting, but I could see a strengthening of the bond between you. Perhaps I experienced a change myself when…" She stopped herself. There were some things that were better left private, unsaid.

"Have you told Henry?" she asked.

"Yes," said Stephen grimly. "He wasn't best pleased. He said we were bloody fools and that it was shameful. That we'd let down you two. And…. And Mum."

She paused. "Well, maybe it's not the right order for you to have done things. Maybe you should have… well, waited. It wouldn't have been long, would it? So maybe he was right and you were bloody fools." She smiled, surprising them. "But what are you going to do next?"

"Get married," said Mary quickly, "soon."

"You'll need permission from us, of course, but that's just a formality. Have you seen the vicar yet?"

This was going quicker than either of them had expected.

"No," Mary told her, "we only discovered this morning."

Susan nodded. "Call him now, from here. Make an appointment. Tell him that you were engaged ages ago…"

"Last January," said Mary.

"I thought it was earlier. Ah well. A lot has happened in the meantime. But also tell him that you're building a house on the mainland and will need to live together in it to run the herd. He'll understand."

"What about the baby?"

"Well if he asks, then of course you'd tell him. But volunteering the information is up to you."

"Well, someone's got to take the buggers back."

"Get the corporal and the man who got the boy out, Sarge. They brought them here."

He looked round at the speaker, who turned away.

The boy was better. He'd spent a month in the white man's hospital. After the first night when his arm had really hurt, he had been sent to sleep my some sort of powerful magic, or so he thought, and when he woke again, feeling sick, his arm was stiff, in white stuff which was like but different from the white things they had used on him down the hole. Even his hand was in it.

Three days later they cut the white stuff off, and the man who could understand them had told him that it was the white stuff that would be cut and then replaced, and not him. Not his skin or anything. And it wouldn't hurt a bit.

He had watched as the blade approached his arm and was scared, but his friend told him it was all right and wouldn't cut into his arm at all.

It didn't. The partial cast was removed and was replaced by a full one.

Three more weeks had gone. He was bored, as bored as he'd ever been in his life. And he wanted to see his village again. Then out of the blue one of the doctors announced that he could return, and explained through an interpreter what needed to happen to make sure the arm returned to strength.

An orderly, a local man, was nearby, ready to start his cleaning duties. He heard every word. That night, once free from duty, he ran with a message to a local house which had a tall tree outside it. One in which there was an oddly straight, vertical branch.

Four of them; Sean, Bob and two others, were rounded up two days later and told to get the boy, his father and the interpreter back to their village. Seeing something like sanctioned time off approaching they agreed readily. This time they took not a lorry but a smaller vehicle, a troop carrier. The boy, because of his arm, was allowed to sit in front. He felt it was almost worth the boredom of the hospital to travel like that, in pride of place.

The tedious journey was made, the vehicle hidden as best they could near the road, and they set off, guided by the father and the interpreter but guarded by the four soldiers. It was about a couple of miles from the road when the rebels struck. Shots rang out. With a muffled cry the boy's father clutched his head and fell backwards, blood emerging from a wound in it. The boy gave a wail and crawled to the man, hugging him, crying.

The others, surprised but remembering their training, did what they should and machine guns flung their curtain of death towards any movement, any rifle fire. The shots from the jungle faltered, then fell silent. They waited. The boy's sobs were the only sound. His father was motionless.

Bob was near the soldier with the radio. "For Christ's sake get on that thing and tell them what's happened," he muttered.

Cautiously the aerial was raised.

Sean: "Chuck something over there, out of the way, see if there's any fire."

Bob readied the smaller of his packs, hefted it and threw it. There was a crack, and the pack changed trajectory in mid air. Machine guns rattled again and the rifle was silent.

"Is that it?" Bob asked Sean.

"I'll try."

Another pack flew through the air. This time there was no reaction.

They waited again. Sean could hear the radio being used as quietly as its operator could manage. At last he stopped.

"All done," he said quietly. "They know where we are and what's happened."

"Are the others all right?" Bob called.

Sean looked round.

"The father's dead, I think. The boy's all right – sort of. Oh – the interpreter's buggered off," he said in annoyance. "I wonder if it was him who told them where we were."

"Shall we go now? Is it safe?"

"No. We wait here until they make a move or we hear them."

'Waiting here until…' stretched into what seemed like hours. There were no sounds from anywhere around them apart from the usual noises from the rainforest. There was a tickling at Bob's left arm, the one underneath him that was supporting him. Idly he flicked at it, thinking it was a leech or a yet another mosquito.

Snake.

A black and white banded snake. As he rolled out of its way he was pleased to see it was startled, and start to crawl away. But there was a shot. A line of what felt like fire seared his arm and he instinctively gripped it with his good hand.

"You ok?" someone called.

"Bullet. Right arm," he said.

There were more rifle shots now, and some returning machine gun fire. Bob took no part in it. His arm was bleeding badly and he could feel the strength ebbing from it. He felt useless, increasingly sick and faint. Dimly he heard shouts; the rifle fire seemed to be more distant, and then there was silence. For Bob, there came blackness.

When he came to, he was on a bed of leaves, and a plantain leaf was swinging over him, dispersing some of the heat. He was conscious enough to recognise that it was being swung by a small boy with his arm in plaster. Bob managed a smile, the boy smiled back and put his finger to his lips. Bob's eyes closed again.

When he woke again it was to find the interpreter sitting by him, swinging the improvised fan. Bob felt a little stronger, though his arm hurt and was throbbing violently.

Bob introduced himself by the simple expedient of pointing to himself and saying "Bob". The man did the same, saying "Farid".

He haltingly told Bob that he'd slipped away when the soldiers' packs were being used to draw rifle fire, and had run to the village. The men had been roused and had ambushed the rebels. "They no trouble us again," Farid said with a grim smile.

"What about the other soldiers?" asked Bob.

The face clouded. "They all shot. We bury. Sorry."

Bob felt an emotional blow, and was silent.

"Tuan father shot too," he was told, as if that would even things up.

"I saw," Bob told him. "Is Tuan the boy? Is he all right?"

"Sometimes."

It was probably the best Farid could do with his basic knowledge of English, but that one word said more to Bob than a whole paragraph of eloquence would have done. He pulled a face.

"Pain?" asked Farid.

"The boy's pain," Bob replied.

Farid nodded, smiled again, and put a hand on Bob's good shoulder. "You good man," he said, and Bob smiled back before dozing off again.

They fed him. At first his stomach rebelled at the diet, and even in his weakened state he found he was having to make a rush into the communally used, elementary latrines. Gradually, over a week or two, he acclimatised, and found, to his relief, that his arm was less painful and that use was returning to his hand. Tuan often sought him out, and the two tried to teach the other his own language, with much laughter. But in Bob's mind was the knowledge that the weeks were slipping away and that he was all but a prisoner of the forest, if not its people.

If only he had a wireless... But surely the wireless set his comrades were carrying would be long gone. Or would it? If the rebels had all been killed, who was there to take it anywhere, unless his hosts brought it.

He asked the question and was answered with a shrug.

"May we look for it? Please? It's the only way I have of getting back."

The man agreed, but refused point blank to let Bob accompany them. "To noisy, still too slow" he was told.

All he could do was to make sure they knew what was needed, what it looked like.

Whilst Farid was away, Bob thought of his comrades. He was aware of an ache, a spiritual pain, that had been with him since his eyes had first opened. How could he get the lads' bodies back to Britain? Would the army do that? Would they face danger in seeking the temporary graves and in digging?

When they returned they told him that the bodies had gone. Dug up and taken away. "By English," said Farid.

"How do you know it was them?" he asked.

"We know," was the only answer. "But we found wireless."

31 – Wedding and the Hannafords

Mr & Mrs Hannaford heard the post arrive. Along with the usual bills was an OHMS [On Her Majesty's Service] envelope. Bob's father opened it with suddenly shaking hands. "We regret to inform you…" he read.

Silently, trying to take it in, he handed it to his wife, who scanned it again and again, trying to make the words say something different. "Missing, presumed killed…" So there was still a chance, then? Maybe? Please?

They looked at each other, each with tears. He crossed to where she sat and put his arms round her.

"He's all we have, now," she said. "But should we…?"

The question was left unfinished and unanswered. She had missed her daughter from the first, when she had been banished having elected to carry her child through to birth despite it being a pregnancy because of rape. They had objected, telling her that her daughter would be a bastard and as such was not welcome in their house. Her home. There had a been a row and she had moved away. Recently she, the mother, had become more and more aware of the hole in her life. And she had never even met her granddaughter, never known if she was healthy, if they were both safe.

"We should tell her," she finished, in a tone of voice that for once brooked no denial.

Later that evening, when the tears had paused, he said: "What do we do with those letters?"

She started, guiltily. "We… we can't throw them away. They have his writing on them."

"I know. But we can't read them, either. That would be wrong."

"Was he just trying to save that girl from being thrown on the scrap heap, or did he have feelings for her?"

"I… I don't know," he answered thoughtfully. "That's more your province. He kept going out with her…"

"But they knew each other such a short time. Can it have been real? And she's yet another girl with loose morals. No woman just allows a man to rape her; we know that. There must have been some acceptance, or the girl would scream the house down and get help. That's what we said when Maud told us her story. And we cannot have a bastard in the family."

"No. No, we can't. It would be wrong. Immoral. But…"

He waited.

"Maud isn't a bad girl, not a good-time girl. Maybe this… this Welsh girl isn't either. And both made the same decision, it seems, to carry… to continue expecting. Should we tell Angharad about Bob?"

He sighed. "I don't know. It's too soon. I don't think so, though. She made a bad decision too. And she's not good for our son, an unknown girl from a small Welsh town."

Susan, Henry, Mary and Stephen found an opportunity when the twins were being looked after by an entranced Angharad, to have a talk in private.

"We have things to sort out," Henry started brusquely. "Mary is going to have a baby, you two need to organise a wedding, sharpish, and we need to decide what to do.

"What? You and Susan?" asked Stephen, alarmed and on the verge of anger and incredulity.

"No. All of us. We need to decide who we invite, who we tell, and what happens afterwards.

Stephen's anger evaporated into mist. They had accepted it, then. They had been so busy since the bombshell had hit that there had been no opportunity to detect their attitude, much less talk.

"We have talked to the Vicar," said Mary. "Saturday, November the thirtieth. I hope that's convenient. But he needs to know that you are giving your permission."

This time they both were startled.

"You have actually arranged it?"

"He is holding the date for us and is waiting for you to talk to him.

Another pause.

"We don't have an option, do we? You've..."

Susan put a hand on Henry's arm. "What he means is that of course you have our permission. It's a formality, really, but a necessary one in the eyes of the law. And we wish you every happiness and success, along with his or hers, of course. And..." She lifted her hand to stop Henry talking. "And even if you couldn't marry before the birth it would make no difference to us. You are ours, and we are yours, and the baby will be yours with us sharing occasionally, I hope. And won't he be good for Alice and Tom? And Angharad's child too."

Every last breeze had been removed from Henry's sails, resulting in a look of astonishment that was almost comical. She turned to him.

"You agree, darling, don't you? After all, whether or not we would prefer that the marriage had come first before... had come first, we cannot wind back time. Our elder children are pledged to each other – they've said so often enough – and they're going to have a baby. We need to accept that we shall become grandparents, just as they have to accept that they will be parents with all that responsibility, as well as being an aunt and uncle to these two."

It was as well that November's short days meant that work on the buildings started later and finished earlier than previously. The long evenings gave time for wedding plans, invitations and for the myriad details that seemed necessary for the wedding of such a well-known couple. Peter readily agreed to act as Stephen's best man. He laughed when the phone call was made.

"Getting your own back, Steve? I couldn't say no, now, could I? And would you like me to lose the speech for you as well?"

"Probably best not," said Stephen, laughing back. "Thanks for agreeing, though. But there's another thing."

"What do you want me to do?"

"It's what it'd be best undone, really." Stephen swallowed hard, wondering how the news would be taken. "You see, we're going to have a baby. And... and we really don't want that to be mentioned."

Silence. Then a long exhale. "Stephen Loft. You old dog. You good old dog. My kid brother and you're having a baby before me. Well, I don't know what to say, not really, but I think probably 'congratulations' might just about cover it, for a start."

There was a seat alongside the telephone table. Stephen found himself sitting on it, quite hard, as a feeling of relief washed over him.

"Are you still there?"

"Yes – yes. I'm just relieved you didn't... start lecturing me. You know, you didn't think we should..."

"Don't talk rot. I'm delighted for you both. Mary ok, I hope? How did Dad and Susan take it?"

"Mary's fine, now she's got used to the idea. Susan was nearly sure something had happened, but said nothing until we told her, and then she was all right about it. Dad..."

He remembered back to the exchanges. His father was still not happy, he knew. But Stephen could do nothing about that. He explained.

Peter was quiet for a moment. "You probably know now, but when I left home it was after we argued, many, many times..."

"I know. I could hear you from upstairs when I was meant to be asleep."

"Did you? Well, I'm sorry. But he's very stuck in the mud sometimes, our Dad, and once he gets his mind set in a rut, the sides of the rut are all he can see. You'll know that he and I are on very good terms now, but it was only my leaving that enabled him to scramble his way out of the rut. Even then it took a long time."

Stephen thought back. It seemed sense.

"His world was in turmoil as well, don't forget," Peter continued. He gave a sudden laugh and startled his listener. "It's in turmoil now too, I should think, with two building sites and a pair of twins to keep him busy. He'll be better after the wedding and better still when he has a grandson or granddaughter to think about. When's the baby due?"

"Next May."

"So... It was when you were in the Lakes."

"Peter!"

"Well, it was. And I can understand even more now. I remember my first time, too." He sighed.

"But you didn't get her pregnant."

"I was older, knew more, and took precautions."

"Precautions?"

Peter explained. At one of the more explicit parts there was an exclamation. "Peter...!"

"Well, you want to know. In fact, you need to know."

The explanation continued.

"Oh...well," said Stephen when he had finished. "That was embarrassing. And I never knew. I'd heard the name, of course; people talked about rubber johnnies at school. But I never asked. If only I'd known... why doesn't anyone tell you?"

"Tell you? Because they don't talk about things like that at school. Certainly not to schoolchildren – and they view us all as schoolchildren until we leave as hunking great brutes at eighteen or so. Don't forget that we're all meant to be good little boys and girls until we get married. And for some time afterwards too, if money's short. You know that no one talks about things like that. Not even between the older boys at school, not really. Not on a farm, not on an island, and certainly not in church. Those are almost the only places we went when we were growing up, you and me. I had to get out; leave the farm and spread my wings. But you loved farming, and that way of life. For me, when I started work I met other mechanics who were a lot more – I suppose 'explicit' is a good word – than you and me. So I kept my ears open, made one or two comments that got me teased, but learnt a lot.

"Now you know about what you might have done to stop it, though, do you regret it?"

Stephen thought. What he'd learnt had coloured his attitude, certainly. Did he regret that they were going to have a child? In some ways, yes. His father's attitude was one factor. What the church had always said about adultery was another. And they were major factors. But did he really wish it hadn't happened? That they were to become parents, Mary and he?

"No," he said decisively. "No, I don't. Oh, maybe if I'd been told about... protection... I might have used it. But somehow it wouldn't have meant so much to us. Between us. It would have felt..." He realised he was about to say 'dirty', but remembered in time that it would have been like criticising his brother's own behaviour.

"More like play, and less like love, you mean?" asked Peter, more gently. "Maybe so. For us, it's been a financial decision, mainly, but also the time commitment. Maybe we should think again."

"I didn't mean..."

Peter cut him short. "Oh no, I'm not criticising you. I'm a bit jealous, really; jealous that you and Mary have stolen a march on us!" He laughed, a natural laugh, and Stephen knew he really was on their side.

Wedding planning took most of their time now, what little of it they could spare from developments on or adjacent to the island. Finally the milking machinery had been installed, tested and approved and it was with difficulty that Henry and Mary stopped Stephen looking for suitable cows to buy so as to build up their herd.

"We have our few which are still being looked after, and there's a lot going on for the next months. At the moment we've hardly got a base to run a milking operation from. Let's get our and the Rawles' cows down first and iron out any problems. Then when we've got used to it, and got them established, we'll add to them. Maybe in the spring."

Stephen thought, and had to agree.

Ian was just Ian, and had more or less got over the fact that he was not needed at the Boatyard during the autumn and winter except on Saturday mornings to do some sweeping and odd jobs. He accepted reluctantly that his own boat would be better being stored safely there as its use would be only occasional while the weather was chancy.

Angharad was helping where she could with writing lists, calling people, and seeing to the little details none of the others seemed to have time for. She felt useful, accepted; she was certainly happy to help these people who had given her so much, who had become both friends and surrogate parents. But a week before the day of the wedding there came a natural halt to the frenetic work, and for the first time in weeks she found she had little to do.

It was then that the lack of contact from Bob really came to worry her. She had heard nothing from him for ages, not since the last letter as he was being sent to Malaya. Perhaps he couldn't write from there. Or… or – she could hardly cope with the thought – had he been hurt whilst over there? Or was he dead?

Although Ted did what he could to keep her company, and talk, or just be there, she was upset. Her sleep began to be interrupted by dreams of him, lying deep in the jungle, bleeding, fainting, dying; or having to endure long marches through insect-ridden swamps and fast rivers. What if he had been swept away? What if he had been lost and was having to fend for himself somewhere? What if…

She brooded on. The worries would come at that stage when sleep has gone, but wakefulness is still to take hold. The stage where the would-be sleeper cannot see that that worry and fear are pointless and could lead to no solutions.

She was sleeping so badly that she found herself becoming absent minded during the day, partly through the worry but mainly through lack of sleep. She found that there were times when she couldn't think properly and would make silly mistakes.

The day of the wedding was better; she had been excited for the first time in ages when she went to bed, knowing that waiting for her to wear was a really beautiful dress she had chosen. She had bought it with her own money, earned earlier in the year from working so hard in the café and in planning for the Kingsbridge shop and café when it would open the following spring. She was nearly her usual self when she rose on the morning of the wedding to make tea for everyone.

She walked up the hill to the church with the others, feeling happy, *en fete*. Once again she was aware that she was being looked at by older boys and young men with the same interest that Bron was being appreciated – even when Martin was by her side. To Angharad's pleasure Bronwen had come down from University for the weekend. Angharad smiled, yet still aware that there was only one young man she wanted there, but who couldn't be. Nevertheless the attention she received, which would a few months previously have horrified and embarrassed her, she now found flattering. And that was even now, when she could hardly hide the fact that she was expecting a baby.

The Service was lovely, she felt. It passed off without a hitch. It seemed a lot more grand than weddings in the Chapels in Wales, but it was lovely for all that. Mary looked wonderful in her dress of sheer white, and it had been a shock to her to see Stephen and Henry in very smart, light and dark suits respectively. And she felt that her floral dress was as good and as pretty as anyone's there.

The newly wedded couple seemed to have a smile for her alone as they processed out to the crash of organ and the clangour of bells. Outside she found, to her astonishment, that she was called on to be in the photographs. Even after all the months she had still had a feeling that she didn't really belong; surely, though, if they included her in wedding photographs the must have meant what had been assured from the beginning, that she was one of the family.

The Reception was once again to be in the nearby Knowle Hotel, whose staff had cheerfully accepted the questions, changes, and checks thrown at them by various in the wider Loft family over the last weeks. Angharad herself had been responsible for many of them and was really pleased by the room, an appearance which she had helped to create. She was even more pleased when, after the session of drinks, the seating for the Breakfast went without a hitch. She had been inspired to have Ted sit beside her, and Ian – who had wanted to attend in his RNLI jumper but was fobbed off with a new, long-trousered suit – next to him. Next to them was Annabelle, then their Uncle Bert. On her other side was Mike Alexander, whom she admired for his natural courtesy. She still felt happy, and was naturally pleased that the arrangements she had helped make were working well.

It was strange, she felt, sitting between the young Ted and the older Mike. Ted was becoming a very good looking young man, and he was old enough to hold intelligent and interesting conversation. Mike was attentive, pleasant, and similarly courteous. She appreciated them.

Yet there was something about Bob that made him special. *Would* have made him special, had he been there.

Stephen's speech was witty and entertaining. He referred to having lost his speech at his father's and brother's wedding, then made a mock-panicked search for his own – only to 'find' it on the table in front of him. When it was his turn Peter turned to Stephen and said in mock severity: "You just used the joke I was going to start with!" That continued the tone Stephen had set, and they were all laughing when he had finished.

Henry gave an emotional speech, referring to having watched both bride and groom grow into the couple they now were. "It's a rare privilege," he said, "and enables parents to know just how suited they are as a couple, and how happy they are together."

It pleased Stephen that the dissonance of a month previously seemed to have vanished. There had been no mention of approaching parenthood, for which he was glad, but then knew that it would be the last thing his father would want made public.

Celebrations continued. Ted and Mike were attentive and ensured that Angharad was never alone. But the feeling of being incomplete stayed with her, worsened, as the evening continued and was still there as she prepared for bed.

Having experienced the church at the wedding she felt drawn to attend it with the others the following day. Salcombe's was not one of the old-fashioned congregations which held a belief that expectant women shouldn't attend, and then be "churched" once the baby was born. Again, the others looked after her. She was shocked when, during a quiet part of the Service, a double explosion was heard, and men quickly stood, made a bow to the altar and left. Martin and Mike were amongst them, and Ian looked longingly on as they joined the town's other crew members in their rush to the Lifeboat station.

It disturbed the others in church, too and once the Service was over there was a buzz of conversation. Angharad noticed a couple talking earnestly to the vicar. There was something about the man's face that struck a chord with her. She was too shy still to approach them as they eventually left, but asked Ted if he could find out who they were.

Ted asked the vicar.

"They're the Hannafords," he told Angharad airily, unaware of the import of the name. Angharad was startled, thanked him, and made herself go and talk to the vicar.

"Hallo, my dear," he said as she was hovering nearby, wondering what to say. "I know of you and was hoping you might come and see us some day. I was told your story, of course, and realised it wouldn't have been right for me to go and see you. In your eyes I'm another man of the church, and probably suspect. Though in my defence I can say that my marriage is very happy and I believe in Christian behaviour."

He was so obviously sincere, unafraid of mentioning her story in a matter-of-fact way, and gentle, that she found herself smiling.

"Thank you. And yes, I could have been upset if you came down as soon as I arrived. But it's better now, and so many have been so kind and understanding." She paused. "One of them was Bob Hannaford. Mary and Stephen, he and I have been out together, and Bob and I... like each other."

"It was the Hannafords, Bob's parents, I was speaking to just now. Do you not know them? I could have introduced you. But... "

He paused. "Come and sit down, would you?"

Suddenly scared, she complied, and he slowly told her that Bob had been reported missing. He saw the wide eyes fill with tears and the face crumple.

"Is he dead?" She asked.

"No one has said. The army say he's missing. But maybe we should prepare ourselves. If I can help in any way, I will. But maybe you should go and talk to his parents. You might be able to support each other."

She shook her head. "They have already sent their daughter away, who was raped. They will do the same to me."

It was the vicar's turn for surprise.

"Surely... are you sure?"

"Bob told me. She lives in London with her baby."

"They never mentioned this. How long ago did it happen?"

Angharad thought as best she could through her unhappiness.

"He didn't say."

"I wonder why they never mentioned it. Maybe we should go down together, you and I, and talk to them. Though... no. Maybe better not, not at first. Should I go down and talk to them, then perhaps a day or two later you – or we – could see them."

"But it's now that I need to know. No letters have come for me since he left England and I was worried. Now I know why."

"It's only recently that they heard from the army. Certainly, though, any letter for you should have arrived from Malaya by now. He had your address, I suppose?"

It was the past tense that tipped the balance. Angharad buried her face in her hands. A moment later she felt a presence at her side. Ted had been watching, worried, knowing that there was something going on outside his experience, feeling powerless. But when his friend was in tears he knew what to do. Others had done it for him often enough over the years.

It took some minutes. Slowly a feeling of resolve crept back into Angharad and she stood.

"It's down to Mr and Mrs Hannaford I am going, now," she said firmly. "I cannot wait. I must know... must see..."

"I think it would be better if I..."

She shook her head. "I go, now. Please tell me where they live."

Ted and the vicar looked at each other, worried.

"I really think..."

"But I *have* to know. I have to find when they last heard from him. Whether he talked about me. Whether there were any messages for me."

The vicar sighed and told her where they lived.

"Should I go with her?" Ted asked.

"I think someone should. I have to finish here and lock the church. I could come down afterwards."

She smiled at the vicar as best she could and turned away. At the door she had to pass Bronwen and Annabelle who had been waiting for her.

"It's to Bob's parents I have to go. They say he is missing. In Malaya." Sweeping past them she headed up the hill towards Allenhayes Road; fortunately for her it was not far. Ted walked beside her, worried at hearing her laboured breathing. She paused in front of the well-founded, detached house, looked, then climbed the driveway to the front door and rang the bell.

Mr Hannaford opened the door.

"Please," said Angharad, "I am a friend of Bob's and I've not heard from him since he was sent to Malaya. I heard he was missing, and... and... I just wanted to know what was happening."

It was all she could do to get the words out.

Mr Hannaford looked nonplussed. He called his wife.

"Is it...is it Bob's child?" was the first question he asked when his wife appeared.

She shook her head.

"Then we don't need to have anything else to say, do we." he stated it: it was not a question

He was closing the door. "Has he written to me? Angharad Pugh. I'm living with Mr Merryweather." The door slowly opened again.

Mentioning the solicitor was the best thing she could have done. The door stayed open.

"One minute." She watched the half open door like a hawk, as if it would suddenly open and reveal the man she really wanted to see.

It opened again. Two letters were held out. Each was addressed to her. "Please forward" was written after her name.

"Did he not leave my address?"

"You have the letters. If you do not want them, please return them. They have our son's writing on them and are precious to us."

"It is to me he is precious as well," said Angharad, with spirit.

"You do not know what you are saying. You only just know each other. There can be no feeling between you. And you are… are… going to have a baby that is not his. That is not anybody's. That makes him a bastard. He will not want it. No bastard would ever be a part of our family."

The door started to close again.

"The baby will belong to me! And, please God, to Bob. It is not my fault I was raped."

It was said in a louder voice than Angharad had ever dared use before. Despite her passionate exclamation the door shut again. To her horror Angharad found she was swearing at it in loud Welsh. There were footsteps behind her. Both she and a horrified and wordless Ted swung round.

The vicar.

He paused. "All is not well, I detect."

Angharad was speechless, she didn't have any words left. She was feeling peculiar, aware of a growing pain in her body which started to horrify her. Ted, aware something was wrong, grabbed her hand. She looked at him as if seeing him for the first time.

"I feel… oh… is it starting?"

She swayed. The vicar and Ted held on to her as she slid to the ground. Ted sat at her side while the vicar went to hammer on the door.

There was no answer. He found the bell and rang it. Nothing. Not for the next thirty or so seconds of ringing and knocking.

A voice spoke.

"Is she all right?"

The vicar and Ted turned.

"I live over there. We could see there was something going on. Can I help?"

"Please could you call an ambulance? I think she is about to have her baby."

"My wife is already phoning. She knows about these things more than I do. The people here can't help?"

"These two have just been talking to them, but they closed the door in their face and now aren't answering it. I imagine they believe it is still the girl and her friend trying."

He nodded. "I'm afraid we have little to do with them. Their children were good, polite kids, and it seems a shame that the daughter chose to go away when… I'm afraid their attitude doesn't surprise me. Churchgoers they most certainly are, but sometimes I wonder whether they are actually Christian."

Angharad was gasping, trying to be calm, but above all she was scared. All Ted could do was to sit with her and hold her hand. Gradually the pains diminished and she was able to look him in the face.

"Good to me, you are."

An ambulance arrived eventually, and it was the clangour of its bell that brought the Hannaford parents back to their front door. The vicar gave them a long, expressionless look before helping get Angharad on her feet and into the vehicle. The two ambulancemen looked around.

"Anyone the father?"

"Long story," said the vicar. "Where are you taking her?"

"Kingsbridge," he said shortly. "After that, who knows?"

"Her home's here."

"Looks like they want her, doesn't it?"

"Not at this house. In the town."

"We'll get details from her, reverend. We need to go now."

"Can I go too?" Ted reluctantly relinquished her hand

"No. You're too young. Go home."

Ted felt angry, crushed. Angharad was his friend. All he wanted was to be with her, to be her friendly face, to look after her. But the two men ignored him and separated, one to the driving seat and the other to the inside of the vehicle. It accelerated away.

The vicar went to Ted and found smouldering, angry eyes.

"I used to hate being dismissed like that."

It was a comment that Ted wasn't expecting. In his experience adults had always just talked down to him. He had come to expect it from his father as part of his impatient ways, even if he now knew the reasons behind the attitude. But at school, almost everywhere, he had found himself put down. The only people who had accepted his input were his Uncle Bert, Aunt Amble, and now the Loft family.

But now, when he knew he had something to do that was important to another human being in trouble, he was being put down again. Except that the man in front of him seemed to know what was in his mind.

"It's not fair," he said, and was aware and ashamed that his voice was trembling. "I can't help being young. And Angharad is a friend. I mean a *real* friend."

"I can see that. And if I'd just been left at the side of a road by an ambulance when I knew I could help her just by being there, I'd be as angry as you. But we both know she's in good hands now, that the ambulancemen are experienced and that she'll be cared for in hospital better than either of us could do ourselves."

"I know. But she needs someone she knows with her."

He nodded. "Then perhaps we should go back and see your family so they can go to Kingsbridge and be with her."

This made sense. "Would you come with me and help explain?"

"I was going to offer."

The sudden smile brought one to the vicar's face too and they walked back together. He had been aware of a contrast between the childish "It isn't fair…" and the maturity of the need to protect his friend. It occurred to him that here was a youngster on the cusp of starting his journey into adulthood; one who seemed already able to accept one of the responsibilities of friendship.

"Oh, good heavens," said Bert when he had heard. "One of us should most certainly be with her. The best person is probably Dolly, but I know Angharad would like Ted there as well, and Ted's made it very clear he should be there. I had better fetch the car, I think."

Once again they made the journey to the hospital. Once again Bert had to be reminded to remove the keys from the car.

"Oh yes," said the Receptionist. "What is the patient's name, please?"

"Angharad Pugh"

"And how do you spell the Christian name?"

Bert obliged.

"And you say she was brought here by ambulance."

"Yes," said Ted, "I watched it go."

"And are you the father?"

Ted didn't notice it was said with a laugh in the voice and was immediately embarrassed.

"No," he muttered.

"I thought not." This time Ted did notice the condescending laugh and stared hard at the woman in dislike.

"She was the victim of a rape when she was employed at my sister's house," said Bert quietly and distinctly, having noted the slight to Ted. "My sister – and Ted here – are now looking after her since her mother has disowned her."

That silenced the Receptionist who quickly dropped her eyes back to the hospitals register of admissions.

"And she was brought here when?" she asked more quietly.

"About half past twelve or one o'clock," Bert replied.

"Today?"

"Yes. Just now."

Another referral to the register.

"There's nothing here showing her yet. Maybe the Midwife hasn't told me yet. Sometimes they forget until everything's been sorted out."

"How do we find her, then?" Bert found that he was still just able to stifle his impatience.

"You could go to the Maternity ward and ask. It's down there and turn right. There's a sign on the door. And ask the Midwife if she'll please tell us quickly about admissions, would you?"

"Certainly," said Bert, "I'll ask her to do so as soon as she has spare time from delivering babies."

He turned away and the others took that as a hint. They followed.

"Wretched woman," he muttered. "Didn't like her attitude at all. Where's this ward?"

They found it, and were welcomed by the sound of crying. Adult crying. Ted hesitated.

It was a long ward. Some of the beds were partitioned by curtains. Nurses came and went, particularly from one of the curtained areas from where the crying was coming. No one came to them and they stood there awkwardly.

At last an imposing woman in a massive head-dress approached.

"Yes?"

Bert felt that he should act as spokesman again. "We are looking for Angharad Pugh who was brought here by ambulance about twelve thirty or one o'clock today."

"And you are?"

"The family who are looking after her in Salcombe. My name is Merryweather, solicitor in the town."

"There are no solicitors in Kingsbridge of that name."

"I practise in Salcombe."

"And are you the father?" It was said with incredulity.

"She was the victim of a rape when living in Chepstow."

The Sister's eyebrows raised. "Oh." It was said with a tone of disapproval. The two looked at each other.

"Where is she, please?" It was Dolly this time.

"She is not here. We have had no admissions this morning at all. It's Sunday, after all."

"It would be most inconvenient for anyone to need to be born on a Sunday, I'm sure," said Bert drily. "Where else would she be taken if not here? She was in an ambulance, I should have said."

"I really cannot say. All I know is that she is not here."

She made to turn away, dismissing them.

"Are you, then, care-less of the well-being of a young, first-time, reluctant mother and of her baby?"

She swung back, eyes blazing.

"I am a Sister in a maternity ward and you ask me that? How dare you?"

"I dare because I am a solicitor and used to dealing with those who prove reluctant under questioning. Such people who may have to answer to a Coroner if harm befalls a mother or newborn if they do not receive the treatment and support needed."

"I am appalled that you should even think such a thing possible. This is 1958. We care for mothers and their babies properly. Look around you."

"We are. And we see no sign of a mother and maybe her baby who should have been brought here by ambulance. I ask again: where else would they have been taken?"

This time she thought, though the look of impatience remained.

"I suppose if the delivery happened in the ambulance and everything was satisfactory, and since the mother by your account is unmarried for whatever reason..."

"She is unmarried because my husband, who committed suicide after the event, raped her," said Dolly from between gritted teeth.

The Sister looked at her. "Oh."

Silence whilst they waited for her to complete her interrupted sentence.

"She may have been taken to one of the special Homes in Plymouth or Exeter," she said. "But I really don't know. Maybe asking the ambulance organisers on Monday would discover where."

"You mean that the ambulance service would have made a decision what to do with her?"

"It happens sometimes if there's a doubt where the mother should be after a successful birth. After all, hospitals are hardly the place for people who need no help, are they?"

"And you are satisfied neither of them needed any help, are you?"

"*I* never saw them. I never knew about them."

"Then you may want to revisit this conversation with the hospital authorities and the ambulance service. Because I shall most certainly be sending them a letter. A Solicitor's letter, if that focuses your thoughts a little. Good day."

32 – Morgan

The ambulanceman sitting opposite her was smoking. It made Angharad feel sick. At least she was lying down now and feeling better. What had happened back there? Had it been the cold? Or was it the baby as she thought?. The movement of the ambulance made her feel strange, almost light-headed. But at least she was safe. Why hadn't they let Ted come with her? He could have held her hand and made sure she was all right. Ted... so young, yet of late he had seemed to grow up, to be almost a young man. And he was good looking...

She stopped herself. Bob was her man. And he was missing. Her heart missed a beat as she remembered. The arguments with his parents came back to her mind, and her anger increased again, and the memory of that pain...

Her mind went round in circles until, on the main road near Malborough, she found that the pains were returning as well as the memories. She gasped. The ambulanceman stubbed out his cigarette and threw it in a bin, then started to look at her carefully.

"Coming, is it?"

"I don't know... Ahhhh...."

He called through to the driver. "Best stop and beg some hot water. Things are happening here."

The ambulance came to a halt.

It had been like a miracle when this warm, slightly squirming, towel-clad bundle was laid gently on Angharad's chest. She instinctively held it, exhausted, strange-feeling and most definitely relieved that she was nearly free from discomfort.

"It's a boy, and he's healthy," she had been told.

They said something else to her but she had time only for the baby. Her son, this miracle of life of which, up to that point, she had had no clue how it might make its appearance. The baby that was now once again asleep on her, having at birth shown that he had a fine pair of lungs, and a voice that she would recognise from any other.

When she woke again it was to find herself being wheeled in to a dark hall on the stretcher. Instinctively she knew it was strange to her, and her arms tightened for a moment around her son.

Her son.

"Room seventeen," she heard, and the journey continued. At some point she was being carried up some stairs, through a doorway and then was laid onto a bed and carefully transferred from the stretcher on to it. She noticed a cot by her side. With little ceremony, and no resistance from her, the baby was transferred into it. He was still asleep. Soon, knowing that babies were meant to be in cots, happy that he was healthy and quiet, she fell asleep herself.

When she woke, seemingly in the middle of the night, the cot was empty. With a cry she swung herself from the bed and nearly collapsed because she had been horizontal for so long. Struggling to her feet she crossed painfully to the door.

Locked.

Panicking, agonised, she beat on it, repeatedly, becoming more frantic by the minute. At last footsteps could be heard.

"Silence, girl! You'll wake everyone."

"My baby's gone!"

"Of course. It's best that way. Then you don't become too attached to it. Go back to bed now."

This made no sense to Angharad.

"But I want him with me. He needs to be with me."

"He is all right. He is being looked after. You cannot look after him while you are asleep, can you?"

"When will I get him back?"

"We will see how you both are tomorrow."

"But I must have him back tomorrow."

"We will *talk* about him, about you both, tomorrow. Go back to bed. You need rest."

"But…"

The footsteps were receding. Angharad was still worried. At least her baby was still well, being looked after. And tomorrow…

What should she call him? She couldn't keep calling him 'my baby'. She needed a name for him. She struggled back to bed obediently and thought of all the names, Welsh names, names that she knew. What would sound good with Pugh? And, within a short time, sleep returned to her.

With the light through her eyelids came the name, as if planted by the sun. Morgan. Morgan Pugh. Once in Welsh history it would have been Morgan ap Huw. Morgan was a good, strong name, and she had heard it in Devon too, she thought. And what of another name? All the posh people had a middle name. She thought of Bob. She thought of Ted. Robert and Edward were not Welsh names, but did that matter? Both had been good to her; Ted still was. She smiled as she thought of him and how particularly he had grown up so much in the few months she had known him.. Then the smile faded as she thought of Bob, and his being missing, and what might have been. But yes, both of their names should belong also to little Morgan.

Planted by the sun the name may have been, yet on this grey, wet day there was no sun to be seen anywhere. She wondered what time it was, noted the still-empty cot, and wondered if she was still locked in the room or whether she could go and see… Morgan Robert Edward. Once again she stood, but with more caution this time. It felt a little better, but she also knew that she needed the bathroom. Soon. Very soon.

The door to her room was unlocked. Outside she heard distant voices. She turned the other way and walked slowly and carefully along the corridor and found a door marked "Toilet".

In her own room she looked for her clothes and slowly dressed, aware with a shock that the special dress that had been bought to hide her 'condition' was now shapeless on her. Vast and unbecoming. Yet it was all she possessed. She put it on and set off towards the stairs in search of her son.

Instead, all she found were two girls, sweeping the main hall, who fell silent when they saw her.

"Do you... do you know where my baby is? Please?"

The two looked at each other. "Probably adopted by now," said one. "When did it arrive?"

"Adopted? But...no..."

Angharad froze, aghast, feeling sick.

"It's what happens to most of them, m'dear. Don't fret. You'll get over it."

"But he's mine! I want him. I need him. He's mine!"

A door opened and a woman in nurse's uniform bustled in, taking in the situation at a glance. She focussed on Angharad.

"Who are you? Oh, yes, you're Ann something, aren't you? Had yours in the ambulance yesterday, didn't you? Well, what do you want? Breakfast isn't for another half an hour, you know."

Nine months previously Angharad would have buckled at the tone and the words, and hung her head like a naughty schoolgirl. Now, she knew she was a cook, a baker, a provider of supplies for a growing chain of cafés, someone who made decisions about what would sell and what wouldn't. She was also going to be in charge of other staff who would run those cafés and sell her cooking. And another thing.

She was a mother.

"What I want, please, is to see my baby. I want to see Morgan..."

"That's a Cornish name. You can't call a baby that here, it'll never be adopted."

"He's not *going* to be adopted. He is called Morgan Robert Edward Pugh and he is my son and I will bring him up. And I want to see him. Now, please."

The nurse tossed her head. "Now he sounds Welsh..."

"He *is* Welsh. So am I."

"I can hear that, and don't interrupt me when I am talking to you. You girls – you have no idea about what it means to look after a baby, what it takes out of you. You'll need to sign the papers and have it adopted. And we'll see to that in the next few days once we know the baby is healthy."

Angharad was now beside herself and said something very rude in Welsh. From between gritted teeth she said "Morgan is mine. I know what bringing up; babies is like – I have two bothers and a sister. And Susan – Mrs Loft – has twins and I help with them. So I *do* know. I will not sign anything."

She was aware that the woman was glaring at her, unused to having one of the usually downtrodden, often guilt-ridden girls – mothers – stand up to her.

"You will in time. You will find that you have nothing you can give to him. Nothing to use to care for him. No home, probably. Now go back upstairs and wait for breakfast, then we will see if you can see your baby."

Angharad breathed deeply, trying to quell the feeling of panic that was threatening her.

"*Arlgwydd Mawr, helpwch fi plis*," [Great Lord, help me please] breathed Angharad. "Why am I here and not in hospital? If I was in hospital I would see my baby. If I was at home I would see my baby. I did not ask to come here. I did not need to be here. I need to go home, with my baby. Now."

"Home! You were found outside your home where your parents had thrown you out. That's why you are here..."

"I was outside a friend's house when the baby started. Not my home."

"That's not what the ambulancemen told us."

"The ambulancemen know nothing about me apart from my name. I live in Salcombe with friends. Friends who know me and have cared for me. One of them was with me when... when I started."

"Ah yes, we were told there was a child involved... I'm sure he isn't the father." She laughed, condescendingly.

"No," said Angharad, "he is not the father. I wish he had been. I was raped." The nurse was only taken aback for a few moments.

"Then you'll be glad to have it adopted, won't you?"

She received such a glare from Angharad that she took a step back. Encouraged, Angharad stepped forward, watched in amazement by the two girls who had stopped any pretence at cleaning.

"I have told you that the baby is mine, that he is Morgan Robert Edward, and my family and I want him and will bring him up. And that I want him. Now."

She was listening to herself speak as she formed the words, words which seemed to be coming from a stranger. It surprised her to hear the vehemence, and to register that yes, it was indeed her own voice.

The nurse had recovered a little and gave an uneasy laugh as if in dismissal.

"You'll get the baby when your family tells me what you say is true."

"*Yn dda iawn*," said Angharad. "Very well. I need a telephone and the number of Merryweather, Solicitor, in Salcombe. He is my family and he will come with my friends to rescue me and Morgan from... from this *place*."

Ted slept badly. The fury at the throwaway remark by the ambulancemen was still with him. The unlooked for desire to be with Angharad was stronger than he was expecting; the knowledge that he could help her just by being there was still strong. He was unable to articulate to anyone what he felt; doing so was completely beyond him and outside his experience. His brother would have been the obvious candidate but he knew without asking that Ian would have no idea how he could feel the way he did.

To the others, during the time between their return from the hospital and his bed time, he was uncharacteristically grumpy; silent and monosyllabic. Bert knew the signs of frustration. He had suffered it himself at the hands of his father although not with the same cause. He felt, though, that even he would be unable to penetrate at that point, not that there was much opportunity.

It was a tired fifteen-year-old who came to breakfast, nearly exploding because of the inaction of the others, as he saw it. Some of the wind was removed from his sails when he heard his Uncle Bert in the hall, talking in Solicitor tones on the phone.

"So you are telling me that there is no record of their detailed movements yesterday? .... And when will they appear and file their log? ... Late turn? But what does that mean? ... Not until then? I see. I have a situation here that you might wish to consider. A ward of mine, a girl of just seventeen, gave birth in that ambulance yesterday. She is, so far as I am concerned, currently missing. In that we knew with whom she was travelling and therefore who was caring for her at the time, it means that technically she has been abducted ..."

Even Ted, listening some yards away, could hear the indignant squawk from the mouthpiece.

"That is not what I am saying. I am saying that technically, under law, that is how the situation reads. It is your responsibility and, I hope your wish, to correct this situation without delay. You can do that by making urgent contact with the crew of that ambulance and telephoning me to give me the simple information I am seeking...

"Yes, I know it means interrupting their sleep and you should not seek to blame me nor the patient. It is the hospital's system of reporting that is responsible for what is, I repeat, an apparent and technical abduction ...

"Hallo? Are you still there?" There had been such a long silence from the other end of the line that he had wondered about the connection.

"Very well. Thank you. I shall not stir from this telephone until you call me back. Goodbye."

He replaced the receiver, and continued looking at Ted.

"I'm doing my best, Ted. I know it's early but I couldn't sleep. I know they would have an early shift and am ashamed to say that I dialled 999 in order to be put through to them. We should probably have done so last night, but none of us was thinking properly."

Ted nodded, feeling a wave of relief wash over him. "I didn't sleep well either," he said. "It was all so horrible yesterday. And losing her was just – just the last straw."

The eyes held his. "That is exactly how I felt, though you had a worse time having so nearly been able to be there with her. You probably gathered from what you heard that one of the ambulancemen is about to receive an early reveille, so although we shouldn't seek revenge it's only human to want to share some discomfort. It is the lack of reporting that is really to blame for our not knowing where she is so perhaps we shouldn't be too harsh. During weekends, crews' reports stay with the crew, and aren't delivered until they are next on duty. Usually it doesn't matter, but on this occasion, it did."

"So where is she?"

"We don't know yet. They will be telephoning back very soon with the news. Would you put the kettle on?"

The phone gave its usual long ring. Both their eyes lit up. Bert lifted the receiver again and gave the number, then listened, then gasped.

"*Angharad!* By all that's holy... where are you? How are you? How is the baby?"

Fifteen or not, Ted was now hopping from one foot to the other in frustration and relief, looking pleadingly at Bert and the phone.

"You're *where?* But why on earth did they take you there? No, look, that doesn't matter. Are you fit to travel? I know it was only yesterday but really that is no place for you. I'm horrified ... Well of course we're going to come and fetch you. Now ... Well of course with the baby too ... Who? The baby ... oh ... bless you, he'll be thrilled. You can tell him – he's here, hopping from one foot to the other just waiting to grab the receiver from me ... yes, of course."

He smiled at Ted. "We're going to fetch them."

"When?"

302

"Now. As soon as I can get the car."

Bert handed the receiver over. Ted found he was suddenly shy and didn't know what to say.

"H – hallo?"

"Hallo Ted. It's glad I am to hear your voice. Will you be coming in the car too?"

"Yes, if I'm allowed."

"You should be one of the first to meet Morgan Robert Edward."

"Who?" Ted almost faltered. Was this another boyfriend? It was only a fleeting thought, though it crossed his mind before common sense returned.

"My son."

"Is that his name? But *Edward* – that's my name. I like Morgan, though."

"But yes, it is after you that I called him, Bob and you."

Once again Ted didn't know what to say, or even how he felt. Any thought of more talk was defeated by the sound of others coming downstairs to join him.

"I… I don't know what to say."

She laughed. There was a scrambling noise on the line and another voice, a Devon accent, older, spoke.

"We cannot pay for a call this long. Really, it is too bad. And just who are you?"

Ted looked at the receiver. "A friend. One minute, here is Uncle… Mr Merryweather."

The phone was handed back and Ted, surrounded now by family, listened as his honorary grandfather resumed Solicitor mode to speak to the Nurse. He listened to protestations about it all being highly irregular and too long a call, and after listening for what seemed ages he said just one word.

"Enough."

It was said in a tone so peremptory that she had no option but to cease.

"The situation is this," Bert continued. "Angharad was brought to you by ambulance without either her guardian's permission or her knowledge. She was not told where she was being taken. I have already informed the ambulance service that technically she has therefore been abducted. If you now try to refuse to release her to her guardian it will compound abduction into false imprisonment. I need hardly tell you how that would be seen by your employers and the general public when it came to Court.

"Please understand that we shall attend your Home as soon as we can physically get there and expect both Angharad and…and the baby to be ready for their journey home."

Silence.

"Hallo?" asked Bert.

"And now who am I speaking to?"

"Algernon Merryweather, of Merryweathers, Solicitors and Commissioner for Oaths, of Fore Street, Salcombe, Devon."

Another silence. Then, as Bert reported later: "Very well. Your… ward and her baby will be ready for collection when you arrive."

"Thank you. Now all I need is your whereabouts."

"I should have thought Ann would have told you."

"Ann? Who is Ann?"

"Your ward, of course. Or have we been talking of the wrong person all this time?"

"If you mean Angharad, then she is the girl we shall be collecting. Along with…"

He looked hopefully at Ted, who was watching him like a hawk.

"Morgan Robert Edward," he enunciated proudly.

"Little Morgan. What is the address, please?"

It was dictated to him; he dictated it to Ted who scrabbled around for a pencil and wrote it on the notepad by the phone.

"We will be there as soon as we can," Bert told the nurse.

"Very well."

Bert looked at the receiver as it gave its final loud pop, hinting that it had been dropped onto the cradle at the other end. "I will go and fetch the car," was all he said. He marched, breakfast-less from the house.

"I'm going," Ted announced.

"I had better come as well," Dolly said, "Though really I should stay here and make sure the office opens on time.

"I'll make some breakfast," Annabelle offered, " then if you're not back it can be left in the oven low. I'll get Ian to school and go and open the office. You go and help with Angharad."

"Are you sure you don't mind?"

"Of course not. And you can tell Bert, if I don't see him, that he needs to drop Ted off at school on the way back through Kingsbridge. I will telephone to tell them he'll be late."

It was yet another journey in the car to Kingsbridge, but this time they had to continue to Exeter. Without being asked, Dolly found a street map in the car and sought out the address of the Home.

"There's a cemetery on the other side of the road it's on," Ted suddenly told them. "She said it's depressing."

"There's a cemetery down that road we just passed," Bert told her. "Should I turn round?"

"No... take the next right, then right again at the end."

At last they found it. As usual Bert left the key in the ignition and had to be reminded by Ted. They mounted the steps of the forbidding looking building and rang the bell. The door was opened after a long wait by a woman who appeared just as forbidding as the building.

"Yes?"

Even Bert was taken aback for a moment..

"Er.. Merryweather, of Merryweathers Solicitors of Salcombe. I have come to take Angharad Pugh and her baby..."

"Morgan," Ted interrupted.

"... Morgan back home. I hope she is ready?"

"I will find out. Wait there."

"I think we should come in, don't you? She is my ward, after all."

After a pause the door was opened wider.

"What is *he* doing here? Is he the father?"

He, in this case, was Ted, who blushed furiously.

"N... no. I am her friend. That's all."

"Then you have no place here. And I was talking to your father, not to you."

That stung Ted, and his eyes swung up to blaze into the woman's eyes.

"My father is dead and I don't want you talking about him. Angharad is my friend and I am here to help take her where she should be. Home."

"Don't be impertinent. She is nothing to do with you."

Bert intervened. "She and he are the best judges of that. He is her friend and he will be accompanying me to rescue her from here. We need to see her. Now."

If he had been startled by the tone of the woman's supposed greeting when she had answered the door, she was now startled at the command in Bert's voice. She backed away. They marched behind Bert into a hallway, waited for her to close the front door and walk past them, then followed her. She led along a gloomy corridor to the reception room where Angharad was waiting.

When he saw her Ted pushed past everyone and embraced her, much to the surprise of both of them, "Are you all right? Where is Morgan?"

Angharad was so glad to see them that she broke down. When she was able she sobbed "they will not give him to me. They say I will not be able to cope with him."

"And why should that be?" asked Bert to the nurse. "Was it you I spoke to on the phone? I think I recognise the voice. I ask again: Why would she not be able to cope with him?"

"She is too young."

"Rubbish. And it is not in your remit to judge. Why would you want to stop her taking her own child, or even seeing him? I hope he is still here. I have heard of places like this arranging adoptions against the wishes of the mother. Even charging for the paperwork – which might be seen as charging for the adoption or even selling the child. Is that what you do?"

There was a gasp. "How dare you say something like that? What do you think we are?"

"In that case you will have no reluctance returning the child to his mother. Now, please. Without further delay. So that I may return to work and start looking into the licensing situation regarding Exeter's Mothers' Homes."

Angharad received Morgan into her arms with a cry of delight, something that caused a previously unknown emotion in Ted. He stood in front of Angharad, looking at the baby who was partly named after him with a benign smile on his face.

"He's wonderful," he said with the utmost sincerity, and received a smile from Morgan's mother which added to this unfamiliar feeling that was making him tingle.

"I think that will be all," said Bert, turning away thankfully.

"We normally receive a donation in cases where the grandparents take the baby," she said in a voice that was suddenly wheedling.

"And does your supporting church know of your normal donations?" Bert asked in a dangerously quiet voice.

"I believe they would not object to people helping with our expenses."

"You exceed your authority, madam. I am not a grandparent, for one;

Angharad was brought here without her or our knowledge; and she has incurred no expenses whatsoever. Nor has the baby."

"There's milk..."

"Which is better ...er ... provided by the mother..." He tailed off, knowing this was forbidden territory. "We need take up no more of your valuable time. Ted, lead the way, please."

"Goodbye Anne..." the nurse was not going to give up easily.

"My name is Angharad, as I kept telling you. I will go now."

As swiftly as possible they retraced their way to the front door. Once outside Bert drew in a breath of pure Devon air.

"That feels healthier," he said. "I feel sorry for any girl who has no opportunity but to be looked after by that place. At least I can investigate it and the others to check on their governance, not to mention their practices."

"They were dreadful," said Angharad. "Why did they take me there?"

"That's something else I shall be looking at. This whole thing has gone wrong from start to finish. It was the ambulancemen who were wrong at the start, as well as their lack of a suitable reporting scheme. But now we need to get you home."

It was a slower journey this time; more of a triumphant procession than a mad dash to provide succour. They reached Kingsbridge. Morgan was asleep on Angharad's lap as he had been since leaving Exeter. Ted spent almost the entire journey looking at him, fondly marvelling. Dolly remembered school and mentioned it to her brother. Ted looked up as he heard his name mentioned.

"We need to drop Ted at school, don't forget."

Bert turned to look at Ted and saw the look on his face.

"I think Ted will be of more use to Morgan and Angharad today, don't you? How he has reacted today has earned him that privilege. If Angharad would appreciate his company, I think we might make an exception for a day, don't you?"

So a smiling Ted was there when the little lad stretched, then opened his eyes. Both he and Angharad felt emotion sweep through them and turned to smile at each other.

No one else saw.

Aunt Amble had been busy. She had telephoned Loft Island. Susan and Mary immediately brought themselves to the mainland with the twins. It was quite a welcoming committee when Annabelle opened the door and Angharad was surprised and flattered by their being there to welcome her. She was glad to hand Morgan to Mary, to find herself ushered to a comfortable chair and to lower herself carefully into it. Tiredly she watched the three babies meet each other. Though on the surface they seemed to be behaving the same as they were when alone, the sounds seemed noticeably quieter as they felt each other's presence nearby.

33 – Bob : Ted

The journey from the jungle put more strain on Bob than he thought possible. The time between finding the wireless, getting it to work and actually making contact had seen his supposedly improving arm grow weaker and more painful again, and it had become swollen, tight of skin and red of colour. He was finding that sometimes he was unable to concentrate on matters around him with a level head. Farid had seen the arm and had looked worried. As had Tuan.

Finally a party of soldiers had cautiously made contact, had agreed a rendezvous point and had been escorted to the village, not without mutual suspicion. But seeing them had been such a relief to Bob that his fever-induced delirium overcame him and he slept. During the journey he was a dead weight and the stretcher bearers cursed his immobility as they struggled back to the track, the nearest point to their patient that the armoured truck could reach. They all failed to see or hear any signs of a shadow that traced their steps all the way; a small shadow with one arm in a sling.

The stretcher was carefully wedged into the vehicle and the soldiers settled on the benches around it. The driver engaged gear and was about to set off when a small boy, one arm in an obviously army-style sling, ran out of the surrounding cover and stood in front of the lorry, looking scared. The driver engaged neutral again. The corporal looked alarmed, but armed with a rifle jumped out and looked around, fearing another ambush. Nothing happened. The boy had remained in front of the truck, looking between that and the rifle-wielding corporal.

"Where are they?" asked the corporal.

"Only me. Hospital. Please. They cured me."

"Hospital?"

The boy pointed to his arm. "Bob knows."

"Bob's unconscious."

The boy looked blank.

The corporal made a sleeping sign with his head on his hands and the boy nodded.

"Fever," he said.

"Fever. Are you from the village?

The boy shrugged. "Tuan," was all he said.

The corporal pointed to him with a questioning look and the boy nodded.

"Why do you need to go to the hospital?"

Tuan just looked at him. "Hospital?" He pointed to his arm again. "Please?"

A soldier emerged from the back of the truck. "Was there a child... oh. Yes, there is. Bob's awake and heard it. He's insisting he wants to talk to him."

The corporal swore. "We're here to be an ambulance service, not a bloody nursery. Get the boy up to Bob, for goodness sake, then we can get going."

Tuan was lifted up to the back of the truck. He went straight to Bob, knelt beside him and touched his face.

"Fever," he said.

"Yes," said Bob weakly. Hospital. You go home. We said goodbye earlier."

"No goodbye. Tuan come too. Arm hurt."

"Bad?" Bob could only mutter the question.

"Bad."

"No one knows you're here."

A blank look.

Bob did his best to point to the village.

"Mother know?"

"Mother dead."

In all that time with them nobody had thought to give that nugget of information to Bob. It would explain why Tuan spent so much time with him. He had no parents at all now. There was just the village to bring him up.

The corporal was listening. "We can't take him," he said.

"We can't just leave him there to find his own way back to the village," Bob said weakly. "You know how far it is. It'd be murder. I've saved his life once, and I'm not going leave him. Tell your sergeant I'll be responsible, will you?"

It was a long speech for someone trying to recover from a fever, and Bob sank back, exhausted. To his relief the truck started off a few moments later and the corporal returned.

"He's not happy, but we can't take him back all that way to the village, he says. So it looks as if you're lumbered, mate."

Bob nodded as best he could and returned to sleep.

At the hospital he was diagnosed with sepsis. The infection in his arm had been ineffectively treated and he hung for a fortnight between life and death.

It was only after the two weeks he started to feel less awful and had less pain whenever he tried to lift his arm. Throughout the time Tuan was by his side, either watching him like a hawk or dozing. The army medical staff fed the boy as well as Bob, making sure he was as all right as he could be. Tuan's arm had been checked and pronounced to be fine – something that caused suspicion with the corporal from the rescue mission whilst on a visit. But a five year old child would be above suspicion, surely?

Gradually, as he recovered, Bob continued to teach Tuan to speak and to understand English. The nurse who was looking after him during the day, a local girl, was at first amused, then impressed, and after a while started helping translate some of the Malay words Tuan used and which Bob couldn't grasp. Bob grew to like her, sharing many laughs with her and Tuan, especially at the confusions caused as each got to grips with the other's language.

When the boy was away, asleep, the two chatted and compared notes about Bob's experiences with Malaysian society and Maryam's with English foibles when she had been at medical college in London. Her English was very good; her understanding impeccable. Bob asked her how it was that she was working in Malaya, almost on the edge of what westerners would call civilisation.

"It is my country," she said simply. "I would have stayed in London – England was good enough to train me and I owe them gratitude. But when the Emergency happened I knew I had to return and help. And..."

She paused. "And when people started talking about fighting in Malaya some pointed at me and it felt as if they were accusing me of somehow being an enemy. It made life very unhappy for me, even at the Hospital. So for many weeks I searched my heart and then knew I had to come home. So here I am, talking to

308

an injured English soldier and a small boy from the Malay jungle who seems to have befriended him."

"I'm very glad you are here, and talking to us," Bob told her.

Over the weeks following they were seen to be talking whenever possible.

Five days following Bob's admission to hospital a letter was read with relief and tears by his parents.

"I *knew* he was still alive," said his mother.

That first day Ted watched over the three babies like a fascinated hawk. Several times he looked anxiously at either Susan or Angharad for confirmation that all was right. It was. Angharad smiled at him each time he showed that he was looking after young Morgan. When the time came for Susan and the twins to head back to the Island he was sad, but Morgan would remain. Perhaps helping to care for one baby was a responsibility he might be able to shoulder, if needed. Completely subconsciously, a thought stirred; helping with Morgan might bring him closer to Angharad.

He was so attracted to the tiny life in front of him that he was almost deaf to calls to come and eat – itself a major astonishment to all the adults and particularly to his brother. Ian knew that Ted, at fifteen, could eat for England.

"School tomorrow, Ted," Annabelle reminded him.

He looked up, worried. "But…"

"No, she can cope. I'm capable of looking after Morgan too, you know."

He smiled, then looked at Angharad, who smiled back. He had been marvellous that day, she thought. And he was a really nice person too… and despite herself was surprised to find that his appearance attracted her. She blushed and felt guilty, knowing that Bob was still away.

Bob! She had letters from him from his parents and she had forgotten them.

After the meal, whilst the others talked around her she fished the letters from her pocket and read them, weeping a little as she read of his struggle with the training and then with the Malay climate which had come as such a shock. Reading for the third time she noticed at last the dates of their writing, and her anger grew at the Hannaford parents who had kept them from her for so long.

Impatiently she sought paper and pen.

School the next day loomed for Ted who tried to think of a reason to stay and help with looking after Morgan. Many may have tried wheedling, but he knew that would have no effect. He could think of no compelling reason he could give that stood a chance of working and reluctantly set off for the bus accompanied by the irrepressible Ian. Returned, late that afternoon, he was his usual, cheerful, old-schoolboy self. Nevertheless he made a beeline for Morgan and Angharad.

That evening Martin was working in his room; this time it was on the correspondence course that was proving at times interesting and at other times infuriating. The interest was in discovering industry-standard techniques and understanding them, and the annoyance was at some of the stuck-in-the-mud attitudes that the course assembly experts so often displayed.

He had complained to Mike about them before.

"You'll be taking an exam in due course, and they'll be looking for their stock answers. You need to give them. You need to learn how to pass the exam. And there will be times when we work together that you'll come up with stock solutions and I'll make it very clear that once you've qualified that's an idea we ditch and go back to your clear thinking. Our clear thinking – I hope!"

He had seen it as a two-edged sword. He needed the exam but was boosted by Mike recognising that he had the ability to innovate. The conflict was resolving itself in his mind when he was interrupted by an explosion. Startled, an ink-blot spreading over his work, he leapt to his feet. Lifeboat? The second maroon answered him and he leapt up, upset his chair and rushed down to the hall. Waterproofs on against the wet, windy December weather he yelled his farewells and vanished, leaving the door to swing behind him.

His first trial on the lifeboat had been in April. Regular training since had seen him grow into a useful, if still inexperienced, Lifeboatman. Andy had been quietly pleased with him, without saying so. As of a month previously he had been allowed to join the rota of spare men who would go out if necessary or if the call was likely to be not too demanding.

Tonight was likely to be a call requiring a crew of experts since the weather was so bad. Even Mike might not make it, he thought. But he still presented himself, just in case.

At the quay there seemed to be more chaos than he was used to, though Andy was trying to calm things down. Eventually he retrieved a whistle and blew a long blast that reduced everyone to silence.

"'Bout time too," he announced. "We're short. Good to see some young'uns though. It's a bugger out there. Force 7 Sou-westerly, gusting 8. So don't be bloody heroes, if you're not up for a struggle to get to this one, say now and we'll get Plymouth out. No questions asked. Coastguard says she's a trawler and they lost their engine 'bout two miles off."

There remained silence.

"Ok, then. Let's get her under way."

The well-rehearsed machine of kitting up, clambering aboard the tender and departing started. Before long only the Station Manager was left in the sudden silence.

At ten o'clock the following morning the doorbell was answered by Annabelle. A strange woman stood there, and Annabelle knew from the expression there was a problem.

"Have you.. have you heard about the Lifeboat?" she was asked.

Annabelle's eyes widened. "No," she almost whispered. "What's happened?"

"We don't know," said the stranger. "They went out last night and haven't been seen since. I hoped... I hoped that being nearer you might have heard."

"I thought that Martin had come back and was sleeping it out," admitted Annabelle. "We have a very new baby in the house now, and – well, let's say that there is little routine as yet. Sorry – I don't think we've met?"

"I'm Mike Alexander's mother, Janet. You must be Mrs Williams."

"No, I'm Annabelle Rawle, Martin's aunt. Please come in?"

Once she had been shown to the living room a similarly anxious Annabelle checked Martin's room, only to discover an unused bed, books open on the table and an upset chair by it.

"He's not returned, either," she admitted to her visitor. "Have you been down to the quay?"

"I never like to," Mrs Alexander admitted. "I always feel like an anxious hen if I do that, fussing too much. But he's very... precious to us, you know."

"They all are. Every one of them. But Martin has told us about you, and I can understand more how you're feeling. I think it would be a good idea for us both to seek news, don't you? Shall I get my coat?"

A few moments later she had checked that Angharad would be able to cope if Morgan woke, and they set off. The weather then was at least dry, though if anything the wind had increased.

They found other, anxious parents and wives at the Lifeboat Station. With the more experienced crews it seemed that wives were more accepting that sometimes delays occurred. Most of those who were crewing her this time were young men; family men, or those still living with parents who were understandably anxious.

Mrs Alexander and Annabelle joined the group, identified themselves and asked for information. It seemed that the Manager of the Gara Rock Hotel, on its cliff between Prawle Point and the Estuary entrance, had chanced to spot red flares and had raised the alarm. The Lifeboat had gone out but once again radio reception from her had proved intermittent. The Station had all but lost contact with her.

"They've asked that Manager feller to tell us if anything's to be seen of her, see," said a very Devon accent next to Annabelle, "but they ain't seen her yet."

They stayed there for ages, or so it felt. Annabelle was worried, but she had faith in the local seamen to deal with anything the sea could throw at them. After an hour she begged Mrs Alexander to stay but to let her know when there was news.

"I have Angharad indoors and it's only her second day as a mother," she explained. "I'm split into two. I need to care for both, but I know where Angharad and Morgan are. Please would you forgive me? But please also call in as you pass when there's anything, anything at all."

By this time they were on Christian name terms. "Of course I will," Janet assured her.

Angharad was in the middle of feeding Morgan when Annabelle knocked at the door and opened it without thinking. Angharad hid herself hurriedly.

"I am sorry," each of them said, and there was a strained laugh.

"Is this... is this how you do it? I have seen only sheep do it before."

Annabelle had no idea. She had had no children. "If he is happy, and feeding, and you are comfortable, then I should think so," she told her. "We really need to ask a doctor or, better, the health visitor. She would be better."

"Yes," said Angharad, "*She* would be. The doctor is a man."

An hour later there was a ring at the front door again. Janet, looking happier.

"She's in Dartmouth," she said. "They're exhausted and hungry, but everyone's safe. They've been told they have to stay there and sleep, then return tomorrow. It was a French boat, she'd lost her engines and was being blown onto the coast, so they saved her and all the crew."

They rejoiced quietly over a cup of tea after Janet had called her husband.

Angharad joined them, with Morgan, and the rest of their morning was complete.

Bob had received a letter from Angharad which said that she hoped beyond hope that he was still alive and telling him why she hadn't been able to write before. The reason angered him considerably, but also set him thinking.

At last he knew he had to write. two letters, one to his parents to tell them the decision reached by Maryam and him, and the other to Angharad to try and explain. It wouldn't wait until he saw her again, and anyway he was scared of having that meeting. Once Maryam had returned home, with an illicit kiss from him which, had it been witnessed, would have meant dismissal for her, he set to.

Christmas was spent in Salcombe. Loft Island was still too much of a wet, muddy building site for anyone to be able to use either house or café. None of the buildings was anywhere near readiness – unless you were part of the dairy herd. Henry, Stephen and Ted made regular journeys to their new land to do the milking and ensure that all was well.

It was a busy time with all of them there, even with Bronwen and Martin away at the Alexanders who had invited them for Christmas Eve and Boxing Day.

Early on January 1st the postman delivered a letter to the Hannafords. Bob's father read it with relief.

"He's coming home," he said with joy. "The army is giving him a discharge in view of his injury. He says there's other news too, but that it would wait until he sees us." He looked up. "I hope it's not to do with that girl. The pregnant one that tried to get in here."

"I heard about her before Christmas," his wife said, guilt in her voice. "She, that boy and the Vicar had been ringing our bell because she was starting to have her baby."

He sat down with a bump.

"Oh… Does that explain why the Vicar's been avoiding us?"

A letter had also arrived for Angharad. She frowned over the unfamiliar postmark, then deciphered "Malaya" and opened it with hands that suddenly trembled.

She read. Her face grew straight, the eyes widened, then brimmed with tears as she read on. The boys were eating their breakfast; Ted happened to look over at her.

In a moment his spoon was on the floor and he was kneeling in front of her, looking into her eyes.

"What?"

She shook her head, still reading a second time, hoping that somehow the words would be different.

With a start she stood, pushed Ted over and ran from the room. They heard her bedroom door slam. Cautiously Ted stood, picked up the lonely envelope and read the postmark as Angharad had just done.

"Bob?" asked Annabelle.

"Yes, it must be, but I don't know what. It's not official, so it's not… not from the Army. It's from him."

"She just needs some time to herself," said his aunt, comfortably. "Finish your breakfast. It's nearly time to get ready."

Ted had hardly heard her. Was Bob all right? Was he coming home? Was he *not* coming home? What was happening? Could it be that he had separated from her... surely not. She had thought about no one else for months – well, not in that way.

But had he thought of her like that? And what was "that way", anyway?

Ignoring protestations he marched to the door, and went upstairs to Angharad's and knocked.

Silence.

"Angharad, it's Ted. Please?"

Silence for a while, then he heard sounds of movement, then a voice that filled him with hope.

"All right."

He took that as permission and went in. She was looking at him, almost without recognition, the letter in her hand still. He stood, waiting.

"*Sbwriel yw pob dyn.*" she muttered, looking at him almost accusingly She had tried to teach him Welsh on a few occasions and it had ended in laughter from them both, but he knew '*pob dyn*' and that it was something about men.

"Is it from Bob? Is he hurt?"

"He is not hurt, not now, and he is coming home. He will leave the Army and return to Malaya and marry his nurse and take on a boy."

Ted's jaw dropped. How could he do such a thing? How could he just leave someone like Angharad? They were – had been – together. Real friends. More than friends. In his eyes it made Bob appear no better than his parents who had ignored a girl about to have a baby. And a boy? What should he want a boy for?

"I don't understand."

"I don't understand either. He has said that because he had heard nothing from me he had thought that I was having second thoughts. He knows now that his parents didn't send on the letters, that they didn't approve of me, and is now – what did he say? Horrified.

"In the meantime he had met this girl, this nurse, and they had got together. And he had rescued a boy from the jungle and he was visiting with her when he could. He wants to leave the army and live with them now."

Crossing to her, he held the hand that wasn't holding the letter. "I don't know what to say. How can I make it better?" He felt inadequate. "I just don't know."

"You can't. Not at the moment. Maybe not ever. I just need to think and cry."

"Morgan will want you."

Reality dawned in her eyes as the present returned.

"Morgan. Yes. Morgan... Edward Pugh. He will want feeding."

Ted, trainee farmer, suddenly made a connection he had never made before. Angharad's absences when the baby cried. Meaningful looks between her and his Aunt. Cows, calves...

Suddenly, he smiled. "And that is something I cannot do for you. I don't have... I'm not... I don't have the... er...equipment."

She looked up sharply and caught the smile, and was almost able to return it. With a start he realised that this time she had not given Morgan the first of his middle names.

"Oh Ted, you should not know about things like that."

"It's a bit late for that. But don't forget that I'm here when you want cheering up, you know."

"I know you are, and you do."

"What did you say in Welsh when I came in?"

She thought. "*Sbwriel yw pob dyn.* All men are rubbish."

He smiled again. "Perhaps, for once, I'm glad I'm a boy."

A shout of "Ted!" came from downstairs.

He was aware he was being looked at.

"I don't think you are. Not now."

He took that in, startled by what he saw as a high and sincere compliment, and felt an inner glow. The silence extended. Another shout from below which he ignored.

"Then I *am* rubbish?"

At last, a shaky smile.

"No."

End of the second part of the story.

The first was told in Loft Island. If you register to receive irregular information from the Author at rw2.co.uk you will hear about the next part's availability before anyone else.

Printed in Great Britain
by Amazon